Beasts of the Night

a Novel

Matejs Kalns

 Friesenpress

Suite 300 - 990 Fort St
Victoria, BC, V8V 3K2
Canada

www.friesenpress.com

Cover design by: Ignacio Andres Paul
Map design by: Machfudz Arif
Author photograph: Austin VanDeVen

ISBN
978-1-5255-8026-0 (Hardcover)
978-1-5255-8025-3 (Paperback)
978-1-5255-8027-7 (eBook)

1. Fiction, Action & Adventure

Distributed to the trade by The Ingram Book Company

For my grandmother, who encouraged me to write
since I was a boy. Paldies Yapapai.

"Slavery is a weed that grows on every soil."
—*Edmund Burke*

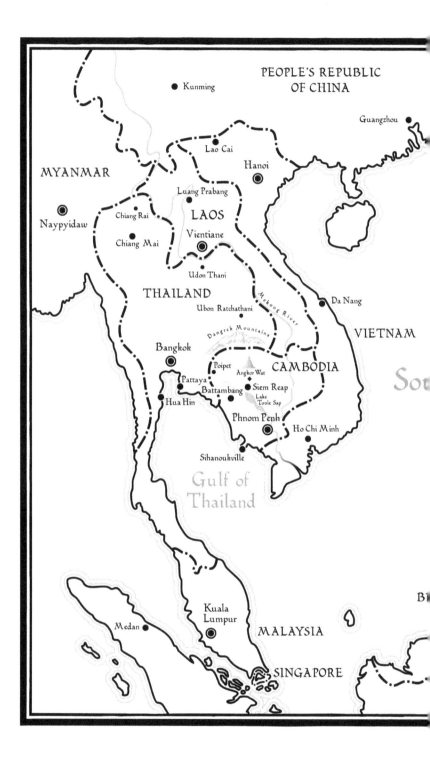

PART
ONE

ONE

Siem Reap, Cambodia,

NO ONE HAD EVER CALLED QUINTON MILLS A COCKROACH before, and it caught him off guard, as one might expect. As far as insults were concerned, the slight was beyond reproach. Brilliantly original, cutting in delivery, a curse made all the more poignant in that it came from the lips of an eight-year-old girl.

Ghonlaat, the Khmer word for these most hated of insects, mythologized since time immemorial in the Western consciousness as a creeping, crawling embodiment of filth. The scourge of cheap restaurant kitchens and dilapidated basement apartments, thought to predate Jurassic reptiles and defy atomic blasts.

It was hardly the most flattering of introductions, a child spitting insults, yet strangely appropriate given the circumstances. Try as he might, he couldn't prevent the smile playing at the corners of his mouth, surely infuriating her—hooded hazel eyes glaring from across the room. It was in that moment that Quinn fell in love with Mei, grass-stained and seething on the dusty wooden floor—her irascible spirit, resilient and enraged, poised to take on the entire world.

Just a month before, the story might have shocked him, but now the business of selling children had become something of a routine conversation. No longer the tragic tale of one family's misfortune but the gradual, numbing realization that the trade was commonplace, the children nothing more than commodities—sold at market for a bushel of maize, a sack of rice.

It was a sweltering day on the periphery of Cambodia's most famous town, the air thick and humid from the afternoon thundershower. The brief downpour, a storm that appeared like clockwork during the rainy season, bringing with it a dark and ominous sky, had cleansed the area, washing away the pervasive dust and sand that matted the red earth. Quinn's shirt clung to his back from morning to night, a constant lacquer of sweat, his cheeks glistening with perspiration no matter the time of day.

Admittedly, his Scandinavian roots weren't particularly well suited to the climate. With windswept blond hair and pale blue eyes, he could have hardly been more out of place. He had a high forehead and slender nose, both perennially sun-kissed from the unrelenting heat, and stood well over six feet tall, towering above most of the locals—a slim physique better suited to office chairs than any task of manual labor. Some of the children at an orphanage in Thailand had taken to calling him *soong yai farang*, loosely translated as "big, tall foreigner." This was later amended to include the term *mun yow*, a reference to how shiny his face became in the afternoon heat.

Noi, his colleague, for lack of a better term, was inside the ramshackle hut dealing with a sensitive situation that she assured him was nothing more than "women's things." The hut itself was a makeshift shelter, constructed haphazardly out of teak pillars and bamboo reeds. With a flimsy thatched roof of dried grasses and spindly stalks, he wondered whether it could withstand the ritual downpours of the season.

He had been visiting various shelters in the region with Noi, who ran her own housing project for disadvantaged youth in the southern province of Battambang. One of the last stops of the day, they made it in part due to its proximity to some of Noi's old friends in the city.

Lost in reverie, listening to the birds chirping amongst the low tree line, Quinn managed a single drag of a stale cigarette before they called his name.

The interior was as bare as expected, even more so. Some faded area rugs, marred with stains and burn holes, covered the dilapidated wooden floor; a threadbare hammock hung against a near wall not far from a chalky concrete wash basin. A ladder led to the second-floor loft, though it too had seen better days, a lower rung still shedding splinters where it had snapped.

Noi called again, her voice a muted sound from above. With some hesitation, he mounted the ladder, which creaked and groaned beneath his weight. As he crested the floorboards, in the far corner he saw three women and a young girl, seated on a rug that had once been a color other than beige. Noi sat cross-legged, the farthest away, and the other woman, whom he assumed to be Chanthavy, rested against an old bookcase that held far fewer books than any bookcase should.

Chanthavy was a local housewife who volunteered her time preparing meals for the young girls, stitching their clothing and even teaching some rudimentary curriculum. In truth, she spent little time at the decrepit shanty, but it was more than anybody else in the community, and for that, Noi was eternally grateful. There were rarely more than a handful of girls in residence and they often disappeared without a trace, no one to follow up on their whereabouts or care where they had gone. Currently, Noi had said, there were only four, all of them taken to a neighboring home a few miles down the road for an afternoon of crafts and pottery.

The two women mirrored each other's folded hands in their laps. Between them, tucked as far back into the corner as possible, practically melding into the wall, was a girl no more than seven or eight, silently hugging her knees. An elderly woman knelt beside her, dipping a wet rag into a pot and dabbing a small wound on the girl's forehead, just below her hairline.

The child was clothed in a faded pink dress embroidered with outlines of white flower petals. Her left shoulder strap had fallen, perhaps torn—it was difficult to tell—the pleated bottom of the dress badly frayed and grass stained. While Noi and Chanthavy searched for the right words, the little girl glowered at him with fierce, suspicious eyes. The older woman cleansed the scrape on the girl's tanned forehead, darker in certain spots from smears of dirt, her hair a bird's nest of twigs and weeds. She had rounded cheekbones, a low-lying bridge of the nose, and lips a dark shade of maroon. Quinn wondered if perhaps she came from one of the remote hill tribes in the Dângrêk Mountains, the range that naturally divided Northern Cambodia from Southern Thailand.

"Quinn, this is Mei," Noi said softly.

He kept his distance, a good ten feet from everyone, and crouched on his haunches to join the others on the floor.

Placing his palms together in front of his chin, he bowed his head to *wai*. "Mei, *suosdey*."

The little girl neither moved nor blinked, holding him with her piercing stare.

"And this is Mei's neighbor, Rom Chang."

He knelt and repeated the greeting, hands clasped together a little higher this time, as custom dictated. Rom Chang gracefully returned the gesture, then rinsed the bloody cloth and started to wipe the girl's knobby, blackened knees.

"Mei has been through, what's this word in English," Noi said, hesitating for a moment, "an ordeal. Actually," she shook her head, "that's putting it very simply."

He placed his hands on his knees, careful not to say or do anything too quickly.

"Rom Chang found her not too long ago and brought her here. Mei just showed up at her house. She says she didn't know where else to bring her."

"Is she alright?" he asked, all too aware of the light hazel eyes still boring a hole into him.

"Honestly, I'm not really sure."

Noi proceeded to ask Rom Chang something in Khmer, the two speaking in whispers for a time. Chanthavy also chimed in, with Quinn struggling to comprehend anything from the foreign tones. Shifting his weight, he was mindful of a small bulge in his pant leg, recalling the granola bar that he had stashed in his pocket that morning.

"Mei won't speak to anyone but Rom Chang," Noi said.

"What happened?"

"We're not really sure. I'm trying not to fear the worst."

She inquired further with Rom Chang, who was seemingly providing context with animated facial expressions and subtle gestures with her free hand. Then Chanthavy rose, brushed herself off, nodded, and proceeded back down the ladder.

With great care, Quinn crept over and took her place by the depleted bookcase, taking the opportunity to remove the snack in his pocket and crinkle open the wrapper.

Eventually, the conversation between the two women dropped off, followed by a moment of silence. Noi turned to him, composing herself, her expression hardening. "They tried to sell her."

"Who did?"

"Her aunt."

"Where?"

She furrowed her thick eyebrows. "I think China. She hasn't said a lot since she came to Rom Chang's home, and she was crying and talking at the same time. It was hard to understand."

"What did she say?"

"Her aunt was telling her about working in the north, most likely Yunnan or Guangxi. Better opportunities for the family."

"Parents?"

Noi shook her head. "She lives with her aunt. They met with a man who Mei said spoke Khmer with a strong accent. Average looking, but she said he looked greasy, very greasy hair, that's all."

"Where?"

"At their house. Mei said she was washing up out back when the man came to talk to her aunt. Mei saw him give her money. She thought it was strange how her aunt was in a rush. She was never in a rush. Then she told Mei to go with him. 'Pack your things, hurry up,' like this. Mei did as she was told; her aunt called him 'uncle,' and she thought maybe he was a distant relative. When she began asking questions, he only grunted.

"They walked to his taxi, and when he got frustrated with her talking, he grabbed her arm and said, 'You're with us now,' or 'You belong somewhere else now,' something like this." Noi frowned. "It's hard for me to translate this expression. Mei said she couldn't understand his accent well, but she understood enough. When he grabbed her, she tried to pull away, and when she couldn't, she bit him. He chased her into the woods, and she kept running until she couldn't hear the footsteps behind her anymore. Rom Chang said she started crying very hard just then . . ."

Quinn glanced at the young girl who, as expected, was unflinching with her distrustful glare.

The story was familiar enough. Recruitment into a black hole of forced labor in Chinese garment factories, privately owned and completely unregulated; or brick kilns, as vast as they were remote, where untold numbers spent their childhoods, overworked and abused, caked in red earth. Though the man could just as easily have been a marriage broker, or so they were called. Perhaps even the buyer himself, though more than likely a middleman. A slippery character with the right connections to move women and children across borders—stock for rural brothels, warmth for the beds of lonely farmers—greasing palms for passage into the lawless sprawl of southern China.

"Did she say anything else about the aunt?"

"Only that she doesn't want to go back. She won't go back."

Mei moved for the first time, wincing slightly as Rom Chang put a bit too much pressure on the raw scrape on her shin. Quinn held the granola bar in his palm, broke off a crumbly morsel, and extended it toward her.

Mei's wrist shot out like a coiled spring, smacking his hand away and sending the piece of granola skittering across the floorboards. She shrieked a brief, unintelligible sound with such vitriol that a few white droplets of spittle flecked her chin, her tiny figure pressed so firmly against the wall that it could have made an imprint. Whatever sentiments she had initially conveyed were nothing but warmth and tenderness compared to the fury that burned in her eyes now.

The women, spurred on by maternal instincts of some sort, scolded the young girl half-heartedly for her outburst, though neither spoke with any real conviction. Quinn turned his gaze momentarily to the floor in apology as Rom Chang gently stroked

Mei's head, the girl's pointy, birdlike shoulders rising and falling with each heavy breath.

"What did she say?"

"It's not worth repeating."

"I just want to make sure she's alright."

"She is. You don't have to worry."

"Noi . . ."

She hesitated for a moment. "She just said to get away from her. Something like that."

"I figured as much. What was the other thing? Gon-something?"

"*Ghonlaat*. It means, well, she said to 'Get away from me, you cockroach.'"

He grinned in spite of himself, in spite of everything. The little ball of rage continued to fume at him from across the room, and like an idiot, he smiled back with admiration. This tiny, helpless child who had no one, not even her own family, and she would scrape and claw and will her way through anyone, through everyone who dared to confront her.

"I suppose that's my cue to leave," he said. "We need to find a place for her. She can't stay here. Does she have any other relatives?"

Noi translated for Rom Chang. "No relatives. Mei is like family to her also, but she doesn't have the means to support her. She has three children, and they struggle to get by as it is. Some days she can't afford to feed them at all. And of course, Mei's rightful place would be with her aunt—she can't take Mei and have her live in the neighboring house."

"Well, she can't stay here," he said, glancing skeptically at the roof. "Look at this place."

"I know. I can ask some questions to other houses here. My friends can help with that."

"What about Battambang?"

"I don't have any room, Quinn. I wish I did."

"I'll pay for everything," he said. "Uniform, books. I'll throw in something just for general expenses too, like hydro."

"You know I won't accept your money, and it's not about the money." She paused. "*Most* of the time."

"I know it isn't, and that's why I'm not giving it to you; it's for her and the girls. I know you don't have much room left, but if—"

"*Any*, Quinn. We don't have *any* room left. I want to help her as much as you, and, of course, I will. *We* will. I'll find her a suitable place."

"I'm not letting her stay somewhere where we don't know the staff. You know better than most what goes on in those privately run shelters." He looked to Mei and then back again. "And she's sure as hell not staying here."

"Of course she won't. And, in a couple of months . . ."

He let her sit in the uncomfortable silence for a moment. "You know what could happen in that time."

"Quinn . . ." she said, placing a hand on his knee. "You can't save everyone by yourself. Believe me, I've tried. You'll lose yourself."

"I'm not trying to save everyone," he said. "I'm trying to save her."

Mei had calmed somewhat, the adrenaline beginning to wear off, the inevitable creeping fatigue of the resulting crash setting in, visible in her heavy eyelids.

"And you've been reading that MoSVY report again, haven't you?"

"I hardly need the ministry to tell me how bad the conditions are."

"In a few months, I might be able to arrange something. Right now a couple of our girls are thinking quite seriously about going to the university. They would live on campus, which would free up a room."

"She doesn't need an entire room to herself. She just needs a clean bed somewhere safe."

"Quinn," Noi said, her tone stern, "I know you're trying to help, but you also have to trust that I know what I'm doing. You talk as if we're going to leave her here. I'll find a place for her. Have some faith in me, please."

"I know, I know. It's just—"

"She's here with us now and probably safer than she's been in years. I won't let her disappear into the system. You know I won't."

Noi's shelter, Jewels of Battambang, was a rehabilitation center that operated in a different stratosphere than the ramshackle construct in which they currently sat. While managed by Noi, it was run primarily by trained teachers, counselors, and a local graduate student majoring in psychotherapy. It had a rigid school curriculum with all the requisite supplies, nutritious food, clean bedsheets, and, as the girls grew older, they were guided into various vocational courses depending on their interests. Many had gone off to college, and many more reintegrated successfully into local communities plying various trades.

One of Noi's golden rules was no more than twenty girls per facility, of which she owned three: one in Poipet, on the same eastward smuggling route as the flagship center in Battambang, and the third in Pattaya, a coastal resort city roughly two hours south of Bangkok. An influx in numbers would not only upset the balance but, more importantly, the sense of community and the amount of attention each girl received. These principles were a cornerstone of her success with all three centers, a success in which she clearly took great pride.

To say it was a preferable alternative to government shelters was an understatement. MoSVY, the Cambodian Ministry of Social Affairs, Veterans and Youth Rehabilitation, had recently released a publication shedding light on the state of orphanages in the country—at least, shedding light for those with no prior knowledge of the subject. Among its highlights was the acknowledgement that the vast majority of youth shelters were operated without any official oversight, completely unregistered, thereby leaving tens of thousands of children unaccounted for across the land. Vulnerable children were housed in essentially anonymous group homes, pagodas, and various makeshift accommodations, the backgrounds and intentions of caregivers as suspect as the lodgings themselves. Numerous facilities had been shut down due to the rampant sexual abuse of the children, preyed upon by volunteers and social workers alike.

As Quinn rose to his feet, his knees cracked in harmony with the floorboards, and he gave a tight-lipped nod of acquiescence to Noi. "I need a cigarette."

"You should stop that."

"Come on, Noi," he said, moving toward the ladder, "you really should learn to pick your battles."

TWO

IN A HUMBLE GUESTHOUSE RUN BY A CHARMING, MIDDLE-AGED Cambodian couple, Quinn woke earlier than intended after a restless sleep. The bedroom was simply furnished: dresser, chair, creaky bedframe, lumpy mattress. A slowly revolving fan was apparently decorative, for it certainly served no other purpose in the stuffy room. His ankles had spent the night dangling over the edge of the bed, as was customary whenever he visited the Far East, though he didn't mind all that much. The room was clean, the neighborhood quiet, and with such gracious and welcoming hosts, he wouldn't dare make a complaint. After all, he could have stayed at the Shangri-La and still tossed and turned for hours. There would have been no blissful slumber that night regardless, not after what Rom Chang had told him.

Slipping out the front door, he followed his nose and the sounds of the early morning village bustle down a narrow side street packed with food stalls. He approached one of the small, expedient eateries, the ground littered with produce shavings. It had a long plastic table, on which sat large bowls of shredded cabbage and noodles, short pillars of stacked serving bowls, and a blackened, wire grill that smoked over hot coals. The cook, an older woman with deep set eyes, held a pair of tongs in one hand and wore a frilly white top—a blouse with billowing flaps that looked as though a cloud had descended and settled just under her neckline. She had an all-too-familiar look: warm, inviting, but tinged with nervous apprehension. At six-foot-three, blond and blue-eyed, he wasn't exactly her typical customer, and her concerns were evident in the wrinkles on her forehead.

He smiled and gave a quick nod, then pointed to a man squatting on a flimsy stool, shoveling rice and pork into his mouth with a plastic spoon.

"*Saum, Bai Sach Chrouk?*"

A toothy smile spread from ear to ear as she let out a high-pitched laugh, equal parts amusement and relief. Along with her assistant—a ponytailed girl in her twenties mesmerized by the interaction—the pair set about assembling his breakfast. The task was filled with lively discussion, punctuated by giggles and glances at the tall foreigner with the terrible accent. While the great ruins of Angkor were internationally renowned, Siem Reap hosting throngs of tourists each year, in the backwaters of the country, in the villages and hamlets and rural heart of the land, a white face remained quite the novelty.

After receiving his breakfast, Quinn thanked the cooks with a confident "*Aw ghon,*" which elicited yet another chorus of giggles across the table. He dropped a few extra *riels* into a silver tray before weaving through the crowd to find a quiet place to sit. He opened the plastic lid and breathed in the *bai sach chrouk*, literally "pork with rice," a must-have whenever he found himself back in the country. Cheap cuts of pork marinated in coconut milk and grilled over piping-hot coals, which, when dribbled with pork fat, hissed and smoked beneath the seared cuts of meat. It was served on a bed of rice along with another personal favorite, pickled daikon radish.

Mei had eventually warmed to Chanthavy after she returned with tea and soup, and following a brief discussion about a trip to the hospital, it was determined the girl needed rest more than anything, her exterior wounds little more than superficial scrapes and bruises. They would take her to the doctor the following morning just to be certain, with Chanthavy and Rom Chang to remain with her throughout the night.

When Quinn returned at dusk with supper for everyone, the adrenaline coursing through Mei's little body had finally dissipated, the events of the day taking their toll, and she slept like a stone. At one point she even began to snore, everyone sharing a welcome moment of levity. *That little button nose, it sounds like a freight train!*

As Chanthavy cradled Mei in her arms, Rom Chang spoke at length about the child's parents, with Noi translating a heartbreaking tale long into the night.

Mei had never met her father, Vichet. Her mother, Sokhanya, was pregnant when he and a few friends left their village in hopes of finding work in the great land of opportunity: Thailand. Vichet, like many rural and impoverished Cambodians, struggled to make ends meet and provide for his family. When Sokhanya finally became pregnant, it was a blessing but one underscored with anxiety for the future. They had been trying to conceive for years using any means possible, from ancient tribal superstitions to whatever modern remedies they could afford, which were few. They had all but lost hope when, after years of heartache and frustration, finally, as if completely by chance, a gentle seed had taken root in Sokhanya's belly. The couple was overjoyed, with Vichet all the more so, privately elated that his mother-in-law had lost her main bone of contention. He would at least have some temporary respite before she inevitably found some other subject to galvanize her endless nagging.

The blessing, however, would come at a cost. Vichet had spent most of their meager earnings on fertility medicines and the like, earnings that barely put rice on the table without the added expenses of elaborate and often unfounded virility treatments. He and his friends had often heard stories about the lucrative opportunities that could be found in Thailand, particularly in its capital city. Bangkok served as the region's commercial and business center, one of the major hubs of Southeast Asia, and as such had infinitely more job prospects than any of its local counterparts. The food industry, whether in restaurants or food preparation; the construction sector and its various low-skilled trades; farming on plantations; general labor in garment factories, there were countless ways to earn enough *baht* to live modestly and still send good money home to the family. That is, of course, if one could afford to get into the country.

For many Cambodians, particularly rural-dwelling farmers such as Vichet, the cost of acquiring a legitimate passport, never mind a genuine work visa, was astronomical. When factoring in recruitment fees, the processing of documents, and the very real possibility of being overcharged for each and every expense simply for being a migrant worker, it could easily take over a year's salary to come up with the necessary funds.

Vichet had less than nine months. However, there was always a much simpler option.

There was a well-known smuggler who frequented his village and other nearby towns, a swarthy and rather duplicitous fellow, as such characters usually were. For a long time, Vichet and many others scoffed at those foolish enough to trust these snake-oil peddlers or any of their fly-by-night schemes. And yet, time passed, circumstances changed, and there he was, desperate for a service that very few could provide. In the end, it may not have been the path one intended on taking. It may not have been a path one was even aware existed, but there, amongst the shadows, it was just this sort of man who shone his dim light.

And so, after much deliberation with family and friends, Vichet and a group of local men paid a far more affordable sum to get across the border, albeit without any papers.

They left at nightfall, traversed rivers and jungle, got lost for a long while, regained their path, and finally emerged at an obscure rendezvous point at the edge of a field where they were promptly picked up by a taxi, the next link in the smuggling chain. Eventually, after being passed from one broker to the next, they found themselves grouped together with various other migrants at a Thai port and ordered to board fishing trolleys. Vichet figured he would be better suited to agricultural work, even construction, but wasn't about to complain at the prospect of hard work for fair wages.

It wasn't long before he and the others realized they had been sold to the boat captain. Hopes and dreams of a new life at sea, earning honest wages as fishermen, quickly devolved into a waking nightmare, illusions of fair pay vanishing with the shoreline. Now they had debts to repay, exorbitant transport costs fronted by the smugglers.

The men were regularly beaten, abused, and forced to work under inhumane conditions. Day and night they pulled nets, sorted fish, and scrubbed the decks, working all hours with nothing more than diluted bowls of foul rice for sustenance. If they lacked strength, they were given a special powder to mix with water. The amphetamines masked the knots in their hungry bellies, dulled the sting of saltwater on their blistered hands.

Over time, Vichet became more and more vocal despite the beatings, even more so when he heard rumors that they wouldn't be docking for another year, maybe longer. Every now and again, a smaller ship would sail by and restock supplies on the open water, a practice meant to keep them from even spotting a shoreline, never mind thinking of escape. Here, the slavers had them too. If they fled, they would be reported as illegals—arrested and imprisoned—depending on how far they could swim, of course.

One morning, Vichet reached his limit and confronted the boat captain. No one could hear what the argument was about, but it wasn't difficult to imagine. To everyone's surprise, Vichet's passion seemed to strike a chord with the man. The crew looked on as the seaman nodded in agreement, shook his head, and held out his palms sympathetically. *What would you have me do?*

He led Vichet to the port bow, an arm around his shoulder and pointed somewhere off in the distance, seemingly providing an explanation. With his free hand he produced a small blade from his pocket, carved into Vichet's throat, and muttered something to himself as he watched the body spasm and topple overboard into the sea.

When the news trickled down to the village and Sokhanya finally received word of her husband's fate, she didn't speak for a long while. Eventually, much to the surprise of gossiping neighbors, assuming her to be forever catatonic, she began to make preparations for her own journey abroad. Clearly not the sentimental type, she resolved not to be as naïve as her late husband and would seek out a better living not in Thailand but to the north, in China. She made arrangements with several other women who would take a bus along a popular route through Vietnam, ideally ending up in Lao Cai on the Chinese border. Many had heard about the job opportunities for unskilled workers like herself, higher wages, possibly even marriage to one of the countless bachelors across the expansive state. The skewed gender ratio, a result of China's misguided one-child policy, ensured that many Chinese men would pay handsome dowries for South Asian brides, particularly in the more rural parts of the country.

In truth, Sokhanya had never been as gullible as Vichet, even before his tragedy. She had heard all the stories before and was wise enough to believe them. Criminal gangs and traffickers who preyed upon the stateless and destitute across the Mekong region were hardly particular about the backgrounds of those they victimized. Over the years a disturbing trend had emerged whereby vulnerable women, impoverished and without any formal education, were lured abroad with promises of plentiful work opportunities and relative prosperity. Such stories were polished and tailored to better suit the traffickers' deceit, and the women—transported in buses and sea craft, through remote mountain passes or corrupt border checkpoints—would end up purchased by Chinese bachelors.

If one asked the right questions and probed the right sources, horror stories abounded. Newly acquired Khmer "wives" made to work as house slaves, raped by husband, father-in-law, and relatives alike. Some were housed in brothels rather than homes and confined to similar routines. No one could deny that bridal trafficking was a lucrative business for those without care or conscience. The risks were low, the rewards considerable. It was rape for profit and far more cost-effective than selling drugs or running guns. The product, after all, was a reusable commodity. It could be bargained for and auctioned, peddled and traded, purchased, sold, and resold again.

Rom Chang didn't know the exact circumstances of Sokhanya's life when she got to China; she heard only rumors. They had an argument the last time they spoke, Sokhanya well aware of the risks involved but stubbornly confident in her own way, determined to earn a better living for her daughter. Rom Chang agreed to help Chaya, Sokhanya's sister, care for Mei but counseled against placing her faith in the Chinese, never mind those who would smuggle her across.

While there were numerous cases of Khmer girls being repatriated after dreadful experiences, not all stories were so disheartening. One girl returned home quite pleased with her current arrangement, newly married to a pig farmer from a small village comprised almost exclusively of bachelors. The farmer could not afford a dowry for a Chinese bride, but—as foreign women came at a fraction of the cost—it was a mutually beneficial arrangement. Upon her homecoming she described her husband as "a fat rice cake of a man," dull and bland and perfectly harmless.

She remembered Sokhanya from the long journey north through Vietnam, the woman who confided that any situation where she could send money back to her daughter was a positive one. Still, she had no illusions and hardly expected any man—not even a penniless Chinese wheat farmer—to pay a notable sum for a widowed single mother. To the best of the girl's knowledge, Sokhanya had also married, but she was uncertain about the circumstances. She'd been wed to a man described as short and squat, a whisker away from being completely bald yet with thick eyebrows, like two giant caterpillars perched above his eyelids. She hadn't seen Sokhanya since the week they were both sold.

Every few months the girl would return to the village, bringing money and gifts for her son, eternally poking fun at her husband's vapid personality, searching desperately for a way to legally bring her boy back to China. The last time Rom Chang had seen her, over a year ago, she asked if there was any news about Sokhanya. The girl hesitated for a moment and turned her gaze, uncomfortable with the idea of spreading rumors to a concerned friend.

Rom Chang insisted.

While shopping at the local night market a month before, she had overheard the raucous laughter of a group of drunks. One man was especially vocal, complaining bitterly about his financial woes, having apparently wasted a small fortune on foreign women. "A scam! A complete waste!" he ranted, much to the amusement of his goading friends. He bemoaned the stereotype that Vietnamese girls were just like Chinese girls, similar in culture yet infinitely more subservient. "Nonsense!" he exclaimed. He had been married twice before, once to a girl from Vietnam and, more recently, had tried his luck with a widowed housewife from Cambodia. Being careful not to stare, casually perusing a rack of blouses, she caught a glimpse of his bald head as she passed. A bald head and a thick, prominent brow.

He had allegedly given up, happy to live out his days as a drunken bachelor, free at last from their incessant badgering. One of his wives had tried to escape no less than three times, on one occasion seeking help from the local authorities and receiving the beating of a lifetime when she was returned to him. He bragged that he sprained his wrist while doling out her punishment and couldn't masturbate for an entire week. More rollicking laughter. Apparently, she had escaped a fourth time, never to be seen or heard from again. The man promptly returned, fuming, to the local broker and demanded his money back. Instead, he was compensated with another wife, an older woman this time, which was more than he deserved according to the broker. This one didn't even last through the harvest.

His first thought was that she had fled as well, the autumn morning eerily quiet, the ground wet with morning dew. A peculiar sound caught his attention from inside the shed, a dull moan that came and went with the breeze. The bare earthen floor was littered with rusted farm tools, and, suspended above, a haunting silhouette; Sokhanya hung from a cross beam by his old cattle reins, skin pale as the morning sky.

When Rom Chang finished, Quinn was somewhat surprised by his own reaction—he wasn't shocked in the slightest. After all, these stories were commonplace. Still, it was the first time all the numbers and statistics, the migration trends, the political and environmental stressors were refined into something tangible. All the diplomatic jargon he had heard or read about in the field, the brutal realities of life in the region, of life for the weak and vulnerable, now had a human face. These weren't maps with migratory arrows and parabolic flows, annual reports with color-coded pie charts and overlapping graphs, ninety-second news segments to hastily bookend television broadcasts. At all the meetings and lectures and conferences, and even in his own work, the lofty and detached ambitions of suits with lanyards were distilled into a singular narrative. It could all be found in the deep slumber of an exhausted young girl—in the dark abrasion on her forehead, in the fray of her weathered dress, in the tragic tale of her family, and in her fierce and unrelenting will to survive.

THREE

Four Years Later
Transit Zone, International Arrivals

THE GREAT HALL SWELLED WITH THE VOICES AND FOOTSTEPS OF hundreds of weary travelers. The air was stagnant, the warm fog of an impatient public: yawning, coughing, chattering in countless dialects. Quinn did his best to block out the hum of voices as his feet trudged along the polished tile floor, obediently in step with the orderly queue of feet in front of him. The line snaked left and right, seemingly endless, dispersing into orderly columns in front of a dozen inspection booths.

Was there anything worse than a busy transit hub? A great mob of people thrusting themselves forward, rushing this way and that, desperate to beat everyone else by mere moments to a suitcase, a lounge, a taxi, or, like himself, a connecting flight. The affair was especially irritating on this occasion, made all the more uncomfortable by a throbbing headache, compliments of cheap airline whiskey and, admittedly, a few other brands from the departures lounge.

Nowhere could one find a person more bereft of social graces than in an airport terminal. Basic manners and any pretense of civility were thrown out as fast as one's favorite shampoo at the security screening, society reduced to a frenzied mass of clamoring animals. The anxiety of a delayed flight, the frustration of a long queue, the dread of lost baggage; it was prison rules, everyone for themselves among the swarm of impatient tourists. Coming or going, it was always the same, looks of consternation painted on the faces of the world, invariably lost in buildings with more signage than, well, anywhere. Directions ubiquitous and in various languages, glowing, blinking, colored, and immense, accompanied by arrows and icons and pictures as well.

And all of it irrelevant, of course, to the tardy traveler—inevitably barreling through the terminal, sometimes in the right direction, sometimes not, and to hell with the ankles and heels forced to suffer the wrath of their baggage carts. Collateral damage.

Aboard the flight it was the same upon arrival, people leaping to their feet, baggage in hand before the aircraft had even slowed, sometimes before the wheels hit the tarmac, eager to deplane. The plan was immediately foiled—the doors yet to open, no gate at which to disembark—and so they stood, lemmings with vacant expressions, pinned against one another while flight attendants rolled their eyes. "Please" and "thank you" were foreign words among all foreign tongues, the principle of *me first* dictating the procession with far more authority.

Airports always made Quinn wonder what people would be capable of in times of real struggle. Sometimes, during strange bouts of reverie, one could almost make sense of it all—even accounting for man's inhumanity to man. Just the thought of a slight delay, a less-than-optimal seat, perhaps even the admittedly gross inconvenience of a missed connection; there were those who became almost rabid, foaming at the mouth while berating ticketing agents and airline staff. A tempest in a teacup, a brief glimpse into the true nature of the human form. How animalistic they remained. How fragile the social order and its conventions truly were.

His conversation with Noi had been brief. After establishing the where and when, he booked the next available flight to meet her. Something had gone terribly wrong. It was evident in the tone of her voice, despite her reticence. He refused to fear the worst, and though the liquor helped with that, missing his connection wasn't an option. Noi insisted on telling him in person, to which he reluctantly obliged, but he could hardly wait any longer. A few more hours out of absolute necessity, but no more.

Surveying the terminal, bloodshot eyes squinting in the fluorescent light, he spotted what could only be described as the physical manifestation of everything wrong with border security. Quinn was too far back to read the officer's nametag, but the man was clearly a supervisor or at least someone of relative importance, judging by the epaulets on his wrinkled charcoal uniform. A great, doughy paunch protruded from his midsection and hung over his belt, two drooping love handles completing the tableau. His pants hung precariously low, though due to the sheer circumference of his waistline resembled more of a parachute than slacks with two separate legs. As if on cue, the man wedged a thumb into the belt loop by his lower back and hoisted his pants a couple of inches, likely out of precaution.

Quinn looked on in disbelief as the man waddled from booth to booth with strained, shallow breaths, distributing papers to every customs officer. To millions of travelers, both international and domestic, this individual's disheveled appearance represented the face of the nation's border control. He was a member of the elite, charged with defending national interests, overseeing the operation that kept terrorists, murderers, and drug dealers at bay. This caricature of a man was meant not only to keep the border safe but inspire faith and confidence in the traveling public that all was well, that they could sleep soundly at night. He was the personification of every government department that Quinn had ever worked for, every bloated bureaucracy that valued political correctness and public opinion over experience, aptitude and ability.

It brought to his mind a time when he had been contracted to work on a project based out of Brussels, a consultation aimed primarily at improving response times for security threats. During a preliminary survey, he had been alarmed to find as many gaps as he had. The assignment was brief, in part because the airport authority ultimately decided to go with a different firm, but also because he had difficulties remaining diplomatic while voicing his opinions. In his mind, sugarcoating the glaring lack of safety protocols and security loopholes, never mind the inadequate training of airport personnel, set a dangerous precedent. If anything, it only encouraged more of the same lack of attention to detail. Apparently, this was hardly the outcome his employers had in mind, the entire survey being something of a formality. There was never any real intention to overhaul security procedures; the costs would have been astronomical, and that, as it turned out, was the quintessential issue all along. A report was required, any report, to tick off one more box along a checklist of items that would usher in a newer, more cost-effective system down the road. A new policy designed to move security screening into the modern age, doing more with less, eliminating redundancies and maximizing profits. His boss at the time, a kindly old man, later counseled him that his temperament was not exactly suited to a job that required, "Well, now, how to put this? A lighter touch."

It was hardly the first time he'd received such advice. It was there in academia, a lifetime ago, while studying a combined degree of political science and international relations. Professors had always told him to remain "grounded" and "realistic" about work in the field, always speaking with a sort of veiled counsel as if portending some bleak philosophical reckoning just over the horizon. As it turned out, he wasn't altogether ill-advised.

While his first internship had been in Beirut, it was in New Delhi that he cut his teeth; a six-month contract as a human rights consultant where he experienced corruption, poverty and general disorder on a near unfathomable scale, and, most disconcertingly, within the very NGO he was working for. This inauspicious trend continued with the following contract, then the next, and onwards ever since. While working for Transparency International he became obsessed with high-level bribery and fraud, particularly corporate fraud, and was praised for his innovative reporting, if not his blunt delivery and vehement calls for action. He moved on to work briefly with WorldVision in Singapore—an experience somehow even more disheartening than India, and later joined several projects under the auspices of the United Nations, the organization which he soon came to recognize as the gold standard in bureaucratic inefficiency.

In just over a decade he'd dabbled in all manner of humanitarian crises—from border security to war crimes, from drug trafficking to refugees—and in that time had become a disillusioned pseudo-authority on nearly every subject. He was paid handsomely for brief contracts—from two-week training seminars in Doha to weekend speaking engagements in Hanoi—which allowed him to intermingle just long enough before inevitably railing against the hypocrisy of the very institutions that were paying him. It wasn't long before he developed a rather colorful reputation; the subject-matter expert with an axe to grind, and Quinn, both incapable and unwilling to tolerate such habitual Orwellian doublespeak, had been grinding the axe down to the handle ever since.

The orderly queue became less so as it fanned out into various lines in front of corresponding customs booths, with counter number four manned by an officer who was neither man nor officer. A pencil-necked young boy with either a pubescent mustache or a smear of dirt on his upper lip sat proudly at his post. Quinn was certain he had adjusted his chair as high as it could possibly go. Despite his valiant effort to command some semblance of authority, the young recruit was preoccupied with an Indian family of five who weren't exactly making things easy. Visibly out of his depth, he struggled to make sense of the assembly before him.

A woman in her early twenties was translating for her elderly parents, both in wheelchairs, while two young children, a boy and girl, engaged in some sort of ritualized hand-slapping contest. The officer fumbled with a stack of passports, stapled together and falling open like accordions, residency cards tumbling across his keyboard.

Quinn strained to hear the conversation but was distracted by a sharp whack to his calf, a six-year-old boy waving a toy airplane behind him. His mother stood oblivious on her bedazzled phone, prattling away as her son yanked her dress, whined for attention, and recklessly piloted the aircraft into the back of Quinn's knee.

For a moment he considered how best to trip the little bastard without being noticed, then thought better of it. Difficult, with the number of security cameras.

The two women in front of him, garbed in floral *saris*, stepped forward and approached the booth, evidently cousins of the family ahead, feeling it necessary to lend a helping hand. The ensuing cacophony of Hindi reached new levels as the entire group tried to make sense of the officer's questions, and the boy, having recently been the victim of a particularly well-timed smack from his younger sister, started to wail in agony.

Struggling to maintain his composure, the officer took a deep breath. "What is the purpose of your trip?" he asked sternly, hoping the added baritone might transcend the language barrier, which, of course, it did not.

The elderly couple smiled and bobbed their heads from side to side while the children were respectively scolded and consoled by their mother.

"Your purpose of travel."

"Wedding," the mother said. "My cousin brother."

"Your who?"

"Cousin brother."

"Well, which is it?"

"Yes."

"Pardon?"

"Yes."

This went on for a time, questions addressed with a series of well-intentioned non-answers before the officer looked to a worn stack of paper, shuffling through faded pages soaked in highlighter. He traced his finger along a passage and blurted out some bastardized dialect of Punjabi, which the family seemed to recognize was no longer English but nothing quite comprehensible either. Seven puzzled faces returned his vacant stare, including the boy, who, having recovered from the earlier assault, was being soothed by a small plastic bag of assorted biscuits.

Quinn pinched the bridge of his nose between thumb and forefinger, willing away the early stages of a dreadful hangover until the officer, apparently satisfied, picked up his stamp and proceeded to wallop each passport with such ferocity that he may well have been tenderizing a steak.

A moment later, Quinn stood before the counter where the boy, now identifiable as one Officer Hankel, couldn't have been much older than twenty. With a youthful face and a shaven head, he had just the sort of protruding ears that one was tempted to grab onto and shake like maracas. His mustache, for anyone who might dare call it that, was curly and sparse yet painstakingly cultivated, matching its wispy counterpart on his chin. Far too thin to fill out his uniform, a stiffly starched collar bobbed loosely around his neck, his frame so wiry that Quinn could have sworn he'd forgotten to remove the coat hanger.

"Passport and boarding pass," Hankel said. He scanned the documents awhile, then plugged away at his keyboard. "Where are you coming from?"

Quinn hesitated, not on purpose but for a moment genuinely unable to recall, a whiskey fog coating his memory. "I believe it's on the card there," he said, rubbing the corner of his eye. "Liberia."

"Pardon?"

"Liberia."

Hankel's brow lifted expectantly. "The country, or . . ."

"West Africa? No, Costa Rica. The flight code is on the ticket stub."

Hankel continued his theater, sizing up his client, conducting an overlong comparison of the passport photograph.

"There's been an outbreak of Ebola in Sierra Leone," he said. "It shares a border with Liberia."

"As far as I'm aware, there's no Ebola in Guanacaste."

"That's fine, sir. Anything to declare?"

"Just a bottle—no, two bottles of rum."

"What size, sir?"

"Regular size."

"Which is?"

Quinn immediately regretted rolling his eyes, the headache leaping straight to the fore. He placed the neatly wrapped bottles on the counter before him. "This size."

Hankel nodded.

Quinn could barely manage to keep his mouth shut, the effects of the mid-flight binge wearing painfully thin, the uniformed vanguard before him practically salivating at the opportunity to assert his dominion. Usually, Quinn ended up learning things the hard way, but best to keep his composure here, he thought. Given the time of day, there was no telling what awaited the poor souls held captive during any additional screening—a stuffy little room packed with wailing children, yappy dogs, entitled businessmen, and more disgruntled humanity.

"I apologize for the questions, sir, but this is an international border," Hankel said, straightening his posture. His tone reflected an almost erotic passion for the authority he commanded. "As I'm sure you understand, we have security regulations in place for a reason."

"Sure."

"Everything alright, sir?" asked a gruff voice by his side. Quinn turned and looked straight into the sunken eyes of the floor supervisor. A heavy sigh escaped Quinn's lips, and he suppressed some choice language before burying a palm into his eye socket, rubbing away the tedious reality.

"If he gives you any trouble . . ." the supervisor began, then casually jutted his chin behind the counter, his neck following suit with a gelatinous wobble.

"No trouble here, sir," Quinn interjected. "I'm a little out of sorts, I'll admit. It's been a hell of a day, the flight, the lineups . . ." Just then, a toddler broke out into a piercing wail behind them. "The people," he added, pointing with his thumb. "I just don't want to miss my flight."

The supervisor shifted his weight. He had plump cheeks and beads of sweat on his receding hairline. "We wouldn't want that, now, would we?"

"No, sir."

After a moment, sufficiently placated by the display, the supervisor hoisted his pants up once more and gave a singular nod, a smug look of satisfaction on his sweaty face. "Good work, Officer," he said, smacking the counter twice. Then, turning to Quinn, "We've all been there. Air travel isn't what it used to be. We appreciate your patience. Carry on, gentlemen."

Quinn returned the nod, for once able to keep his comments to himself, a humility that had come with age, perhaps. The thought amused him and left a certain look on his face, one that confused Officer Hankel, who stamped twice but said nothing more.

Waiting by the luggage carousel, he could hardly stand still. Shifting his weight, crossing and uncrossing his arms, he was increasingly concerned about his meeting with Noi. He had a habit of rubbing the pad of his thumb against forefinger whenever he was anxious. Each time he caught himself, try as he might, he was back at it within moments, starting a fire in the palm of his hand. He looked on as the conveyor rumbled along, still bare but for a single, navy suitcase, marooned from a previous flight.

It wasn't long before his thoughts returned to the two officials—the scrawny officer, green, having just departed from his mother's teat, and his pompous, slovenly boss. He wondered what rank the man held, the embroidered epaulets on his shoulders signifying some division of upper management—perhaps superintendent, or chief—though the designation hardly mattered. In his experience, it placed the man invariably into one of only two categories, a relatively straightforward classification clouded only slightly on this occasion by age.

He was in his late forties, maybe older, but not quite senior enough to fit into the first category of organizational fossils: men employed since the dawn of time, now jaded, disgruntled, unable, and unwilling to change with the times, and in most cases, utterly inept. Still, they weren't quite offensive enough that one could simply get rid of them—after all, one could make a career as a government official by being an imbecile. Inevitably, the next logical course of action was promotion. Relocation elsewhere to a post with more authority, an inflated salary, and an inflated ego to match, yet still someplace relatively out of the way. Talents redistributed to where they would cause the least amount of harm, a position invented out of thin air if need be. Distracting a kitten with a ball of yarn.

The second category of managerial leadership was far more insidious and consisted of much younger officials. Eager upstarts with a penchant for flattery, their only inherent skill seemed to be the ability to lodge their wagging noses so firmly between the buttocks of their superiors that one might wonder how they were able to draw breath. When they weren't preoccupied with throwing their colleagues to the wolves or giving confident opinions on subjects well beyond their comprehension, they too would find their stock rise quite regularly through promotion. Given their practiced habit of puckering up to the backsides of executives and directors and presidents on high, eventually, one of these organizational demigods would reach down to wipe themselves, and who would they find but the fawning parasites themselves, gleefully holding a wrap of toilet paper.

On and on it went, this carousel of incompetence, no matter the organization, no matter the state. A distant memory came to mind. An older gentleman, something of a mentor, had once told him that he was far too young to be such a pessimist, but that was many years ago now, many contracts come and gone. Better to be a realist, he thought and, more to the point, better not to be delusional. If one always expected the worst of their superiors, life wasn't as frequently disappointing.

FOUR

Montreal, Canada

THE ICY WINDS OF A BITTER STORM LASHED THE WINDOWS OF THE Café Bientôt, the howl alone enough to send shivers down the collars of the cozy, red-cheeked patrons inside. Every now and again, the old glass rattled, bracing itself as fierce gusts blew past, rivulets of condensation streaking the panes.

Sipping a watery, overpriced coffee, Quinn sat in an armchair and pondered how long it would take his shoes to dry, the soles soaked through from navigating wet slush. A decent cup of coffee would have been a start, and he longed for it—something Turkish, if possible, molten hot, thick enough that a spoon could stand erect in the center of the *kahve finjani*. Coffee in its purest form.

His shoulders still stung, freckled and raw from the Latin sun, the warm tropical breeze nothing more than a distant memory now. Winter had come early, and the first blizzard of the year had caught everyone off guard: heaps of gray snow piled by the roadside, cars whipping by, spraying waves of dark sludge onto the sidewalk, a slick, translucent layer of ice coating the pavement, lying in wait for unsuspecting passersby.

Noi was late, though he didn't begrudge her that. He wondered how she was faring in the brutal Canadian weather. Bracing himself before stepping outside, he turned his back to the cutting wind and lit a cigarette.

The pair had first met years ago at a conference in Bangkok organized by UN Women. A rather busy affair, almost a year in the making, its aim was to gather representatives of various NGOs, community organizations, charity groups, anyone and everyone working to help impoverished women and girls in Greater Mekong. Napatsorn, or Noi, as she liked to be called, was working at the shelter in Battambang where girls were taught silk weaving and sewing alongside a basic curriculum: arithmetic, hygiene, hospitality essentials. Noi was one of the founding members of what would grow into a humble but highly reputable organization, establishing contacts with various donors, charities, and other well-funded foreign aid departments in the field. She was consequently invited to the Bangkok initiative—the sole representative for the newly dubbed Jewels of Battambang—with the aim of forming a tight-knit network of highly motivated actors in the region.

The conference was held at the InterContinental in Patumwan and was an impressive affair with attendees from over thirty organizations in Indochina. Quinn had been invited as a guest speaker to discuss the role of corruption in law enforcement, the challenges of nepotism and bribery, as well as the complicity of border officials in the trafficking of vulnerable persons. A routine contract for the quasi-diplomat; a jack of all trades who lent his "expertise" on the subject *du jour*, popping up at various forums like a gopher in suit and tie.

During a midafternoon recess on the first day, he and Noi exchanged pleasantries over tea and lemon cakes. By the third day, they sat at their own table for lunch, exchanging views on the current state of trafficking affairs in Cambodia. He was captivated by her passion for the girls and the selfless nature not only of her work but her entire lifestyle. She came across as a modern-day Khmer Mother Theresa, so much so that he felt a pang of guilt for initially doubting her, wondering how one person could be so genuinely charitable, determined, and kind. The guilt only increased thereafter, pondering his own contributions, or lack thereof, as he nudged a deviled egg around the rim of his plate with a fork.

They became fast friends and, following the seminar, he changed his return flight to add a small detour—a quick trip east across the border to Battambang. The facility was modestly constructed, but the palm trees and sprawling gardens gave it a welcoming, if homely charm. He didn't have the chance to meet many of the girls as they had taken a field trip into the city, but he did meet one who made a lasting impression. She had yet to meet any of her sisters either, and would soon become the newest member of the Jewels of Battambang family.

It wasn't long before a brash gust of wind drove him back inside, butting out half a cigarette in the bin as he went. He repositioned his seat, avoiding a draft from the windowsill, and covertly tipped a few splashes of whiskey into his mug, tucking the flask back into his jacket pocket. Biding his time, he was begrudgingly forced to accept that his mood was particularly foul. It had been months since his last contract, perhaps close to a year, though the respite had done little to improve his outlook. Not that he was in any frame of mind to look for work—joining this organization or that agency, this division or that department, passing through titles and time zones on some infernal phantom merry-go-round.

Still, this malaise, it was no longer on the surface. Now the cynicism had taken root somewhere much deeper, in his *bones*, permeating all facets of life. Had he really become that browbeaten, clichéd diplomat? The jaded, alcoholic attaché, forever brooding in the back corners of lecture halls, chain smoking in the stairwells of the Hilton, the Marriot? That same man he spotted at every conference: faded suit, dwindling hairline, ageless, pallid, and weary. The rabbit hole was widening now, but it was either dour self-critique or the haunting specter of Noi's visit.

A string of silver bells jingled in the doorway, and a diminutive Thai lady, buried in the folds of an oversized winter coat, heaved open the front door. Hair blown about in every direction, she spotted Quinn in the corner and gave him a sympathetic smile, lips tinted a bluish gray from the frosty winds.

She rushed over to him as politely as she could, tears already welling in her tired brown eyes. He embraced her through the frozen synthetic puff in which she was wrapped as she pressed her cheek into the middle of his chest. They stood for a moment in silence before she looked up at him, the same labored smile etched across her face.

"What is it?" he asked, taking her by the shoulders. "The call was bad enough, but now you've really got me worried."

She pressed the pads of her fingers beneath her eyes, blinking, and inhaling deeply.

"Sorry, are you alright? How was the flight? Let's get you a coffee first."

"It's fine," she replied, straightening her posture. "I'm alright, really. Let me just get a cup of tea. No, no"—she motioned for him to sit—"I'll be right back."

He tried to maintain his composure, fearing the worst, though he wasn't quite certain which "worst" he should be dreading. A nightmarish game show played out in his head, his thoughts racing from the demons behind door number one to the horrors behind door number two, so on and so forth, deeper into the chasm. He distracted himself by leveling the wobbly table next to his seat with a folded napkin.

Noi returned with a steaming mug of green tea. She looked well, if a bit drowsy, creeping shadows beneath her eyes, but fourteen-hour flights took their toll on just about everyone. She was barely five feet tall with a stocky physique, her jet-black hair tied in a hefty ponytail revealing large, naked earlobes. Her full lips had regained their color, and her nose—still a touch red from the elements—had a soft bridge with wide nostrils that flared whenever she laughed, though he doubted there would be much humor today.

"It's great to see you. It's been, well, too long since I've been out your way. Lots to catch up on, but this is obviously serious. I can't remember the last time you were in my neck of the woods."

"I was planning on coming in the spring to look at some schools, maybe study my master's here. My French, it's mostly gone now, but I would love to use it again. If not here maybe Toronto." She took a small, cautious sip from her mug. "But you're right; that's not why I'm here."

"What is it? Is she alright? Is she sick?"

Her eyes misted over once more, and she let out a wavering breath, composing herself. "I didn't want to tell you over the phone. I wasn't sure—no, I *was* sure of how you would react, and I knew you—"

"Noi. Please. Just tell me."

She gathered herself for a long moment before saying the words. An eternity for Quinn; he had never seen her so conflicted. Noi was exceptionally good at keeping her emotions in check, containing them, compartmentalizing all the pain and hardship that she had seen back home and then using it as motivation. She harnessed the fear and frustration and transformed it into focus and drive, using the energy to make positive and lasting change in the world around her. And yet, despite all the love and sensitivity she possessed, one could never see it written on her face. She was eternally stoic, unreadable, and maybe that was why she hesitated, for fear that the words would sting too harshly when she spoke them. In the end, it hardly mattered. Somehow, he knew before she said anything at all.

"They took her. She's gone."

FIVE

A TWISTED KNOT FORMED DEEP IN THE PIT OF QUINN'S STOMACH, taking most of his strength with it. It wasn't the sudden news so much as the dreaded confirmation. His subconscious had whispered it as he slept the night she called and again while on the plane, in the taxi, in this very café. He already knew, yet hearing the words spoken aloud brought on a wave of nausea.

Noi rested her hand on his as they sat quietly for a time. Through the window, gentle, drifting flurries had replaced the strafing winds. Couples at nearby tables spoke in hushed tones, reflecting the changing mood outside, jazz piano tinkling softly overhead.

Finally, he spoke. "Tell me. Tell me everything. I need to know what you know."

She nodded, taking another sip of tea. Her eyes darted around, probing for the right words, as if they might appear written on the ceiling, the wall, the counter of creams and sugars.

"They came in the night. I didn't even hear about it until the next day. Pichai called me. He woke up in the morning, unconscious the whole night, alone in the grass, in the ravine. He could have died . . ."

"Who's Pichai? Who's they?"

"Pichai has been helping us for some months. I don't know why I didn't mention him until now. He's a nice man, a very kind heart, from near Siem Reap. He volunteers as a caretaker for us. He's very helpful, always fixing things when he doesn't have to—the children's bicycles, the sewing machines. Now he stays overnight to make sure the girls are okay."

"He stays overnight?"

"He's a good man, Quinn, and I trust him. You know, just last month he fixed the reading lamp in Mei's room."

"In her room now."

"He sleeps outside by the front gate there. You know we don't have any real security, so he stays more for, how is it—appearances. The recruiters, those . . . those *snakes* have been getting more and more bold lately."

He had been kneading his armrest compulsively for some time, her cadence changing when she noticed—a momentary pause.

"He's a family friend of Prang," she continued. "You remember Prang. Pichai's wife, she died last year. Two years before that, his daughter passed away. He's a kind man with no one now. He's helping us, and we're very grateful. You don't need to worry about Pichai. You need to trust more."

"Who do you expect me to trust right now? What else?"

"He barely remembers anything. He was asleep when he heard some trucks on the dirt road that comes in, you know, from the main one. Nobody drives on it. So he went outside of his hut to see. It was dark until they turned the headlights on and it was blinding for him. When he asked who was there and what they wanted, they started to hit him. He said he only remembers maybe one or two hits, that's all. Then he woke up in the grass in the morning. Well, almost morning—it was still dark, he said."

Quinn leaned forward, burying his face in his hands, working his brow with his fingertips as she continued. "When he woke up, he went to check the dorm rooms, but the beds were empty. Some were as if no one had even been there. Everything in the same place. Mei's room . . ."

He lifted his head.

"The chair was tipped over, the covers were everywhere. The desk was also moved a little bit, like maybe someone had pushed it. I think . . . I think she did not make it easy for them."

In his mind he pictured the scene unfolding. The creaking door, the ruffle of sheets, the muffled screams followed by toppling furniture and the pull and chafe and tear of stressed fabric. He felt the faintest sense of pride as he visualized the chaos. She wouldn't have gone without a fight, tooth and nail.

"They're getting more braver all the time," she said, her voice rising an octave, the adopted English exposed with the heightened emotion. "Always there are stories about them talking with families, recruiting near the schools, the way they usually do, but now if they don't get the answers they want, they just take! We were doing good for a long time, the activists and our partners, they're having more and more influence. Even Phnom Penh is starting to take things more seriously. Did I tell you they sent Bunthan Lim to the conference in Beijing? With UNDP and the new five-year plan. We're not just guests now with these projects, Cambodia is starting to play a real role. It's really good, really."

The eternal optimist, she was never one to get too carried away. She wouldn't say such things if she didn't genuinely believe them, that the country was making real progress. It was difficult to watch the pendulum swing back and forth.

"But underneath, so many things are still the same. The police are as corrupt as always, maybe worse than ever. And now that the people are getting more education about migrating, the dangerous work and the risks, it's getting harder for recruiters, so they're becoming more aggressive. The police, too. That's how I know we're doing better, making a difference, because those . . . those *bastards* are getting more braver." For a moment Noi ashamedly tucked her chin and lowered her gaze. She rarely cursed. In fact, he couldn't recall ever hearing it before.

"I have to talk to this Pichai. He didn't say anything else? Nobody saw or heard anything?"

She shot him a look for doubting her. "What I know about that night, now you know. Nobody heard anything except Pichai, and even though he was there, I think he knows less than us." She let out a heavy sigh, turning a ponderous gaze to the floor.

"What is it?"

After a moment, her lips parted hesitantly. "On the plane, I was thinking . . ."

"What?"

"I don't know. I'm not sure it's important, but now I keep thinking about it, so maybe you should know. About a month before, maybe longer, Mei had a fight."

"What kind of fight?"

"An argument with some friends. We had three new girls come not long ago. Two were around Mei's age, but one was older, and she was in a very bad situation. Many of the girls, well, you know how they are, from broken families. Most have been abused, some of them trafficked, but this girl . . ." She looked away, a wistful sound escaping her lips. "She had been through too much, I think. I don't like to say this—sometimes I think it's unfair to even think like this in my position—but girls like her, you can see it in their eyes. I don't know how to help them. I don't know if anyone can help them. Sometimes I would watch her in class or during meals. She could be so very mean toward the others. Tricking them, teasing them, and enjoying it. She was still a child, but her innocence, the warmth, you know, with children, it was completely gone. I think maybe they were grooming her to be a *mama*. Rajitkaew was her name, Kaew."

"Sounds Thai."

"She was, from near Bangkok."

"How did she end up with you?"

"She never said, but we don't ask too many questions. It was obvious where she had been or at least what she had been doing. She was very, what is this word . . . damaged. We don't ask a lot because we don't want the girls reliving those experiences if they don't have to. It's not always healthy for their recovery, a sort of *re-victimization*," she said, trotting out the syllables carefully.

"Of course, Mei became friends with them very fast. You know how she is, like a tour guide the first day they came, showing every-body around, sharing her favorite books, introducing them to the other girls. She even told them about her secret reading spot behind that pile of wood with the small pond. You remember?"

He nodded, a faint smile as he recalled the pictures she had sent.

"Then one day there was some kind of fighting, arguing. I didn't see it happen, but I heard Mei crying in her room. She was very upset. She wouldn't tell me very much, only that Kaew and the other two girls were making fun of her for being young and child-ish, something like that. They weren't much older, but you know Mei. She has a strong spirit, but she can be very innocent. They said she spent too much time at the flower shop doing children's things instead of learning to be a woman." Noi shook her head. "They can be so cruel at that age, you know."

"What was her name again? That girl at the flower shop."

"Areum. Mei looks up to her a lot. She goes over as often as we can let her." She pinched her eyes closed, wincing slightly. "She *was* going over a lot." Pausing for a sip of tea, she cradled the mug in her hands. "Mei never said what they fought about. She was upset, and she was honest with me, but still she avoided some of my questions. I don't know why. They can be secretive at that age about all sorts of silly things. But whatever it was, she didn't like it or didn't agree, and because of that, they sort of broke up. For the next few days, she spent most of her time by herself, and you know her, always so cheerful and friendly with everyone. She was very down. She didn't want to talk to anyone, not even me. She had no interest in seeing Areum either." Noi sighed heavily, sinking back into her seat. "And then, one night about a month ago, they just left."

"Who left?"

"The girls. All three of them. They disappeared in the middle of the night, ran away. If you ask me, I think it was Kaew's idea. I don't blame her, the poor girl. That life is all she's ever known. I think maybe she was more comfortable before she came to us, as strange as that sounds. She needs help that we simply cannot give. We just don't have the resources, the funding, we don't have so many things. And, of course, we can't make anybody stay against their will."

"Why didn't you tell me any of this?"

"I'm telling you now," she said curtly. "This isn't the first time it's happened. Girls leaving, I mean. And Mei was writing you another letter. I'm sure she would have said something. Or maybe not. I don't know."

"I didn't mean it like that."

"I wish I could tell you that this was something unusual. Some of the girls, they just disappear like this. Runaways. Or long-lost parents and relatives appear, pretending to be family." She gave a contemptuous shake of the head. "They show up with paperwork that I know, I just *know* they have paid for, some corrupt policeman helping them. It's just that this time, Mei was involved. I did try to contact you, remember? It was you who didn't answer me right away. Were you on vacation? Quinn . . ."

"Hm? Oh." He gave a perfunctory nod. "Something like that."

"You look tired."

"Mm . . . so do you." He forced a grin, and in turn, so did she.

They sat in silence for a moment as the busy hum of the café surrounded them—murmuring chatter and the occasional snicker over the tinkling of cutlery, baristas clanging glasses and steel containers, intermittent gusts of steam. The door jangled open and a gust of cold air rolled in, sending a chill down the backs of those seated nearby, sweaters and scarves adjusted accordingly. Noi thumbed the edge of her mug while Quinn, lost in thought, stared beyond the smudge marked window into the gray cityscape.

"I have to go down there."

For a long while, she said nothing at all, staring at her lap. "I knew you were going to say something like that."

"I have to, Noi."

"I know," she replied, reluctance in her voice. "I suppose, in some way, I already knew this. Even before I got on the plane." Taking a breath, she met his eyes again. "What will you do? When you get there, I mean."

He shrugged. "Don't know. Talk to Pichai for starters, see what he says."

"Quinn, be gentle with him, please. He thinks of our girls as his own daughters. The guilt he feels, I can't imagine."

"If you trust him, then so do I. But that doesn't mean I'm not going to talk to him."

"Then *talk*, don't . . . interrogate him."

"I need to see the place, the dorm, her room. I can't just stay here. What can I do from here?"

"I'm worried you're going to get your hopes up. I know how much you care for her. We all do. I don't want to sound like I'm giving up hope, but we both know, in these situations . . ." She trailed off, leaving the words unspoken. "I have been through this before."

"I have to do something. I can't just abandon her."

"You're not. You can't think like that."

He scoffed.

"Quinn, listen to me. You can't protect everyone. This will sound terrible, and I'm only saying this because . . . the chances of finding her, any of them . . . I just want you to be realistic."

"You sound like my mother."

"Sometimes I have to," she said softly.

He leaned forward in his seat. "I can't just stay here. Sit here and what, not even try? Just give up on her? We found Mei together, you and me. How could I ever look myself in the mirror again, knowing that I did nothing, hm? That she's out there somewhere, and I did nothing."

"Don't you think I feel the same way? We are looking, Quinn, of course we are. But life, life is cheaper back home than it is here. Much cheaper."

She pursed her lips, eyes glistening faintly. The slightest chink in her armor, the emotional shield that she had developed over the years. It was the only way she was able to work as she did, with a full heart yet keeping a certain, necessary distance between herself and those she cared for. It was the endless tragedy, the sheer trauma experienced on a routine basis that made it necessary, this bulwark allowing her to ease the pain and suffering of others without absorbing it herself. It was similar to soldiers, detectives, and paramedics; those who would seemingly make light of the horrors they witnessed, their comments and jokes crude and distasteful to strangers within earshot but for themselves a form of therapy, a vital coping mechanism. A delicate balance had to be maintained or one risked losing themselves. And this, Quinn thought, was where they truly differed. He was never capable of maintaining that distance and, to his own detriment, which he had long ago accepted, always ended up taking things personally.

Noi collected herself. "I know you mean well, but this is a different world than yours; you know this. There are no missing children reports in Battambang. We don't have those pictures that go on the drink boxes or the lampposts or even the news. Not for children who have been missing their entire lives. Stateless children. I loved her like my own daughter, all of them, but for you this will be like looking for a grain of rice in a paddy."

He turned his wrist, revealing an open palm. *And?*

"I'm worried you're going to do something impulsive. Dangerous."

"Don't worry about me. You have enough on your plate. But you're right; I have no idea what I'm doing. I don't know where to start or where to look, but we're all the family she has. This isn't about what the chances are. She deserves someone to go looking. She's out there, and she's a fighter. We should fight for her too; she deserves that much for what she's been through." He downed the rest of his coffee, cold and bland but with a welcome sting. "How long are you here for?"

She gave a look of resignation before she answered, defeated, as if she had foreseen the entire conversation before it unfolded. "Only a week. I can't be away for much longer. Especially now. I was planning to come in the spring, like I said. I have some relatives here who I haven't seen in a long time, and I'm going to meet with one of the professors I've been speaking to. We're going to discuss my proposal. It's hard to feel enthusiastic about the program right now. And my relatives, that will require some special patience this time. What will you do?"

"I'll catch a red-eye tonight. Should be several flights with connections—who knows where—but I'll get there eventually. If I'm lucky, I'll snag an empty seat on standby."

SIX

She was lying. That much was clear. Not that it was some grand and nefarious deception, more of an offering meant to spare his feelings. And not that Quinn was particularly astute at detecting this sort of theater, least of all when it came to women. With Noi, things were a little different—it just wasn't all that difficult to tell. Dishonesty wasn't a character trait that came naturally to her. Even the most innocuous little fibs, meant to soften a rash remark or placate a tender ego, deceit of any kind seemed to grate the very fiber of her being.

She wanted to deliver the news in person; it wasn't a conversation to have over the phone. Her relatives, the professor, that was all well and good, but it wasn't why she had traveled such a distance. The spontaneity wasn't like her, even under the current circumstances. She had come for something far more personal: to console him, to help him grieve, to provide him with closure. She had come to deliver Mei's eulogy.

When faced with the breadth of Noi's experience, his naïveté was undeniable. After all, this was her country, her world. She had spent her entire life living among these very circumstances, known friends and acquaintances who had suffered in the same vein of corruption and cruelty, and had dedicated her life to stemming the bleed. She was too kind to deceive and far too wise to ignore. Somewhere deep in his psyche, he refused to engage with a voice that callously intimated that he *should* be more realistic, just as she had said. But this voice would be given no quarter. Noi's intentions were good, perennially so, but he would not, could not, entertain any contrivance of last rites in a French café.

She had also come with a warning. Had certainly prepared some cautionary speech, well rehearsed and abandoned as soon as she stepped through the door. It begged him not to get involved, to leave it be. For his own sanity, perhaps. She said very little in the end, glimmers of disapproval showing here and there, imploring him with silence rather than any pleading lecture. An air of futility hung over every word she spoke that afternoon, as if she knew exactly what he would say before he said it, making an effort without hope because it was the proper thing to do, expectations firmly checked.

Stupidity was predictable, he mused. Or stubbornness. Some restless combination of the two, and yet she had flown across the world to make her point regardless. The more he reflected on their conversation, the more he heard the whispers from somewhere amongst the weeds: *She's right, you know.*

In a laggard airport queue, he stared at the photograph in his hands. Himself, Noi, and little Mei, eyes as wide and bright as her smile. It was a keepsake he always took with him, a source of inspiration. He thought about all the letters she had mailed in neatly wrapped bundles, snapshots of her life across the ocean. Letters she had sent over the years, first in brief, rudimentary English, and then, the adorable and life-affirming correspondence of a young girl relishing the exciting new chapters of her youth. Little Mei—his much younger kid sister; his distant, adopted daughter—the other half of the strange yet wondrous relationship they had formed.

He took the greatest pride in watching her grow, in listening to her aspirations, her challenges, and her dreams. He watched over her from a distance, like some accidental, haphazard benefactor, knowing that despite everything, at least here was something positive, something tangible that he'd contributed. It wasn't much, but on certain days—those that began with that encroaching, seemingly perpetual gloom—it was these letters of scribbled, broken English that helped him rise and face the world anew.

There was room on the flight—an exorbitant price—but he paid it gladly and settled into the lounge, grimy and disheveled, in desperate need of a shower. Hygiene would have to wait.

He hated flying. He didn't mind it as a child, but things changed as he got older—things usually did, he supposed. The blissful ignorance of childhood gone, the invincibility of adolescence overcome, now forced to accept that he was placing his life in the hands of strangers navigating some scrap metal with nuts and bolts through the sky and across an ocean. The entire notion was insane no matter how many people tried to convince him otherwise, tried to rationalize the concept over the years. Friends and colleagues would hopelessly describe the physics of lift and drag, Bernoulli's principles of flight, Newton's laws of motion. Quinn's eyes would inevitably glaze over, partly unable to comprehend and equally unwilling to try, his own scientific theorem much more to the point. Airborne in a giant metal canister, hurtling through the air at 40,000 feet with no more than a seatbelt for security. The liquor helped, as did the occasional tablet or capsule—any color would do—especially when downed together. One would think the years of international travel would have at least dulled his anxiety. "Turbulence is completely normal," they would say, "like paddling through choppy water." Newton and Bernoulli could go straight to hell. In one of their own goddamned airplanes too. There was nothing normal about being shaken up in a sardine can soaring above a mountain range.

He tilted back the last of his drink as the hollow metallic announcement was made, urging all dawdling passengers aboard. The dimly lit ramp may as well have been a trudge along the green mile, but rather than prison guards waiting to put him out of his misery, two emerald visions appeared at the end of the tunnel. The flight attendants, identical East-Asian statuettes, stood on either side of the entranceway with gleaming smiles and thick, black lashes, rouged cheekbones and matching ruby lips. They were impeccably dressed in polished leather shoes and black leggings, knee-length dresses—thinly striped, a muted shade of green—and vests a touch lighter overtop, necklines plunging to three golden buttons. Their raven hair was pinned back, hands folded in front, bowing ever so slightly in welcome.

As the ramp flattened out, Quinn stumbled a few feet from the door and stared vexingly at the ground as if the carpet were to blame, surely not the steady procession of rocks glasses that had come and gone with the long evening. The twins voiced some professional concern, ushering him aboard, though if they'd been permitted to roll their eyes, they surely would have. *Wonderful, a drunk already.*

The crew, expeditious to a fault, had everyone buckled and bags stowed within minutes, whether they liked it or not. One of the senior flight attendants approached Quinn, presumably to take his drink order, until she launched rather abruptly into a heavily accented monologue regarding the safety protocols that accompanied his exit-row seat. Nerves already on edge, he chuckled uncomfortably, which seemed to confuse her—tired eyes and a stern expression—and then replied that during any emergency he was far more likely to soil himself than escort any passengers safely off the aircraft. Something was certainly lost in translation, yet apparently this was an acceptable response. She gave an uncertain little smile and was promptly distracted—an unsettled family, restless and spilling into the aisle, were swiftly chastised and returned to their seats.

A few sobering minutes later, the plane began to taxi along the tarmac, a long and torturous harbinger of what was to come. Quinn loosened a sweaty grip on the armrest just long enough to unbutton his collar, then forced his eyes closed and cursed every ludicrous Zen-like platitude he had ever heard.

Inhaling deeply, he tried to mentally transport himself elsewhere. Sparkling crystal waters, shallow waves lapping at a pristine ivory shoreline. The first pitch at a ball game, the splitting crack of a Louisville Slugger, the roar of the crowd, the manicured green expanse of the outfield. The quiet serenity of a fishing trip, cloudless skies, reflective glass waters, the gentle splash of a float bobbing up and down with the current.

The twin jet engines roared to life, thrusting him back into his seat. Pinned against the cushion, he felt the tingle of fresh sweat beading across his brow. The fuselage shook, tray tables and overhead containers vibrating, fueling the growing cacophony. He held his breath as the plane picked up speed, rattling along, the scream of the turbines almost deafening now. It would come soon—the metal would lift, the shaking would cease, and his stomach would fall out from under him. Any moment now, and they would rise. After that, simply a routine fifteen hours in the sky, soaring to the far side of the world.

SEVEN

Battambang, Cambodia

The six-hour bus ride from Phnom Penh was less jarring than he remembered but still ragged enough to keep anyone from a decent bout of sleep—anyone aside from the seasoned locals, of course, well accustomed to the constant gyrations of the journey, the wheels suffering fresh blows with every new ditch and streamlet that scarred the gravel road. Across the aisle, an age-old man— soy-spotted hands and skin like rice paper—slept blissfully: jaw slack, mouth fully agape, eggy head bouncing harmlessly against the headrest.

With tired, listless eyes, Quinn watched the rural countryside as it passed, drifting in and out of a jet-lagged haze, a sort of international trance where time ceased to have any meaning, nodding off and being brought back to life with every fresh pothole, the warm breeze from an open window swirling his matted hair.

Whenever his attention returned to the wild countryside, he inevitably began to question why he still lived in the city. There was so much beauty in the simplicity of life here, the virgin land untouched, isolated from the rest of the scurrying, busy world. The history captivated him, and he often found himself in reverie, wondering whether the people, the structures, the landscape looked the way they did hundreds, thousands of years ago. The rice paddies, waves of lush green shoots swaying gently in still ponds, did they look now as they did then, in the ancient days of the Khmer empire? And these two farmers tending their fields in conical straw hats, were they also there when the great Asian armies of days gone by waged war against one another, carving the land into new colonies and kingdoms? It was difficult to daydream back home, convenience stores with fluorescent lighting on every corner, the world rushing about at breakneck speed, everything built the day before yesterday. There was a tranquility here that he never felt back in Minnesota, even in cottage country, miles from the urban sprawl. This countryside had a quaintness, an ancient serenity that was familiar and soothing even in spite of the old bus's whinging suspension.

Jewels of Battambang wasn't an especially long walk from the bus station, but given the time of day, he was thoroughly drenched with sweat by the time he arrived at the front gate.

He didn't expect much in terms of security, and he wasn't surprised. Squinting into the distance, he spotted mature fruit trees flanking the red dirt promenade and a yellow school bus parked by the main residence. Apparently there were visitors, voices carrying in the wind. Perhaps the gatekeeper was tending to the new guests. He hardly expected Fort Knox, and Noi would have wanted him to give Pichai the benefit of the doubt.

The layout was as he remembered, and well maintained. Each of the four buildings had a reasonably fresh coat of paint, the grass was cut, and the branches of the orange trees were pruned back along the main thoroughfare. On his left he passed a vegetable garden, a project still in its infancy, a handful of humble sprouts. Farther on, a pair of bicycles lay on their sides, abandoned in haste by a hillock. As he approached the main hall, a couple of young boys materialized behind him and raced past, shouting after one another, shirtless and old enough to be missing some baby teeth. They sprinted to a group of people congregating around the bus, which he saw had a white dove for a logo, though he couldn't make out the writing beneath. Missionaries, perhaps.

There were maybe thirty in all, mostly Khmer but a few white faces sprinkled amongst the crowd. The oldest was a man who, judging by his mannerisms and the circle gathering around him, was leading the introductions. Noi often encouraged meetings between brother and sister organizations, sharing best practices but most importantly giving the youth a chance to make new friends. It was a great idea, though Quinn held reservations about some of the more zealous Christians who participated and, in his estimation, laid it on a little thick at times.

He blended effortlessly into the crowd, another one of the visitors. It turned out they were, in fact, a charity organization, led by a priest and his missionaries, stopping in for the afternoon. A weekend workshop was being held in Siem Reap, a few hours to the north, and they had planned a day trip to come and see the grounds. The participants chattered away, making introductions, sharing well wishes, and Quinn made seamless small talk with a few of the older ladies—a Sister Josephine and Sister Something Else—making sure to be pleasant but not lingering. Everyone appeared to be rather preoccupied, which worked well in his favor. He needed to find Pichai. He needed to see Mei's room.

"Hello, young man!" came a cheerful voice, followed by a soft touch on his shoulder. Quinn turned to face a white-haired man with a bulbous red nose and a broad smile. His collared shirt was a shocking shade of pink. "I don't believe we've met. I'm Father Marco."

"No, sir, we haven't. Quinn. Nice to meet you."

Father Marco had a delicate handshake, though just as he began to speak, one of the frenzied women nearby interrupted apologetically and reminded him of the upcoming service. They were already running a little late, and the audio equipment was finally working.

"You'll have to forgive me," he said. "Duty calls, as they say. Will you be joining us for the service?" It seemed that Father Marco had already determined that Quinn was a little out of place, observing him with a speculative raise of his eyebrows.

"I wish I could, Father, but I actually have some business to attend to. Maybe next time."

"There is always a seat for you, my son." Once again, a gentle hand on his shoulder. Quinn nodded respectfully, as one did.

A middle-aged Khmer woman took the lead in near flawless English and began to direct everyone inside. After the service, lunch would be provided in the dining hall, followed by some group activities listed in the daily itinerary. Did everyone have their copy? The crowd shuffled toward the main doors, counselors herding the children together, a fidgety queue of adorable little faces assembling against the wall. While everyone busied themselves, Quinn took the opportunity to slink around the corner, now just a few paces away from the dormitories.

It didn't take long to find Mei's room. Each door had a hand-scrawled name lanyard and was plastered with all manner of artwork and crafts. Mei's door was a mural of assorted pencil sketches, a few he recognized from photographs that Noi had sent. Inside were two single beds, one in each corner, white sheets tucked beneath a thin mattress, a beige blanket folded overtop. Beside them were twin off-white nightstands and an old bookcase on its last legs, one of which had been replaced by two strips of scrap wood. The walls were painted a light pastel blue, and the window faced out onto lush, green foliage. A perfect room: simple, clean, and bright.

He cast an inquisitive eye over anything that could be of importance, though clearly everything had been rearranged long ago—likely by the police, then tidied by the staff. It wasn't as if anyone was going to put up yellow tape for something like this. Had the authorities even bothered to investigate? Incompetent at best, at worst—accomplices, which worried him far more. Though what did he really know about such investigations? Assuming that anyone had taken the time. Tidbits here and there from his policeman father and a couple of true crime novels. The first forty-eight hours were crucial, and that window had come and gone. Contamination of the crime scene was a foregone conclusion. Then again, maybe he was so late that everyone had simply moved on. This was Battambang, after all.

Mei's side of the room was obvious: a leaning tower of used books piled precariously high on the left side of the nightstand. Her sketchbook lay next to them alongside a potted orchid. A bulletin board by the window was a collage of pinned photographs: a birthday celebration, a field trip to Tonle Sap Lake, friends in uniform, friends making silly faces. She hadn't mentioned a roommate in her last letter, and the few keepsakes on the right indicated that, whoever the roommate was, she was a fairly recent arrival.

He leafed through the sketchbook, opened the drawers, and examined the bookcase, hoping to find some sort of diary she might have kept. Didn't all girls have one of those? His search was thorough and yet half-hearted, the voices of doubt already snickering in the background. *And just what do you expect to find here? A ransom note with a map?* Noi had mentioned that argument with the other girls. It weighed on her; she wouldn't have said anything otherwise. There might be something there. Then again, there might not. *Children fight all the time. What do you expect to gain from that?*

He sat on the edge of her bed for a few minutes, sketchbook in hand, a rough pencil draft of a horse in mid-canter. Then he rose and hoisted the mattress from the bedframe. No diary beneath, but he did find a few folded papers spread along the weathered plywood. He couldn't read Khmer, much less a girl's handwritten notes in Khmer, but it seemed to be nothing more than doodles and gossip. One note had a bunch of hearts and stick figures holding hands—simple drawings, likely hidden there for some time. A crush? Wasn't she too young for that? Amongst the pages he unfolded several letters addressed to him, thankfully, in English. They must have been the latest in a batch she'd written but hadn't had the chance to send. He took a deep breath before reading one of them, uncertain of what to expect. For some reason, it made him uneasy, this phantom letter.

Ghonlaat,

How are you? I am fine. These days the weather is too hot here. I want to come to Minneapolis and see the snow. I know I always say this but one day I will do it. I asked Noi if she will take me. She said she will think about it but I think she is thinking no. But that's okay. These days I go a lot to Siem Reap with Auntie Thom. Every time I can we take the bus together so I can work at the flower shop with Areum. I love it there. I get to smell all the different flowers. Areum teaches me how to plant the different ones in different ways. Some need more water. Some need more sun or more shade. I don't know how their names are in English. But my favorite one is the orchid flower. Every color of them. Last week Areum gave me my own orchid flower in a pot to bring home. You can see the picture I sent you. Okay, bye for now. (I learned this expression in one of the books you sent. It's good right?)

Mei

He glanced around for the picture but couldn't find it, though the orchid itself was tall and splendid. A single stem, white blossoms with a lavender fringe, three buds still lying in wait. He gathered the letters and other scraps of paper and tucked them into his shoulder bag. Unless he was missing something, this was likely as close to any diary as he was going to get.

A gentle knock on the doorframe.

"Hello? Sir?" came a timid voice from the hallway. He turned and vaguely recognized one of the live-in staff members, a hunched woman with a round face and plump figure carrying bedsheets, a disconcerted look in her eyes.

"Oh, I'm sorry. I'm Quinn, Noi's friend, and Mei's . . ." *What was her name again?*

"Yes, Mr. Quinn! Ah, so nice to see you again!" She clasped her free hand to her chest. The one-woman performance continued: a look that had lingered on the edge of panic swept away by relief, then thin lips and full cheeks slipping into remorse, reality slowly dawning. Her gaze shifted to the floor, all too aware of why Quinn was seated on the edge of Mei's bed. "She was our little angel," she said. For a moment he resented her for speaking with such finality. "Are you coming to collect her things?"

"No," he replied, shaking his head slowly to no one in particular. "No, I'm not. Actually, I came to find her. I don't suppose there's any new information about what happened?"

Her smile, well-intentioned as it was, gave everything away. Forced from the side of her mouth, it conveyed a sort of patronizing sentiment, pitying the poor foreign man's misplaced hope.

In the main hall, the chaperones took swift note of the new face among them, ushering him to a table and insisting that he join them for supper. Introductions were made courtesy of Sister Josephine who, given the way she continually patted his arm, already considered herself a dear, old friend. They sat with Sister Isabella and Sister Lizeth, both Colombian and having lived in the region for too many years to mention; Malee, an energetic Thai woman and one of the group leaders; Samnang, the seamstress; as well as two of the local day staff, shy and very reserved, as if convinced that someone had surely made an error and seated them at the wrong table.

A humble meal of chicken and rice followed—the meat simply seasoned with coarse pepper and fresh lime—providing Quinn with an opportunity to canvass opinions on Mei's friends and the night of her disappearance. He didn't learn much. There was a great deal of overlap with what Noi had told him, though everyone was clearly still devastated by the news: a somber tilt of the head, eyes searching around the table, heavy sighs and offers of prayer, everyone aware of some great secret that could not be revealed.

Mei did have a fight with her friends, Samnang said, but none of the staff seemed to think much of it—children will be children, after all. Yes, some newer girls had some behavioral problems, but that was nothing out of the ordinary. They were far from the only ones and had regular sessions with the trauma counselor who, regrettably, was away on business in Pattaya. Anyhow, nobody thought it had anything to do with Mei and the *snakeheads*, as Malee called them. It was a term he recognized, though usually in reference to Chinese smuggling gangs. The police had been called as a matter of procedure on both occasions—the night Kaew and her friends disappeared and then again when the girls were taken a month later. Predictably, they offered few signs of encouragement.

He fought the urge to roll his eyes. Across the country, law-enforcement agencies had budgets spread so thin that they hardly covered the meager wages of the officers themselves. Most of them subsisted on about two or three dollars a day. Any additional funding for investigations, vice units, or any other specialized training was essentially nonexistent.

Apparently, when the officers finally arrived, several hours after being contacted, they could have hardly seemed more disinterested. Upon learning that the shelter didn't have any reserve funds to inspire a proper investigation, they took a brief and reluctant tour of the dormitories, spent less than five minutes in Mei's room, had a cigarette, and, without any further financial incentive, left. Even one of the day staffers, timid as a mouse up to that point, gave a contemptible snort.

Once everyone around the table had taken their turn, offering their two cents, Quinn found a degree of consolation in that the officers came across as lazy and indifferent more than anything else. He hadn't ruled out the possibility that they could very well have been participants, and on that point he had yet to make up his mind. The inherent poverty throughout the country meant that most officers on the take collected the majority of their salaries through bribes and other payoffs. They were hardly going to get any worthwhile sum from a victim's shelter. They would have known that long before showing up, but then again, selling the girls to a third party would certainly have put a few *riels* in their pockets. He couldn't afford to rule anything out just yet.

For dessert, pouches of fresh durian and mangosteen halves, served alongside hefty chunks of sweet sticky rice wrapped neatly in fragrant banana leaves. While getting up to pour himself a coffee, Quinn finally bumped into Pichai, who turned out to be as disappointing a source of information as he was a security guard. Still nursing a sizeable welt on his forehead, a glossy balm applied to the purple gash and its yellowing periphery, he had a gangly frame and meekly bowed shoulders, some sparse, grayish hair slicked down across his head. He wasn't some bumbling fool, as Quinn had assumed, and by the end of their conversation, he felt a twinge of guilt about his earlier judgment. A kindly old man with a sincere heart, he had become quite spiritual following the recent loss of his wife and daughter. For Noi and the girls, he did what little he could, a wholesome and rewarding arrangement for all parties.

As the meal drew to a close, Quinn made the error of mentioning Areum's flower shop in Siem Reap and that he might pay her a visit in the coming days. An offhand comment meant for Sister Isabella, Malee seized on the opportunity from across the table.

"You should come with us," she said, eyes wide as tea saucers. "We have plenty of room!" The rest of the table joined in—brimming smiles and insistent nodding. They were heading back to Siem Reap anyhow—surely, it would save him quite the hassle.

The thought of a four-hour bus ride with a group of excitable Christians made his head hurt, though it was far too impolite to decline, and he wasn't quick enough to think up a plausible excuse. If he could endure another juddering excursion along the washed-out dirt roads, he might be able to find a bar once they got to the city.

An hour later, as the crowd bid their farewells, and Father Marco gave his blessing, Quinn propped himself up against the bus, jet-lagged and pensive, smoking a cigarette. Not for the first time, a creeping gloom lingered in the back of his mind, not quite overwhelming, not yet—merely toying with him, a steady current making its presence known.

He had hardly anything to go on. He had gathered Mei's letters, class notes, and drawing books, then made photocopies of anything even remotely relevant from the files in Noi's office. It didn't feel like much of a start. What was it she had said at the café? "A grain of rice in a paddy."

He would comb through the papers on the way and then, first thing in the morning, pay a visit to the flower shop. He already harbored suspicions about Areum, despite Mei's glowing words. It wouldn't have been the first time that a charming young woman had recruited an unsuspecting girl into the trade. From the little he did know, it was a growing trend in the industry—desperation, years of grooming, Stockholm Syndrome—women were coming to the fore in this business, victims descending into predation.

He took a slow, meaningful drag, then watched in horror as two women approached the bus, bubbly personalities with a spring in their step, each with an acoustic guitar clasped firmly in hand. They hopped up the steps to scattered applause on board. The profanity came too easily sometimes, the words nearly slipping from his lips despite his concerted effort. Sister Josephine was one of the last to board. Somewhat unsteady on her feet, she latched onto his forearm, rheumy eyes smiling up at him from behind smudged glasses. He helped her to the door where she patted his arm once more and gave him a curious look, a twinkle in her eye. "Tell me, Mr. Quinn, you look like a baritone, yes?"

EIGHT

Siem Reap, Cambodia

THE CATHOLICS HAD MONEY. CLEARLY, THEY HAD SPARED NO expense for their annual symposium. As Quinn stepped into the lobby of La Résidence Angkor, the atmosphere was warm, welcoming, and richly elegant. Massive teak pillars rose like tree trunks to the ceiling, where elaborately carved beams crisscrossed the canopy. Aside from the polished marble flooring, everything was wooden: rustic chairs and coffee tables with whittled décor, bamboo shutters—handmade and charmingly imperfect—and ornamental lamps that hung luxuriously from the rafters, emitting a soft glow from above. The expansive room received guests like a cozy French chalet nestled among its tropical surroundings.

A young Khmer girl with a sparkling smile stood at the entryway offering cool refreshments for parched throats. Another, who could have passed as her younger sister, sat next to her and played a cheerful melody on a *Roneat ek,* a traditional xylophone made of bamboo. A few tourists were still mulling about after a long day in the unforgiving heat, wearing hats of varying sizes with red, sun-kissed cheeks to match. As dusk approached, the heavy, humid air was scented with a refreshing aroma of herbs and citrus, numerous citronella candles shimmering throughout the foyer.

Most importantly, just beyond the lounge in the left-hand corner, was a well-stocked bar, five empty stools lying in wait. The bartender, a rather tallish girl with dark skin and high cheekbones, took his order and promptly dropped a couple of ice cubes into a tumbler.

"How are you tonight, sir?" Her voice was soft and slightly raspy.

"I'm well," he said, squinting at her nametag, "Nary?"

She nodded happily, hovering a bottle of Black Label above his glass. "Scotch?"

"If you insist." As she tipped the bottle, he said, "Nary, do you know what a 'home pour' is?"

"I'm sorry, sir, no."

"Call me Quinn, please. Where I'm from there's what we call a 'home pour' and a 'bar pour.' When you go to a bar, usually you pay for a single, a double, whatever you order. Bars, or sometimes beautiful hotels like this"—he cast his hand in an arc—"they measure out how much they give you. But a home pour, that's a little different. You see, when you're at your house with family or friends, you pour yourself a single, but maybe you sort of, *forget* to measure." He tucked a folded bill into the empty tip jar.

"I understand your meaning," she said, flashing a conspiratorial smile. "I think we can do special Siem Reap pour." Another inch of amber liquid splashed into his glass.

"*Aw ghon jrern.*"

"Oh! You speak Khmer?"

"Unfortunately not, but I'm learning a new word every day. Don't let me bother you, Nary. I have some papers I need to read here. Maybe you can help me with some words if I don't understand?"

"No bother, Mr. Quinn. Of course I can help. Would you like

to see dinner menu?"

"I'm alright, thank you. But every once in a while I might need a top up." He wobbled the glass in his hand.

She nodded dramatically. "Siem Reap pour."

Leafing through the photocopies he made at the shelter was slow going. Painfully slow. There wasn't much in terms of background on any of the five girls who were taken, but that was to be expected. Names, birthdates, only one had contact information for some distant relatives in Sihanoukville. Blood types and allergies, vaccination records, and medical reports. With every page he turned, the same nagging questions. What exactly was he hoping to find? Clues of some sort, but leading to where? To what? A letter of distress, a precise location of her whereabouts? It was difficult to focus, pushing forward page by page, an impending sense of futility as he trudged onward without direction.

Mei's schoolbooks weren't of much use either. If ever something caught his eye, he called over to Nary who would translate the scribbled Khmer as best as she could, though it was never anything relevant. Nary was the best sort of bartender, charitable with her bottle and never asking too many questions.

After a couple of hours, he couldn't tell if it was the whiskey or the sobriety that was getting on his nerves. Reading and rereading the notebook and loose-leaf papers only served to focus his mind on the worst possible outcomes. Each page seemed increasingly irrelevant, mocking him as he went: *What did you expect to find this time? Something different?* He drifted in and out of conversations with Noi, memories of speakers at anti-trafficking forums, his sodden mind conjuring horrific images and statistics.

It had been almost a week since they took her. By now she could be anywhere in the country—even the continent. Had he failed her before he'd even begun? Thoughts tormented him. Young girls with bloody fingers, blistered hands chafed and raw from handling cloth and thread. Painted smiles on young faces caked in makeup. Costumed little dolls singing forlorn songs in dimly lit karaoke bars. Amateur back-alley surgeons sewing and resewing genitalia to be sold at virgin prices to the pond scum of the world. The stuff of nightmares an all-too-familiar reality for countless millions.

The foyer had long emptied and Nary was wiping down the bar when Father Marco made a late appearance, hobbling down the timeworn wooden stairs in a navy robe and slippers, smelling peculiarly of some sort of floral lotion. He apologized for the late hour and, pulling up a stool, ordered a jasmine tea with a heaping spoonful of honey. "It helps me to rest," he said with a warm smile, the dim lighting accentuating his enormous ears and prominent nose. Nary was kind enough to top up Quinn's glass a final time for the evening, and he reminded her that his tips were to be used exclusively to buy some candy for her two boys, even the youngest, little Samang, regardless of his cavities. His were only baby teeth, after all. She shook her head, chuckling softly to herself, and bid both men a restful night of sleep, leaving them amidst the silence and stillness of the deserted hotel lobby.

"And how are you this evening, Mr. Quinn? It seems we are the only night owls of the group."

"Would seem so," Quinn replied, taking a sip. "Not to be rude, Father, but, tomorrow is Sunday, isn't it? Don't you have an early start?"

"I always rise with the sun, but I enjoy the evenings just as well. It gives me time to catch up on things, to be alone with my thoughts." He smacked his lips rather loudly, savoring his sweetened tea. "Though I will admit it makes certain sunrises arrive a bit too soon."

"Burning the candle at both ends."

"Indeed."

Quinn motioned with his chin at the teacup. "Trouble sleeping?"

"Oh, this? No. Just a habit, I suppose. My mother used to make us chamomile tea before bed or some warm milk with honey. Usually because we were too rambunctious, my brothers and I. But in recent years I've developed a taste for jasmine. Most likely a symptom of having spent so many years in the region now. I seem to have forgotten my roots," he said with a chuckle. "Truth be told, my biggest weakness is I end up settling in with a good book, and I can't seem to put it down. I enjoy the calm of the evenings as much as the early mornings." He looked around, drawing Quinn's attention to the tranquility of the vast, empty room. "Although I wish I could say the same for you."

"How's that?" Quinn replied.

"If you don't mind my being so bold, I'd say you drink like a man seeking to drown his sorrows. I can tell you from experience, it's not so easily done."

Quinn couldn't help a smirk. "No kidding."

"What I mean is, the answers you're seeking—I hardly think you'll find them at the bottom of a bottle. But you already know this, of course."

"Listen, Father, don't take this the wrong way, you're very welcome to sit, of course, but now's not really a good time for, well, whatever this is . . . a lecture."

The old priest raised a hand ever so slightly, bowing his head with a smile, apologizing for any affront, and doing so with the delicacy and grace that only a man of his station could. "Of course not, of course. I only meant to say that I know the look of a man who's struggling with his thoughts. Conflicted, perhaps. If nothing more, perhaps I could lend an ear. Some would say we're quite well known for being good at that sort of thing." The familiar warm smile illuminated his face.

"Thank you, Father. I appreciate the sentiment, though I doubt you'll be able to help." He let out a heavy sigh, rubbing his eyes with the pads of his fingers. "And I don't mean to offend the, you know"—he opened a palm to the sky, glancing at the ceiling—"the powers that be, but I'm not really sure anyone will be able to help at this point."

Father Marco had wispy white hair, thin and receding, some-what unremarkable and thereby at odds with his rather largish facial features. Puffy bags hung suspended beneath his bluish-gray eyes. Natural signs of aging, inevitable, not the telltale signs of a life filled with excess, a life of drink and smoke. There was a certain health and vitality that accompanied his advanced age. And now, even in his velvety blue robe and moccasin slippers, he maintained an air of decorum; approachable and wise. He folded his hands on the bar and, with a nearly imperceptible inclination of the head, sat patiently, saying nothing, yet all the while inviting his new friend to unburden himself.

"Even at this hour, you're still working," Quinn said reluctantly, swishing the liquid around in his glass. He sighed heavily. "Well, Father, if you must know, I've lost someone. Someone very close to me. It's not a romantic affair—my marriage isn't falling apart or anything like that. There was a young girl, like family to me. You could even say a daughter, in a way. And she's gone. Disappeared . . ." His glassy-eyed gaze passed through the bottles behind the bar, through the painted brick wall, beyond the pond outside, alive with all manner of evening creatures, off somewhere into the wild Cambodian countryside. "And I'm not sure there's any way to get her back."

Father Marco paused for a delicate moment before speaking. "I see. I'm wondering, did she run away, perhaps?"

"No. They took her"—he met the priest's eyes—"when they came."

"Ah, yes," he said, putting it all together now, "she was one of the girls who disappeared last week."

Quinn nodded.

"I'm so sorry. I don't know much of what happened, a tragedy to be sure." He paused again, as if out of respect, and Quinn was struck by how genuine the gesture seemed. "I was informed by one of the sisters that they suspect it was the modern slave traders. 'Traffickers,' I believe they're called."

"That's right."

The priest paused once more, treading carefully around the subject matter. "Forgive my ignorance. My work is that of the Church, so I'm not very familiar with this world, only to say that it is a most unfortunate business. Truly, a great tragedy. And you are trying to find a way to locate this young lady, yes? May I ask her name?"

"Mei."

"Mei. Beautiful. And the police, I don't suppose you could contact them about the disappearance? Or surely they've already been notified."

Quinn scoffed a little too loudly. "Sorry, Father. Don't take that personally. And no, the police won't help. Not here, anyhow." Father Marco's forehead creased, brows pinching together. "How long have you been in Cambodia, Father?"

"About three years now."

Quinn tilted another mouthful and cleared his throat. "This was probably a bit before your time then. I can't remember the dates exactly, but maybe it'll help give some perspective. There was a police chief; I think it was three or four years ago. Not an officer, not a sergeant, a *chief*. He worked in Phnom Penh, heading up the anti-trafficking unit—humans, not drugs. Apparently, while he was supposed to be overseeing a department dedicated to protecting vulnerable boys, girls, men, and women, he was doing just the opposite. He would take bribes, kickbacks from brothels, warn them of upcoming raids, even help smuggle new victims into town if the selection got a little stale. Day after day, year after year, he spent his time protecting those who stood to make a profit from selling women and children to sex tourists. And, of course, he profited quite well himself."

Father Marco fingered the rim of his teacup, listening intently but giving nothing away.

"Eventually, as all good things must come to an end, he slips up, and they get him. He's actually arrested, charged, even convicted. A police chief of the anti-trafficking unit convicted *himself* of human trafficking. Sentenced to seven years. It was a coup."

He tugged at his nose a couple of times, then met the priest's eyes. "Would you like to know where he is now? He still works in Phnom Penh. A kind of deputy police chief now after the charges were overturned. Don't even ask me how that works following a conviction. Claims he's some sort of legitimate businessman." He shook his head in disbelief. "That's the level of corruption at the *top*, Father. A highly publicized case, all over the news, and still swept under the rug like it was nothing. If guys like him, in the spotlight, are getting away with it, what do you think the rest of them are up to? So, no, to answer your question, I highly doubt the police are going to be of much help."

Father Marco remained silent for a long while, measuring his response. "We can't allow ourselves to be enveloped by things beyond our control. This story is . . . shocking, to say the least; however, it's out of your hands. Of course, I don't mean to suggest that you do nothing, but we need to learn to let go of that which we cannot control, learn to take comfort in that which we can. This is too large a burden to take upon yourself. You cannot be the judge, jury and executioner. You'll forgive my tired clichés, but that is the role of a much higher power."

"Your higher power sure has an interesting take on things, letting this man walk free."

"I wish I had some answers for you, Mr. Quinn, truly I do. But what I do know is this: you can't take on the world's problems on your own. Not by yourself, not without faith."

"Faith isn't going to help me find Mei, Father."

"Perhaps not, but it will help lighten your burden. With Mei, this police chief, and seemingly this entire bureau, if what you say is true, you're taking the world's problems upon your own shoulders. This is too much for one man to bear on his own."

"I'm hardly taking on the world's problems."

"Yet you drink like a man doing just so."

A brief silence lingered, and Father Marco shifted slightly in his seat, as if wondering if he had overstepped his bounds. For Quinn, it was getting late, and the whiskey was stripping most of his filters, the hour thinning his patience.

"I prefer the solution in my glass. Next you're going to tell me that He works in mysterious ways."

"An expression for children, Mr. Quinn. We both know that's a naïve way to approach such a topic."

Quinn raised a brow. "You know, I'll give you credit, Father, you're a lot more level-headed than I thought you'd be." He poured back the last of his glass, a slight wince as the single malt stung his throat. He felt the soft touch of a hand on his forearm.

"My son . . . you're destroying yourself."

"Thanks for the company, Father," he said, sliding off his stool. "You should get some rest."

NINE

He woke at first light, tossing and turning for a while, unable to fall back asleep. Once downstairs, he located the hotel café, had a cup of black coffee and a banana, and waited patiently until the business hour for the front desk to call him a taxi.

Areum's flower shop wasn't difficult to find—in truth, he could have easily walked the distance had he known, which also happened to explain the curious look he received from the driver.

From the back seat of the cab, he observed the bustling morning routine along Sivutha Boulevard, eventually turning onto Oum Khun, a tranquil side street with faded French colonial buildings and weathered balustrades. They stopped before a strip of humble storefronts amidst a veritable jungle of shrubbery, bamboo trees sprouting from the concrete, motorbikes and *tuk-tuks* parked in disarray along the curbside.

Beneath a gray awning speckled with fallen leaves, a white door was flanked by two large display windows with stenciled blue lettering. Inside, hand-woven baskets with simple yet elegant arrangements sat alongside exotic bouquets in lavish ornamental vases, the rows of colorful blooms visible through dusty panes besmirched with the grime of the city.

The front door opened easily, accompanied by a jingle from the tiny bell that hung above. The air was humid yet revitalizing, fresh and fragrant next to the urban soot and traffic exhaust outside.

He cleared his throat. "Hello?"

"Yes, hello!" came a voice from somewhere amongst the foliage. "Just a minute please!"

A moment later, a young woman emerged from behind a colorful wall of perennials. She had a thin, petite frame beneath her airy blouse, a light-blue handkerchief pinning back her dark hair, and wore a pair of ratty, old gardening gloves blackened with potting soil. She had narrow eyes and delicately arched eyebrows, cream-colored skin blemished only by an inadvertent smear of dirt above her cheek. That, or she was readying herself for a game of football. She beamed at him, clasping her gloved hands together, a warm and completely disarming welcome.

"Sorry about that—looking for some flowers today?"

"I am, yes," a hesitant reply, despite the fact that it wasn't a particularly difficult question.

"Do you know what you're looking for?"

"Not exactly, but I need a small bouquet. For a friend. Maybe you can help pick something out for me."

"That's what I'm here for," she chirped. "Any specific requests?" He shook his head, and she hurried off back into the maze of blossoms. "I'll be right back!"

He had prepared himself for the unexpected the moment he stepped onto the bus in Battambang, hardly certain of what he was doing or where it might lead. And yet, he already felt lost. Miles from where Mei had disappeared, he now stood in a flower shop without any genuine plan, wracking his brain on what to make of the florist. There was something peculiar, something undefined about her. He couldn't place his finger on it just yet, but it was still early. She hardly struck him as a recruiter, the type of woman who, traumatized after years of abuse, targeted vulnerable girls herself, perpetuating and prolonging the cycle. Those who did manage to leave that world, recover, rehabilitate and start their lives anew, carried their scars forever, sometimes visible to the naked eye, sometimes not. The signs weren't particularly difficult to spot if one knew what to look for, but that was hardly his area of expertise. And to complicate matters further, all of this would involve a woman, an area in which he had even less expertise, if that were possible.

The young woman, whom he assumed to be Areum, returned cradling a veritable rainbow of petals and bulbs, prickly stems and decorative brush, and went about arranging the bouquet—snipping here, tying there—as the pair made idle small talk. He figured it was best to develop some genuine rapport prior to revealing the true purpose of his visit. It would hardly be the most graceful of transitions. *Those tulips are lovely. What do you know of local kidnappings?*

The conversation was effortless. Areum held a distinctive allure: charming, clever, not afraid to make a sly remark or two, and he wondered if perhaps she had studied abroad. Her accent aside, she had an excellent command of the English language. Yet all the while, despite her poignant little quips, she remained somewhat reserved. Charismatic to the point that certain exchanges lingered provocatively on the edge of flirtation, or so he thought, she would then retreat back into her shell: the quiet girl next door, well-mannered, humble and shy.

At one point there was a lull in the conversation as she looked around for her scissors, which he found beneath some discarded stems of leatherleaf fern. As he handed them across the countertop, his fingers innocently grazed her blouse just above the cuff, yet she withdrew her arm in a flash as if pricked by a thorn. She flushed for a moment before regaining her composure. "Sorry about that. I can be a little jumpy."

Quinn responded with a casual shake of the head. *Don't worry about it.*

He had always been a good judge of character, an instinct that had served him well throughout his career and in life in general. Still, there was something about her that he couldn't quite quantify. He needed more time. After all, who was he to make such snap judgments? Now and again, through the brief glimpses she permitted behind the curtain, he cobbled together his preliminary impressions.

Holding her scissors with surgical precision, a flick of the wrist shaved and curled the flowing yellow ribbons. "Voila! What do you think?"

"Lovely. Thank you. You're an artist."

"Oh, I don't know about that. Not yet, but I'm getting better."

"I never got your name."

"I'm Wendy," she replied.

He gave her a puzzled look. "Alright Wendy, do you have another name?"

"Oh? Another name?"

"I've never met a Korean girl named Wendy. Maybe that's the name your English teacher gave you in a *hagwon* years ago, but I doubt that's what your parents call you."

"Ah, so you know I'm Korean too? Are you a detective?" She smirked, giving him a sideways glance.

"The big *Hangul* letters on the window sort of give it away."

"Ah, yes. What do they say?"

"I have no idea."

She laughed. "Choi Areum." She bowed her head slightly, almost mockingly. "Nice to meet you . . ."

"Quinn."

"Queen?"

"Not exactly. Quinn. Try the word 'win' but with a 'K' at the beginning."

Her eyes narrowed as she pursed her lips. "Queen."

"Sure. Something like that."

As Areum punched the order into an old cash register, he insisted on giving her a tip for her efforts. She refused several times until he stated she would have to accept the full amount or nothing at all. He tried to be playful, laying on the charm, only to be stonewalled, Areum vexingly immune and oblivious. Each time he thought he had gained a foothold, he was politely rebuffed and had to start over again, trying to piece it all together.

There was no easy way to bring up the subject. There certainly weren't any convenient segues available, at least none that came to mind. Honesty, he found, was hardly ever the best policy, particularly in diplomatic circles, but the saying had still hung around after all these years so maybe there was a grain of truth to be found.

"Areum, I haven't been completely honest with you—the flowers are lovely, by the way." He inhaled deeply from the bouquet. "But that's not exactly why I'm here."

Her expression gave nothing away.

"There's a young girl who works here from time to time. Helps out, anyway. Mei, of course you know her. I'm, well, I'm looking for her."

He regretted his poor choice of words immediately, even before they hung awkwardly in the air between them. Areum was silent, suddenly fascinated with the countertop.

He raised his hand. "Let me rephrase that. I've known Mei for many years. She's basically like family to me, an adopted daughter, you could say. I was there the first night Noi found her—you know Noi, of course—she runs the shelter. In Battambang."

Areum shifted her gaze, lifting her eyes to meet his. Despite the skepticism, he could tell that her confusion was genuine.

"I'm sorry, maybe you haven't heard. Noi's been away, and . . ." He reached into his pocket, pulled out a pack of Camels, and held one between his thumb and forefinger. "Do you mind?"

She shook her head, crossing her arms across her chest, closed off yet paying close attention. A puff of smoke swirled into the air between them.

"About a week ago, some men came to the shelter in the middle of the night. They kidnapped several girls, and Mei was one of them. I've been trying to find . . ." He trailed off, running a hand through his hair. "I've been trying to find something, anything, a kind of clue that might lead me to her. I spoke to Noi in Canada when I saw her, then came straight here. I was at the shelter. I saw her room, and I talked to people there. The police, I mean, it's a waste of time." He met her eyes, speaking slowly. "I hate to say it, Areum, but you're pretty much my only lead at the moment. She spent a lot of time here with you, and she looked up to you very much. I thought maybe you might know something."

Areum was motionless, arms still crossed, the wheels turning behind her furrowed brow. When she finally spoke, her voice was low, soft. "When did this happen?"

"Thursday. Last Thursday."

She looked around searchingly, still unsure what to say. Maybe unsure if she should say anything at all.

"Listen, you don't need to trust me, and I wouldn't blame you," he said. "I know this is completely out of the blue. But Mei is gone, and someone has her. I don't know who, and I don't know where. I'm already running out of time. I promise you, I'm here to get her back. I came here to find her, but I need your help. Whatever you think of me, of all of this . . ." He paused as Areum dropped her gaze to the floor once again, shifting her weight, visibly conflicted. "I need your help. *Mei* needs your help. You might not trust me, but why else would I be here? How would I even know who she was?"

He took a drag and blew a thick plume of churning cloud into the air. "I'm sorry, I know it's a lot to take in." He looked to the door and back. "I'll go, and you can sleep on it. Are you free tomorrow?"

She looked at him, uncertain, then nodded. "Why?"

He gave the most casual shrug he could manage. "I've never been to Angkor Wat."

It seemed to help. She pressed the back of her hand against her nose and sniffled quietly. Shifting her weight once more, the faintest hint of a smile tugged at the corners of her mouth.

"I've heard the sunrise over the temples is a must-see," he said. "The view from just behind the pond or something like that."

Areum nodded absentmindedly, eyes on the floor, expression still guarded, balancing her emotions.

"Meet me there tomorrow. At the front gate."

That caught her attention.

"I have something I want to show you," he said. "I think you'll like it. Puts a smile on my face every time." She took a deep breath as if about to confess something, and he made sure to intervene. "Sleep on it. Think it over," he said, picking up his bouquet.

He turned on his heel and walked to the door, worried that if he gave her the chance to speak, she might turn him down. She would have the entire day and the evening to let it simmer. He could always come by the shop again tomorrow if the gamble didn't pay off, though a change of scenery was certainly needed.

He couldn't be sure, but he wondered fleetingly if her reticence was about protecting Mei and not just herself. A good sign, regardless.

The bell jingled as he held the door ajar, and he paused for a final roll of the dice. "The orchids," he said. "Were they always her favorite?"

That did it. Areum's face was so full of emotion that he felt ashamed for being the one responsible. Her brown eyes shimmered, the faintest quiver in her chin. She gave a single nod.

"She really loved the one you gave her," he said over his shoulder, "the white one, purple edges. I made sure to water it before I left." And with that, he let the door slip through his fingers and disappeared back into the streaming sunlight of a cloudless morning sky.

TEN

IN THE MORNING HIS EYES WERE SWOLLEN AND GRAINY AFTER another sleepless night, a night filled with dark dreams and cold sweats. Still, on this occasion the jet lag actually worked in his favor, his body already expecting to wake at an ungodly hour before the Cambodian sunrise.

He arrived at the grand temple complex of Angkor Wat by *tuk-tuk*—or at least assumed that's where the driver had taken him. It was far too dark to make out his surroundings.

After paying the entrance fee, he stumbled a long way through the darkness, crossed a still, black moat by way of an ancient stone bridge, passed towering, ornately carved gates with columned walls, continued beyond crumbling ruins, and finally walked through dew-soaked grass to where a small crowd had gathered at the base of a pond. The air was cool given the season, and the shadow of the morning sky teased hints of purple hues on the horizon. He walked a few paces from the crowd, far enough not to force his cigarette fumes upon anyone, and meditated on the lily pads, water blossoms, and little bugs that skittered erratically across the surface of the water.

As the minutes passed, the crowd swelled, sightseers streaming in at regular intervals while he made a conscious effort to stop glancing at his watch. If she didn't show, he would drop by the flower shop again, though it would be unwise to force the rapport. Another unwarranted appearance after she had clearly made her point would be far from ideal.

From the crowd, muted chatter replaced the early morning whispers, an occasional yawn or a cough carrying over the still air of the complex.

He butted out his cigarette on a nearby stone. In the distance, a solitary figure stood apart from the group, and as he looked on, it began to approach. Hardly recognizable as she navigated the wet grass, Areum wore a large afghan whose corners hung low, draped over each shoulder, the bulk of the fabric covering her midsection and hanging between her knees. Wrapped in the knit, she was the silhouette of an abandoned kite, hovering closer and closer in the darkness.

"I wasn't sure you'd come," he said a little prematurely.

"I'm here for Mei," she replied, arriving by his side, cordial but to the point.

He nodded. "So am I."

For a while they stood, side by side, gazing ahead in anticipation of dawn, taking in the tranquil majesty of the early morning. The murmur of the crowd grew louder in anticipation, photographers repositioning their tripods, hulking lenses at the ready.

"So, how long has it been since your last drink?" she asked.

He turned to face her, but she stared straight ahead at the gray sky. He found himself kneading his palm with his thumb, self-conscious, as if doing so might relieve the tremors.

"How did you know?" he finally asked.

"My father used to drink. I remember his hands shaking like that. When I was a girl, I called them his 'dancing hands.'" She smiled strangely at the memory. "He loved to drink *makgeolli*. Do you know it?"

"No, I don't think so."

"It's sweet—like a sweet milk but made from rice. And it tastes best on rainy days. You drink it from a bowl, like soup."

"Sounds nice."

"Except for the next morning. The sweetness has a little devil that hides inside, he used to say." She lifted a flap aside and reached into her purse, pulling out a thermos and two cylindrical logs wrapped in foil. "Hungry?"

"You brought breakfast?"

She nodded. "My grandmother always made *kimbap* when we would have class trips in school or when we went hiking. This one is her special recipe, with tuna and extra cucumber." She handed him a roll. "So, even if you don't like it, don't say anything bad."

"I wouldn't dream of it. Thank you. And thanks, for coming."

"Yesterday, I was . . . maybe a bit strange. I didn't know who you were, and then I didn't want to believe what you were saying. It was very confusing for me. I was very suspicious of you, and then I was angry! I don't know why. I think I wanted to blame someone." She mumbled something in Korean. "I think I just needed some time to be alone and make sense of everything."

"Don't apologize. You took the news much better than I did. And here, in case you're still skeptical," he said, reaching into his pocket. He handed her a folded letter that Mei had written along with an old picture, creased in half. "This was taken a few months after we found her."

Areum smiled at the photograph. Against a tableau of tropical green, Quinn and Noi stood behind a beaming young girl in a crisp new school uniform, a white blouse and a navy skirt.

"She looks so young here," she said.

An enthusiastic photographer called out excitedly as the great stone spires cast their silhouettes in the pale purple sky. Rays of sunlight crept out from beyond the temple, their golden beams shimmering on the still water. Thin wisps of cloud, magenta and royal blue, provided a majestic backdrop as the five great towers, sprouting upwards like lotus bulbs, stood proudly in the sky as they had for centuries. The pair gazed quietly in silent appreciation of the wonder before them. The grand temple, the jewel of the ancient Khmer empire, noble and magnificent.

Afterwards, they breakfasted, and Quinn shared a genuine compliment about the famous kimbap recipe: refreshing cucumber complementing the salty seaweed. Areum had brought two plastic cups, apparently having thought of everything, and poured her favorite brand of genmaicha, a green tea blended with roasted brown rice.

When they finished, they decided to take a walk around the grounds, agreeing that *tuk-tuks*, particularly *tuk-tuks* at tourist sites, were the absolute bane of existence and should never be encouraged. They talked for a while about Mei, sharing humorous and uplifting anecdotes, and then about Kaew, whom Areum had never met, though she was hardly a fan.

"Mei started to ask questions," she said, "questions girls should not be asking at that age, so I did my best to explain things to her. About girls and boys, where babies come from. Kaew wasn't a good influence on her, but Mei was very curious. Kaew was older. Children look up to the older ones, you know."

After a time, the conversation settled into a natural rhythm, drifting aimlessly for a while, and soon they began to share more personal stories of how they came to know their feisty, little Cambodian friend.

Areum was indeed Korean, but it wasn't quite as simple as that, she remarked, adding that her family were, in fact, *Joseonjok*—a distinct ethnic group that many considered to be more Chinese and often viewed with some disdain. She was born and spent the early years of her life in Yanji City, in the Chinese province of Jilin. Though she had never known her mother, she was absolutely certain of two things: one, her mother was incredibly beautiful, a veritable fact attested to by a couple of old photographs; and two, that she had been her father's one true love and had left him brokenhearted.

As she recounted her story, Quinn chimed in here and there, peppering the conversation with his own confessions, if only to keep her from becoming too self-conscious. She maintained a noticeable physical distance, yet he was surprised by how transparent she was about her past; about everything. At first he was quite pleased with himself for winning her over, but as the morning wore on, he realized that he had little, if anything, to do with it. At times it seemed as if she simply needed to unburden herself and might not have had the opportunity in quite some time.

They meandered along pathways without map or agenda, stopping here and there to observe whatever caught their eye: grand temples whose ornate carvings and chiseled pictorials fought against timeless enemies—erosion, and the occasional vandal. Each ancient structure was decorated with intricate designs and figurines: bejeweled deities, either dancing gaily or grimacing; illustrated depictions of famed Hindu tales and folklore. While Areum admired the artistry of the bas-reliefs, Quinn was absorbed with the natural overgrowth of the forest, which imposed itself on the crumbling structures. Trees as old as time stretched their enormous roots in all directions, strangling pathways and enveloping monuments. Twisted wooden limbs, thick like Amazonian serpents, descended from on high, slithering over walls and through cracks in the stone. Others wove like cobwebs, creeping eerily across a façade, vines like tentacles approaching an unsuspecting nymph or a dozing Buddha.

It wasn't long before he was sweating profusely, and though he blamed the rising sun, Areum countered with a remark about his withdrawal. Yes, her father was indeed an alcoholic, she admitted, though she despised the term, which carried far too many negative connotations. While he drank heavily, he was always a pleasant drunk: chatty at first, then hungry, then sleepy. She had heard all the stories before about other men who drank, those who spent the family savings or became violent, but not her father. He was always a gentle, loving man, even when seeking the answers to life's riddles at the bottom of a bottle of *soju*.

When Areum was still a child, they moved, the two of them, to Seoul. Growing up in Seoul was an uncomfortable experience, and one that only seemed to get worse as the years progressed. Although the *Joseonjok* were ethnically Korean, their ancestors had emigrated to nearby China during the Japanese occupation a century before. She explained that they were viewed essentially as immigrants in Seoul and treated as second-class citizens. She was often bullied in school, had difficulty finding a decent job despite her excellent grades, and had long ago given up on thoughts of marriage, having been ridiculed far too many times. Only backwater farmers and other country bumpkins married girls of mixed backgrounds.

While she had a close relationship with her father, the only other person who ever treated her with genuine kindness was his mother, Baek Su, her sole grandparent, who owned a humble flower shop in Hapjeong-dong. Areum would go there after school to do her homework and visit on weekends when Mr. Choi was away on business. Each time she pushed open the door, the fragrance of a thousand blossoms lifted her off her feet, and in an instant, she felt right at home. Eventually, as the business struggled to turn a profit, her father hatched a plan for Baek Su to move her shop to Cambodia. He was frequently there on business, it was far more affordable in every way, and he was fond of the small but welcoming Korean expat community in Siem Reap, mostly retirees escaping the chilly winters. Despite Baek Su's initial reluctance, it was a rather smooth transition abroad, with Areum flying down every year to spend the summer months with her grandmother. Over time, she began to feel more at home in Siem Reap than in Seoul, taking on a bigger role at the flower shop until finally moving to Cambodia five years ago.

"And you like it here?" he asked.

She smiled to herself. "Yes, I really do. The summers are awfully hot, and I miss the cherry blossoms in the spring, but," her smile broadened, "this is my home now. It has always felt more like home than Korea or China or anywhere else."

As the hours passed, the conversation was bittersweet. At long last it finally struck him that every doubt he harbored, every nagging suspicion that vexed him, had more to do with her personality than anything else. She was quite introverted but also a rather quirky sort of girl. A kind and natural beauty chock-full of little idiosyncrasies that had surely confused many a smitten young man over the years.

Whatever lead he was hoping to follow with Areum wasn't there; that much was certain. Thoughts of an association with traffickers, smugglers, or lawbreakers of any sort were ludicrous. And if she wasn't connected to the disappearance, it left him to simply gather any information she might have, a disappointing notion that hardly spurred him onwards. Traveling all the way to Siem Reap had been a long shot from the beginning, whether he fully admitted it to himself or not.

And yet, speaking to Areum that morning did serve another purpose, something most unexpected. It was different with Noi. Perhaps the incident was too recent, and she, from a kind of professional necessity, a form of self-preservation, always maintained an emotional distance. With Areum, there was no hiding their shared love for Mei, and the sting of her loss was dampened when they faced it together. While he needed answers and was desperate for any clue, it was comforting to simply reminisce, to trade stories. The humorous incidents that Mei wrote about in her letters—a dramatic first bee sting while potting gardenias, a triumphant scuffle with a teasing young boy. It was therapeutic for both of them, a welcome conversation amidst his own extended bouts of self-medication. And in that, for the better part of a dreadfully humid morning, they at least found some temporary comfort and solace together.

ELEVEN

As the long shadows cast by the afternoon sun stretched across the city, Quinn peeled a strip of pastry from his croissant, buttery flakes sprinkling across his dish. Seated on the humble front porch of a café-cum-guesthouse, he waited for Areum as he indulged in some of Cambodia's French culinary influence. His hands no longer trembled, at least not as much, though having mainlined several espressos, his entire body seemed to be idling at a low hum. Areum had declined his invitation to join him for dinner, only to playfully suggest that they dine together the following evening instead. It was a bit late notice, after all. She did, however, promise to drop by for coffee just before dusk—after scouring the shop and her home for any belongings Mei might have left behind. She wasn't particularly optimistic. Mei didn't have many possessions, and those she did, she treasured immensely, but a thorough search would be conducted nonetheless.

The sun was immense as it dipped, nearing a distant horizon of palm trees. A cool breeze drifted across the porch, across Quinn's damp forehead, lulling him into a dozy, late-afternoon trance. On the sidewalk, a procession of monks, young boys with heads shorn like kiwi fruit, robes the color of persimmon.

He opened his eyes, blinking heavy lids when he heard the sound of gentle footfalls, Areum climbing the front steps. She wore a flowing, yellow dress and a broad-brimmed sun hat, and was clutching a woven handbag, beaming with the same heartwarming smile that she always seemed to possess. Such was their awkward duet. Encounters always pleasant, now even somewhat familiar, though underscored by an irrepressible tone of despair.

She plopped into a rattan seat, the faintest twin wrinkles creasing just above her nose. With narrowed eyes she looked at him, then at his demitasse, back to him once more, before leaning forward to inhale the rich aroma of roasted espresso.

"It smells like coffee," she said.

"What did you expect?"

She looked to the sky, mouth slightly agape. "Oh, tequila?"

"Come on, Areum, don't be ridiculous," he said, taking a sip. "Everyone knows you can't find good tequila in this part of the world."

"Ah, is that so?"

He shrugged. "Even God rested on Sunday. Figured maybe I should give it a try."

A waitress shuffled past to the only other couple on the porch. On her way back, Areum ordered a latté and lemon biscotti.

"So, I found a few things, but she didn't leave much at the shop. I don't think it will be much help," she confessed, placing her handbag on the table. She removed a faded purple tank top, a book, some postcards with pictures of the Eiffel tower and Notre Dame, and a few other trinkets.

"Where did she get these?"

"I don't know. Sometimes tourists come into the shop, and Mei tries to practice her English with them. Maybe they gave them to her."

He flipped one over. "There's no writing."

"I think she just liked the pictures of Paris."

He picked up the tank top, turned it inside out robotically, and wondered what it was that he expected to find. The book was a hardcover with dogeared corners. While the title was written in Khmer, the boy wizard on the front cover was universally recognized. He flipped through the worn pages absentmindedly, his heart sinking. Areum met his eyes. *Now what?*

He shook his head, slumping back into his chair and letting out a heavy sigh. "This is everything?"

She nodded. "I feel so helpless. She spent a lot of time with me. She was so chatty, and now that she's gone, I don't even know the first thing to do. I feel I should have more to tell you, or, I don't know . . ."

"She didn't ever mention having a fight with some of the girls at the shelter, did she?"

She shook her head. "We didn't talk much about the shelter or anything that happened there. It was almost like she pretended to be someone else when she was at the shop. She wasn't Mei, or at least, she wasn't Mei, the young girl. She wanted to grow up. More and more lately. She liked to hear stories about Korea, and China, anything about traveling. Or she would gossip with me about my magazines. Lately, she was asking more about boys, about, you know, more adult things. But like I said, these were ideas that Kaew had put in her head. We didn't usually talk like that. I could tell she wasn't comfortable asking but was curious because—" She paused as something appeared to catch her eye.

"What is it?"

Putting down her biscotti, she reached across the table, fingering the inside sleeve of the weathered book. Lifting the cover, she removed an old water-stained flyer of sorts folded into the front jacket.

"What's that?"

She regarded it thoughtfully for a moment. "I remember this. She used it as her bookmark. I remember the pink color sticking out from the pages, but I didn't think anything of it. It's just a bookmark, right? Then one day I saw it more closely and told her not to use it anymore. I bought her a new bookmark the same day, made from a nice fabric." She handed him the worn card, and he studied what little remained of it. "I guess she must have tucked it away and forgot about it."

Even with the creases and water stains, it was obvious—one of a million Thai leaflets handed out on the streets of Bangkok promoting soapy massages and sex clubs. Several girls were front and center, posing in bikinis amidst frothy bubbles, advertising cheap draft beer for a few *baht*, though the date of the noted specials was lost to wear and tear, as was the name of the venue. He could make out one of the giant fishbowls in the background where men could select the women they wanted, likely a massage parlor.

"How long has she had this?" he asked.

"A couple of months? I haven't seen her use it for a long time. I thought she threw it out, like I told her, but she must have put it away and forgot about it."

"Where would . . ." He turned his gaze, the wheels in motion once again, the answer clear as day. When he met her eyes, he could tell she was with him. "The girls."

"Kaew."

"They were Thai."

"I don't know about the others, but she was, yes."

"I think Noi said she was from Bangkok too, or the outskirts. Brought in maybe. I can't remember."

He squinted, trying to make out the faded block lettering at the bottom of the flyer. It was impossible to tell. He flipped the card over and back again and then tilted it forward, just so, the light catching something. Holding it at just the right angle, there it was, the faintest imprint of the address: Sukhumvit *Soi* . . . something. *Which soi?* Sukhumvit was the longest road in the country, but which side street?

"Do you see something? What does it say?"

Manipulating the card, he exhaled with relief when he didn't see the numbers 4 or 23, the most notorious *sois* in all of Bangkok. For a moment, he didn't fear the worst.

Then, from beyond the distant tree line, the last rays of daylight shone for a final time, the glow rising for an instant, glinting on just the right spot. And there it was. The faintest debossed outline from the once-sparkling silvery ink. Twenty-three. *Sukhumvit Soi 23.* He dropped the card on the table and buried his face in his hands.

"What is it?" Sliding the card from the table, she examined it once more. "Mei would never go to a place like this," she said, her voice firm.

He rubbed his eyes. "You're right," he said, voice muffled as he spoke through his palms. "She wouldn't. I don't think she's ever been down that way, but those girls have."

He grasped at the straws inside his head, though speaking it aloud helped to lay the pieces together with a bit more conviction.

"I think maybe they went back. The girls. I think they went back and told people about Battambang and how to get there. That there were lots of girls, no security." He tried to look at the situation rationally, objectively, removing Mei from the equation. "Like shooting fish in a barrel. And from Bangkok it's not a great distance to travel either, considering the potential revenue."

Areum's face took on a look of determination. "I don't know about these girls, but I know about those people," she said. "Noi and I have had many conversations over the years. A lot of the girls are sold and have to pay back their debts, right? Family debts?"

He nodded.

"Maybe that's what they're doing."

"Paying off their debt by going back?"

"By going back and telling them where they can find *other* girls. Even more money."

He pulled a cigarette from a wrinkled package and put a flame to it. "Maybe. I mean, it's certainly possible. But it still doesn't make complete sense. This is a long way to come and recruit. They're not known—"

"But Quinn, they're not recruiting here. They're just taking. Easy. Fish in the barrel, remember?"

He let the smoke churn deep in his chest as he fidgeted with his demitasse and considered how likely the scenario was. Areum had a point, the same one that Noi had stressed in Montreal. These weren't recruits; there was no grooming process. These were damaged girls being taken right back into the life. Victimized girls had a staggering rate of being exploited all over again. Returning to the only life they'd ever known, a misguided sense of comfort in that, in the familiarity.

However, it still could have been a local gang. But then, why risk employing the girls locally? Siem Reap wasn't that big a city. Sure, there would be some local demand, but how much would they make? Peanuts compared to the market in Thailand, and it would hardly outweigh the risk of keeping the girls so close to the shelter. There were always prying eyes, rescue attempts, NGOs hard at work.

"You said you used to work catching criminals like this, right?"

He shook his head. "No, not exactly. I know a little bit from Noi. I worked for a while on border corruption, concerns with law enforcement, but this is different. If they took them, if they took Mei to Bangkok, it's a whole new problem. The city is too big now, too infamous. The gangs operating down there aren't just satisfied with local Thais and sex tourists anymore. They have international operations, moving girls across borders. The volume, the variety, it's a massive industry now."

"I can tell you one thing for sure—this card, she didn't get it from anyone in Siem Reap. I'm almost positive she brought it with her one week during a visit." She hung her head. "What do you think?" she asked quietly. "In your heart, you think she's there?"

"I don't know. But I do know that, unfortunately, this is the only lead we have. If I can find this place"—he picked up the leaflet—"if I don't find her, at least I can find some answers that will point me in the right direction." He nodded to himself, certain of at least this much. "I have to go."

"Yes. You do."

They locked eyes for a moment, both uncertain of what to say next. Somewhere within, a small part of him wished he could linger for a while longer. She forced a smile, affectionately placing her hand on his and, after words unspoken, patted it with finality.

"I'll see you again," he said, rising from his seat.

"Quinn," she called out as he made his way down the front steps.

He stopped and looked back.

"Good luck."

Ghonlaat,

How are you? I am fine. Actually, today I am not so fine. Today I am being very annoyed by one of the boys. His name is Ponlok. He always wants to ride his bicycle with me to school or market. Every day he is like this. He really likes me a lot, I can tell. I don't like him. He always plays roughing around with the other boys and is always covered in dirt. Always dirty. Then when he talks to me he has water coming out from his nose. I don't know the English word for this, but it's disgusting. Dégoûtant this word is in French. Yesterday we got new pencil crayons from Noi and a special teacher teached us how to draw. It was really fun, but my drawing was not so good. I think I need a lot of more practice. Today I will go to my secret spot by the pond to practice drawing but I don't know what to draw. Anyway, I hope it will be dandy. Do you use this word "dandy"? I learned it in my book, but Noi says this word is old. I like it. Dandy. Okay, bye for now.

Mei.

TWELVE

Bangkok, Thailand

STEPPING OUT OF THE COOL, CLIMATE-CONTROLLED TERMINAL OF Suvarnabhumi Airport, Quinn inhaled the thick tropical air. There was something unmistakable about the city's muggy scent: the salt from stale canals that meandered through miles of concrete, fried palm oil from a million woks, dense smog from dense traffic, ripe sewage and pungent durian fruit. It was the yin and yang of smoldering grills and fragrant incense, fiery red chilies and smooth, cool coconut milk. The sights, the sounds, the ferocious pace—the Thai capital was an assault on the senses from the very outset. *Krung Thep,* as the locals called it, was not for the faint of heart.

"Thong Lor?" asked the cabbie.

Quinn nodded, handing over an address scribbled on his boarding pass. As they pulled away, he leaned back and gazed out the window, absorbing the essence of a city that he hadn't visited for some time. Any thoughts of a speedy trip across town were firmly checked once he noticed the time—midafternoon—the notorious city traffic at its height. So much for nostalgia.

They proceeded to sit in gridlock for an hour and a half, Quinn cursing under his breath while his driver, more than accustomed to the local pace, tapped his fingers to the latest Thai pop songs playing on the radio.

Bangkok was modernizing at a staggering rate, its skyline filled with condos and skyscrapers, barely recognizable from the city it had been only ten years before. Glitzy shopping malls, futuristic sky trains, and Michelin-starred restaurants contrasted with the poverty that the city had left behind. Migrants were housed in slum dwellings built of corrugated metal, while the homeless hunkered beneath bridges, sharing their real estate with motorbike taxi mafias in their bright orange vests.

Every few minutes the motorbikes would whizz past, weaving between the gridlocked vehicles at breakneck speed, darting fearlessly between lanes, occasionally tapping their brakes as a mere formality. Quinn particularly enjoyed watching the businesswomen who sat sideways, undaunted, across the backseats of the two-wheeled demons. Gripping the seat with one hand, texting with the other, legs crossed and heels dangling precariously above the asphalt as the driver sped through the streets, skirts and blouses fluttering in the wind, hair to be dealt with accordingly upon arrival.

It was early evening when they arrived in Thong Lor, the city's trendy East-Asian district, punctuated by Japanese *izakayas* and Korean barbecues on every corner. His shirt clung to his back as he stepped into the lobby of a chic boutique hotel, the temperature plummeting by about fifteen degrees.

"*Sawatdee-kaa*!" A harmonious welcome from the three clerks behind the front desk. "Welcome to Bangkok. Checking in today?"

He nodded, handed them his passport, and turned to find a young lobby boy had sidled up to him holding a polished silver tray with a damp cloth and a citrus beverage.

"*Kop kun krap*," Quinn replied, inclining his head.

BEASTS OF THE NIGHT

A moment later a young lady came around the counter, apparently charged with taking his belongings upstairs, rather insistent despite the fact that Quinn had only one bag.

It was her vocal cords that gave her away, vibrating just a half octave too low, but she was a striking woman with a grace about her that took him by surprise. Cindy, as she introduced herself, spoke like an auctioneer—rapid and direct, swallowing consonants like only Thais can—and he strained to understand her. "Where you from? First time Bangkok? Where you go tonight?" She shot him a mischievous look when he mentioned Soi 23, but he reassured her he was simply meeting an old friend.

He tossed his bag aside, had a quick rinse in a cold shower, and, hair still wet, fly still down, buttons mostly left unbuttoned, rushed out of the room just as dusk began to creep its way into one of the most vibrant and notorious cities in Southeast Asia. Bangkok was coming to life once more, and he had no time to lose.

It wasn't a far walk to Soi 23, and he spent most of it trying to recall whether it was Nana Plaza or Soi Cowboy that gave the area its seedy reputation. Not that it made much of a difference; they were completely interchangeable in his mind, though surely some of the regulars, connoisseurs of the evening's pleasure houses, would disagree. He could still picture the bright neon sign that hung above what was once a tranquil and unassuming backstreet like any other: "Nana Plaza: World's Largest Adult Playground."

He barely broke stride for a couple of barbecued pork kebabs from a street vendor, wolfing down the succulent grilled meat as he went. With every passing minute, every new street that he crossed, the city's atmosphere began to shift. The blue haze of the evening sky darkened, and the city, at least this part of the city, seemed to resurrect itself from its daily slumber.

There were no more chic boutiques or trendy eateries, and while the street vendors remained—tables crowding the sidewalk from either flank—they catered more to tourists than local Thais. On display, tropical fruits and street food, pirated Hollywood films, and football jerseys all gradually underwent the same transformation—tank tops with vulgar slogans, adult films, sex toys, and erectile pills.

The clientele changed as much as the climate. It was as if an invisible sewing machine followed him across every intersection, lifting skirts, adjusting hemlines, and adding an inch or two to women's heels as it went. Thai businessmen and women, walking with purpose after a long workday, were replaced by foreign men with beer guts and receding hairlines, wandering tourists and backpackers, and women, lashes pressed, faces painted, readying themselves for the evening shift.

He overshot Soi 23 and found himself at a chaotic intersection across from the sky train station. Then, a few paces north, he heard the bustle and hum of the infamous alley and needed no further direction. A small backstreet, once quiet and humble like any other in the old Thai capital, was illuminated like the Sunset Strip. Flashing neon lights strobed from all angles, accompanied by pounding bass rhythms from warring speakers. It was as if he had entered an outdoor nightclub.

He proceeded down the gauntlet of go-go bars, girls in various stages of undress hollering and catcalling at passersby. Each venue had its own distinct theme: girls dressed in spacesuits, girls dressed as police officers, girls dressed as nurses, girls in fluorescent bikinis. Each establishment promoted one drink special or another, a happy hour that apparently lasted the entire evening, while TV screens projected football and rugby matches.

It was a carnival of lights and sounds, and it teemed with all manner of life: dusky men in cheap suits hawking fake watches, ladyboys in their cliques aggressively pinching wide-eyed single men, prostitutes, old and young, male and female, all manner of individuals who were only brought back to life with the setting sun. Every now and again, he caught a glimpse of an overwhelmed tourist, shocked and appalled, having clearly taken a wrong turn and desperate to escape. A visibly offended couple with Tilley hats and oversized camera lenses marched their adolescent son and daughter hastily through the crowd, shielding their eyes from the horror.

Soi Cowboy, once a small cluster of bars catering to American war veterans and expats, was now an entire strip, throbbing with an infectious energy on a busy Saturday night. It wasn't hard to see why it was such a draw: bright lights, liquor, and sex, not only plentiful but cheap, half-naked young women cooing and tugging at shirtsleeves. They didn't mind thinning hair, and they didn't judge soft physiques. They listened to men's stories with fascination and giggled provocatively at their clever jokes. Their clients were no longer shift workers with basement apartments but emperors among their consorts, no longer divorced and paying alimony but wealthy bachelors who had found paradise.

The shiny veneer was effective if one didn't look too closely. It distracted people from thinking too deeply about what lay beneath. And why would anyone want to think about that? Better to live amongst the dream than wake now, realizing it was all an illusion. Like a cheap coat of glossy paint, if one scratched too hard, they might accidentally reveal the dirt and grime hidden beneath the surface.

Snaking through the crowd, Quinn avoided most of the unwanted attention, a difficult task being male and single, accosted here and there by the more desperate predators. Nearing the end of the lane, he made a left onto Soi 23 and, a few steps later, caught a glimpse of one of Bangkok's many amusing contradictions in an abandoned parking lot.

Directly behind Cowboy's last watering hole, in a shadowy corner on a small patch of grass, a solitary woman was making an offering. She stood before a small spirit house, a Buddhist shrine set atop a pedestal. It was the size of a dollhouse and in the shape of a traditional *wat*, with golden *chofas* like miniature spears pointing skywards. Shadows danced across her face from the light of a small candle, her head slightly bowed as she held some incense between her palms, the smoke coiling upwards, undisturbed by the still night air. He could still hear the static bass echoing from the go-go bars, the guffawing of drunk men from the last corner pub, and yet there she stood, her evening ritual undisturbed, a simple bowl of fried rice placed as an offering to the guardian spirits.

Down the street, eyes darting around for the numbers matching his flyer, Quinn got closer with every step. He crossed to the other side and marched on, past some pubs, massage parlors, and a classy Italian restaurant in a very poor location. Counting down the street numbers, he was only a short block away. In all likelihood, All Night Massage was the corner building on the right side, a pale red light casting its ambient glow onto the sidewalk.

He quickened his pace. Legs pumping, he propelled himself forward, an awkward gait now, clumsy with anticipation. He wondered if maybe, on the other side of those doors, he might even find her: running errands, fetching towels, changing oils. He couldn't bear to imagine Mei doing anything more. The thoughts spurred him onwards, as did the pounding in his chest.

By the time he reached the bewitching red lamps, his pace had quickened to a near canter. He narrowly avoided a taxi as he jogged back across the street, two angry honks blaring through the dormant neighborhood.

He came to a stop in front of the corner building, momentarily dazed. He checked the address again: 18/2 Soi Prasanmit, Sukhumvit 23. The right address. This was it—at least what was left of it. The glowing red lamps illuminated the sidewalk, and several massage girls mewed at him from their seats, but they were several feet to his right, seated along the stoop of a neighboring building. He stared straight ahead at the decrepit remains of a brick structure—a massage parlor, a nightclub, whatever the venue happened to have been before it went belly up, neglected and abandoned. The paint from the overhead sign was long faded and washed out, a giant gray smear hanging above a thin vinyl canopy. Rusty air conditioners above matched the rusty metal gates pulled shut across the storefront, a giant padlock securing the entryway.

He stood, staring, unresponsive for a time. Eventually, an apparition took form before his eyes, and only then was he aware that he'd been gazing straight through another person. An old woman with natty gray hair and painfully stooped shoulders stood behind her food cart. She stared straight back, her face withered by time, utterly perplexed, as a medley of bean sprouts sizzled in a giant wok.

THIRTEEN

"Handsome man! Handsome!"

"Want massage?"

"Cheap! Cheap! Really good, really cheap!"

Slender fingers wrapped around his bicep pulling him nearly off balance, his feet awkwardly sidestepping along. The sudden jolt stole his attention from the deserted storefront, his eyes relaying new signals to his brain as it struggled to comprehend its new surroundings. It continued to buffer, synapses firing, processing the vacated building.

"Relax massage!"

"Look like Captain America!"

"Ohh, handsome Captain America!"

He glanced down at the painted nails that shook him, then up at the painted face of the owner. A homely Thai girl with crimson lips, she pulled with one hand and pointed with the other at a neighboring establishment that was anything but vacant. Outside were a half dozen girls, some striking poses in the luminous red doorway, others seated provocatively along its tiled front steps. They wore matching tank tops and pleated pink skirts that were, in certain cases, little more than belts. The homely girl and her friend, a farmhand with muscular forearms, were the most forward, tugging his arm and pushing him toward a menu of services displayed in the window. A couple of the others giggled amongst themselves, exchanging whispers and calling out suggestions amongst a chorus of snickers. Another pair sat on stools, quietly looking on, knobby knees apart, exposing white undergarments beneath the rose-colored ensembles.

Gradually, he came to his senses, nodding along and thanking the girls for their flattery in an attempt to deflect their attention. He wasn't sure what he was saying, but he muttered something to buy some time and piece everything back together again. The farmhand momentarily lost interest when a tall African man walked past, cooing a most endearing racial slur. "Chocolate man! Want massage? Handsome chocolate man, cheap massage!"

His mind slowly began to refocus, rattled and thrown disconcertingly off course but refusing to accept this new reality. All Night Massage, whatever seedy enterprise had once occupied the dilapidated building was gone, but it *had* been there once. It could have been there for years, a mainstay of the sordid Cowboy back alleys. For all he knew, the lively establishment in front of him could be its new location, the business having relocated for cheaper rent, better real estate. He stepped back to read the sign: Sakura Massage and Spa.

The fact that he remained standing in Sakura's red glow served only to encourage the girls, who had now formed a trio around him, pointing at the various services available, batting fake eyelashes and pouting their lips. He scanned the list for keywords of interest but found none.

"Ladies," he said, pointing to the tarnished, empty storefront, "do you know what happened there? All Night Massage? Do you remember?"

Unfazed, their sales pitches hardly wavered, instantly pointing back to their own establishment, nodding suggestively. He shrugged off the tallest of the bunch, who had circled around and begun to rub his shoulders.

"Alright, alright, a massage would be great, but what about *there?* Did you know this place? Did you work there? How long has it been closed?"

"Finish!" the homely one said. "Closed, all finish!"

"Sakura special massage for handsome man."

"Happy, happy Sakura massage," chimed in another.

His patience was running thin, which hardly mattered now, the communication barrier effectively unbreachable, the other parties clearly occupied with a very different set of priorities. Nodding and smiling like a fool, he pushed open the front door—a cheering chorus of approval from the girls outside—in hopes of finding a *mama-san*, or an overseer of any kind.

Inside was crisp and revitalizing: lights dimmed, the air scented with fresh lemongrass. Leafy bamboo reeds stood in various corners, a trickling stream flowed across some elevated stonework, emptying into a small pond to his left, and a serene melody played in the background, the brass strings of a *khim* being plucked like an exotic harp. One could have been forgiven for thinking it was a genuine spa.

He heard footsteps descending a well-used wooden staircase and waited patiently for someone with answers, but instead met another white-on-rose uniform and her client, a stocky man with glasses who walked straight past, refusing to make eye contact. The masseuse smiled and continued down the hall, a jumble of soiled towels in her arms.

A moment later, a somewhat officious woman appeared—middle-aged, thin, and scarcely more than five feet tall. She was garbed entirely in black and approached with a weary smile, permed black hair curled stiffly into place, massive nostrils like prehistoric caverns.

"Welcome Sakura Massage. Can I help you?"

"Yes, the shop next door," he said, pointing through the wall. "All Night Massage? Do you know how long it's been closed?"

The manager's eyes flickered for a minute, unfamiliar with the peculiar line of questioning. Then, after some initial hesitation, she nodded. "Oh, All Night Massage. Yes, is finish now. We are Sakura Massage. You like see menu?"

"No, no"—he waved his hand—"do you know *when* it closed down, when?" He tapped his watch. "How long have you been here?" She made a face and handed him a greasy laminated price list. "Have you worked here a long time?" he asked. "One year? Two years?"

"One year," she replied, rather unconvincingly. He was beginning to get the impression that she would say anything now to be rid of him.

"And you don't know when All Night Massage closed?"

She gave a brisk shake of the head and tapped the price list with a bright-red acrylic nail.

Quinn muttered a few expletives and stared blankly at the ceiling. There was nothing here. He felt it in the pit of his stomach, felt it before he'd even asked, before the trickling stream and the lemongrass, before the scantily clad greeting party outside. Nothing about the place felt right. Nothing that even hinted at the use of minors. Located slightly off the main drag, it had minimal lighting and was not as obviously promoted, but that was essentially where the similarities ended. The list of services posted in the window were standard, with no mention of words like "Lolita," "innocent," or "fresh"—euphemisms that spoke the secret language. No underworld symbols of teddy bears, blue triangles, or colored butterflies, arcane signals for the occult community. Not to mention the fact that every girl outside was easily in her mid- to late-twenties and, therefore, according to industry standards, a grizzled veteran not long from retirement.

The manager was talking again. He watched absentmindedly as her lips moved, something about a two-for-one discount. There was a time when Bangkok was a mecca for predators seeking to take advantage of vulnerable youth, an international haven for abuse. Now the Thai capital's world-renowned red-light district had become so famous that purveyors were forced to take far more precautions. With the sex industry worth billions, estimated by some to account for over 10 percent of the country's GDP, the added spotlight wasn't always welcome, especially in an area like Cowboy. In lesser-known locales, such as the border provinces of Udon Thani in the north and Ubon Ratchathani to the east, in the debauched coastal city of Pattaya, the underbelly wasn't as difficult to find, if one knew where to look. Perhaps, like many others, they had simply moved their exploitative practices across the border to Cambodia, Laos, and the lawless regions of Myanmar. Working amongst the shadows in less regulated tourist enclaves in the karaoke bars of Vientiane and the notorious beer gardens of Phnom Penh, away from the prying eyes of inquisitive journalists and human rights activists.

"Maybe want two girls, four-hand massage? We make special tonight for you."

He waved a hand dismissively, turned on his heel, and shoved open the front door, nearly clipping the wing of the homely mother hen outside.

"Where you go, handsome? Come back massage."

"No fun, cheap man!"

"Handsome man, no fun!"

The voices of ridicule gradually faded into the night as Quinn marched toward the main strip, his eyes focused on the bright lights of a corner bar. He felt himself flush with anger, fuming and on edge, ready to lash out at the entire world. He resented the fact that he had grasped so tightly to such a tenuous lead, a faded leaflet from a bankrupt massage parlor. Pulling it from his pocket, he examined it once more. *This* was his great hope? The clue that would solve all the riddles of her disappearance? *Did you really think it would be that easy?*

The bar, its canopy lined with Christmas lights, was little more than a patio with a few cheap plastic tables. It was mostly empty. A couple of white-haired men sat watching a soccer game, an occasional critique leveled at the screen in German. Behind them was a pair of jaded working girls, likely hired companions for the weekend, sharing some pomelo. Pulling up a stool, he ordered three shots of whiskey and a bottle of Singha.

The monotonous electronic rhythms boomed all around him, accompanied by the flashing lights of the go-go bars. The street was packed, the laughter and shouts from the crowd competing with the bass from innumerable speakers. Quinn downed the first two glasses, relishing the singe at the back of his throat. A young Thai boy, barely old enough to see over the bar, reached across and hovered the bottle spout over the empty glasses.

Quinn nodded.

FOURTEEN

As he lowered himself unsteadily from the barstool, Quinn's legs danced an unintentional little jig, causing him to stumble backward into a passing group of backpackers. "Easy there!" one said as they chuckled along their merry way.

Time had stood still at the bar—quite a bit of time, as it turned out, until eventually, anguished thoughts of Mei overruled his feelings of self-pity. The whiskey had dulled his senses, but the respite had at least given him time to formulate a new plan, though even his saturated conscience knew that, in truth, it was nothing more than a drunk's last resort. Still, for the time being, it was all he had.

The massage girls at the parlor couldn't tell him a thing, but they were hardly keeping secrets or party to some conspiracy. They were typical of the industry, long-serving employees at the rub-and-tug *du jour,* but so was everybody else along the strip. While many of the provocatively dressed bar girls were rather young, many were quite a bit older than even the country bumpkins from Sakura Massage. Perhaps they knew a thing or two about the darker side of the business, steeped in the local surroundings for years. Surely some of them could speak to the more particular requests, the unique tastes and back-page menu items that could be provided with a subtle wink and a few extra *baht.* He could canvass the bars, turn a stone or two, certain he would gain some information in return for a hot meal or some extra cash. The prospect of being paid for a few tidbits of common knowledge rather than servicing yet another drunk foreigner would surely turn some heads.

He tilted back the last of a warm, frothy beer, and paid his tab. Not much of a plan, he thought, but something.

The unrelenting bass throbbed in his ears as he sat on the farthest end of a red, pleather sofa, his eyes adjusting to the shadowy ambiance at odds with the laser show on stage. A long, elevated platform ran the length of the bar with a dozen brass poles rising from the glowing white floor through the sparkly, decaled ceiling. A ring of barstools encircled the dancefloor, where half-naked girls moved to the beat of the bassline. The dancers, dressed in white bikinis, didn't so much dance to the music as sway in a sort of bemused shuffle, sidestepping back and forth to the rhythm, or some simply at their own off-kilter pace. Each skimpy string bottom was adorned with a circular button and number, making it easy for customers to identify their preference for fourteen or twenty-seven. Patrons of all ages and backgrounds guzzled their drinks and debated amongst friends which girl would be the evening's lucky recipient of their undeniable sexual prowess.

Despite the varying outfits, the most constant feature, identical from one bar to the next, was the emptiness etched across the girls' faces. At first glance, brimming lip gloss and smoky eye shadow completed the sultry look for every exotic seductress. But the eyes themselves stared into the distance, devoid of emotion. Glassy and dull, they gazed beyond the customers, beyond the walls, perhaps even beyond the city, far away from the lights and sounds and the catcalls of drunken men. Quinn had never seen such vacant, life-less expressions.

Dipping in and out of various clubs, he struggled with his poorly laid plan. Wracking his brain on how to investigate the loathsome underworld he sought, he tried to figure out how to engage in the secretive exchanges. Drug use in Thailand still carried the death penalty, but anyone who thought they couldn't find a few grams of this or that, especially in Cowboy, was mistaken. Minors were also taboo, even in a spot like this, but the arrangements took place somewhere; that much was certain. There *were* people behind it, offering the option if one knew where to look and how to ask.

"You look like a first-timer! A deer caught in the headlights!" Quinn looked up from his seat and saw a pair of men smiling down on him from the tiered benches. "No need to be shy about it. I'm envious. I remember my first time in one of these joints. Thought I'd died and gone to heaven. I'm Jim, this here is Carl." He motioned to the spot next to him, "You wanna grab a seat?"

Quinn considered the question for a moment, then nodded casually. "Sure, why not."

They were Americans—Southerners, judging by their accents, and seemed keen on playing the role of big brother. Quinn had been eyeing a different man across the stage, rehearsing introductions in his head, but this would work just as well. They were well dressed, relatively speaking, khakis and polo shirts, well groomed, and if he had to guess, a couple of middle-class bachelors on vacation.

"Like I said, no need to be shy here. This is all for us, you understand? Just pick whichever one you like, call over that cranky lookin' lady in the black there, and she'll take care of the rest. She's the *mama-san*."

"The what?" Quinn glanced over at a conservatively dressed woman, nearly identical to the manager of Sakura Massage: older, thin smile, holding a clipboard. He decided it was best to pretend he was completely naïve, allowing the two men to do most of the talking.

"*Mama-san*, it's Asian for boss lady or somethin' like that. Basically, she's the one you pay. Now look, you've pretty much got your two options: short time or long time. Short time, you get to take her for a few hours, have yourself a good ol' roll in the sack, and then you get on about your day. Long time is for the whole night. You get to keep her till morning. Costs a little more, but then again," he opened his palms, "you get your money's worth." He chuckled.

"But you can't be an ass about it. You'll have to buy her dinner at least," Carl added. "Hell, probably breakfast too, but it's well worth it. Don't think you can't be turned down in a place like this either. Me, I like a girl who's a little bit more seasoned, speaks a bit of English at least. The younger ones, it can get a bit dull after a while."

Quinn nodded along, happy to play the part of the innocent tourist out for his first night in the big city. "Is there a different price for the younger girls? I see a couple over there who look like they're straight out of high school."

Jim made a face and shook his head. "Not that I know of. And those girls, they ain't goin' to no high school. Like he said, we tend to prefer the women who speak the language. Makes for a more relaxing evening. Some of the younger ones do, but the subject matter, well, to be honest, it gets on my nerves. What do you talk about with a girl half your age?" He cocked an eyebrow at Quinn, "Now, I know what you're thinkin', 'I'm not really here for the conversation.'" He let out a hearty guffaw, pleased with himself. "But still, after a while, it can get a little dry. Carl here, he's got himself a steady one. How old is Lek, early thirties?"

"Yep. Thirty-three."

"What do you mean 'steady'?" Quinn asked.

Carl was busy ordering another beer, so Jim carried on. "He's based out of Hong Kong at the moment, so he pretty much comes up here any chance he gets, takes her out for a week or two, maybe down to one of the resorts in Hua Hin. It's a long-distance kind of thing."

"You can take them out for that long?"

"Well, sure, if the price is right. Anny is my girl's name. She's kind of a free agent, so to speak. I take her out, we spend some time together whenever I'm here, and when I'm back at work, I send her some money from time to time, for her and her family. She's got a kid back home up in Chiang Rai. It's peanuts for me, but they really appreciate it. I'm actually hoping to relocate down here eventually, maybe even retire up north. It doesn't cost much to build a house up there. The material's next to nothin' and the labor's 'bout the same." He sighed and tilted his head, contemplative. "I kind of miss her, actually. She's up there with her family right now."

"So, what brings you to paradise?" Carl leaned in, fresh beer in hand. "I never got your name, boss."

"John, sorry 'bout that," Quinn said, shaking hands. "First time. It's all a bit much." He paused to take a long sip of his beer, searching for an acceptable backstory. "Like you said, paradise. A couple of buddies at work have been raving about it for years. I just finalized my divorce a few weeks ago and figured, why not? Might as well go and see what all the fuss is about."

"Attaboy!" A heavy mitt smacked his shoulder. "Well, you came to the right place. These Thai girls, they'll treat you well. Treat you like a man should be treated, like back in the good ol' days. None of that new age feminist shit down here. Women back home, some of them don't even know how to fry an egg. Hell, I know my ex sure couldn't."

"Mine neither," Quinn added. "Hopeless in the kitchen."

He cringed inside, almost embarrassed by the pathetic character he was inventing. However, it seemed to do just the trick. His comments served as the catalyst for a prolonged debate about the drawbacks of marriage. Both men appeared far more eager to disparage the women they'd left behind than pay attention to the topless entertainment shimmying on stage. Each time one would complain about alimony payments or child support, the other would inevitably dredge up a story of even greater hardship, confirming that he was, in fact, the far more pitiable victim. This supremacy would last for a few brief anecdotes until the conversation swung back in the other man's favor once again.

The one-upmanship continued until Quinn finally found a moment to interject, saying he wanted to explore the rest of the strip and uncover all that paradise had to offer. The two Southerners hardly matched his criteria, and the strange man across the stage had also left in the middle of Jim's rant about divorce lawyers.

As he wandered along the strip, dipping in and out of nightclubs, every venue consisted of a rather similar clientele. Some were young and curious, a false confidence betraying their youthful fascination with the bare breasts on display. Others, much older, were lonely, visibly there for the companionship as much as anything else. A kindly presence to remind them what it was to feel young, to listen to the hardships that inevitably came with age.

Most, however, were simply there for cheap drinks and cheaper sex, many sharing the same crude, demeaning jokes and predatory grins—endured by their scantily clad hosts as a matter of course. From club to club, a fresh drink in hand and new patrons to question, the lights became increasingly blurred, the sounds muffled as he tiptoed dangerously along the edge of the rabbit hole. His mind well and truly sodden, he looked more and more the part of the debauched Bangkok sex tourist.

"What, that one there with the tattoos all over her back?" A voice stirred him from a shallow slumber. He felt a cool sensation on his thigh and realized he had spilled his beer. Chin up, glancing around in an inebriated haze, he was at yet another club—bright lights and mirrors, colors and sounds. He didn't recognize the men around him, but it seemed as if they were all together. The voice had come from just behind, a man with a fringe of brown hair, thinly framed glasses, and a boiler of a belly. He had the thick, arthritic hands of a former boxer.

"Look at all that ink. Forget about it, mate," he continued in a heavy working-class accent, though Quinn wasn't especially adept at placing English intonations. Still, if there was anything left of the class system in Britain, this louse had certainly crawled out from somewhere beneath the pyramid.

"Listen, a girl like that wants nothing to do with your teensy little prick and button-mushroom balls. You couldn't handle her. Look at those eyes. Maneater. Eat you up like a fucking pudding. What she needs is a proper cock. The type of cock that still got the belt in his younger days, knows what it means to take a beating. Kind of cock you'd be scared to meet in a dark alley in a bad neighborhood. And a set of mean, old balls to match. Fucking stones. Hard, bristly fucking balls."

"And I suppose you're just the man for the job, then?" another voice said.

"Believe it, son. I'll have her walking bow-legged for a week."

Quinn caught a sharp elbow in the ribs. "This one runs his mouth all day and is always the first to bed—usually on his own. All talk. 'All night she takes it, bareback, every position, begs me for more.' It's a miracle he doesn't get dehydrated flapping his gums the way he does."

"Bareback? Are you joking? With that one? Look at her. Half the pricks in Manchester have been up in there. I'd be double wrapping at the very least. Get me one of them plastic suits like they wear in those space films." A rumble of laughter rippled through the small crowd.

"She looks a little old for me," Quinn said, trying to jump in as nonchalantly as possible. "Kind of run down. I'm in the mood for something a bit younger tonight, I think."

"Aren't we all. Well, there's plenty to choose from up there," the man replied, jutting his cleft chin at the stage. He had lively green eyes, a snub nose, and sour, reeking breath. "And then there's this one here." He leaned forward as number seventeen walked past, slapping her right buttock. "They don't get much younger than that!" Seventeen cocked an eyebrow and wagged a finger disapprovingly.

"Nah, you don't want that one," the boxer chimed in. "Look at her; she's fresh off the farm. You want one from the city—more urban, polished, lighter skin."

"You ever had one of them farm girls cook for you?" asked a third man. He sported a slick side part and goatee, and kissed his fingertips with delight. "She can toil the fields all day as long as she makes me a curry!"

"Listen, lads," the boxer said, on his pedestal once again, "what you want is a nice city girl. One of them posh nannies. She'll treat you right. She can run around, do the shopping, doing her Mary fucking Poppins routine." He took a gulp of beer and wiped his stubbled chin. "Polish the silverware and then polish my knob!" He roared, the others joining in a chorus of laughter.

"Suit yourself," Quinn said. "I'm never settling down again. Forget it. It's the bachelor life for me. I just don't see anything I really want here tonight. I need something a little . . ." He paused and searched for the correct word. "Younger. A little *fresher*." He stifled a wave of disgust once again.

"How fucking young you want to go?" the goatee asked from behind. He pointed to a giggly pair on the right side of the stage. "Those two are barely legal as it is." He chuckled. "I mean, I like 'em young too but no younger than my daughter. There's just something wrong about that."

"Which daughter? How many little bastards you have running around Thailand anyway?" the man next to Quinn teased.

"Try out the place down a little ways, the girls wearing the space suits," the goatee said. "We were there earlier in the night, and it didn't look too bad. Still . . ." Leaning forward in his seat, he hungrily perused the showcase on stage, nodding his approval. "This is the place to be, mate, far as I'm concerned."

As the evening slowly devolved into its more debauched hours, the strip unfolded like a slideshow before Quinn's sagging eyelids. Each venue flashed before him, a series of still frames—painted faces, fluorescent lights, sweaty flesh, greasy beer sleeves. The more he drank, the more he talked to everyone around him, only serving to underline what a hopeless effort it truly was. The only ones more concerned with making money than the dancers were the *mama-sans*, and neither party, young nor old, had any desire to entertain his perverse questions about underage girls. The men, on the other hand, were all, unfortunately, cut from the same cloth. What he needed were patrons with truly dirty laundry. They were nowhere to be found, preferring anonymity, and for good reason. Avoiding detection was half the goal, even at midnight in Bangkok.

At one point he was tipped off by a group of Australian rough-necks about a Russian-owned nightclub not far from the main drag. Apparently, it consisted exclusively of imported European escorts rather than Thais and catered to all manner of depravity. He stumbled down a side alley in near darkness until he found the place, a blue neon sign illuminating the shaven head of a herculean bouncer in a black suit.

Inside, beyond a black curtain speckled with cigarette burns, Slavic techno music boomed at a volume that made him wiggle a finger in his ear. With the exception of a steep cover charge and exorbitant drink prices, it was a typical go-go bar.

Not long after being seated, he found himself the center of atten-tion from a pair of redheaded Muscovites, who could have easily passed as sisters. Even in his stupor, he placed the girls somewhere in their mid-twenties and was again stymied with every attempt to gather information. Eventually, a bristly man with a thick Ural accent recommended, with little subtlety, that if he wasn't going to pay the girls for their time, perhaps he should stop wasting it.

Quinn mulled this over for a while and noted that he had become rather indifferent, all part of the evening routine now, the fumbling questions of an amateur either tolerated or ignored, inevitably culminating in the same futile outcome. And then, in a rare moment of clarity, he realized he didn't much care for the bristly man's tone either and found it all rather amusing. The vodka was the cheapest item on the menu, and it flowed freely.

A few songs later, or possibly further along in the same blaring monotony—who could tell?—he found himself seated next to a rather belligerent character, possibly even more inebriated than himself. As obnoxious as he was obese, the man, evidently the proudest Ukrainian to have ever lived, hurled critiques at every new dancer who took the stage. With the chest of a champion bodybuilder and the belly of a pastry connoisseur, he was particularly vulgar when a stocky brunette began her routine, teasing and caressing the brass. After each heckle, he craned his thick neck around to see if anyone had taken note of his wit, chuckling to himself, vying to be the center of attention. To his right sat a stooped, anemic friend, laughing along and encouraging the show, the two alternately singing verses of folk songs about the glory of Kiev and then comparing the dancer's thighs to various livestock.

Descending further into darkness by the minute, Quinn couldn't be bothered to hide his displeasure or his lingering, droopy-lidded glare. When the man noticed the unwanted attention, he jerked a square jaw in his direction, muttered a guttural "*Chto?*" and then went back to lobbing insults at the dancer who, having finished her routine, was unceremoniously collecting discarded lingerie from the stage.

Quinn slurred an analogy of pots and kettles and shades of black that failed to fully translate, though the Ukrainian seemed to grasp the message well enough, shifting his weight and bellowing something unintelligible in Russian. Not a moment too soon, Quinn felt a soft hand take his wrist and gently divert his attention—rescued from an almost certain altercation by a stunning Moldovan blonde.

Escorted up to a private room, he briefly made friends with the angel-faced, blue-eyed dancer, who at first wanted nothing more than to keep the peace yet ended up quite taken with his knowledge of Eastern Europe. She was particularly intrigued when he mentioned a trip to Chisinau years before, and they talked at length about the exceptional vintages of the capital's famous wine cellars. On a plush, velvety sofa, hidden behind goblet-pleated curtains, they got along rather well until he inquired, less than tactfully, about where he might find a slightly younger selection of girls. She helped herself up from his lap in an instant, her sneer of disgust matching every other grimace he had received that evening.

After she demanded payment for her time, he stumbled back down the stairs and, rather predictably, came face to face with the Ukrainian, who'd clearly been biding his time. During the ensuing tirade, Quinn understood little more than some of the more common Slavic vulgarities, but then again, little else needed translation. He heard the panicked voices of several women, and even in his state, anticipated the heavy swing of a fist as it flew, avoiding it cleanly, though not the weight of the man throwing it—both of them toppling backwards onto the stage and crushing the fragile ankles of a Russian beauty. The girl shrieked in pain, slapping at the pair of them, until Quinn was hoisted back up into the air. Bracing himself for another swing, he spotted the Ukrainian crumpled on the floor, realizing only then that two hulking bouncers were dragging him away by each arm.

Quinn floated effortlessly through the air, arms outstretched, feet dragging lazily along behind. Like a bald eagle, he soared through the night, wings propelling him forward into the breeze, the world falling away beneath him. He embraced the majestic flight until it ended, rather abruptly, the two men heaving him forward, using his forehead as a battering ram against the door. A heavy thud echoed through his skull and sent vibrations down to his toes, the slideshow flashing its final frame of the evening, the music and the entire world fading to black.

Ghonlaat,

How are you? We are good here. This week there is many new girls here. Loung is my new best girlfriend but I like Rangsei too. I think we are three best friends. Some of the new girls are really mean. Kaew is the worst one. And she's the prettiest one too, so everybody likes her and does what she says. When we were swimming she saw my birthmark on my leg. She said it looks like a rotten durian fruit. But she also has a birthmark on her face, but it is so smaller. She said hers is called a beauty mark because it is on her face and that's what they are called when it is on your face. She even showed me a picture from a magazine where a model has this beauty mark. I eat lunch with Loung and Rangsei now but even sometimes they like to spending time with Kaew. I hope you are coming back to visit soon. It is feeling like a long time since you came. Tomorrow I will go to Siem Reap and visit Khun Areum at the flower shop. I am excited for tomorrow. I think it will be a fun day. Okay, bye for now,

Mei

FIFTEEN

QUINN WOKE TO THE CLATTERING OF A STEEL SPATULA IN AN OILY wok, female voices murmuring somewhere beyond the darkness, his ankles knotted amongst twisted sheets. He slid a speculative hand along the wall, elbows and knees ricocheting off various sharp corners as he fumbled through the black. His eyes adjusting, he caught sight of a backlit door, then pushed and pulled on a doorknob until he fell forward into the beaming sunlight.

The early afternoon rays blinded him. His eyes stung and his temples throbbed, the room so cavernous that he imagined a few bats might have followed suit, fluttering out from behind him. Squinting back at the sign—Fall Inn—he grimaced upon realizing it was a rent-by-the-half-hour brothel, stifled something that rose from his stomach, and coughed some pasty spittle onto the pavement.

The movement was jarring. He put a hand to the tender spot above his hairline, still sensitive to the touch, swollen from a few nights before at the Russian nightclub. How he made it to his room that night remained a mystery, just like the previous evening and the evening before last. The days didn't turn to night so much as the nights simply bled into the next, seemingly endless, the lights of the spectacle only dimming for intermission. The colorful characters of the soi slunk away like vampires at the first rays of dawn before inevitably re-emerging at dusk, the carnival resuming exactly where it had left off. Now, however, any sign of the teeming, vibrant strip was long gone, the alley all but deserted. A couple of greasy food carts and supply vans, the scrape of a street cleaner's spindly old broom, the rattle of glass bottles, a gurgling hose.

He crossed the street stiffly, cursing when he stepped abruptly off the curb, a jolt of lightning splitting his forehead, and helped himself to a shaded stool at the rail of an open patio bar. Burying his palms into his eye sockets, he methodically rubbed the night away, speckled lights and stars flooding his vision.

A fan clicked along in a semi-circle, the breeze cooling the back of his neck as a heartbroken woman from a Thai soap opera moaned from a distant television set. The theme song of the melodrama filled the empty bar until the anguished woman's voice was overtaken by that of another, although this one spoke English. Then, from somewhere, the saccharine fragrance of vanilla and patchouli.

"May I sit?" the voice asked again. A rhetorical question, apparently. A petite woman in a short floral skirt slid into the adjacent seat, peeking up at him behind fluttering lashes.

"Christ."

"Oh?"

He continued rubbing his eyes for a time, kneading away reality before glancing over to see what was keeping the waitress.

"Just waking up?"

He grunted in reply, and somehow she seemed to understand perfectly.

"The hair of the dog, I believe you gentlemen call it," she said, then cooed something in Thai toward the bar.

"Listen"—he cleared his throat—"I'm not really looking for any company, so you might be better off not wasting your time."

"Oh, now don't be silly. Everyone needs company. How lonely would it be to go through life all on your own? Like a lost little lamb."

He met her eyes for the first time: an Asian woman with classic features, though remarkably plain, roughly in her late thirties, perhaps early forties. Behind powdery, white foundation he could still make out some faint pockmarks, and her unusually angular nose had clearly undergone at least one procedure. Sparkling blue contact lenses looked over his face, her pink lips curling into a playful smile.

A young waitress appeared, placing a frosted mug of beer before him, disappearing just as quickly.

"Well . . . maybe not a lamb in your case," she said, dipping a napkin into the mug and dabbing at the crust that streaked his chin. "A lion perhaps." She squinted mischievously.

He pulled away, his head aching with the sudden movement. "Alright, alright. Enough. Like I said, I'm not really in the mood for company, okay?"

"So disappointing. And here I thought you looked like a gentleman. You know, a *true* gentleman would at least buy me a drink." She sighed dramatically, head tilting to the side. "It would help ease my heartache."

"You're laying it on a little thick, don't you think?"

She shrugged. "Rejection is never easy. It stings, you know. Stings just the same every time."

He sighed. "What do you want."

"A cosmopolitan!" she chirped.

He nodded, pinching the bridge of his nose. "You order it."

"I knew you were a gentleman." She winked and then sang a few notes in Thai at the passing waitress. Quinn gulped his ice-cold pint like an elixir, the woman seeming content to carry on the conversation singlehandedly.

"I always drink cosmos, just like in Sex and the City. Such a glamorous show. Have you seen it? No? I love that show. I've always wanted to see New York. Are you American?"

"Listen, I don't mean any offense, but I'm really not in the mood, alright? I know I may look the part, but I'm not exactly your typical john looking for a good time."

"But that's wonderful! Typical is so boring. I like to keep things interesting. People can be so dull sometimes, don't you find?" She shifted in her seat, craning her neck like a swan, and extended a thin wrist. "I'm Ling."

He rang her dangling fingers like a tiny bell.

"So, what brings you to Bangkok, Mr. Not So Typical John?"

Given her age and rather obvious profession, she might as well have been in a nursing home. That, and she wasn't exactly out hunting during prime time either. A lifetime in the trade, he thought, and she certainly used it to her advantage. While she wasn't particularly attractive, simple and rather ordinary features all around, she possessed an undeniable charm, a sensuality surely gained through years of experience. Every movement was delicate, precise, demonstrating a mastery of her craft. Propping a wing upon the table, palm cradling her pointed chin. Smooth, porcelain legs gently rubbing together as she draped one across the other. The way she tilted her head, wiping a napkin slowly across her bottom lip, every action subtle yet full of purpose.

He had to admire it. She knew exactly which strings to pluck, tugging playfully at the strands of a marionette. Lust and sexuality reduced to a mathematical equation. One could hate the numbers all they wanted, but the formula was practically foolproof.

"It's a long story. Too long for this early in the day."

"Well, I'd be happy to hear it. I've been told I'm an excellent listener, you know."

"I'm sure you are," he replied, the waitress returning with a veritable rainbow in a cocktail glass. "You're not too short on confidence, are you?"

"Should I be?"

"I suppose not, in your line of work."

"And what line of work would that be, Mr. Not So Typical John? You should be careful not to assume. I might get offended."

"We wouldn't want that now, would we? I have to say, your English is excellent. Where did you study?"

"Who says I studied?"

"Do you always answer a question with a question?"

She crossed her arms on the table and leaned in, a conspiratorial glint in her eye. "Don't you know? It's one of the secrets of remaining mysterious."

"You didn't pick up that kind of language around here, working as—"

"Hm? Working as . . . ?"

He took a rather large swig, avoiding the question.

Ling broke into a smile, letting him off the hook. "No, not at all. You're right. One doesn't simply *pick up* this vocabulary as a courtesan. I had private lessons, of course."

He couldn't help a smile. "Courtesan. Nicely put."

"We are delicate flowers, after all. And I like that term. For the life of me I can't remember where I first heard it. But I've got plenty—lady of the evening, mistress at midnight, I've heard them all." For a moment, a shallow wrinkle creased her brow. "Most are too crass for my liking."

"I'm starting to think your English might be better than mine," he said, finishing his beer. "These lessons, something from a past life or a more recent undertaking?"

She smiled to herself, nostalgic, perhaps. "It feels sometimes as though it was a lifetime ago. And I suppose, in a way, it was." She paused to order him a fresh beer. "I was in a relationship with an English man. He insisted I take lessons to improve. Our time together didn't last, as it turned out. As is the case with all wealthy men, eventually, they tire. They want something younger, a newer, shinier toy. Still, I'm grateful for the lessons." She hesitated, then continued in a moment of seemingly genuine vulnerability. "We had some very good years together. London, *ahh* . . ."

"Well, they do say everything happens for a reason, don't they?"

"*They* seem to have so much advice, don't you find? I would very much like to meet one of *them* one day. They must have the answers to all of life's riddles. Still, I much prefer making my own mistakes. What's the point of living life according to someone else's directions?" She sipped her rosy concoction. "And now that you know a little something about me, you still haven't answered my question."

He scratched the stubble on his chin, turning the query over in his head. "I'm trying to find an old friend. We've lost touch, and, well, I'm starting to think I might not see her again."

"Mm. When was the last time you saw her?"

"About a year ago."

"And I suppose you don't have her contact information?"

"Not exactly. It's a little complicated."

"Maybe she doesn't want to be found. Hard to believe you don't even have a phone number or address. Or maybe she won't return your calls." She folded her napkin and pointed it at him. "Are you some sort of stalker?"

"It's not like that."

"Of course it isn't. Look at those baby blues. Your eyes give you away, you know. You're far too sweet for all that nonsense." She shifted gracefully in her seat, her collarbone exposed like a royal jewel in a display case. "I wish I could help."

"Well, actually, who knows? Maybe you can."

Ling had clearly been working in the industry for years, perhaps even decades. She likely had a million stories to tell, and knowing the tricks of the trade, she likely knew a few of its darker secrets as well.

"I'm at your service," she said, a familiar glint in her eye as she dragged an index finger the length of his forearm, which he, carefully, so as not to offend, pulled back.

"Ling, how long have you been working here? I mean . . ." He drew a halo in the air with his finger. "Around here."

"In this neighborhood? Quite a while. Though a lady never reveals her true age."

"Down the street here," he said, pointing, "maybe five or six blocks, there's a massage parlor. Sakura Massage. You know it?"

"Mm . . . I might."

"Think. Sakura."

For a moment, she pondered the word, or at least affected the display. "Ah, yes. On the corner, there."

"Just about. That's right. Well, the building next door, it's abandoned now, completely closed down. Used to be called All Night Massage. I don't know how long it was there or when it closed, but that was the address. Anyway, I think my friend might have been involved with that place. Working there. Do you know anything about it?"

Ling hesitated, though he couldn't tell if she was stalling or simply couldn't recall. Either way, she seemed uncertain.

"It sounds familiar. These types of shops come and go all the time. Was your friend a masseuse?"

It was as good an opening as any to test her. She didn't appear to be particularly nervous, a bona fide doctorate in mind games and flattery, and so he held the attention of her bright, blue eyes.

"Not exactly. My friend is twelve years old."

Master seductress she may have been, but a skilled liar she was not, at least not on this occasion. Ling glanced at the table just long enough, a near imperceptible shift in her demeanor before she recovered. "Oh," she said. "That's rather strange. I don't really know what to say. Is this a relative of yours, perhaps? I'm sorry, Mr. John, this is hardly the type of place for a young girl."

"You're absolutely right."

He kept his eyes on her, the tension proving too much for Ling, who looked away and raised her glass to her lips.

"You're a charming woman, Ling, I'll give you that, but you're not the best actress. Not today, anyway. And you can stop making that face. What do you know? What happened there?"

She took a moment to gather herself, swishing the pink liquid around in her glass, buying time. "Do you play billiards? Let's play billiards."

"What?"

"Billiards, pool? You know." She mimed the sweeping motion of a pool cue. "Let's talk over a game."

"I'm not really in the mood for games, Ling."

"All the more reason to play!"

She was up and out of her seat before he could utter another word, scooping her glass and floating away toward the back of the bar.

He followed her to a dimly lit back room, well hidden from the mid-afternoon rays that streamed in from the front patio, Ling already plucking colored balls from each knitted pocket.

"We'll play bigs and smalls," she said matter-of-factly. "I don't play snooker. Or was it stripes and solids for you Americans?"

He placed his palms firmly on the edge of the table. "Listen to me. If you want to shoot some pool, fine, we'll play. But this is serious. If you know something about that place, if there's any chance they were employing minors, I need to know. I'm not a cop, and I'm not looking to get you into any trouble. I'm just trying to find a young girl who's gone missing, and this is the first clue, even half clue, that I've found in a long while. That is, if you're not full of shit. I don't mind paying for the information."

Whether he had tugged at some deeply hidden emotion or simply raised the prospect of a few extra *baht*, Ling appeared to drop her guard momentarily. The faintest hint of conflict flashed across her eyes before another dramatic flutter of her thick black lashes.

"Mr. Not So Typical John," she said, laughing to herself, her fingers sweeping her collarbone, "you really stay true to your name! Not so typical at all. One game and then we talk, okay?"

He said nothing, staring back, trying to read behind the façade. After a moment, he nodded. "One game."

"Excellent! So, how much should we play for? Five hundred, one thousand *baht*?"

"I'm not much of a gambler, Ling."

"Where's the fun in that?" She shifted her weight and flicked a lock of hair over her shoulder. "If we're only going to play one game, we should make it worthwhile, wouldn't you agree?"

"Five hundred *baht*. One game."

"Wonderful," she replied, leaning forward to rack the balls in a weathered wooden frame. She took her time, arching her back just so, bending low enough to make sure he got a proper view of her humble cleavage. "Would you like to break?"

"Go ahead."

"If you insist," she pipped, snatching a cue from the stand on the back wall. On a nearby table she found a half-empty container of baby powder. Releasing a puff of white smoke, which she stroked across the length of the cue, she released a second burst for her hands, ensuring the wood slid smoothly between her fingers. Making her way back, she squeezed herself rather unnecessarily between Quinn and the table, swinging her hips wide and casually brushing the front of his pants. As if on cue, the floral notes of her perfume lingered in the air.

The balls snapped, clacked, and rumbled. Fifteen colorful orbs spun outwards and ricocheted against one another, flowing across the baize. Ling pouted dramatically as none dropped off into a pocket. After Quinn stepped up and slammed a green stripe into the left-middle pocket, he bumbled his following stroke and stood aside.

It was at that point when Ling, ever so casually, chalked her cue and embarked on such a masterful run that after the first deft stroke into the near-corner pocket, he knew the outcome was inevitable.

The diminutive Thai, in her sundress and platform heels, meandered around the table, filling pocket after pocket with such ease that at times, even for all her sultry pouting, he swore he spotted glimpses of boredom. A yellow blur caromed here, a blue streak whizzed there until finally, the slow and merciful roll of the eight-ball disappeared off the edge, plopping into the soft netting.

Ling gave a childlike smile, eyes wide, the very picture of innocence, and Quinn wondered if years ago her mother hadn't birthed her right there on the green felt.

"I should have known."

"Beginner's luck!"

SIXTEEN

Ling's playful act was wearing thinner by the minute. She insisted on another game, sulking like a child, and when he refused—hunger pangs, whining that she had worked up an appetite. He pressed further, to no avail, Ling clinging firmly to her well-rehearsed pixie routine.

Quinn had no qualms about paying her for information and was more than prepared to pay handsomely. In truth, he would have been surprised if she hadn't tried to extract some kind of reward for her services. After all, in her line of work, nothing was free. She clearly had something he wanted, or at least feigned as much, and it, like everything else, came with a price. Still, he was beginning to form the impression that she was merely working him like any other lovesick client, playing all the right notes in an attempt to fleece him right down to his pocket lint.

When their meals arrived, two identical bowls of green chicken curry and jasmine rice, even he had to admit it was a good idea. He couldn't recall the last time he had eaten a hot meal, or any proper meal at all. He drowned the mountain of rice with a fragrant, spicy stew of chili paste, zesty ginger, and fresh lemongrass, tender chunks of chicken marinating in coconut milk.

"Let's cut to the chase, Ling. Finding this girl doesn't have a price. I'll pay you; I don't mind. But I'm through messing around. Understand? Tell me what you know."

She pursed her lips once more, childishly mocking his tone. The more she simpered, the more frustrated he became, until the exchange culminated in an ill-advised hand grazing his inner thigh. He slammed his palms on the table, rattling bowls and cutlery, beer splashing and foaming over his glass. The sudden clatter attracted the attention of the bartender and a couple of nearby patrons, but judging by the dumbstruck expression on Ling's face, seemed to have the desired effect.

He closed his eyes and exhaled, then slowly removed a wad of colorful bills from his pocket, peeling off three five-hundred-*baht* notes, and slid them across the table. He lowered his voice. "Tell me what you know, Ling. No more games."

Her demeanor had changed somewhat, either pleased with the easy money that she had just made or perhaps a newly awakened sense of prudence having pushed her latest client to the brink, the wisdom to know when to cash in her chips.

"I don't know what you want me to say," she said, reaching for her purse. "I told you, I don't know very much." She removed a cigarette from a sleek stainless-steel case and hung it from her lips.

"But you know something—more than I do," he replied, applying a flame. "Anything will help at this point. You knew *something* was going on at All Night Massage, right? Something . . . illicit."

She rolled her eyes and blew a thick plume of smoke from her nostrils. "Sweetheart, this is Bangkok."

"Even Bangkok has its rules. You can't have kids out on the street corner. You have to be more subtle than that. What was going on at the parlor?"

She turned her hand inwards, examining the glowing amber tip of her cigarette, blowing away some ash. "I don't know anything for certain, just rumors."

"So, tell me rumors."

She took another long drag, followed by a shrug. "I had a friend, a girl in the business, like me. A beautiful thing, an angel. She was maybe twenty or twenty-one but with such a petite figure. We're blessed with remarkable genes, Asian women, wouldn't you agree? You want to know the secret to guessing our age? Any pretty face you see, just add ten years. Except me, of course." She winked. "Ageless."

"Get on with it, Ling."

"Well, like I said, an angel, but with a very young face, you know? She was working there for a little while. We would have lunch from time to time. We girls, we share stories." She opened a palm to emphasize the obvious. "She said it was very different than the other places she had worked before, back in her village."

"Different how?"

"The clients. Clients who wanted younger girls, *much* younger girls. Some of the men, they were very shy, but some of them were also quite cruel."

"Go on."

"That's it, really. She hated it. Like I said, she was the tiniest little thing. You wouldn't think that she was twenty-one, but in that place, she was criticized. I saw her toward the end, the way she dressed, barely any makeup, she looked maybe, fifteen? Sixteen? And some nights, afterwards, the men would refuse to pay, complaining she was too old, things like that. She told me she was the eldest there by far. I saw some of the other girls, and believe me, I can tell." She shifted in her seat and tapped her finger twice above the ashtray. "Everyone has an opinion about our line of work, and most of them are negative. Especially about us. Damaged girls, you know—corrupt, immoral. But we all have our rules, our codes, the lines we don't cross. And *those* girls," she pointed down the street, then met his eyes, "they shouldn't have been working there. They shouldn't have been working at all."

"Where's your friend now?"

She shook her head slightly. "I haven't seen her for a while now. She was with an Australian man the last time I spoke to her. Always together, going on trips. She wanted to settle down with him, get out of Bangkok. She would talk about Melbourne like it was some kind of dreamland."

"Where does she live?"

"If I had to guess? With him. I really wouldn't know. She was very excited about leaving all this behind, I wouldn't be surprised if she has. I saw her last, maybe, three months ago?"

"And that's it. That's all you can tell me?"

"You asked if I'm afraid of getting in trouble—I'm not. I make my own way in this world, and I have for a long time. I work for myself. No one tells me what to do or frightens me into doing it." She inhaled another puff of gray. "Yes, I like the finer things in life, like any other girl"—she folded the *baht* notes and tucked them into her violet clutch—"but the things I heard about that place, the girls I saw, the requests—this is not my line of work. This is not anyone's line of work. This is something else completely."

"So, you *do* know more than you're telling me."

"No, but I'm not stupid. I can see things for what they are. You learn that quickly in my profession. I should hope for your friend's sake that you can put two and two together as well."

"What happened to the place? Why did it get shut down?"

"You said it yourself; even Bangkok has rules. It's not like the old days. They need to be more careful now." She stubbed out her cigarette, examining his face a moment, the ashtray smoldering between them. "You have a kind face," she said, almost to herself. "Wounded, but kind. And now that we're talking plainly, who is this *friend* of yours? If you're looking for a massage girl in Bangkok, you're looking for a needle in a haystack."

"Just someone I know, more like family now. Me and some others helped her out a long time ago. Who knows—she may have even ended up here if we hadn't found her back then." Something caught in his throat for a moment. "I just need to bring her home."

Ling studied him, tilting her head, the hint of a smirk spreading from the corner of her mouth. "You know, I'm really starting to believe you, Mr. Not So Typical John. You actually seem like one of the decent ones." Then she took a breath, her eyes narrowing. "I don't know if this will help you or not, but, well, I never liked him anyway. A real creep, but he might know something. Whether he'd tell you anything . . ."

"Who?"

She looked out into the street where the local traffic had picked up, delivery trucks rumbling past, a group of motorbike taxi drivers in reflective orange vests laughing raucously as one of their colleagues held court. Given the hour, the sun was undeniable. The smog that hung perpetually over the city had cleared, at least relatively so, allowing the rays to stream down, unforgiving, broiling the asphalt.

"I've never really been a fan of Louis Vuitton, you know? Not that I can't appreciate the style, but it's so common now. Everyone has an LV bag. And in Bangkok, you can get everything fake, cheap as well, and some of them look very authentic. I mean, truly, what's the point?"

Quinn sighed, combing back his hair with his fingertips, reaching into his pocket yet again.

"Personally, I've always been partial to Hermès. Do you want to know why?"

"I have a feeling you'll tell me," he said, peeling off three more notes.

"The oldest luxury brand in the world—did you know that? Well, in France, anyhow. And everyone knows the French put the *class* in *classique, non? Mais, oui!* Founded in 1837. Of course, I *do* have a soft spot for Chanel. What good woman doesn't? But Hermès . . . ah, they are my one true love."

He placed the bills on the table and held his hand firmly overtop. "Talk."

Ling cleared her throat. "Well, there was this man, as I said, a disgusting man." She shuddered. "He would hang around the storefront sometimes, always hitting on the girls, but he was so cheap, always wanting something for free or a discount."

"Where was he from?"

"Not a tourist; he was local. Not Thai either, but local. A couple of times he was trying to sell his disks around there, but it's not such a busy area, not many people. He usually has his table in the market, by Nana."

"Table? What table?"

"You know, all the shops and stands they have in the evenings, selling T-shirts and trinkets to you tourists who waste your money. The night market along Sukhumvit. He sells disks, DVDs. Adult ones. Many do, but he also sells ones with children. And I heard he has a big collection. Even when he wasn't working or trying to get a free massage, he was always lurking around the shop. I could be wrong, but he might have had some business with them, but now

I'm only guessing. He was there often. My friend said he would be in the office sometimes, relaxing like he was a boss."

"Business with whom, the owners?"

She nodded.

"How do I find them?"

His question was met with a hiccup of a laugh. "You don't. Now you're truly dreaming."

He considered that for a moment. "What about this guy?"

"Like I said, the night market. Go down and look for the most disgusting man you can find selling movies. He's usually closer to Nana, around there, but I can't remember exactly. He moves around."

"Name?"

She shook her head.

"You don't know his name?"

"Why would I?"

"What does he look like?"

"Nothing special. Short. Creepy. But maybe that's just to us girls. You might not think so. But truly, he's . . ." She pulled a face. "And his tongue, it's too short for his teeth."

"What does that mean?"

"You know, he can't make 's' sounds. His tongue is too short."

"He has a lisp."

Ling shrugged indifferently, reaching for her purse and applying some lipstick. "Well, Mr. Not So Typical John," she said, rising slowly from the table, "I must say it's not often that I can have an interesting conversation with a gentleman such as yourself. I enjoyed it, something a little bit different. 'Variety is the spice of life,' *n'est-ce-pas*? It's been a pleasure, but I have an appointment."

"The pleasure was all mine, I'm sure," he said with a beleaguered sigh.

"Not entirely . . . but yes." Glowing once more with the familiar smile of the seductress, she reached for a folded napkin and, pursing her lips, laid a sensuous kiss on the cheaply embroidered serviette. Placing it carefully on his thigh, a thick, symmetrical smudge of mauve across the middle, she leaned in to whisper in his ear. "So you don't forget the shape of my mouth."

And with that, she tossed back her hair, making sure he caught a final whiff of perfume—one last memento—and was gone. Her heels clicked like a metronome down the length of the bar, changing their pitch when they hit the sidewalk, the staccato rhythm gradually fading away into the bustling noise of the city.

SEVENTEEN

THE HOURGLASS HAD BEEN EMPTYING LONG BEFORE CAFÉ Bientôt, and if he was chasing shadows then, what did it say about his odds now? Pacing along the same stretch of pavement on a muggy Thai afternoon—sweat on his brow, another once dry shirt sticking to his back—he found himself with just the opposite problem: too much time.

Too much time to worry and wonder if he hadn't already strayed at some unforeseen crossroads. Too much time to second-guess the minutiae of every decision, to consider every subtlety he might have missed, and if maybe one of his worst fears was already being realized, there, at that very moment, drifting further and further off course with every step.

Had he overlooked any vital clues in Battambang? He should have spent more time in Mei's room, combing through her belongings, digging a little deeper, talking to more of the staff instead of rushing off so hastily to Siem Reap. Had he been right to follow such a flimsy lead to Bangkok, countless miles away, another country, no less? Impetuous, a "lead" by only the most generous of definitions, a decision based on nothing more than a faded leaflet and biased intuition. Was it wise to trust his instincts in a situation such as this—hope and fear, side by each, clouding his judgment?

And then there was Ling. A reliable source of information, or was it he who was reliable, the easy mark, manipulated from the very beginning? She sold fantasies, after all, did she not? Reading him like a tarot card, weaving the exact tale he wanted to hear for a few extra *baht*. An effortless payday, comfortably collected while still on her feet, no less.

He decided to ignore the cruel voices that festered in the back of his mind. They grew louder, bolder with each passing day, whispering their arguments and propositions, always grounded in rational thought—logical, impartial, and absolutely damning.

And with them, something more, from deep within, coursing with adrenaline, countering with the only argument he required, the only rationale worth considering: What were Mei's odds? What were her chances four years ago, living—no, existing, *enduring* in that destitute village? What were her chances then, an eight-year-old orphaned, betrayed, sold off like livestock? If she could somehow overcome all of that, surely he could turn a few more stones, no matter how slight the chances. If she possessed the will to fight through such a tragic beginning, he would ensure it wouldn't end like this. And that, for him, was enough.

He trudged back and forth the length of Sukhumvit Road, starting at Asok Montri, at the edge of Cowboy, and all along the busy thoroughfare to the edge of the market at Nana station. He towered above the locals who sold their routine wares, drawing looks of curiosity from shopkeepers as he meandered to and fro along the already trodden stretch of sidewalk. At first he tried to look as inconspicuous as possible, paranoia gnawing at him. On the one hand, with his light hair, height, and skin tone, he stuck out like a sore thumb. On the other, he was unshaven, exhausted, and wandering the heart of the red-light district, and therefore fit in rather seamlessly with the droves of foreigners gathering in the downtown core at dusk.

As the blurred orange sun faded behind a tawny horizon, the crowds grew in size, as did the number of sidewalk vendors setting up their makeshift stores, until eventually the lanes were choked with pedestrians and peddlers. They hung all manner of clothing from propped-up metal gates—shirts and jackets, bathing suits and bikinis—draped upwards to the sky like floating walls of cheap cotton and polyester. Others displayed watches and belts, purses and bags, socks and undergarments blanketed across flimsy display stands. Some popped up like discount pharmacies, arranging packages with everything from Panadol to Prozac, Viagra to Cialis.

The sidewalk, formerly occupied by convenience stores and fruit stands, was transformed into a hawker's gauntlet of knick-knacks and knock-offs, merchants on either side, crammed together like sardines wherever they could squeeze a clothing rack and a mannequin, a folding table and a footstool. At certain points, tourists and locals alike spilled onto the street to avoid a congested impasse, sharing the road with a gridlock of pink and yellow taxis, and the whizzing motorbikes there among.

Quinn focused upon each display, doing his best to memorize the face of every last vendor—an impossible task, while filtering through the crowd in search of the nameless salesman, the one man who might possibly lead him to another clue. He tried not to think about any other possibility, his hopes feebly tethered to a discarded flyer and the word of a professional temptress.

A guava vendor and her friend, viciously mashing pungent ingredients with a mortar and pestle, giggled and chirped every time he passed, studying him curiously from head to toe. Farther along, by Soi 11, a foursome of men, stooping in front of a tableau of football jerseys and scarves, gambled on a checkered board with bottle caps and tiny seashells. One of the men appeared to be chewing betel nut, his mouth stained a deep crimson with matching blotches of spittle on the pavement. They glanced up for an instant, "Here, here, my friend!" one said, gesturing half-heartedly to their wares. In Bangkok, everyone was Quinn's friend, and everyone had a deal.

At the entrance to a small stairwell, he couldn't help but smirk at the old man who squatted on his haunches, waving enthusiastically as their eyes met. The man's humble arrangement of sandals and flip-flops was laid out before him on a knitted blanket, a poor selection of sizes and a worse selection of colors. He had a wilted head of hair, and his sunbaked face, creased with ancient wrinkles, radiated every time he spotted Quinn amongst the crowd. One might have thought he was showcasing the crown jewels of King Bhumibol the way he proudly waved his hands and gestured toward his merchandise.

The first table that Quinn spotted with pirated DVDs was closer to Asok, near to Soi 17, though he approached with little expectation. He caught sight of a young girl helping her mother meticulously arrange each plastic sleeve, covering the length of their table. Once they finished, she pressed "play" on a scratchy boombox, which began wailing pop melodies. No one else seemed associated with the pair, and when he strolled past to take a closer look, he found the film sleeves to be exclusively of live concerts by Korean and Japanese idol groups.

Farther west, between a mountain of cell phone cases and waves of sunglasses, another stand had an equally impressive collection of the latest Hollywood blockbusters. A slender man crouched on a plastic footstool, slurping noodles against a vivid backdrop of action thrillers, animé adventures, and every genre in between. Quinn spoke to him briefly, and after determining there was nothing particularly suspect about his speech, asked if he had any adult films hidden away. An industrious salesman, the man shoved forward a cardboard box from behind the overhanging tablecloth, doing so without even looking up from his bowl. He motioned to the box with his chin—*take a look*, the gesture said—though a cynical man might have interpreted it differently. As Quinn leafed through the sparse collection of mainstream pornography, the man paid him no mind, fixated on his meal, gulping the leftover broth in his bowl.

Occasionally, a diminutive Thai man would emerge from the shadows of a quiet soi or materialize from a nearby crowd to offer colorful leaflets for soapy massage parlors and "ping-pong shows." Quinn brushed them aside one after the other like gnats. He hardly had the time or the resources to poke his head into every quasi-brothel on the strip, and he risked veering even further off track, chasing ghosts across all of Bangkok.

As the night wore on, the nagging voices in his head grew louder still, and he decided to expand his search radius slightly further, wandering along the side streets that fed off Sukhumvit, exploring the area in greater detail.

Back at Asok, the pulse of Cowboy was alive and well, vibrant lights and frenetic sounds emanating from the nightclubs as he walked north along Asok Montri, eventually swinging east and returning by way of Soi 23, passing the familiar glow of Sakura Massage and its mewling concubines. Crossing the busy main street, he continued south on Ratchadaphisek, though now felt certain he was drifting in the wrong direction. The bustle of Sukhumvit and its throngs of tourists gave way to enamored couples walking hand in hand, groupings of mischievous teenagers basking in the serenity of Benjakitti Park and its shimmering pond.

Making his way back west, he wandered up the various winding sois, tributaries that bled into Sukhumvit, littered with food stands and drink carts. Some of the alleys throbbed with crowds, billows of smoke and steam rising from bubbling pots and hissing grills, open makeshift bars where backpackers drank luminescent cocktails—street concoctions in plastic bags, curly straws, and bobbing glowsticks. Other sois were relatively deserted, dark and silent, a few residential buildings with lights on low, a couple of garbage dumpsters rotting beneath the drooping branches of a neglected palm.

Past the sky train station he took a detour to Nana Plaza, Cowboy's western doppelganger, then circled back north through the Muslim quarter, passing shisha bars and shawarma shops as he strolled through Soi Arab, as the street was known. Forcing his eyes awake, he found nothing of any great significance. Several stands sold identical DVD selections, and even those with pornography didn't seem to have any additional inventory hidden away from the public eye. Eventually, with heavy lids and aching feet, he returned to his usual route, the crowds of hijabed Malays and Indonesians and traditionally garbed Emiratis thinning in numbers as he plodded eastward back toward Asok.

It was late when he realized the pounding bass rhythms that grew louder throughout the evening came primarily from between his own temples. He bought some aspirin and chased a small handful with a can of Singha, purchased from a convenience store that just happened to be situated next to the enthusiastic sandal salesman. Head throbbing, he sat down by his side, offering his pack of cigarettes. The old man cupped his hands together obligingly, and the pair sat puffing in silence as the crowds shuffled by.

The tethered rope to which he clung was beginning to fray, along with his wits. Not for the first time, he wondered whether he should have expanded his search beyond the night market, taking him well outside the area that Ling had described. He removed his shoe, rubbed a raw, swollen toe, and eventually dismissed the thought.

Then, in an unexpected moment of inspired resolve, he focused his thoughts and determined to use his stubborn nature to his advantage. Ling hadn't provided much detail, but this was surely the place. It *must* be the place. Naturally, one could find illicit goods farther down the road in any direction, which meant facing the very real prospect of drifting farther from where he needed to be, deeper into the tangled web of the city. If he cast the net too broadly, he risked any number of clues slipping through his fingers, closing his fist on grains of rice. He was exhausted, worn so very thin from the market and the nights spent at Cowboy. It was both foolish and, admittedly, impossible to scour the entire city. All things considered, it was better to trust what Ling had said, dubious as her words may have been, than to take on all of Bangkok singlehanded.

He would remain there at the market for as long as necessary. He would remain until he knew the life story of every salesman along the strip—their names, their origins, what they sold, and why they sold it. He would tape his blistered feet, redouble his efforts, and leave no stone unturned.

EIGHTEEN

THE HOURS PASSED SLOWLY, AND QUINN FELT HIS BODY GIVING way as he continued his pilgrimage, shuffling laboriously along. He had a permanent grimace now, dragging one stinging foot behind the other, back aching, shirt saturated with wet salt. There wasn't a film stand that he hadn't found and inspected, leafing through collections of pirated disks, harried now by many, mistaken as a drunken pervert who simply fawned over their wares but never purchased a thing. He no longer ventured east past Soi 19 unless he cut a wide detour. Two Indian men situated nearby had made quite the scene, now pointing and shouting each time he came near. He felt like some homeless degenerate, shooed from park benches and posh hotel lobbies.

Much later, he again found himself seated on a quiet concrete stoop when a gentle nudge interrupted his thoughts, the old man with his assorted sandals offering a small plastic bag of grasshoppers, crisply fried in soy. Quinn raised a hand, politely declining, and so the man shook the bag. *Appetizing, no?* Then he placed it between them, open and accessible should Quinn change his mind.

Quinn had seen the food carts of fried insects before, platters of silkworm larvae, bamboo worms, and the eye-catching scorpions, always assuming it was merely a gimmick for Western eyes. Apparently, he'd been wrong. His new companion sat next to him, munching silently with a smile on his face, occasionally pausing to pluck a leg or two from his teeth.

"Hello, my friend!" a man said as he passed by. "My friend, how are you?"

Quinn glanced up and recognized one of the gamblers from the previous block just east. It was not an easy face to forget, his mouth still stained dark red from chewing betel.

"My friend, this is my uncle, Soothai. You are friends now, yes?" He nodded toward the old man, who smiled, a stubborn insect limb still clinging to his gums. Between the two of them, they would have given any reputable dentist a coronary.

"He's not really my uncle, like you say, but we all family here," the man continued, muttering something in Thai that amused the old man. "What are you looking for tonight, my friend? My uncle's sandals are not for you. You want better deal? You come to my shop." He motioned with his head. "My sandals are better quality, more cheap. These no good in Thailand!" he said, pointing to Quinn's shoes. "Too hot Thailand!"

"I'm alright," Quinn replied with a dismissive wave, his current state of mind hardly lending itself to good manners. After spending hours in the market, all the street vendors sounded the same, so many "friends" with so many "bargains."

Unconcerned, the man turned his attention back to Soothai, speaking in Thai once again. Quinn watched as he removed a small, tin canister from his pocket, arranging its ingredients on a windowsill. He sprinkled a green betel leaf with some slacked lime, holding it in his palm as he added areca nuts and a few strands of tobacco. Then he rolled the leaf into a tight little quid and deftly tucked it into his mouth, something he likely could have managed while blindfolded.

Quinn caught himself staring at this curious man, intrigued by his unmistakable accent, which he couldn't quite place. He spoke Thai; that much he could tell, but he did so with a strange cadence, an offbeat rhythm that gave Quinn pause. Not that a foreign sales-man in Bangkok was something to be noted; the city was known for its underground immigrant economy. And yet, something that Ling had said resonated with him as he watched the man reenact-ing some humorous anecdote for his "uncle," then showing off the sparkle of his wristwatch.

What was it, exactly? *His tongue is too short*, she had said. A lisp, he assumed, and then something else as well. Something about his pronunciation? Maybe. He couldn't remember. Could an accent be considered a lisp? And what had she done when he mentioned it? Shrugged. Shrugged, yes? Or, more than likely, had pocketed her money and couldn't have cared less. Shrugged without meaning.

This man had been selling sandals and was now modeling watches to his friend. Quinn had walked past them several times, the gamblers, rolling dice by their stand of sportswear. Were there any other stands nearby? He couldn't remember that either.

His tongue is too short. Not just a lisp; it could have been any speech impediment. The man's oral hygiene was so poor, stained lips and a rotting, receding gumline. Was that what she had meant? He had an accent, sure, but not Thai, nor some rural, provincial intonation. Foreign, certainly. Certainly? Now he was getting ahead of himself. *How can you be sure?*

He must have been boring a hole through the man's head as he sought to wedge the crooked puzzle pieces together in his mind.

The salesman, who seemingly possessed a sixth sense for such curiosity, spat a gob of crimson onto the ground and began his pitch all over again, spouting off the numerous items that he could procure at bargain prices. The speech was half-hearted, as it always was, until Quinn snapped out of his trance.

"Watches," he said, motioning to the man's sparkling wristband. "You have Omega?"

Leave no stone unturned.

The salesman's eyes lit up. "Yes, of course Omega, my friend! Omega, Rolex, Cartier, Breitling, Tag Heuer! Come, I show you!"

Ling hadn't provided much detail about the man, if indeed this was the man at all—breathlessly reciting his inventory, stressing the quality of his wares, and beckoning Quinn forward as they weaved amongst the crowds.

She described him as a "creep," a repulsive man, and this fellow certainly fit the bill. His black hair was short and matted in a greasy smear over his forehead, a dusky complexion well suited to his rheumy, jaundiced eyes. He had an incredibly thin physique, jagged in the shoulders and knees, a collared shirt floating atop his spindly frame.

Quinn was good with accents, always had been, though this one was proving difficult to pin down. The man's mouth was grotesque: everything a deep shade of maroon, pebble teeth enveloped in tar, clinging by their roots to raw, inflamed gums. He might have even had some minor speech impediment, but between the obscure dialect and masticated betel nut, it was impossible to tell. He looked like a vagrant with no true home, a foreign national, likely foreign even within his own country. A man birthed in a village of crossroads and artificial boundaries; a small patch of dirt measured out long ago, designated and divided into sections by silver-haired men in foreign capitals puffing fine cigars and sipping expensive cognac.

After a couple of blocks, not far from Soi Arab, the salesman led Quinn down a dark alley behind some empty stalls where a table, somewhat obscured from the main drag, displayed exactly what the man had so fervently advertised: wristwatches. He nodded to an elderly hijabed woman who had apparently been keeping an eye on things, and Quinn turned his attention to anything else in the vicinity, scanning up and down the barren street. He had hoped the display of fake wristbands would lead to something more promising, but there he stood amongst derelict shops with corrugated metal siding, abandoned display tables, and sheets of rotting plywood.

The woman gathered a sad collection of overripe fruit from a blanket that she had laid on the ground, folding the tattered cloth, waving away fruit flies as she went.

"This is it? What else do you have?"

"Everything, my friend, just wait," the man replied, ducking behind the table and reappearing with a briefcase, latches snapping before it splayed open in front of him. Inside were more watches, luxurious faux Bulgaris and Piagets gleaming in what little light shone overhead.

Quinn brushed his hair back over his damp forehead and exhaled heavily through his nose, mouthing a few choice expletives directed at no one, and everyone. Nothing else in sight seemed to belong to the greasy peddler, not even sandals, and in a passing moment of raw, hard-boiled frustration, he contemplated flipping the entire table into the air. When the salesman sensed his irritation, he began another speech about the discounts offered to his very best friends, only to see his customer turn on his heel and storm back toward Sukhumvit.

Upon reaching the intersection, a Thai man with a sparse pencil mustache and ponytail appeared before him waving yet another flyer for a soapy massage. "Beautiful, yes? You like?" Countering Quinn's step left, then right, he pressed the leaflet against his chest. "Sexy, very sexy." Quinn was spent, tired of chasing ghosts, so exhausted he might well have fallen asleep on his feet had the watch salesman not grabbed his arm from behind.

"My friend, you like girls? Yes?" He tugged his arm, insistent. "Come, come, I show you." He jerked his chin in the direction of the alley. Quinn yanked his limb away and opened his mouth to speak when—

"I have movies. You like movies?" the betel-stains asked.

"No, my friend, here live girls, live!" The leaflet fluttered again and found its way into Quinn's hand. "Cheap price for double massage," the rival said.

"American movie, Japanese, Thai, I show you, what you like?" the salesman countered, his voice full of confidence as he waved a hand dismissively at his competitor.

Quinn's mind woke from a sort of jaded slumber, hibernating, conserving what little energy it had for when something warranted his attention. Suddenly, he found himself waking, synapses firing, eyes focused and alert once more.

He allowed himself to be led back down the deserted alley-way, following much farther this time, past the sheet metal and fence line that guarded darkened shops, beneath a tangled canopy of electrical wiring, along storefronts with faded overhead signs written in cursive Arabic scroll.

Quinn looked on as the slender man scurried down a narrow passage between two buildings, a dark corridor with black puddles and a small mound of garbage bags. On the right side, an ornate shisha bar glimmered with gold décor even amongst the shadows, as did a perfumery to the left, where the salesman was tinkering with a padlocked door toward the back of the shop. Stepping past the pile of refuse, Quinn eyed the rusty door, which hung errantly from a single hinge. The salesman paused to give him a sly wink before the lock clicked open, the door's metal frame letting out a painful squeal.

Quinn's heart rate quickened, the pulsations robust as he wiped his sweaty palms across the seam of his pants.

Once inside, his eyes flashed over what appeared to be a closet, a bedroom, and a business all in one. The interior was two hundred square feet of cracked tile, complete with an ancient kneehole desk, a metal cot beneath a soiled mattress, stacks of cardboard boxes, and a single naked lightbulb that flickered and hummed. The sharp odor of mothballs stung his nostrils. Rummaging in the far corner, the salesman returned with a shoebox filled with DVDs.

"You like American, yeah? I have everything—American, Russia, Japan—what you like?"

Taking hold of the box, Quinn nodded theatrically and turned away, pretending to comb through its contents as he cast an eye over the desk to his right. The room was mostly bare, with the exception of various tools scattered across the misfit mahogany workspace. He squinted to make out what appeared to be sheets of plastic laminates—likely for the DVDs—scissors, and other indiscriminate utensils, maybe tweezers, some pens, and possibly a scalpel.

Quinn slid a couple of disks out of the box, turned them over in his hands, feigning interest, then handed them back. "What else do you have? I have enough American."

His chest was pounding now, thumping so loudly that he wondered if the salesman could hear the deep echo. Upon receiving a new box to inspect, he continued his dramatization and began pacing around the room as casually as he could manage.

The salesman, meanwhile, was waxing lyrical about his films, as if buying pornography required some sort of detailed explanation of what to expect. Regardless, it was clear there was more to be uncovered than simply mainstream adult films. There was a reason he kept the disks locked away instead of selling them openly on the street. There was a reason that, publicly, he sold watches, and had a visible display to maintain the façade.

Quinn moved close enough to the desk to glance at a collection of papers strewn together in a pile. Most were calculations of budgetary expenses, spreadsheets, a couple of waybills for exporting products from the United States, bulk goods apparently shipped through containers in Bangkok, ultimately destined for Vientiane.

His ears perked up. Through the man's incessant rambling, vulgar and heavily accented, a certain phrase caught his attention, and he turned his gaze back to the salesman. "You have something younger?"

"Ayy, here is Bangkok, my friend. Don't be shy! Yes, yes, don't worry, I have. Let me find you." Lowering himself onto his belly, he reached beneath the sagging coils of the cot and dragged a large, black duffel bag out from underneath.

Quinn already knew what the contents would be. He felt his stomach turn a couple of times as he heard the grate of the zipper, followed by hands shuffling inside the bag. Without hesitation, he took the opportunity to reach for one of the desk drawers, keeping one eye on the prone salesman. A bead of sweat escaped his hairline, trickling down the length of his cheek. Taking hold of the handle, he slid it gently outward. The old wooden drawer, warped by age, let out a noticeable screech when it snagged and jerked open.

"Ya—what you doing?" the man exclaimed.

Everything moved in a blur. Quinn reached inside the drawer to find stacks of assorted passports, various colors wrapped with rubber bands, sheets of scribbled paper with phone numbers and flight itineraries. Behind him, the man's friendly tone had changed, his voice on edge, practically shouting. Quinn heard only muted sounds, the rush of his own blood deafening between his ears.

He grabbed a loose passport with a faded blue cover, golden lettering and Arabic script. Afghanistan. He quickly thumbed it open. The front page was about as genuine as he'd ever seen, with the glaring exception of an empty square hole where a picture ought to have been.

He felt a rush of adrenaline as the salesman grabbed him by the shoulder, pawing at him, screaming now, hysterical. He was surprisingly strong given his diminutive frame, but Quinn, surging with new life, held him off, clenching a mittful of his collar and steadying him with an outstretched arm. Hands swatted at him as they grappled, grunts and foreign curses escaping through the man's clenched teeth. It bought Quinn just enough time to yank open a second drawer, revealing exactly what was missing from the first.

Photographs. Portraits.

Quinn howled, reactive, flailing as a row of teeth sank into his shoulder blade, jagged little fangs piercing cloth and skin. Somehow amidst the commotion—the lightning in his shoulder, the swinging of limbs, the clutching of hair, and the scuffling of feet, his mind registered what his eyes had just seen.

A drawer full of pictures, cut neatly to specific dimensions by precise instruments. The faces of the subjects themselves—mostly Asian, some African, some wearing hijabs.

But one distinct, unifying feature stood out amongst them all. One commonality amongst each photograph, carefully cropped, and professionally framed. They all gazed at the camera with glassy eyes. They all held the same vacant expression.

And they were all children.

NINETEEN

A MUFFLED ROAR, DROWNING ALL EXTRANEOUS NOISE, FLOODED through Quinn's ears like a cascading waterfall. The waves rumbled on, swirling and crashing, trapping him within his own lucid dream. As he contemplated the sound, almost soothed by the intangible echo, a distant, steady beat emerged from the fog, softly at first, then louder, swelling into a powerful, almost deafening crescendo. Slowly, he emerged from his trance, as if realizing it truly was just a dream, his own dream, willing himself awake. He recognized his own heartbeat pounding in his head, drumming steadily within his chest, pulsating through his limbs. Gradually, a dull pain drew his attention to his right hand, trembling out of sync. He glanced at his knuckles—scuffed raw, swollen, and bright red, shaking like a rattlesnake's tail.

Then, another unfamiliar sound emerged from somewhere amidst the ether. A strange, melancholy sound: the tortured moan of a wounded animal, wheezing, struggling to draw breath. From the corner of his eye he sensed movement, then spotted the salesman. Shirt torn at the collar, barefoot, having lost both sandals, propping himself unsteadily on all fours, swaying.

Quinn blinked a couple of times, gasped, and then snapped back to consciousness. He rushed to the door, slamming it shut, cursing at how loudly it clanged, then turned his attention back to the desk. He tore each drawer from its runners, dumping their contents across the tabletop. An assortment of counterfeiting tools—primitive but effective—lay among the pictures and passports. Glossy, translucent stickers. Stamps. Pens. Razors. Ink pads. He picked up a stamp, tried to read the inverted characters, couldn't make out most of it, then read the letters "UAE" clearly enough.

Scanning the passports, he realized they were almost exclusively from Middle Eastern states. The majority were Egyptian, their pale green covers standing out amongst the darker documents, navy blue and maroon. The photographs were, in fact, photograph sleeves, portrait sets of six identical shots, most with one or two pictures neatly cut out and removed.

He stared back and forth between the children's faces, then looked at the cowering salesman, contemplating what to do next. The adrenaline coursed through his veins, and he fought hard to ensure it didn't cloud his judgement, his mind racing. Incredulous, he struggled to make sense of it all, having stumbled across . . . whatever this was. Had Ling been telling the truth after all, or at least some version of it? Had she been referring to this depraved weasel, writhing on the floor? The lisp, the films, and perhaps some sort of business with the massage parlor. He'd been seen in the office before. Ling's friend had said as much.

Then, the passports. There was no denying that some form of smuggling was taking place. Children, no less. Forced labor. The containers en route to Laos. He glanced around for the waybill somewhere amongst the pile. His mind flashed pictures of sweat-shops and textiles, the garment industry, running shoes. The massage parlor could have been a front, or was that too bold? The shop was abandoned, maybe bankrupt, shut down? A raid, perhaps.

Mei was mixed up right in the middle of it; he could feel it, her presence hidden somewhere among the right questions, the correct puzzle pieces. He saw her in each and every picture strewn across the desk. The eyes, no matter what color—caramel, chestnut, a deep, sea green—all lost. The same listless expressions, gazing far off into the beyond, past the camera lens to a different world. One picture resembled her so much that, for a pained, nostalgic moment, he forced himself to take a closer look. The eyes were tired, unnatural, dark circles on a youthful complexion; at once the primary subject and star of the portrait yet somehow as removed from the image as possible, there in body if without spirit. Her hazel eyes, almonds with shadowed contours, stared straight through the camera, past the photographer, as if asking for his attention.

Then, he looked closer. At the eyes and then the nose and the chin. And again, the eyes, nose, chin, cheekbones.

Imagination. Delusion.

He stared, focusing on every detail: the curve of the jaw, the height of the cheekbones, the subtle peak of the hairline. How many hours had he been awake, pacing the city, drowning his fears, nerves frayed into loose threads?

He rummaged for his wallet, hands patting every pocket, fumbling, pulling out his most recent picture. He compared the images, holding them side by side, scrutinizing every feature:

The bridge of the flat button nose.

The soft arc of the brow.

An earlobe exposed by a rogue lock of dark hair.

For a moment, he didn't breathe, simply stared at the picture in amazement.

Mei. Or at least someone pretending to be Mei. A version of her, a sister. A bleary-eyed and blank expression, identical in each of the four remaining photos in the sleeve. She had a scrape along her right cheek, arcing toward her mouth, a swollen, purple lip.

The salesman had crawled to within a few feet of the door, but his progress was halted by a hollow thud escaping his midsection as a shoe blurred through the air. The kick was venomous, making contact directly beneath the ribcage, flipping the gangly man onto his back, limbs flailing like an overturned potato bug.

Quinn grabbed a handful of his torn collar, which ripped further still, coming apart in his hand. He tried once more, both fists now, pulling him close, ignoring the hot, sour breath from the salesman's panting face.

"Where is she? Tell me where!"

The salesman wriggled on the ground until a heavy fist caught him squarely in the jaw, the cracking sound that followed echoing along the tile floor. He wailed, whipping his head from side to side. "I don't know! I don't know!"

Quinn connected with another swing, this time glancing off a sweaty cheekbone, the man's bony fingers shielding his face.

He grabbed the photograph from the ground. "Look at the picture before you start telling me 'no.' Look at it! Where is she?"

"I don't know! Don't know! All look same—I just make passport!"

"What passport? Did you make one for her?"

"I don't know! I just take picture!" he shouted, squirming from Quinn's grip and jabbering in a foreign tongue.

Quinn dropped the picture and reaffirmed his grasp, raising a fist before sending it plummeting forward. Once. Twice. Then everything slowed, still frames of clarity as he waited for an opening between the man's waving hands. He connected cleanly just above the jawline, the salesman letting out a howl once again, his mouth glistening a brighter shade of red. Quinn shook him to attention. The man sputtered something unintelligible, a blackened molar tumbling from his open mouth and rattling like a marble across the floor.

"Tell me!"

"I don't know! I swear I don't know! I just make passport for them!"

"For who?"

"No names! I don't know names. They just bring girls, so I take pictures and make papers."

Quinn grabbed the man's jaw and pinned his head to the floor. With his free hand, he held Mei's picture a few inches from the man's face. "Look. This girl right here. Where is she? That's all I want to know, and I'll let you go."

The salesman's eyes were wild, bloodshot through the yellowing sclera. After a moment, he took his eyes off his attacker and peered, cross-eyed, at the photograph. He glanced back and forth, twitching while examining the picture, wary of another blow. "This one," he said, his voice muffled as he spoke through Quinn's palm, "this one I think Egypt. Yes, Egypt. But I don't know one hundred percent. Everything Egypt now."

Quinn jerked the man's torso upright and rotated his shoulder, readying himself to throw another fist.

"No lie, no lie! I tell you true!" Pinching his eyes shut, the man braced himself. "Egypt! Cairo. Cheap flight now. Cheap, cheap ticket!"

"What the hell are you talking . . . Egypt? Why would—" He stopped, his mind catching up with his mouth. His head had been working it out as he surrendered to his baser instincts. The man wouldn't have any answers. Why would he? That sort of information wasn't the privy of an alley rat. He was a forger and nothing more. And yet, the Middle East. Quinn couldn't make heads or tails of that.

"Why Egypt? Tell me!"

"I swear!"

"Look again, this girl. Look *closely.*"

"I don't know. All look same, I just—" He wailed again as Quinn dug his fingers into his jaw.

"Tell me the truth!"

"*Wallahi*, I tell you true!"

"Where? Cairo, Alexandria, just Egypt?"

"I don't know nothing. I don't know who bring them. One man bring, different man come take them. I don't know. I just make passport."

"For *this* girl?"

"All girls! This month, before month, all Egypt. All Cairo!"

"Where is she now?"

"I don't know! I don't know!"

"You have her picture!"

"Yes, she here but only for picture, then they leave!"

"Leave with who? Give me a name. What does he look like?"

"I tell you, no names—"

A blur from the right side, knuckles snapping against the man's nose, splitting cartilage. "No names!" he sputtered. "No names, no names, just dark man, Arab man. Always same man!"

"You swear you don't know? *Wallahi*, you don't know?"

"*Wallah!* No names."

"You're *sure* it was this girl? Look again."

The salesman squinted once more at the photo sleeve, blood dribbling into his gaping red mouth. "Yes, two picture already use. Look. Finish now. Finish this one."

"When? This week? Last week?"

The man's jaundiced eyes rolled backwards in thought, then flickered with an idea. "Yes," he said, nodding quickly. "I have schedule." He pointed to the desk.

Quinn turned his attention just long enough. The salesman seized his opportunity, twisting to the side and heaving a pointed kneecap into Quinn's genitals. He felt the wind go from his lungs, his organs thrust into a vice. In an instant the culprit scrambled to his feet and across the room, shouting once more in his foreign tongue. He ripped open the door and bolted out into the darkness, a rat disappearing through a crevice.

Quinn remained on all fours for what felt like an eternity, nauseous, retching through shallow breaths, glands of spittle dangling from his mouth.

He crawled toward the pile of documents on the floor, clumsily scraping them together with swollen hands, bundling the mass of loose papers and passports in his arms. Struggling to his feet, eyes full of constellations, he paused momentarily for yet another breathless convulsion. And then another. He scanned the room to make sure all the passports and photographs had been gathered. He had most of them. He had Mei's.

He stumbled through the doorway and back into the night. Wary, he crept along the dark alley, half expecting to be met by a crowd of smugglers and gangsters, rattling chains, fluttering butterfly knives. He imagined it unfolding like a film.

But there was no one.

He pinballed through a crowd of confused tourists, feeling the eyes upon him, papers occasionally drifting from his arms up and into the night as he staggered, making his way. He stepped into the main road and braced himself against the hood of a taxi, the driver laying on his horn, yelling something, gesticulating wildly with his hands. Quinn slid across the side of the cab, jerked open the door and collapsed into the back seat.

TWENTY

A GOLDEN STREAM OF THAI WHISKEY FILLED HIS GLASS, SPLASH-ing across the rim and onto the coffee table. The nub of a cigarette dangled from his lips, smoldering just above the filter. With stiff fingers and bruised knuckles he awkwardly pulled a fresh one from the packet, pressing it against the glowing stump of the first, a curl of blue rising into the air.

In the lobby, Cindy was still working the night shift and had shown obvious concern when he'd arrived—flushed, limping, and disheveled. He made sure to give her a sizeable tip for some fresh towels and the procurement of a decent bottle of liquor. Anything would do—*really, Cindy, anything at all*. He thumbed a few extra notes at the door when she returned a half hour later, beaming, ever so pleased to serve him, only to offer a more subdued smile, courteous but unable to hide her disappointment that he planned to drink alone, without her.

Fanning the counterfeit documents across the glass coffee table, he began to examine them in earnest. It wasn't long before, after some initial doubts, he realized they weren't counterfeit at all. As he handled them, truly felt them, each passport appeared more authentic than the last. While different countries employed a variety of security features, there were many consistencies as well.

Most contained the standard watermarks and security fibers one would expect embedded in authentic substrates, the micro-printing of numbers and lettering as clear as could be—at least for his blurry eyes and, regrettably, without a magnifying glass. Even the embossing was crisp and precise, the tactile features cool to the touch. They were either authentic travel documents or exceptionally good replicas. The more passports he examined, the more he became convinced of the former, the only altera-tions appearing within the front biodata page. Some laminates were damaged—peeled up at the edges, the plastic curling or nicked here and there by an untimely slip of the wrist. Others, prepared with more attention to detail, were clearly being readied for photo substitution by the accompanying picture sleeves. The black Jordanian passports were the only documents he thought may have been substituting entire pages rather than just the pho-tographs themselves.

Egyptian and Syrian passports were heavily in the majority. If being used to traffic false identities across borders, the Syrian docu-ments seemed the logical choice. They were by far the easiest to attain and also one of the most commonly forged documents in the region, given the country's continual instability. Almost everyone cast a slightly more sympathetic eye toward a Syrian passport. A solemn expression to match exit stamps from Damascus always ensured a little less scrutiny at the border, even among those who pretended otherwise.

It was the Egyptian documents that were puzzling. The rat from the alley had little stake in the operation, hardly even a middleman. Of that much Quinn was certain. A low-level peddler, a back-alley forger making amateur-quality fraud documents. It wasn't a par-ticularly difficult task altering a genuine passport, and given the number of scratched laminates and over-blotted ink patterns, he didn't appear to have much of a talent. The most he seemed capable of managing was photo alteration, and given the evidence on hand, it was hardly something at which he excelled.

Pinching the cigarette from his mouth, he stood, tossing aside an especially butchered document from Sudan, and paced around the room.

This salesman, few would allow him entrance to their inner circle, and why would they? With this level of production, amateurish as it was, he was a liability at best. As long as he kept fulfilling his end of the bargain, there was no need to provide him with any further insight; an undue risk for all involved.

And yet, he was adamant that the girls, Mei among them, were going to Cairo. He seemed certain of this, and in so far as that matter was concerned, Quinn believed him. He was a duplicitous little rodent, but what a strange thing to say. Egypt. It was in the man's eyes—wide and panic-stricken, but not false. Not then.

It wasn't entirely unheard of, not exactly. The region as a whole—the Arabian Peninsula, the Levant—had an unenviable reputation for exploiting East and South Asian countries for labor and often for sex as well. Domestic servants, caregivers, construction workers, general laborers—they came in droves in search of stronger economies and remittances. Often they were overworked, underpaid, mistreated, and abused in every capacity.

But the girls in the photographs were much younger, and the vast majority were minors. Too young to be nannies or domestic workers, too young for anything, unless Quinn permitted his imagination to truly delve into the darkness. For now, if for no other reason than keeping his sanity, he pushed that thought from his mind.

What really stayed with him from the evening was the sales-man's strange exclamation, a reactionary *wallahi*. Quinn had spent his early career in the Levant, mostly in Lebanon, and it was a term heard frequently. In Arabic, the exact definition escaped him, though it was something akin to "I swear to God" or, more accu-rately, "I swear to Allah," a term used expressly by Muslims.

He sat back down, collapsing into the couch.

It was not a phrase used lightly. Rather, it was not a phrase rou-tinely employed by non-native Arabic speakers, casual Muslims. Not a saying that one simply "picked up." There was an outside chance that the salesman could have inherited the expression from the "Arab man" he dealt with, some sort of imitable flattery, though the thought felt unnatural. It came with such ease, blurted out so freely in a moment of fear, pain, and candor.

Quinn poured himself another glass, raising it to his lips. What was the connection? The man could have spoken Arabic, but he was certainly not an Arab. Employed by them, perhaps. A rudi-mentary grasp of the language, not unlikely for a man like that, a swarthy vagrant conversant in a dozen tongues.

It was more likely that he was Muslim, to speak like that, to use that expression, as if second nature. It was also another reason why he might have worked for an Arabian man, a natural kinship, perhaps. Though how anyone could call themselves Muslim doing what they did was another matter entirely.

Then there was the betel nut. The only place he had previously witnessed such obsessive chewing of betel was in Mandalay while overseeing some training workshops; ironically, for secure docu-ments and fraud. There wasn't a taxi driver in all of Myanmar who wasn't spitting dark red saliva from his window. It was practically a national pastime.

So then, Burmese. The accent was a strange one, no hope in placing it, but the country did have its fair share of Muslim minorities. From Rakhine, perhaps, Rohingya. The Bamar Muslims, and the Panthays as well, though his features, ethnic as they were, didn't appear particularly Asiatic.

He turned his attention to the scraps of paper that he had collected. Invoices, a bill of lading, a few papers with jotted phone numbers, scribbled either by a six-year-old or someone without a formal education. Thai area codes. He shuffled the papers neatly together, perused them one by one, front and back. Different phone numbers now, a page with new area codes. Strange writing, a child's scrawl of Burmese, not Arabic, but barely legible, even for someone who might recognize the symbols. Slanting rows of semicircles with little tails.

On the back were three more sets of numbers, the first two clearly identified in printed, block letters: "GULF AIR" and "ETIHAD." He tried dialing each of the numbers on the front page, but they were all out of service. He called down to the lobby, and Cindy answered after two rings. Did she have access to the Internet? Would she mind searching for this area code? After a moment, the keyboard clacking, she gave him a confident response: Egypt. Yes, Egyptian area codes. He thanked her and hung up. There was no need to call either airline. Both would have direct flights to Cairo.

He threw back the last of his drink, lit another cigarette, and inhaled deeply, letting the fumes billow in his lungs. He walked to the open window, felt the warm, humid air on his face, the temperature perfection now. From somewhere below, the passing scent of spring onion frying in palm oil as he listened to the vibrant and indulgent sounds of the buzzing city.

It was ridiculous, wasn't it? And yet, the more he turned it over in his mind, let it simmer, it became increasingly difficult to deny. The puzzle pieces, dog-eared and misshapen, strangely began to fit, forming a most unexpected pattern but a pattern, nonetheless. Each sign pointed in a similar direction, less scattershot, more direct. The photographs and the passports. The stammering of the crooked salesman. The area codes. The airlines. The mysterious Arabian man.

In retrospect, the alley itself made perfect sense. Soi Cowboy, All Night Massage, they were both east of Asok. But where had he ended up? On the opposing side of the market, by Soi Arab, in the heart of the only Middle Eastern enclave in all of Bangkok. He recalled the perfumery, selling glistening bottles of exotic *oud*, where the salesman stored his wares. The *shawarma* restaurants all around, the signs for halal groceries, the traditional clothing stores, *abbayas* hanging in the windows. If there was a connection to be found between Bangkok and Cairo, it only made sense that it would be found there, within the confines of Little Arabia.

Still, he hesitated. What was he thinking then? Mei, dragged from the jungles of the Mekong and, what—bundled off to North Africa? To what end? The smuggler's end. The trafficker. For profit, for labor, the purpose irrelevant, as long as any customer paid the requisite sum.

He looked at her portrait again, two cropped photographs neatly cut from the sleeve. There was no doubt, the pictures had been used for a passport, perhaps a visa. And yet, considering it now for the first time, just the thought of stepping onto another plane didn't feel right. The flight itself was trivial. He would gladly endure it time and time again if that was what it took. He would fly to the farthest corners of the globe.

It was leaving Asia that felt unnatural. Every trace of her now pointed, absurdly, to North Africa, though he couldn't shake the feeling that leaving Bangkok would only drag him farther away. Though perhaps it was just that—farther away but not from her, only farther from where she ought to be. Farther from her rightful place, where she belonged. It was just like he had felt in Siem Reap.

He sat down once more, sifting through the pile of documents on the table, searching for a specific piece of lined paper. There was one phone number he had yet to dial. He had his suspicions, though he should have guessed before a courteous and robotic automation answered the line. He pressed a couple of buttons and waited patiently for a human being as he rubbed the sleep from his eyes. After a few moments, one finally answered.

"*Marhabaan,* good evening. Egypt Air."

"I need a flight to Cairo. As soon as possible."

PART

T W O

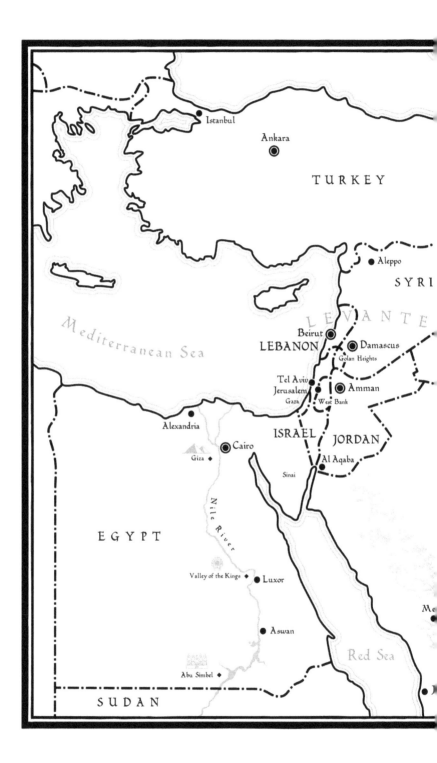

Ghonlaat,

How are you? I am doing fine. Today I am not writing very much because I am very tired. Khun Noi asked me if I'm sleeping good because I always look tired in the morning. She doesn't know that it's because I stay awake after lights off reading. I using my flashlight under the covers to read the Chamber of Secrets books you sent me. Loung said she was going to tell on me but I let her borrow one of my old Nancy Drew books so now she said she will not tell. We both read together sometimes but she almost always is falling asleep. Sometimes there is a lot of water that comes out from her mouth when she sleeps so I take my book back so it is not wet. It takes me a long time to read the English. The Khmer words is easier I think but I will continue. But sometimes the story gets scary and I have bad dreams so now I think I will read in the daytime. Last week was Merry Christmas so I am saying Merry Christmas and here is a picture of all of us at Christmas dinner.

Mei

TWENTY-ONE

Cairo, Egypt

EVERY TAXI IN THE MIDDLE EAST SMELLED THE SAME. IT WAS THE scent of stale smoke, saturating the leather upholstery, and just a hint of cardamom, perhaps nutmeg, from an aromatic cup of rich coffee. The odor was dense, lingering beneath smothering wafts of *oud*—the musky scent of sweet agarwood resin masking sweat, old and musty, other times ripe and pungent.

They sounded the same too. Either filled with animated male voices, harsh, throaty discussions seemingly always on the brink of an altercation, or the feminine, melismatic notes of a classic Arab melody playing on the radio. Quinn much preferred the latter. He found the singsong vocals and rhythms of a traditional *takht* almost hypnotic as he drifted in and out of sleep, his head resting against the dusty window. It was dark outside, the sky still an inky shade of indigo blue, so there wasn't much to see as the taxi sped along the Nile corniche toward the affluent suburb of Maadi.

He had hardly slept on the journey over. Though it was cool in the pre-dawn hours, his shirt was still damp, a reminder of the heart-stopping turbulence during the final hour of his flight. His back stuck to the faux-leather seats while the driver bobbed his head to the melody on the radio, tapping chubby fingers on the steering wheel to the beat of the *riq*.

Quinn had been to Cairo only once before, and only for a few days—an invitation from a UNICEF planning committee organizing a workshop on juvenile justice. He had been based out of Beirut at the time, working on a project with a similar theme, and flew in with a colleague for a brief consultation, a discussion on potential partnerships in the future and, perhaps, a brief spot as a guest speaker. Despite being the major hub of the region, the beating heart of North Africa, he had never had the opportunity to return and carried only a vague recollection of the historic city.

Maadi stood apart from most districts in Cairo, a quieter, more sheltered suburb of the chaotic capital. With wider boulevards, lush trees and foliage, it catered primarily to the wealthier class of Egyptian society as well as to expatriates, predominantly diplomats, aid workers, and the like. He had managed to rent a room in a villa just off of Al Nadi Square, not far from the Maadi Sports and Yacht Club, founded by British expats nearly a century before. Given the number of embassies and humanitarian missions in the area, it was as good a starting point as he could have hoped for, considering how limited his contacts were.

Beirut had been his first posting during his initial stint with the United Nations, working with a side project of the Development Programme. Having completed graduate school only a few months prior, he had been officially brought on as a project assistant, though in truth, handled the workload of a director for the salary of an intern. He looked back on his time in Centre Ville quite fondly and in the end had tallied more friends than adversaries. Still, that was many years ago, and he had far fewer contacts in the region than in most others, certainly less than Southeast Asia. The list he drew up on a cocktail napkin mid-flight was much shorter than he would have liked.

The women he had worked with in Lebanon had all moved on to greener pastures, many of them building upon their successes with the Roumieh Prison project, a rehabilitation effort targeting youth in Beirut's most notorious jail. Of the three he knew best, Leila, a mother of four, was the only one who remained in the city. She was born and raised in Achrafieh, he remembered, and by all accounts prioritized family over her career and didn't plan to leave any time soon. The two others, whose names he could no longer recall, went to work, respectively, at headquarters in Vienna and at UNICEF's regional office in Nairobi.

Hannah was by far his best bet, a German specialist in prison reform and juvenile delinquency. She was still based in Cairo, as far as he knew, and had spearheaded the conference on youth justice years before. A veteran of the Egyptian diplomatic scene even then, they had promptly solidified their friendship on the first day, having uncovered a mutual love for midday sangria.

In one sense, she was an absolute catastrophe: a perennially disorganized person, always losing her wallet and misplacing her keys. Her work station resembled a post office that had just endured the full brunt of a sandstorm. Papers littered the floor, and occasionally the desk, half-full cups of mint tea resting on this shelf or that radiator, presumably as an emergency measure in the event of a water shortage.

On the other hand, she was a remarkably efficient project officer. Capable, somehow, of making perfect sense of the chaos around her, she consistently delivered results no matter how meager the resources or how incompetent the staff.

He recalled her tedious battles with a Sudanese assistant in Juba. According to Hannah, the man was as arrogant as he was inept, and she was perpetually on the phone, dumbfounded by his actions or, more pointedly, lack thereof. Every time she got a call from poor Ahmed, her jaw would slacken, light-green eyes rolling to the back of her head, and Quinn would promptly leave the room with a smirk in search of a fresh cup of mint tea to soothe her.

After Hannah, the list on the napkin grew fairly thin. Raymond Ward was a military contractor and an old friend, though his whereabouts were as unpredictable as his phone numbers. The soldier of fortune didn't keep them for long, and he had four of them with area codes from Damascus to Dubai. He frequented Cairo, but how frequently was anybody's guess.

There was another number for a South African couple who had taught English once upon a time. The pair had a particular fondness, as he recalled, for Turkish *hammams* and Moroccan hashish and not much else. He also had an email address for a John Bennett, presumably an American working for USAID, though try as he might, Quinn had no recollection of who the man was. The most difficult aspect of moving about in diplomatic circles was trying to remember everyone's name, and heaven help you if they switched organizations.

The final name on the list was Hamed Hossain, and only as an afterthought, in case Quinn failed to make any inroads with law enforcement. Hamed wasn't so much a colleague to approach as one to avoid, primarily due to his notorious obstinance. He was based in Amman, having moved up the ladder of the Jordanian national police force rather swiftly. This rapid accession was, he never shied from telling people, due to his keen intellect and detective's intuition, though most others would inform the newly initiated that his father was a highly respected officer, and Hamed had the good fortune of being birthed with a prominent surname. In truth, he was the worst sort of idiot, completely unaware of his bumbling ignorance yet desperate to assert his authority in any given situation.

He also happened to be directly involved in the youth justice conference; however, not in the way that was intended. Upon his return to Beirut, Quinn had received a call from Hannah, eager to vent her frustration. Apparently, on the second day of the event, when Hamed was scheduled to speak, he was nowhere to be found. When he finally arrived, two hours late, he was in quite a huff, railing at the notorious city traffic. Hannah had spoken to the driver after dinner, a few other details emerging that slightly contradicted Hamed's narrative. It seemed the proud Jordanian officer had gotten wind of a more efficient route to Zamalek, and upon having his suggestion politely rebuffed, *insisted* that the driver follow his directions regardless. They inevitably ended up precisely at the military roadblock the driver was seeking to avoid, Hamed managing to delay proceedings even further by endearing himself to the soldiers at the checkpoint, asking in a less-than-cordial tone if they had any idea who he was.

Hannah was forced to scramble at the last minute to find another speaker, holding a brief Q&A session instead, and Hamed, rather than apologizing for his tardiness, directed most of his frustrations toward the overcooked chicken kebab at supper.

The cab rolled smoothly to a stop in front of a large, enclosed villa with a rose-colored brick wall and an entranceway delimited by a wrought-iron gate and two marble pillars. An old sycamore tree stretched upwards from a hole in the cobbled sidewalk, almost reaching the top of the three-story residence. Owned by the Shafiq family, as was evident by the rectangular gold placard affixed to the wall, it almost seemed a bit lavish upon first glance, but it still fit in rather inconspicuously with the neighboring buildings.

Quinn had made prior accommodation arrangements with Mr. Shafiq while en route and was told that the caretaker, a relative, would see to all the practical details upon his arrival. He presumed it was this very relative's attention that the driver was attempting to summon when he laid on the horn.

Quinn stepped out, grabbed his bag, handed the driver a few wrinkled notes, and fished around in his pockets for his cigarettes. When the driver leaned on the horn for the third time, Quinn was well and truly awake, and half deaf in his right ear. A few minutes later, following a great deal of mumbling from inside the taxi, across the street an elderly man shuffled along the tiled walkway and up to the gate. The driver pointed, nodded, and grunted something, indicating that, finally, this was the man for whom they were waiting.

"Mahmoud, this Mahmoud," he said, pointing with a stubby finger.

Quinn nodded a curt "thank you" and had hardly taken a step when the driver revved the engine and promptly sped off down the street. The large gate swung open with the turn of a key, his receptionist standing invitingly at the entrance. He was a fairly small man, short and rather thin, and looked to be around sixty, which probably meant about forty-five. He had short cropped white hair, almost translucent in spots, and a bristly mustache. It too was a clean shade of white and contrasted quite noticeably with his rust-colored teeth. His friendly brown eyes carried heavy, swollen pouches beneath them.

Mahmoud had the excitable yet confused face of a man who seemed to be on the very brink of saying something and having realized just then that he didn't quite know which sounds to make.

With an enthusiastic exclamation on the tip of his tongue, he nodded repeatedly, and smiled.

"Mahmoud?"

"*Aywa*, Mahmoud!" he exclaimed, gesturing for Quinn to follow.

Mahmoud led him down an open-air corridor lined with a variety of potted plants until they reached a rustic bureau in the foyer. Quinn handed over a deposit and watched some muted Egyptian military propaganda on a grainy television set as Mahmoud groped around for a room key in a drawer.

Following the old man up three flights of stairs, each room they passed—doors wide open—was either undergoing some sort of renovation or had furniture draped in plastic sheeting, coated with a thick layer of dust. He couldn't help but notice Mahmoud's feet, rather dusty themselves, calloused and deeply cracked like two pieces of driftwood. They shuffled along in sandals likely stitched together during the time of the pharaohs.

Mahmoud unlocked the door to a suite far larger and more luxurious than Quinn required. He stepped forth into a gusty vortex, several large fans blowing from opposing directions throughout the living room. After affecting interest during a brief and entirely silent tour, Mahmoud left him alone to savor his first moment of peace and quiet since the hotel in Thong Lor.

He walked around the unit, methodically switching off a total of five fans, which at last made the space feel more like a home than a wind tunnel. He decided against a shower and, after splashing some water on his face and dragging a damp cloth beneath his arms, changed into the only collared shirt and respectable trousers he had brought. The shadows beneath his eyes weren't as dark as he'd expected, and he could have shaved, but then again—he appraised himself in the mirror—*to hell with it.*

TWENTY-TWO

THE LEAFY BOULEVARDS OF MAADI WERE IN SHARP CONTRAST with most other neighborhoods in the city: quiet, cool, and green, though just as dusty. Mature, soaring trees lined the roads and formed a welcome shady canopy that shielded those below from the blistering Egyptian sun. Cars were parked on either side of the street wherever there was space, many draped in tarpaulins to ward off grit and grime.

Though despite the abundant foliage, there was still no respite from the thick, stifling air. Even now, at midmorning, a palpable smog hung over the city, visible in the distance. Cairo was hardly the only regional capital that dealt with waste by incinerating it in large rubbish piles, but when the smoke combined with the sand, dust, unrelenting heat, and the flood of noxious emissions spewing from idling vehicles, it choked the very breath one drew.

After passing a few landmarks from a lifetime ago, he finally caught sight of the nondescript building. But for the cars out front giving it away, it was hardly recognizable as the local office of the UN Children's Fund, blending seamlessly with the other multistory apartments along the street. Two identical black jeeps were parked in the shade adjacent to an unremarkable security booth resembling a cottage country outhouse. Next to it, an African man in a white *thobe* and matching turban sat reading the paper and drinking tea.

With a purposeful stride, Quinn gave the man a perfunctory nod, which seemed to demonstrate just enough gravitas—the nod was returned—and proceeded into the foyer.

A security guard made him sign the appointment book and step through a metal detector, the electrical cord taped together at the socket. Without even mentioning Hannah's name—or any name at all, for that matter—he took the stairs and wondered if a dark-haired Egyptian man would have waltzed inside with the same ease.

The first floor was nearly deserted, though he followed his nose to a closet-sized kitchen, where a couple of men were huddled over a stove. He exchanged pleasantries with Saad and Fares, driver and office caretaker, respectively, who were busy preparing a breakfast of tea and *ful*. They informed him that Fares had by far the best recipe, a simmering stew of fava beans, to which he added cumin, lemon juice, and a few other choice secrets, which, Allah forgive him, he just could not reveal. They insisted he have a taste. The *ful* was even better than Quinn expected, and he made sure to get their contact information before asking for Hannah's office. If his career had taught him anything, it was to always befriend the local staff—drivers, cooks, and anyone with keys to the building.

The second floor was more lively, a couple of young men typing in their offices, a threesome engaged in a morning briefing in a small boardroom. He couldn't help but notice the building had evolved quite a bit since his last visit, at least judging by some of the door placards. One office was clearly designated for UNAIDS, and the larger, empty boardroom seemed to have been repurposed into an office for UNODC, Drugs and Crime.

When he climbed to the third floor, framed posters and certificates were all linked by a common theme and a common gender emblem: UN Women. The building appeared to have transformed into something of a head office for the organization, each department buzzing in its own little section of the regional UN hive.

Walking farther down the hall, his attention lingered on one of the posters until he nearly collided with a young lady stepping out of her office. Startled, they both instinctively apologized, then paused.

"Quinn?"

He tried his best not to look bemused, scrambling for her name until she smiled and put him out of his misery.

"Maha . . . from Beirut?"

"Of course!" He rolled his eyes. "Sorry about that. It's been a while. It was on the tip of my tongue, I swear."

"Oh," she said, waving his comment away, "no need to apologize. It's been, what . . . seven years?"

"Maybe more."

"You really startled me." She laughed nervously, placing her palm to her chest. "What are you doing here?"

He rocked on his heels, puffing out his cheeks. "Isn't that the million-dollar question. It's, well, it's a bit of a story."

"Hold that thought. Let me drop off this file with my colleague, and then we'll chat, alright? Do you want some tea? I'll bring some tea." She motioned to an empty chair inside the office. "Have a seat. I'll be right back."

The office was impeccably organized, a place for everything and everything in its place. He thought back, longer than seven years ago, to when they had first met, both wide-eyed young interns in Lebanon. She was familiar, vaguely so, a sketch of a memory, not quite filled in. What he did remember was a shy, introverted young girl, diligent and hardworking but never really socializing with the group outside the office. They had been intermittent colleagues, working agreeably side by side when required, usually amongst a group, and then moving about in their own circles when the task was complete. If he hadn't have nearly bowled her over, he may never have given her a second thought.

A while later, Maha returned carrying a small silver tray with two steaming glasses of golden tea stuffed with fresh sprigs of mint.

"You know, I was just thinking, the last time I saw you was in Fawad's apartment, just before you left. I can't remember what we were celebrating, or rather what *you* were celebrating, but the two of you were drinking some kind of, some *poison* that he had brought from his relatives—boasting that it came from up in the mountains. Something about the climate or elevation. I can't remember."

He smiled at the memory, carefully lifting the scalding glass with his fingertips. "I think you might be mistaking me for someone else."

Maha made a face, wafting an imaginary stench in the air. "I can still smell it, *ach* . . . like petrol."

She looked different than he remembered, faintly as he did— just as conservative but more self-assured, perhaps. No longer the intern, now very much the officer. A heavy chestnut hijab hung loosely around her shoulders, draped over top of a navy blazer, and beneath that, a cream-colored blouse. She had delicate, simple features: dark eyes and darker brows, shaped precisely into confident arches that faintly kissed where they almost met, just above her slender nose. She had a small mouth, lips slightly chapped, a thin crescent scar on her chin.

"Well, I have no recollection of that."

"*La*—I wouldn't think so. Both of you probably have brain damage."

"And you? When did you leave? This place sure has changed, a floor for every department."

"Tell me about it. It's a zoo whenever we have visiting delegations, but it's great for collaboration. I work for UN Women now, obviously. I have for a few years. The building is terrific if you want to bounce ideas off people from different fields, brainstorm new proposals. It was really helpful in the beginning, getting our feet under us. We relied on the experience down the hall quite a bit."

"I can imagine."

"But, to answer your question, I left the project not too long after you. Homesick, I guess you could say."

"Egyptian?" He narrowed his eyes.

"Born and raised right here in Cairo." She smiled. "Over in Giza. Beirut was my first work opportunity away from home." She paused and carefully sipped her tea. "It's funny, looking back now. I was so nervous about moving, and really, Lebanon, I mean, we're practically neighbors."

"The first one always gives you the jitters. I barely slept the week before. Beirut . . . at least *you* could blend in."

A quiet, little laugh.

"Well, it seems like you've got it all worked out." He cast his eye around the office, raising his glass. "You've come a long way from free labor."

"And you? What have you been doing the past few years?"

He shrugged. "This and that. After Beirut I sort of bounced around for a while. A long while. Short consultancy contracts here and there, building up a bit of experience. I wasn't really making the impact I wanted, so I moved to the private sector not long after. I guess I had my moments, but in the end, it just wasn't for me. I'm sort of between contracts at the moment, I suppose you could say."

"Ah, so you wanted the full humanitarian experience. No roots, no commitments, a new country every few months . . ."

"It wasn't exactly the plan. Things just sort of happen, don't they? I just kept searching for where I could have an impact, make a difference, you know? Don't you ever find it frustrating, all of this?"

She raised an eyebrow. "I work for a women's group in Egypt. What do you think?"

"Point taken."

"I should show you some of the initiatives we've been developing, some of the projects we're involved with. They're *fantastic*. Really, they are. Poverty is still a major focus for us across the country, violence against women, what you might call the more traditional areas, but we're focusing so much more on education now, female health education especially.

"And the projects—not just basic funding for generic goals, *equality*, or something like that. But we have real investment now, projects with strategically linked themes and positive multiplier effects across our mandate. And they're not only our programs but new ideas too, all sorts of community-based organizations springing up, more and more each year with their own proposals for empowerment, especially political empowerment."

Her enthusiasm sputtered for a moment, and she let out a beleaguered sigh as she sat back in her chair, the excitement waning upon reflection. It occurred to Quinn that he had never heard her speak so passionately or for so long.

"And then, when you finally meet with the ministers, the CEOs, even the police—all men, of course—they're just so . . . so . . ."

"Supportive? Understanding?"

"Patronizing! Patronizing."

"Your English has certainly improved."

"Don't you start. But yes, that's exactly what they're like. '*There, there, little girl, that's a nice idea. Now go on back to your chores.*' They're not all like that, but the majority are. Honestly, at times I could just . . ." She pursed her lips, making a strangling motion with her hands.

"Sounds about right," he said, chuckling. "Still, even if they wanted to help you—and I'm not saying they do—the size of the bureaucracy with all of this." He waved his hand about. "You know what it's like. You can't turn a ship on a dime."

"Dime?" she repeated, her eyes narrowing.

"A coin. It's a metaphor."

Maha took a sip of tea and shook her head. "*Bas*, enough, I'll only get myself worked up." She cupped her hands around her glass. "So, what brings you to Cairo?"

"I'm happy to tell you, but like I said, it's kind of a long story. I was looking for Hannah, actually. They said her office is up here somewhere?"

"Oh." Her face changed. "It is, but she's in Germany at the moment. You didn't have plans to meet, did you? I think she's on leave for at least another week. Is there anything I can help with?" she asked, sensing his frustration.

He rubbed his jaw, held back the words not suited for polite conversation. "How busy are you?"

"Busy. We've got a workshop beginning the day after next. I can make some time tonight though, if you're free?"

"Sure. Let's grab a bite when you're done."

"In fact," her eyes drifted in thought, "maybe you can help me out a little as well, for old time's sake."

He hesitated. "What did you have in mind?"

"One of our guest speakers just dropped out—a family emergency, apparently. We have a slot to fill at the end of the first day." She winced theatrically. "Would you mind giving a brief talk?"

He shifted in his chair.

"Please? Very brief."

"What about?"

"The workshop is based on our Safe Cities project, but I was thinking, maybe a case study about Roumieh? Just the highlights, a focus on our rehabilitation efforts with the girls, reintegration into society, that sort of thing. Just something light to round out the afternoon."

"You still have those reports?"

She nodded.

"Alright, sure, I can do that, but I'll have to call in this favor right away. I hope you don't mind."

"Not at all. Your turning up is already one thing off my to-do list," she said with a smirk, flipping open a journal and scribbling a note. "But can we talk over dinner? I'm late for a meeting. Actually, oh," she tapped her pen, "I might have some bad news. I'm supposed to brief our rep on the latest developments with the workshop, and, well, once I mention your name, I'm sure he'll want to see you."

He shrugged. "That's fine."

"Maybe. It's Archie Belanger."

TWENTY-THREE

THE OFFICE WAS SIMPLY FURNISHED, VACANT IN THE WAY AN office usually was following a transition—only the bare essentials, its former owner hastily departing for greener pastures. It had a desk, some mostly empty shelves, dusty blinds, an embattled air purifier that wheezed, and a half dozen chairs around a circular table where Maha was already seated. A young woman sat in the corner with a laptop, all freckles and red curls. She might as well have been wearing a nametag that read "Intern."

"Well, look who it is. I thought I smelled something!"

"The ghost of Ramadan past. How are things, Archie?"

"Ah, you know I'd complain, but nobody listens." He rounded the desk, hand outstretched. "Least of all my wife."

His horrid sense of humor hadn't improved, surely the first of many lame quips that Quinn would be forced to endure, already regretting the detour. He shot Maha a subtle glance, but she didn't notice.

"Well, I sure as hell wouldn't put up with you. Why do you think I left?"

"Come on now," Archie said, chuckling, "don't hurt my feelings."

"I see you two are picking up right where you left off," Maha said. "Sir, can we go over a few things about the workshop first?"

"Sounds good. Quinn, you remember Marchand?"

That was his name. He nodded a curt acknowledgement to the short, stocky man standing behind the desk, Archie's personal lackey, the two forever joined at the hip.

He and Quinn had never gotten on, but then again, the man was once some type of military policeman—something of the like, anyhow; Quinn had never really listened—and who the hell ever got on with one of them? The man never failed to work some form of military lexicon into the conversation, just in case anyone had momentarily forgotten the fleeting authority that he once possessed and now so desperately craved. He wore silver-rimmed glasses, a button-down shirt that was a size too small tucked neatly into his khakis, and busied himself shuffling papers about the desk as if they held some particular importance at that moment.

"And this is our newest intern, Heidi. Heidi, Quinn used to work for me years ago. Maha, too. We're reuniting the old team."

The timid redhead smiled politely for just long enough, then went back to typing her meeting notes.

"Maha says you're in town for a bit and are going to fill in on the first day for us. The morning slot, right?"

"Right before lunch," Maha corrected.

"Happy to help," Quinn said.

"It'll have to be pro bono, of course," Marchand said. "We're way over budget."

Quinn shrugged. "Like I said, happy to help the team." Marchand puffed out his chest for some reason. Shoulders pulled back and chin firmly tucked, he resembled a frigate bird with a goatee.

"Sir, most of the embassies have replied, but we're still waiting on Switzerland and, I believe, the Germans. I don't expect more than two representatives from each, so we're still fine in terms of numbers, about twenty in total. Other than that, I think we're looking good. My team can handle all the last-minute details." Maha turned a page in her journal. "Also, I think we need to get moving on the program analysis. I believe you said Vienna needs it next month? Do you know when, exactly?

Archie furrowed a brow. "End of the month, I think."

"Would you mind confirming, please?" she asked, her tone respectful yet direct. "It's going to take some time to assess the reports from each pipeline project. The budgets, too."

It wasn't that Quinn disliked Archie; it wasn't personal. It just happened that the man was the complete embodiment of a bloated and inefficient bureaucracy, a walking, talking reminder of everything wrong with the organization.

The new head of the regional office was big, well over six feet, and doughy throughout. His blond hair was cut short, accentuating his oversized melon, with bright pink cheeks that were clean-shaven. His chin disappeared into his neck rather seamlessly, his features working in tandem to make him appear less like a grown man and more of a forty-five-year-old toddler. Irksome at best, maddening at worst, he was tolerable in small doses, though one would have still preferred the vaccine.

For a few months, Archie had been their hastily appointed supervisor in Beirut and had clearly done well for himself, now managing multi-departmental offices in at least a dozen countries across the Levant and Sahel. The appointment was typical of a growing narrative and the very reason so many held grudges against him. Though Archie meant well, he was completely unqualified and equally inept, but in some perverse and everlasting twist of fate, this only served to propel his career forward. He would stumble and fall backward into promotion after promotion, much to the annoyance of his colleagues and essentially anyone who had ever worked alongside him.

Quinn had heard Archie's name mentioned a few times over the years—now leading this project, then speaking at that conference, here heading this committee, there managing that department— an unstoppable upward trajectory completely at odds with rational thought. His bumbling approach to any dilemma was fascinating to watch: floundering about with indecision, a sweaty look of consternation on his face, staunchly held beliefs shifting direction with every passing gust of wind.

Quinn felt a wave of nostalgia as he observed the theater unfolding before him. Maha was going over timelines for donor reporting, and Archie's subtle nods did their best to convey concentration and approval. After a while, Archie's eyebrows began to soften, his eyes glazing over, followed by the slow blink and all-too-familiar stare. Maha seemed perfectly accustomed to this behavior and, ever the consummate professional, flew through the briefing more out of courtesy than necessity. It was evident that she didn't require his input, approval, or anything else, for that matter. The briefing was thorough and concise, every task accounted for, every responsibility delegated.

"I'm still waiting for contributions from Tunis," she said. "I'll follow up with them again this afternoon, and Juba's expenditures and implementation rates from last quarter . . ."

Archie's head bobbed along, and Quinn entertained himself by picturing a cartoon monkey in the echoing void between the man's ears, stomping around and crashing cymbals together, an adorable little fez on its furry head.

Maha seemed to be wrapping it up, which provided Archie with his window of opportunity. "So, Quinn," he said, "what are you doing these days? You're not here looking for a job, are you? We could use the help."

"Thanks, but I'm already spoken for. Just doing some freelance consulting at the moment."

"Here in Cairo?"

He nodded.

"For who?"

"Anti-terror with the Gulf Council."

"They're looking to do more work in the region?"

"Parts of it. Mostly the territories."

Quinn caught sight of Archie's half-eaten lunch on the desk: a baloney sandwich with white bread, a smear of mustard, identical to all the others in Beirut. Archie always sought to embrace the local cuisine.

"Last I heard you were in Manila, something to do with immigration?"

"A couple of years back. Wasn't really a good fit."

"I heard you got fired," Marchand said.

Heidi's laptop momentarily stopped its click-clacking, silence filling the room. Quinn looked at Marchand, a smug expression painted across the man's thick face.

Archie's lapdog had always been especially uncomfortable around him. Whether it was simply insecurity or some form of misguided envy, Quinn had never really known—or cared.

"You heard right." Quinn shrugged. "A misunderstanding."

"Are you kidding?" Archie asked, chuckling. "What happened?"

"Something about insubordination, I heard," Marchand said.

"Is that right?" said Archie.

"Ah, you know how rumors spread," Quinn replied. "I wasn't insubordinate. I was . . . educating someone. Insubordinate means I was disobeying orders."

"Well, *were* you?"

"Archie . . ." Quinn groaned theatrically. "I'm offended you would even ask."

The big man chuckled again while Heidi smiled nervously, her eyes darting back and forth across the room. It was Maha who caught Quinn's attention. She was staring at the floor, clearly uncomfortable. The fact that Quinn appeared unflappable seemed, for whatever reason, to grate on Marchand, as if some old score required settling, one that only he knew about.

"I heard you told your boss that he had his head up his ass."

The room would have fallen silent once again had it not been for Archie, giddily oblivious to the tension, who found this all to be rather amusing. He giggled convulsively, uncharacteristic for a man of his size, and stared wide-eyed at Quinn, awaiting a response.

"Well, did he?" he asked excitedly.

"I mean, no more than Napoleon over here has his head up your ass, only with less purpose."

Archie tried to stifle another bout of laughter, failing miserably, then swiftly followed the effort with his best impersonation of a man in control. "Oh, come on now," he scolded, his voice lower than usual.

A sidelong glance at Marchand showed the man had flushed, a red hue spreading across his face like a rash.

"You're right. Sorry, the jet lag." Quinn made a face. "I get irritable." Archie's expression sympathized. "I sure could go for a coffee. Anyone else?"

"Maybe a little more respectful next time," Marchand said, his tone menacing.

"Gentlemen, please," Maha said, "this is not some locker room. Can we at least try to behave like adults?" She bored through both men with steely eyes.

"Oh, these fellas are just messing around," Archie said, as usual lacking a full grasp of the situation. "What about it then, coffee? Tea? Heidi?"

"No, thank you."

"I'm fine, thanks."

Marchand hid it well, surely wishing the floor would have swallowed him whole when Archie nodded—the painful realization that it was he who'd been nominated for the afternoon catering. Quinn considered asking for cream and sugar, then caught sight of Maha's glare and thought better of it.

Just then, the telephone on Archie's desk rang, breaking the tension with impeccable timing, allowing Marchand to save face by slipping away as his boss moseyed over to answer the call.

Quinn leaned in to Maha. "Quite a temper on him."

She hissed something and rolled her eyes, unimpressed. "What is it about men? Like children, all of you. You remind me of my nephew."

Quinn nodded. "Clever boy."

"He's eight, Quinn. Eight."

TWENTY-FOUR

Following a brief and conspiratorial consultation with Saad, the department's gruffly affable wheelman, Quinn hailed a taxi and directed the driver to a small cluster of shops along Road Nine. There he found a small liquor store, hidden away on the second floor of a dimly lit plaza, doing great business with expats and other locals in the know.

When he returned to his villa, he considered cracking the bottle open in broad daylight, waiting an eternity for Mahmoud to appear at the front gate. There were no doorbells or knockers of any kind, forcing Quinn to shout from the street like a madman to announce his arrival. Apparently, given the tense political climate, security was tighter than usual and manifested itself at the Shafiq residence in the form of an elderly Bedouin in faded blue robes, shuffling along clutching a gate key, a wave of apology, sleep lines creasing his stubbled cheek.

Quinn decided to freshen up properly with a shower and a shave. The water was cold and sputtering, faintly brown, and accompanied by a strange crackling noise from somewhere down the hall. As he spun the shower taps, a thunderous explosion shook the apartment, rattling the walls, and he stumbled backwards, nearly vaulting himself into the bathtub.

He proceeded tentatively down the hall to the kitchen, where a gas water heater, rusty and decrepit, was mounted on the wall. Turning the kitchen faucet, he heard the familiar crackling sound as noxious fumes enveloped an expired piece of flint that struggled to spark, the air choked with natural gas before the heater finally ignited—a fireball tearing through the heater once again, bending the metal as tremors rumbled through the room. While there seemed to be no visible damage, he wiggled a finger palliatively in his ringing ear.

The cold shower was revitalizing, and afterward, he splashed a few fingers of whiskey into a short tea glass before calling Noi to update her on the latest developments. He left a brief, self-conscious voicemail about red-light districts, international smugglers, and a Middle Eastern capital before tossing the phone aside.

Tipping the bottle once more, he removed one of Mei's pictures from amongst the stack of fraudulent passports and lay down on a dusty couch, staring at the documents in hopes that they might reveal something tangible—hoping that one might just speak to him. Even a whisper.

It still felt like a fool's errand—in Egypt, now more than ever. His thoughts swung like a pendulum from hope to cynicism, from sense to absurdity. One moment he was on the right path, all signs pointing in a single, obvious direction, and the next he was helplessly adrift, treading water in the darkness, slowly drowning.

From the start it seemed strange that Mei would end up in Bangkok. No, not just strange—crazy. He felt the same even after meeting Areum. And yet, it did *fit*, somehow.

The smart money was always on somewhere local: a different town in Cambodia, or farther, Phnom Penh, perhaps. Still, Bangkok made sense if, and only if, this was a far more sophisticated operation than he had initially presumed. One with a greater reach. Longer tentacles. Regional influence if not international pedigree. It was a ludicrous thought at the beginning, even after crossing into Thailand, leaping to conclusions at best. But now? The passports? The documents all but proved an operation of a much grander scale, the idea far less speculative.

If Mei had ended up in the hands of lowlifes fabricating travel documents, then Bangkok, Cairo, these international cities, regional hubs, they made more sense than anywhere. A local operation, small-scale and full of amateurs, wouldn't have gone to the trouble. The region didn't have borders; it had guidelines—streams and forests, mountains and valleys. State boundaries were more fluid than the great Mekong River itself, the water steeped in as much dirt and filth as the border guards themselves. One hardly needed a passport to smuggle innocents across those lands. All one needed was cigarettes, whiskey, bribe money, or an offer of ten minutes in a secluded roadside thicket with some of the cargo.

All business, above board and below, flowed through the Thai capital. It was the region's central hub no matter what—or whom—one was buying or selling. The same could be said of Cairo. Whatever he had stumbled upon back in Soi Arab was part of something much larger, the exposed root of an expansive web, rotting beneath his feet.

In the midst of his reverie, he heard a deft click as a rolling blackout plunged his surroundings into twilight, the long shadows of dusk stretching across the living room. Muffled exclamations of surprise drifted through an open window in the neighboring building. He watched as the lone ceiling fan spun its final revolutions, its momentum only carrying it so far until it too gave in to the stillness of the early evening.

As the sun dipped in the western sky, it illuminated drifts of cloud cover, swirls of orange and gold, the faintest outline of twin peaks, the ancient pyramids of Giza rising above the cityscape on the distant horizon. The air was warm, accompanied by a soft, soothing breeze, offering its apology for the stifling heat of midday.

Quinn kept an eye out for landmarks as he walked, and it wasn't long before he passed the roundabout at Port Saeed Square, where traffic congested and sheet-metal boxes with wheels honked and swerved.

Along the southern curve, a contingent of soldiers stood by two armored vehicles. Some were rigidly at attention, shoulders back, chests out, though most were rather disinterested, leaning against a barricade or sitting atop the strategically positioned IFVs (infantry fighting vehicles). Their desert camouflage blended seamlessly with the beige of their vehicles, assault rifles held carelessly or simply left dangling across their chests as they casually surveyed the roads. The gunner, perched on high in his bird's nest of sandbags, propped his chin against the turreted machine gun that cast its threatening gaze across the intersection.

Quinn turned down Al Sad Al Aalie until it intersected with Street 81, then waited patiently across from the Venezuelan embassy. He lit a cigarette, putting out the match with a flick of his wrist. Rising above the clamor of local traffic, he listened to the distant call of *azan*, the guiding melody of the *mu'azzin* beckoning worshippers to prayer.

It wasn't long before he spotted a familiar silhouette. Squinting in the near darkness, ambient light peeking through trees lining the main street, he hardly recognized her. She wore a headscarf, though this one was light and silken, beige in color, resting delicately on her dark hair as if it had floated down from the night sky. Beneath a full-length cardigan, drifting just above the dusty street, she wore flowing trousers and a fitted café au lait pullover that matched her wedged sandals. Even with the slight heels, she barely rose to shoulder height. A stylish leather shoulder bag hung casually by her hip.

"I didn't know men still used matches," Maha said.

"Most don't."

"Ready, Freddy? We might need those matches where we're going."

She turned as abruptly as she'd arrived, and he followed her down the darkening street, the light swallowed by ancient tree trunks and their dense, leafy canopies. The street, which was more of an alley, led behind a silent row of houses to the front of a brick home, the walkway lit by stone lanterns whose soft amber light reflected against the low-hanging tree branches.

The hum of voices and the tinkling of cutlery grew louder as they stepped through the doorway, a heavy red velvet curtain parting, ushering them into the dining room. Inside, a feast for the senses. Patrons chatted amongst themselves at busy, crowded tables, dining on an array of heavily spiced dishes. In a distant corner, a group of men lazed amongst mounds of embroidered pillows and silver pipes, clouds of shisha smoke hovering in the air. Their host, smartly dressed in a maroon jacket, led them past sandstone brick pillars and thick archways, the walls lined with decorative mosaic tiles and the odd artisanal rug. Candlelight flickered softly within towering brass lamps, the perforated lattice casting long shadows and brilliant designs upon the walls. The room was filled with a medley of exotic aromas—warm cumin and robust pepper, the fragrances mingling with the fruity smoke of tobacco soaked in molasses.

Maha insisted on ordering, arranging for a platter of various tastings and opting for Egyptian wine, more for thematic consistency than personal preference, she said. They had hardly settled into their heavily cushioned seats before the dishes began to arrive: warm breads, liberally floured, with a dizzying array of dips and spreads, smoky vegetable mezzes, and creamy tapas drizzled with golden oils.

"You know, I don't remember you being this cynical," she said, nibbling a piece of fried aubergine.

"We must not have known each other that well."

"Mm, no, you've definitely changed. Not entirely for the worse," she said with half a grin. "It's not all bad, seeing you again, but you weren't this bitter before."

"Is that right."

"Not being critical, just an observation."

"A critical observation then."

"Not that I would blame you. It doesn't take long to become discouraged in our line of work."

He nodded in agreement. "You don't seem that affected. Maybe a little, a hint of frustration there, back at the office, but I wouldn't say bitter. And if anyone has reason to be, I mean, the work you do, the place you do it, I'd be tearing my hair out."

"Believe me, sometimes I wonder how there's any left." She patted her headscarf delicately.

"So, how do you do it?"

She exhaled, took a sip of wine, then leaned forward, cradling the glass against her cheek. "One day at a time," she said, more a question than an answer.

"Fair enough."

"I'm waiting . . ."

"For?"

"What changed? Turning so bitter. You're not getting out of this so easily. It wasn't so long ago that we were going to change the world, remember?"

He chuckled. "Feels like a lifetime, doesn't it? But no, I wouldn't say bitter. Maybe a touch cynical, but just a touch. Problem is I'm at an age now where I can't tell if I'm upset for any good reason or if I'm just slowly becoming an old, curmudgeonly bastard."

"A what?"

"Bastard?"

"No, the first one."

"Curmudgeon." He looked around the room, searching for an example. "Like a grouch, a grumpy old man. Scrooge."

"Ahh, Ebenezer Scrooge, yes, I remember him." For a moment her eyes wandered, then she nodded. "Dickens."

"You've read Dickens? Nobody reads Dickens."

"A Christmas Story," she said assuredly.

"Christmas Carol."

She shrugged. "I was curious what all the fuss was about. My English tutor in university was from Chelsea. And I never said I read it." She dipped a sliver of bread into a spiced purée. "But the film was quite good."

"A classic."

"So then, give me an example, Mr. Scrooge. What makes you think you're turning into such a grouch?" She raised a finger. "And it can't be about work. That's cheating. We're all frustrated with that."

His lips parted in reply.

"And then afterwards you can tell me why you've come to my beautiful city."

He swished the wine in his glass, chewing his lip thoughtfully. "I'm sorry to disappoint, but it's nothing you don't already know," he said with a shrug. "And despite the rules, it's mostly work related. Was, anyway."

"Something specific?"

"Just the opposite. All of it. Years of trying to accomplish what we set out to accomplish—initially, anyhow. As you said, out to change the world. Make a difference. All that."

"You don't think we do?"

He began to answer, then thought better of it, self-conscious upon realizing the words would confirm her playful accusation. "Not often enough. Not as much as we should, which, I'll admit sounds very . . . oh, I don't know . . ."

Maha let his words hang there, the thought unfinished, the conversation awaiting a breath of new life. She kept her eyes on him, tucking another morsel of smothered bread into her mouth.

"Alright, in a word? Bureaucracy. At least the way it's constructed."

"We joined the UN, Quinn. What did you expect?"

"I don't know. Not this. The layers of politics, getting bogged down in it." He sighed.

"Sounds a little naïve."

He tried again, searching for the right words. "I think we knew what we were getting into, just not the scale of it. The snail's pace, that's what we expected, what everyone expects. Like I said before, you can't turn a ship on a dime. But the incompetence, the nepotism, the residual effects. In fact, here's a perfect example." He leaned forward, intertwining his fingers on the table. "Archie Belanger, Regional Representative. Go ahead, say it out loud." He winced at the thought.

"That's not bureaucracy, that's . . . *wallah,* I don't know what that is."

They shared a brief chuckle at the man's expense.

"You start off inspired, motivated, you mean well. Of course, you're a rational person too. You know you won't change the world, but you'll play your part, humble though it might be. And then you find out what kind of people actually make the decisions, who greenlights the projects, who even bothers reading the briefings, how some of them make it into these positions, I mean it's . . ."

"He means well. Archie."

"I was there in the office, you know. It was you giving him guidance, bringing him up to speed. It's supposed to be the other way around."

"It is," she conceded with a nod, "but truly, I don't mind."

"You don't find that frustrating?"

"Not for the same reasons. When *you* look at him, you see—

"A moron."

"*Ayshh.*"

"He is."

"Listen to me." Her tone was gently scolding now. "For me it's different. It works in my favor. The way he is, his personality, he lets me run my projects my way. He doesn't interfere. All he asks is that I keep him updated, and you know Archie—he doesn't *want* any extra responsibilities. So, I'm free to do as I wish. How many people can say that about their work? How many *women* can say that about their boss? *Yanni*, I'm sure you understand, but I don't know if you can fully appreciate this. For a woman here in Cairo, it's nice to work for a man who isn't telling me what to do at every moment. Who doesn't correct me. I have the independence to do my work as I like. He doesn't bother me, and he doesn't talk down to me."

"That's because he knows you'd put him in his place."

"True," she said, playing along, "but you know what I mean."

It was his turn to concede the point with a nod, taking another sip of wine. His gaze drifted, fixating on a floor lamp in the corner of the room, a robust piece of metallic artistry, nearly table height. The soft light filtered through elaborate cutwork, diffusing a myriad of glowing shapes and patterns on the shadowed walls.

"There was an officer I knew, an attaché for the Germans while I was in Manila. Gunther." He shook his head at the memory. "He wasn't the sharpest fellow to begin with, but there was a shortage of staff at the visa post, operational requirements"—he opened his palm—"you know how it is. So, he got an acting position. Promoted basically out of necessity, but at least it was only temporary. Did it for three months, and of course, he was just this side of useless. He didn't know the job well before, and by the end of the three months, the staff were begging for him to go. Organizationally, the place was in shambles."

"Sounds familiar."

"I was on leave, taking a couple weeks off—I think I was in Malta—and apparently, within that time, a vacancy came up. I still don't know how he managed to fill in the P-11 himself, but regardless, he threw in for it, and by some miracle, actually convinced the board that he knew what he was talking about. Nobody could believe it. It was a running joke at the office before it came true, and suddenly, the joke wasn't so funny. The post was still recovering from the mess he'd left behind the first time around, and now he had a permanent position.

"Anyhow, a couple of months went by, and by then not only had he alienated his staff but all the senior management as well. You know, the ones he might have wanted to use for counsel, for their experience. The man was a complete liability. So, what to do?

They had created a monster that they couldn't get rid of. Naturally, they moved him up again. Another acting position this time but managing a much smaller unit—visa fraud, I think it was. The man couldn't do proper assessments to save his life, but now he was in charge of overseeing investigations. You can imagine how that went." He paused for dramatic effect, leaning forward in his seat. "Would you like to guess what happened the following spring?"

Maha smiled from the side of her mouth.

"A lateral move this time. Shipped off to Kuala Lumpur," he said before she could answer. "A bigger office with another special assignment, but at least they could control him. Isolate him somewhere basically for damage control." He shook his head in disbelief. "He's still there, as far as I know. The man has been promoted so many times—which used to mean something, by the way, something positive—and now he has to be effectively quarantined, so he doesn't infect others with his idiocy."

She smiled again, a private dialogue taking place in her head. "No, no, not bitter at all." She pursed her lips but in the end couldn't help herself and began to laugh. He gave in as well, swatting the air dismissively as he finished his glass of wine.

"I'm only joking," she said. "Unfortunately, I know exactly what you mean. I have to admit I was a bit naïve as well when I started. Many people warned me against it, my mother most of all—'Find yourself a nice man. You're a great cook.'" She rolled her eyes. "'Did you know Omar is studying to be a doctor?' Actually, my father was one of the only ones who encouraged me, but he warned me about the politics. Here, there is a lot of it, and I mean *actual* politics. Promotions have a lot to do with who you support." She paused. "Depending on who's in power at the moment," she added in a hushed tone. "People end up in jail all the time for, how do you say, *trivial* things. Not to mention religion. If you're Coptic, you can forget about any kind of advancement. I can't tell you how many Christian friends of mine have emigrated to the United States, Canada. Like you, I knew all of this before, but it's different, *yanni . . .* seeing it yourself." She mumbled something in Arabic. "You have to learn to let it go."

The waiter appeared, clearing dishes and inquiring about desserts. They ordered Turkish coffee, and Maha, momentarily indecisive, settled on the apple-flavored shisha. "The grape is too sweet for tonight," she said.

"It's all too sweet for me," he replied, pulling a cigarette from the pack with his lips.

When the waiter returned, he carried a shimmering tray: two elegantly engraved silver *zarfs* cradling porcelain cups, a matching sugar tin, and a steaming *ibrik* with a polished wooden handle. As he poured the thick coffee, another man arrived with an opulent pipe, tall and curvaceous, placing three coals neatly atop the clay bowl. Maha puffed from the slender hose approvingly, shuffled the coals about with metal tongs, then turned her attention back to Quinn.

"As I said, you have to learn to let it go. But I suppose it wouldn't be much help telling you to just accept things the way they are . . ."

"You suppose right," he said. "Now who's being naïve?"

"You remember our favorite Arabic expression, don't you?"

"*Khalas?*"

"*Insha'Allah.*"

"God willing."

"Exactly. I'm not as devout as my family wishes I was, but I still have my faith. I don't believe that going to mosque or praying for something will make it so, but a degree of peace comes with the ritual. You know, I was in Jerusalem last year with a friend. We went to the church where Jesus was crucified."

"Sounds like a strange place for a crucifixion."

She clucked her tongue at him. "Quinn. Anyhow, the church, I don't remember the name, but it was built on the remains of where he was crucified. Ah, Golgotha, that's right. Honestly, how do I know more about this than you?"

He shrugged, eyebrows lifted in defense.

"As I said, we were there, and in the lowest chamber, very far down, the closest to the remains of the site, there's an altar with candles and flowers. It was very nice, actually. People paying their respects in their own ways. And then I saw on the wall, someone had carved into the stone: 'Jesus, please help me with my money problems.' Can you believe it? Honestly. Even as a Muslim, I was offended." The pipe gurgled as the water churned, Maha inhaling deeply from the serpentine hose.

"Acceptance is the most important," she said, blowing a long trail of smoke into the air, "accepting that some things can be changed, and this is where you work to make a difference, do what you can. The others, there is patience, a *wisdom*, to recognize what is out of our hands and in the hands of . . . something far greater than ourselves." She read his expression and looked at him inquisitively. "You don't agree?"

"Partially. If you never make the effort, if you never try, how do you know what can't be changed? I have the free will to sit here, drink this coffee, stand, go somewhere else. At any moment I can alter the situation. So, how am I supposed to know what can or can't be changed?"

"I suppose that would be the *wisdom* part," she said dryly, looking him up and down. "Like most men, only hearing what you want to hear." Her eyes flickered mischievously. "Still, *wallahi*, I'm serious. I find it very comforting. It allows me to focus my efforts. And that's exactly what I mean with faith or spirituality, whatever you want to call it. Believe me, I've had plenty of frustrations trying to help women in a patriar, partical—"

"Patriarchal."

"—society like this one, but I try my best to accept what I can do, and leave the rest. We used to be so liberal, you know. The hijab was a rarity when my mother was in school. I've seen pictures of her in party dresses with flowing hair, I even saw one where she was wearing a bikini! Can you imagine? On the beach, in Alexandria. She was beautiful." She sighed. "Women were far more free to make their own decisions. But, I'm only one person, and I take comfort in that. I work hard to make improvements, focus my efforts, and when I get frustrated, angry, or upset, I embrace my faith and accept that some things—many things, are simply out of my control." She gave a subtle shrug. "A glass of wine doesn't hurt either."

For a little while, Quinn felt something that he hadn't felt in quite some time: a fleeting sense of normalcy. Pleasant company, a conversation over dinner; it stung when thoughts of Mei returned to the fore, and he considered how Maha's personal mantra would have to wait.

A curling plume of smoke drifted above her head, and she looked as though she had read his thoughts, speaking almost on cue. "Now, what can I help you with? What brings you to Cairo?"

He exhaled heavily through his nose, stubbing out his cigarette in a silver tin, and met her eyes across the table, patient, expectant. There was no simple way to begin, but his hesitation seemed to set the shifting mood. She looked at him differently now, a hint of concern across her face. Resting his elbows on the table, he locked his hands and stared into the darkened garden, entranced by a glowing lamp that hung from a tree branch.

"Hear me out, from the beginning. I need you to have an open mind." He shook his head wearily. "At this point, I don't even know where, I don't know if I'm . . ." He lit another cigarette and tried, in vain, to attract the attention of a nearby waiter. Maha caught the man's eye with a wave, ordering a whiskey.

And then he told her. She remained still—sunk into her chair, a perennial halo of fruity smoke hovering in the night air—as he recounted everything from the beginning. The day he met Mei, disheveled and abandoned in a ramshackle hut. The yearly visits to Battambang, the tutoring and the letters. Then the night it all changed. The kidnappers, if one could call them that. Smugglers. Traffickers. He skirted around the whiskey-soaked days that followed. To Cambodia. Areum the florist, the good fortune of a clue, and the even better fortune that it actually led, in a roundabout way, to something tangible. Ling, the forger, the passport. All the passports.

As he recounted everything aloud, he was caught between two minds. The chain of events made sense—sequential, charting a logical path to follow, and he was buoyed by the possibilities. And then, like the shift of a desert wind, the story began to transform; chock-full of desperation and misguided hope, an alcoholic finding clues where his pickled mind had created them the night before.

"And, aside from Noi, you're the only person who knows about any of this." He took a deep breath, tipped back the last of his whiskey, and motioned to the waiter, who was more attentive this time. "A double. *Shukran.*"

After some moments of quiet contemplation, Maha spoke slowly in a comforting tone. "You're not crazy. At least no crazier than I already knew," she said, trying to lighten the mood.

"Tell me, am I losing the plot here?" he asked. "I feel I've used up all my good luck already, and still, everything points to here. To Cairo. As unbelievable as that may sound."

She nodded, thoughtfully. "It's incredible. Mm . . . it is. But, I don't think you're entirely wrong, Quinn. I didn't know you had, well, why would I—and now, following her like this. You said it yourself, what was the expression—needle in hay? At first it can sound unbelievable, but it's not *that* unbelievable. Asia is not my field, but here in our region, trafficking is a real problem as well. We both know how it works—South Asians brought over for labor, the nannies and domestic servants. Sex work also. This is nothing new."

"Exactly."

She leaned in, locking her eyes on him—no tears, no quivering bottom lip, her expression hard, determined. "Quinn, whatever I can do to help, just let me know. This is my field and my city, I have contacts. I'll look into it, of course, if you'll allow me."

"At this point just telling me I'm not crazy is enough."

She shook her head. "Honestly, I don't think you are." They sat in silence for a few moments. "And I would tell you."

The waiter reappeared and placed a glass and a napkin on the table.

"In fact, I may have another piece of good luck for you."

He nodded.

"I'll reach out to some of my colleagues, find out more about how the trade works here, specifically with foreign victims—we tend to focus more on domestic issues, of course. A lot of what they call 'summer marriages.' But I do know a man who might be able to help you. He can be difficult sometimes but nothing you can't handle." She gasped unexpectedly with a chuckle. "A true *Scrooge*, this man. But a good one, nonetheless. He was like a mentor to me when others were encouraging me to choose a different path.

He's much older now but still an authority on the subject—human smuggling, trafficking, these sorts of abuses. I can set up a meeting for you. I'm sure he will make himself available. He has nothing else to do."

"That would be great, Maha."

"I'm warning you; he can be a grouch, but this is his specialty. He's the man you want to speak to."

TWENTY-FIVE

Thunder reverberated in his chest, and the crackle of lightning jolted him upright from his bedsheets. A veneer of cold sweat was slick across his forehead, his heart pounding, nerves on edge. For a moment, utter confusion. Was he awake or still dreaming? Where was he? Cairo. The Shafiq residence.

Once more he heard the distant rumble of clattering noise, unrecognizable in the dark, disorienting room. He listened. No rain. No droplets. Then it came again, the piercing staccato explosions, the chanting of a thousand monks, the wailing of banshees.

He flung himself from the bed, fumbling in the dark for the light switch. He flicked it on, then off, then on again. *Rolling blackouts.* He felt his way along the wall, eyes straining through the black toward the dim light at the end of the hallway. He concentrated on the commotion outside, the crescendo of unexplained sounds as he glided his palm along the cool wall. The living room came into a grainy focus, the moon providing a glimmer of light through the windows. Crouching to peer through the glass, he stopped, cursing softly in the darkness, a radiator abruptly halting the stride of his big toe.

His eyes adjusted. With two fingers he moved the curtain aside and peered out into the street, scanning the mob of citizenry that marched in unison. A belligerent crowd of men and women, swaying and heaving like a living creature, flooded down the narrow street between adjacent rows of parked cars. These were no monks, but the chanting was real, each of them shouting slogans in unison, faces angrily contorted, fists pumping in the night sky. Some held banners, red and black cursive Arabic scrolled on white placards, while others waved Egyptian flags, fluttering large and small. In the midst of the great moving creature, a car sounded its horn every now and again, adding to the symphony of protest, competing with the marshal at the front, who led the proceedings. He marched with purpose, a thick beard and spectacles, conducting his orchestra with a megaphone in one hand, saluting aggressively with the other.

Quinn straightened himself and breathed a deep sigh of relief. He ran his fingers through his hair, damp now at the roots. The procession went on for several minutes—at once full of passion and vigor yet disinterested in casual onlookers such as himself—until the last stragglers brought up the rear, a dispersed group of young men seemingly attending more out of boredom than any noticeable enthusiasm for the cause.

Quinn's heartrate slowed, steadied, and finally returned to a resting pace as he collapsed back into bed, the sheets cool and damp from perspiration. He stared at the ceiling as the cacophony outside drifted farther and farther away. The static of the megaphone faded, the chorus of voices barely a hum, the great creature fading back into the recesses of the night, back into the dreamless slumber from whence it came.

A restless night was followed by a restless dawn. At a simple teashop around the corner, he breakfasted on Afghan milk tea and crisp falafel before making his way to the UN building once more. He poked his nose into Maha's office, picked up a few documents—including the final project report on Roumieh Prison—in order to cobble together a preliminary outline of a lecture.

The conference was hardly a priority, but he had reserved part of the afternoon to draft some semblance of a speech until he was informed that Maha, with remarkable efficiency, had already arranged a meeting with her so-called Uncle Youssef for that very evening. He would never admit it, she said, but the old man, long since retired, was rather flattered and eager to feel useful once again.

Afterward, Quinn spent the better part of an hour on a deserted café patio making notes on the project's methodology—activities, measurable outputs, monitoring, and evaluation—while a host of flies buzzed relentlessly around his espresso cup. The rest, he figured, he could manage off the cuff, rounding out the hour with a brief question-and-answer period.

With the spare laptop that Maha had lent him, he conducted some exploratory research on domestic trafficking issues facing the country, cross-referencing journal articles and scholarly pieces online with a pile of documents collected from Hannah's office.

Many of the news articles centered around the relatively recent execution of an infamous local criminal nicknamed Al-Tourbini. A street gang leader put to death for the rape and murder of over thirty children, his moniker derived from his preferred method of abuse: torturing and then pitching the bodies of his victims from the roofs of express trains.

Beyond such sensational headlines, there wasn't a great deal of information regarding summer marriages or any particularly unique trends in relation to prostitution and vice. Many arrangements took place, as one might expect, in hotels and short-term rental units. Combing through maps of the seamier pockets of the city, he couldn't help but chuckle at some of the apartment names he came across: *Deluxe* this and *Luxury* that, and, not to be outdone, the chain of *Luxury Deluxe* hotels, evidently the most extravagant of them all.

Later, he took a grimy walk in the oppressive heat along El Nahda Street to Koilet Al Nasr Square, a dizzying roundabout whirring with local traffic and situated just to the south of the Grand Maadi Mall. At the mall entrance, a couple of thin, mustachioed security guards wanded patrons with metal detectors, checking purses and handbags, even a young girl in an *abbaya,* a child no more than eight or nine. When they spotted Quinn climbing the stairs, they gave him a perfunctory nod and let him pass—his pale, Scandinavian face apparently all the affirmation they required.

Inside, the Grand Maadi Mall was far removed from the grandeur of its title. It was drab and run-down, a handful of shoppers meandering throughout. It had a café and a smoking lounge on the ground level where the ever present fumes had managed to permeate the walls, tawny blotches staining the tile floor as well as the high ceiling, stories above. For the conference, he picked up a shirt and slacks, not bothering with a tie; a pair of boots to replace his worn shoes, and, on the way out, made a detour past the florist where he purchased a bouquet of sunflowers and hypericum.

He hailed a taxi from Al Nadi Square, another frenzied intersection where multi-colored vehicles jostled for position, warring horns clamoring for attention. While it didn't take long for a driver to oblige him, the state of the vehicle left much to be desired. The driver, an elderly man with a *taqiyah* cap and matching white stubble, agreed, somewhat reluctantly, to take him across town but remained visibly anxious about the distance to Heliopolis.

Squeezing into the sunken passenger seat, Quinn's knees rose nearly to chest height, the worn fabric beneath resting just above whatever sheet metal separated his pants from the asphalt. The door's inside paneling was missing, wires and levers exposed, the side-view mirror tethered by a fraying strip of duct tape.

His chauffeur seemed keen on making good time, flooring the gas pedal with purpose whenever an opening presented itself, then inevitably stomping the brake only moments later, the momentum folding Quinn's torso like an accordion. With a firm grip on the wheel and a sweaty sheen on his forehead, the man whispered a prayer before every speed bump or pothole, then another swiftly afterwards, pleading with the divine for the car not to smoke, stall, or crumble altogether.

The traffic wasn't as bad as anticipated—thankfully, without a single checkpoint—and Quinn tipped his chauffeur generously—a look of grateful relief having spread across his face—when he was dropped off along a wide, tree-lined boulevard. The building and the entire street was constructed in a unique Neo-Islamist style: handsomely rounded archways and ornate balconies lending a feeling of timeless elegance, the neighborhood embodying a classic style all its own. Much like Maadi, Heliopolis had its own distinctive character amongst the dense, expansive sprawl of the indefatigable city.

Inside, he climbed the stairs while a couple of *burka*-clad young women descended, eyeing him curiously through black lashes and giggling, hand in hand, once they passed. On the fifth floor, he knocked three times at the door and fiddled with the sunflowers, which were clearly struggling with the midday heat.

He heard some shuffling behind the heavy door before it swung open, revealing a middle-aged woman with a beaming smile and warm, inviting laugh lines. She wore a tightly wound cream hijab and a pale-blue abaya, a strip of golden embroidery down the middle.

"Mr. Mills?" she said excitedly.

"Quinn, please. And thank you for inviting me. For you."

"Ahh, so beautiful! Come in, my dear, please, please, come. I am Noor. Youssef is just in the den. Youssef?" she called.

The home smelled of baked spices, cinnamon and coriander, the air warm and enveloping. The living room was large, featuring antique dressers, an enormous bookshelf overflowing in every capacity, and a lengthy dining table with crisp linen and a fruit bowl. An accent wall of ashen brick held a large mirror framed in elaborate gold trim and reflected a glass chandelier that pulled the room together. It was clear where Youssef spent his time; a weathered, beige armchair with a prominent dent contrasted with a maroon sectional adorned with decorative pillows. In front of the chair was a matching footstool and, by the wall, a small television showing a muted football match on a grainy screen.

"Let me get a vase for these beauties," she said, shuffling into the kitchen. "Maha tells me you are old friends from work?"

"Yes. We met in Lebanon a few years ago."

"And so handsome. Tell me, Quinn, are you married?"

"Enough, enough," came a gruff voice from down the hall. "The man is hardly through the door, and already you're asking."

"Just making conversation," she replied, a teasing smile for both men.

"You don't have to answer that. Quinton Mills. Youssef Nasser," he said with an outstretched hand. A firm handshake.

He was much older than Quinn had imagined and not in particularly good shape. He wore a white *thobe* that had seen a lot of use, billowing outwards where his belly protruded. His left hand rested on a varnished wooden cane, gripping what appeared to be the bronze head of an eagle. He was not a classically handsome man. He had sunken, pock-marked cheeks and a prominent, hawkish nose, though his smile was proud, and there was a genuine warmth in his eyes, half hidden by tired, drooping lids.

"Nasser. Any relation?"

"No, but you should meet my brother, Gamal Abdel."

"You're serious."

"He was born the day he took power. My father named him in his honor."

"Those are some big shoes to fill."

"Indeed. Though we should both consider ourselves fortunate. I was almost a Ramses."

Noor set the bouquet on the table and then rejoined them, whispering something in Youssef's ear.

"*Hayati*, please, English in front of our guest."

Noor tsk'ed him with her tongue. "Your *thobe*, look—you couldn't have worn a different one?" She pointed to two small holes in the worn fabric. Youssef raised an arm to inspect his right side.

"What?" he replied, palms open and pleading. "It's for ventilation."

"*Ya lawhi*," she shook her head, first at her husband, then apologetically at Quinn, before gliding back down the hall.

The old man's beleaguered shuffle led them to the living room where he stopped in front of the television and muttered something derogatory in Arabic. The match, apparently from the Egyptian league, had one team in jubilant celebration.

"Fools. Utter fools. Unbelievable. Do you follow football, Mr. Mills?" he asked, still facing the screen.

"Not closely, no."

"No matter." He waved his hand dismissively. "For the best. My doctor says it's not good for my blood pressure. And by doctor, of course, I mean my wife." He jutted his chin toward the kitchen.

"Who's playing?"

"Al Ahly." Facing the television once more, brow creased, he scrutinized a replay. "Fools, truly. Ah, no matter. Come, have a seat."

He carefully navigated the coffee table with his cane and plopped down into the armchair with a heaving sigh of relief.

"Would you mind?" He gestured to the footstool, which Quinn obligingly positioned, before taking his own seat on the adjacent sofa.

"Everything you need to know about my country you can learn from football," he said, shaking his head toward the screen. "Everyone wants to be Messi, Ronaldo, Salah. Everyone wants to be the hero. They ignore the most vital aspects of the game. Defending, positioning, tactics. And now look—a team full of strikers with fancy tricks and losing because they play selfishly like this. Never as a *team*. Two nil this late in the game; it might as well be ten." He finally turned his attention away from the match. "And this is Egypt, Mr. Mills. Everyone pulling in different directions. A lack of unity for the common good."

"Already with the politics," Noor said, sweeping back into the room. She carried a bronze coffee tray stacked with a teapot, cups, and sweets made from honeyed pastry and pistachios. "My husband can be so very negative sometimes," she said, rolling her eyes.

The couple exchanged a few words in Arabic, Youssef inquiring about a certain tin of biscuits that had sadly disappeared, though Quinn's rudimentary Arabic failed to interpret the rest of the conversation.

"You'll stay for dinner," Youssef said. "Yes, of course you will." A rhetorical question, apparently, followed by more Arabic and Noor nodding in agreement before disappearing down the corridor.

"So then, tell me, Mr. Mills, what brings you to Cairo? I should apologize for the current state of affairs. I hope you didn't have any trouble getting here, roadblocks and such things."

"No, not at all. Much quicker than I expected, actually. Maha said sometimes it takes her up to three hours to get home from work."

"Yes, unfortunately, this is the way things are at the moment, and for some time now. We have been in a state of, turbulence, one might say, since 2011. In some form or another." He shook his head. "But that's not why you're here. What exactly did Maha tell you?"

"That you're something of an authority in your field and that she holds your opinion in high regard."

He smiled from the corner of his mouth. "Maha, sharp as a whip, that girl, and a tongue that can sting just the same. Though I'm glad she hasn't forgotten my advice about old men."

"Which is?"

"That we're never too old for a bit of flattery," he said with a wink. He strained to lean forward in his chair. "Help yourself, please, and pour me one with a splash of white, if you don't mind."

Quinn did as he was told.

"And just what did she say was my area of expertise?"

"I guess they call it a lot of different things these days," Quinn said, reaching for the cream. "Trafficking in persons, modern slavery."

"Mm . . . yes. Slavery. Such an old-fashioned term. Though I must admit, I prefer it to this *human trafficking*," Youssef said, making a face. "Anyone who hears this word, 'trafficking,' all they think about is narcotics. Pablo Escobar and the cartels. Why not simply call it what it is? Slavery! This is Egypt, for heaven's sake. Land of the pharaohs. They had a few slaves themselves, you might have heard. Long before this new, fashionable terminology. Anyhow, thank you," he said, reaching for his cup.

"How were you involved? Your work, I mean."

"You know, it was a most unexpected thing. I'm a physician by training; that's how I began my career. By the end I was advising on a number of issues, working very closely with the NCCM—the Council for Childhood and Motherhood—the big Western NGOs that are here now, the local ones as well. But it was during my early placements that I learned just how poor the country's health system was—the poverty and, of course, the desperation that comes from this.

"I did my early work in remote villages, rural communities. The lack of education was worrying and remains so, and the poor treatment of women was evident in my practice. Women and children becoming quite ill, contracting various ailments, many dying because of simple hygienic problems. Easily avoidable, you know. Yes, and a very poor understanding of a woman's physiology as well." He made a sound somewhere deep in his throat. "And all of this, when combined with a basic understanding of Islam, how can I say, a *rudimentary* interpretation—it was an education in many ways.

"Tell me, Mr. Mills," he continued, taking a sip of coffee, "what is it that's on your mind? Your company is welcome, of course, but Maha was quite vague on the telephone. She said that I should ask you myself why you've come to Egypt and why you're inquiring about such a topic."

Quinn nodded, looking upward with a heavy sigh, palms open. "Where to start? I have reason to believe that someone close to me was brought here against her will. To where exactly, I don't know. How? I don't know that either. And as much as I want to find her, I try not to think about the reason why. I'm familiar with some of the smuggling routes in Asia, how the networks operate, but here, in Egypt, I'm out of my depth."

Youssef gave him a contemplative look. "A man lost at sea. Or in the sand, I should say."

"Something like that."

Youssef cleared his throat and exhaled loudly through his nostrils. "I'm sorry for your burden. I wish we were meeting under different circumstances."

Quinn gave a nod of thanks.

"You haven't considered going to the police?" the old man asked, eyeing him closely.

"With all due respect, I don't have much faith in your authorities. If what I believe did happen, I'm more than certain they were complicit, border officials at the very least. I have reservations about involving anyone in uniform, to be completely honest."

Youssef held his gaze for a long moment, studying his guest. "You're smarter than you look, Mr. Mills."

TWENTY-SIX

Noor had prepared a feast and distributed the dishes with pride across the coffee table. Grilled chicken legs with lemon, rosemary, and thyme; chilled eggplant *fatteh*—roasted aubergine smeared with yogurt and topped with pine nuts; an accompanying bowl of coriander hummus, emerald green, served with warm pita and a steaming pot of yellow tea. As they dined, Youssef, quite content to have an audience, lectured on various themes, his thick lips glistening with chicken fat.

"In addition to the corruption, our borders make the situation even more complex. We have become something of a transit point, a hub for Africa and what you Westerners insist on referring to as the *Middle* East. These routes are hardly new, of course; they go back to ancient times, as you may well know. We have a rich trading history with what was then Mesopotamia, the same caravan routes later employed by the Romans. Goods have always been traded across these lands." He paused thoughtfully for a sip of tea. "For better or for worse.

"For these traffickers, as they're called, humans are moved in much the same ways. Many end up in Israel, for example. Girls from Eastern Europe, they're often brought south and, for a price, through Egypt to be sold in Tel Aviv. The opposite is also true—Asians, Africans—moved north through our borders into Europe, and after that, who knows where they might find themselves in the end? With the ongoing troubles in Syria and Iraq, there are increasing avenues—trafficking *flows,* I've heard them called—into Turkey, our historical bridge between the continents.

"The Sinai presents its own challenges, a particularly lawless stretch of land, but the Bedouins, many of them are so deeply involved in such matters that it has become tradition. No one knows the desert like they do, how to avoid detection in the sand, the mountains. They serve as guides, and they're well compensated. Perhaps if you told me a bit more about who you're looking for, the circumstances, I could be of better assistance."

Quinn was listening intently, staring at the floor, processing, trying to put the pieces together. He wiped his fingers with a napkin, then reached into his pocket for a passport and a photograph, handing them across. Youssef didn't bother with a napkin, glancing around instead for his glasses, a set of smeared bifocals with rectangular frames, and made some deep and knowing sounds as he examined the front page of the document. It was a miracle he could see anything at all through the smudged lenses.

"Is it genuine?" he asked.

"The picture, yes. The passport? I'm not so sure."

"I'm hardly an authority, but it looks fairly good."

"If it's not real, it's an excellent fake. I have others. They've substituted the pictures. Some are still blank though. I'm not sure what else they've altered."

"And she is . . . twelve?"

"Yes."

"Hm . . ."

Noor reappeared with the same iridescent smile, asking about the meal and clearing plates, returning a moment later to place two crystal dessert bowls on the table: rice pudding atop a layer of crushed dates, finished with a light dusting of cinnamon.

"How much do you know about summer marriages, Mr. Mills?"

Quinn shook his head. "Not much. Similar to marriages of convenience, I'm assuming."

"A one-sided convenience."

"Of course."

"Similar, yes, but not identical, not exactly. Let me get back to my early practice. You see, the lack of education in these rural communities meant that, in addition to domestic abuse and battery cases, I would see many young girls as a result of gynecological concerns. Rather simple issues often with simple solutions—poor hygiene, infections—these sort of matters. However, there were also a great many complications resulting from circumcisions, those that weren't done properly. If you can call such a thing *proper*."

"There's been a law passed, somewhat recently . . ."

"There has, but you know as well as I do that the practice continues. Especially in these communities. I cannot recall the numbers offhand. It varies depending on whom you speak to. Still, eighty, ninety percent of Egyptian women have undergone this FGM, as they call it, female genital mutilation. It's tradition for these people, and an important one, in their minds, ensuring their daughters remain pure and chaste. Many men prefer their wives this way."

He gestured with his hand, getting off track. "As I was saying, this is the approach to women. Instances of rape, domestic assault, all of this is related. It is a symptom of poverty, desperation, even ignorance. For instance, these families, they sleep together in close quarters with little privacy—a bedsheet, perhaps, drawn across the room. A boy, he sees his parents making love, so what does he do? The next day he finds a young girl and does the same as his father. And why not? No one has taught him that he's doing anything wrong.

"Soon, I began making note of more peculiar cases, as if these issues weren't concerning enough. Young girls, nothing to do with genital cutting or menstruation but rather, sexual abuse. Girls, not women, having engaged in intercourse, clear signs of penetration, suffering from a variety of physical wounds. Not to mention the psychological trauma. It became quite routine, occasionally the same girls several times over the course of a summer.

"Perhaps I was naïve. I studied hard, buried my head in books much of the time. My passion was seeing the problem for what it was, addressing it there and then with a keen medical eye. I was not, how would you say, a *counselor* of any sort. It wasn't my business. Still, as a medical professional, I was concerned. Curious . . . and concerned."

Quinn struggled to control his thoughts, at once relieved to finally converse with someone who had a knowledge of the right issues yet increasingly anxious about the direction Youssef was heading.

"So, I asked others in my field, other practitioners. The families themselves said little, the girls barely saying anything at all. Later, I learned this was a form of secondary trauma. Having them recount the events can be quite distressing if done incorrectly. Regardless, after some time, it was clear that the abuse was resulting from a form of this *human trafficking*—at the time I had never heard the expression. Still, trafficking it certainly was, only a different version. Different in its application and the way the trade functions but the same principles."

"Tell me," Quinn said.

"Well, you see in Islam, one cannot simply engage in intercourse if one is not wed—it's a sin, of course, disappointing as that may be." Youssef's eyes twinkled mischievously for a moment, a fleeting glimpse of a much younger version of the doctor.

"And yet, there are ways to get around such a predicament. Summer marriages, or temporary marriages, as I've heard them called. Pleasure marriages, even, for those who lack subtlety. The concept is quite simple. A rich man approaches a destitute family in one of the many impoverished areas I've mentioned. Sadly, there is no shortage of such neighborhoods in my country. They stand out, these men, driving their luxury cars along dirt roads, vehicles worth more than all the real estate in the village. I was blind not to have seen it before."

For a few moments, Youssef was lost somewhere, a memory reaching out from the past, latching on and holding his attention until he blinked heavily, removing his glasses, free of its grasp.

"And then they simply conduct a transaction. They pay a sum for a young girl, often underage, and proceed with this as a pretext to marriage. The negotiated price is something like a dowry, you could say, and then he is free to consummate the marriage as he pleases, usually until his vacation is over and he returns home. At times these men even travel with their families—one villa for the wife and children, the other a private villa for him."

Youssef shook his head in disbelief, polishing his glasses in the fold of his *thobe*. "So then, what to do? The poverty is so widespread—generational poverty, you must understand, Mr. Mills. And with our tourism industry suffering as it has for years now since Mubarak, it is difficult to imagine. Most families are grateful. They've never seen this sort of wealth before. The transaction is often viewed as a worthy sacrifice for the good of the family. And it is the *family* that benefits. The daughter will rarely see any of this so-called dowry, which is itself going against Islamic tradition, but as I said, who is really concerned?"

"And this is primarily Egyptians? Egyptian families?"

Youssef nodded.

"What about foreign girls? Are they brought in for these sham marriages as well? Or is this only a local trend?"

"Foreign girls as well, yes. In fact, did I not mention, it's mostly foreigners who engage in the practice. Oh yes, the Gulf States primarily—Saudis, Kuwaitis, rich Emirati businessmen—these are the main clients in the country. But women are smuggled in from all over, near and far. Men too, also trafficked. Sometimes for sexual purposes, other times to meet more common labor needs."

"Domestic servants, construction, that sort of thing."

"Yes, exactly."

"What happens to the brides?"

"It depends. The union is nullified as soon as the men return to their countries. Sometimes they only last for a few days, and the girls, they adjust to their new lives. They are no longer considered virtuous enough to be married off to any reasonable suitor; no man will have them. Often they are remarried to other buyers, again and again in a cycle of these temporary unions. The luckiest ones remain indoors, helping their families. Social stigmas being what they are, there is no place in society for them any longer."

Youssef was talking matter-of-factly now, his head tilting this way and that as he recounted all his learnings, jaded and dismally acceptant of the tragic reality.

"Those who become pregnant have other dilemmas, as you can imagine. These marriages are not recognized in any true, legal capacity, hence why they are nullified when the *husband* departs.

No rights extend to any children produced by these unions. Born from children themselves, essentially; they are illegitimate, and they cannot attend school. To put it another way, they don't really exist. Some are taken back to the Gulf States or wherever the man is from, forced to work as servants for the true spouse. If the man is local, an Egyptian man who happens to marry them, it's often to lure the girl into a life of prostitution. Pimps, I believe, in English."

Quinn leaned forward in his seat, burying his face in his palms, rubbing his eyes until all the galaxies of the universe danced before him.

"I am sorry for your troubles," Youssef said. "It isn't an easy subject, particularly given your situation. I tell you this because you asked, and I believe you want to know. However, it's not to say this is the reality for your friend."

"It's fine."

"One must be careful with hope. She can be seductive, and her temperament alone can be enough to crush a man. However, the situation may not be so terrible. Street children here are often targeted for begging, to earn money for gangs. Obviously not an ideal situation, but given our topic of discussion . . ."

"How would I go about finding kids like this? If I were looking, not in local slums but for girls brought in, sold for whatever purpose."

"That I cannot tell you. I've heard of these groups working with border officials; I'm certain there are arrangements being made there. The greasing of palms, as they say. And I believe they employ code words, call signs to move their victims from location to location. Hotels, apartments, even mosques."

"What about online? Social media, Internet adverts?"

"I'm certain there are some, but how prominent these are, of that I'm not sure. I have heard some organizations are using these methods to address the demand, locating the offenders online."

"Terre des Hommes, with Sweetie."

Youssef narrowed his brow, intrigued.

"Artificial intelligence. Terre des Hommes is a Dutch NGO."

"I'm familiar, yes."

"They've created a lifelike simulation of a young Filipino girl; they call her Sweetie. It's nothing more than a computer program, but it talks, it moves, and it's helped identify thousands of pedophiles engaging in WCST."

"This term I've not heard."

"Webcam sex tourism, essentially. Men from the West use computers to exploit girls in the East, paying them online. It's cheap, it's profitable, and it's incredibly difficult to prosecute because it's transnational."

Youssef leaned back in his chair, emitting another deep exhalation through his nostrils. "This, I'm afraid, is beyond my experience."

Quinn sighed in return. "Mine as well. I've been trying to do some research, but I haven't found much." His shoulders slumped in resignation.

"It never ceases to amaze me how new technology can be manipulated. Just as much evil comes from the good. But, unfortunately, if you're looking for more modern insights, *social media*, you've got the wrong man. Even I can admit there are limits to my expertise."

"I heard that, you know," said Noor, floating by once again, gathering the dessert bowls and pouring more tea. She glanced surreptitiously at Quinn while refilling his cup. "I'm never going to let him forget that one."

"I'm nothing if not humble," Youssef replied.

"Oh, but of course, my sultan." She cast a sly wink in Quinn's direction. "Can I get you anything else? Some baklava?"

"No, no, the meal was terrific. *Shukran*."

"And what about me?" Youssef inquired.

"The baklava is for the guests, my love," she called back, already leaving down the hall, the sultan left to sulk theatrically in his armchair.

For a time they sipped their tea in silence, each considering the weight of the conversation. Quinn retreated deep into himself, evaluating the new insight, considering how to proceed, the best course of action. Eventually, Youssef released another heavy sigh of reflection. "They are beasts of the night, you know. I have always thought of them like this, these men. Hyenas. Mm . . . what do you know of them?"

"Hyenas?" Quinn replied, somewhat puzzled. "Not much. What I've seen on the nature channel, really. Scavengers. Descended from wolves, I think," he added as an afterthought.

Youssef made a low grumbling sound, an acknowledgment, but the question was rhetorical. "Vile creatures. Nocturnal, you see, only appearing in the dark of night. Sometimes you see their eyes in the shadows." He made a face, squinting left and right. "Staring at you, watching. They roam the cities now, not only the desert. In the old days, stories told of them sucking the blood of the living, like vampires. They will eat anything, not just garbage but flesh and bone, usually dead and rotting but not always. Eating their own kind. They've even been known to snatch children from their beds." He noticed the shifting expression on Quinn's face. "Oh yes, dragging them from tents in the middle of the night. Treacherous things. Preying on the innocent as they sleep. I'm not a superstitious man,

Mr. Mills, but these creatures, there's something different about them. From another world. From beyond . . ." He grunted, shaking his head. "You understand my meaning."

Quinn nodded slowly.

"These people, they prey on the most vulnerable. Sometimes alone, sometimes in packs. And when they've captured their prey, the things they do are as inhumane as the animals themselves. To do such things to your own kind . . ." The old man's shoulders sagged, as if carrying the weight of the world, and he wiped his mouth with a handkerchief, stuffing it back into the pocket from whence it came. "You know," he said, nodding to the picture on the table, "as soon as I saw her photograph, I knew this would be a difficult conversation. I am truly sorry I could not be of greater help."

"Not at all, Mr. Nasser. I appreciate your honesty. I'm under no illusions. I'm aware of what's happening. But I do have one more question."

Youssef straightened his shoulders with a nod. *Please.*

"Do you have any contacts within the government who might be able to help with the passports? Someone maybe in the Ministry of Interior who could check if they've been reported stolen, missing, anything like that?"

Youssef pursed his lips and considered this for a moment, his eyes moving across the wall as he spun a mental rolodex in his head. Finally, he threaded his fingers together in his lap. "Years ago, perhaps, but now? Nobody I would trust. I don't mean to imply that there is some vast conspiracy; however, these days you never know who is doing what or which agendas are being served. Our country has been in one form of turmoil or another for many years now. The military wrestling with the Islamists, wrestling with Western influence, with corruption. Many are doing what they can to profit from a little *baksheesh*, and their loyalties shift like the desert winds."

"Again, I appreciate your candor."

"I only wish I could be of more assistance."

"Not at all. This has been very helpful, Mr. Nasser."

"Youssef, please. And allow me to offer some parting words of advice, if I may."

The old man leaned forward, reaching for his cane and placing it in front of him, hands resting atop the kingly eagle's head. "Take great care with this endeavor. These people, to violate the young, to violate our most innocent as they do, there's no telling the limits of such beings. You can never underestimate them. And remember, what we are doing, we—those who oppose them—we seek to take away their livelihood. You must never forget this.

"This is a business—sinister and immoral—but a business just the same. They view the vulnerable as raw materials for import and export, products for sale with a specific market value. By interfering with this system, you seek to take the very food from their children's plates. They will not let things go lightly." He paused to take a deep breath. "Naturally, if I can be of any further assistance, you need only ask."

"I understand. And thank you for your concern. I don't plan on advertising my presence here more than I need to."

"You would be wise not to. These are strange times, even for us Egyptians. Given the political climate, it can be difficult to know who to trust." Then, ponderously, he added, "I imagine it may have even been difficult to come to me."

"It wasn't about you. I trust Maha."

He smiled, thick lips and heavy eyelids. "Smarter than you look, Mr. Mills."

TWENTY-SEVEN

He lurched back and forth in the passenger seat—incessant honking, interminable potholes. For two hours Quinn
endured the perpetual stop-start of the vehicle, not a singular
smooth transition from gas to brake but rather roaring, ambitious
thrusts, followed by poignant, jerking halts.

The driver, Saad, sat behind the wheel, ever vigilant, eyes scanning for brief openings amongst the vehicular chaos, darting into
space without hesitation, followed by the occasional hand gesture
at no one, and yet everyone.

Saad had been pleasant company, chatty for most of the drive,
but he was fading now, the commute finally getting to him,
perhaps. His small, round glasses were perched on his wide nose,
his dark African features contrasting with the white speckles in his
frizzy, graying hair. His family was originally from Sudan, from a
small village no one knew, he had said, but close to Abu Simbel.
In Egypt he was able to make more money for his family—a wife
and three small children—and traveled home often, his parents
advancing in age. His long, thick fingers gripped the wheel as he
peered into the traffic like a hawk.

"How are you holding up?" Quinn asked, following a lengthy
sigh from the driver's seat.

"Ah, this traffic, I am used to it. I can drive with my eyes closed. But a long evening, last night." Saad had a deep and perennially raspy voice, a throat full of gravel.

"You sure? I can take the wheel for a bit."

Saad shot him a look, acknowledging the mildest of insults. *And that's the last time we'll ever speak of that*, the look said. "If you can drive in Cairo, you can drive anywhere," he continued, the truck barreling forward into an open lane. He handled the maneuver confidently, working the gas pedal and flying onto Qasr El Nil Bridge, merging with new traffic as they soared past the famous bronze lions, the massive sculptures stoically guarding the entrance.

"I'm a driver. This is my job. Easy. But yes, today, this morning, I'm a little bit tired."

"The long night," Quinn said, watching the sunrays shimmer on the Nile flowing below.

"Short night. No sleeping."

"Kids?"

Saad let out a groan, then smacked his forehead dramatically. "You have children?"

"Me? No."

"It is a blessing. I give thanks to Allah every day for them, but sometimes"—he raised a finger in the air—"I think they will kill me." He guffawed, a hoarse sound, catching on something as it came out.

"The oldest, my son, now he's better, but before, he was the most loud of all of them. Now it's like a game we play making them go to sleep. I take one, my wife, she take one, and we hope the third one stays sleeping. And if my wife is tired or sick or something, then I am doing all of this. Yesterday night it was like this. My girls, I sing to them both, I get them sleeping, but then my son is awake. So, I go to my son—again, singing—make sure he's asleep. When he is quiet, maybe after one hours or more, again my youngest daughter is crying." He breathed a sigh of exasperation.

At the edge of the bridge, they followed a roundabout, circling the Saad Zaghloul Statue and continuing down the river embankment along Montazah Al Giza.

"You know what I am always thinking about this? Throwing the balls up in the air, like this." He pinned a knee against the steering wheel, holding it momentarily in place, and made a juggling motion with his hands. "You know, the silly man with the painted face? He is always doing this, with the balls. I don't know the English word for this."

"A clown. Yeah, juggling."

"Clown! Yes. Yes, this is how I feel with my children." Once again his arms flailed, a panicked look on his face.

Quinn laughed. "You must be getting good at it, so much practice."

"Maybe, I don't know." Saad nodded toward a small cluster of soldiers ahead who were stopping cars. "Let us see what my friends want."

The truck drifted alongside a row of pylons, the cones guiding Saad until he slowed in front of a security booth and a small entourage of men in fatigues. He chatted for a few moments with the lead officer, Quinn giving a casual wave as the man ducked to look inside, another peering through the back windows. They waited as a third soldier circled the vehicle, using a steel rod with a bolted mirror to scan its underbelly. He nodded his approval, the other uniforms stepping back as Saad rolled the truck forward, down the narrow lane, braking at the entrance of a luxurious hotel.

Saad checked his watch. "We're late. I hope Maha is not angry with me."

"We're not—I don't speak until after the break. She runs a tight ship, doesn't she?"

"She's the boss." Saad smiled, dark shadows visible beneath his spectacles. "Now, you must go—*matara shayala!*"

"Sorry?"

"It is a saying in my country. In Sudan, we say *matara shayala*, it is meaning, 'Hurry before the rain is coming, hurry, faster!'"

Quinn smiled and opened the passenger door, politely waving away a nervous bellboy. "You should go home. Get some rest."

"You know, my wife, she says this too. She says I work too much, and I need a vacation. You know what I say?" He leaned over the center console, looking up at Quinn. "This," he tapped the steering wheel, "*this* is my vacation." He barely got the words out before the thunderous chortling took hold.

Inside the grand lobby, early morning rays beamed through a palatial arched window that stretched from the marble floor to the polished chestnut ceiling. Golden curtains were drawn to reveal a splendid view of the mighty Nile, the occasional felucca drifting along its current. The light sparkled, reflecting off a grandiose chandelier. Just below, a magnificent Steinway—raven black with a tuxedoed gentleman tinkling its ivory keys. An elderly couple, presumably tourists, sat on a sofa amongst tropical plants and ornate Egyptian décor, sharing a newspaper and a pot of tea, the woman seemingly quite enjoying the pianist's latest melody.

It was difficult to miss the colossal, winding staircase that led to the second floor, the dark wood jutting into the foyer as it rose.

Quinn followed its red velvet steps until he heard the soft rumble of voices. The chorus grew louder as he passed several signs with the partnering logos of Egypt and the United Nations, before stepping forward into a sea of suits and colorful ensembles in the main banquet hall.

Looking over the hundred, perhaps hundred and fifty attendees, he was swiftly called to attention by three hijabed women seated at a registration table. He penned his name, accepted a booklet and conference agenda, and then wove his way through the crowd. His progress was slow, involving calculated shuffles and sidesteps as he passed through a haze of cigarette smoke and heavy fragrance, the room alive with hushed murmurs and the chime of cutlery on porcelain. By the side wall, a long table draped with fine linen and covered with platters of assorted pastries and croissants was bookended by two delicately balanced pyramids of cups and saucers.

The crowd was varied: jackets and ties, scarves and hijabs, crisp uniforms with polished medals and epaulets. Some of the faces were animated and engaged, leading passionate dialogues, while others noticeably feigned interest, eyes darting round as they plotted routes of escape.

For the briefest of moments, Quinn accidentally met the eyes of a tall Caucasian man in a dithering threesome. Though he glanced away immediately, the damage was done. Quinn stood alone, coffee and saucer in hand—a soft target. The man was already in full stride, eager to introduce himself. Quinn cursed his luck, dreading the prospect of compulsory small talk.

James Hutchinson—whose friends apparently called him Jimmy, as he was informed—had a firm, sweaty handshake. Quinn gave him a once-over as they exchanged pleasantries. His features were sharp and angular, a high forehead and bristly gray hair, strangely parted down the middle like an old book forever splaying open to the same page. A rather imposing figure with dark, piercing eyes, he didn't make for very pleasant company.

"Quite the turnout, isn't it?" Jimmy said, scanning the room and nodding with approval. He stood awkwardly, shifting his weight from side to side.

"Looks to be."

"Who are you with?"

"I suppose you could say I'm with the hosts. The UN side."

Jimmy nodded. "USAID. I guess I should be thanking you for the invitation."

"Not mine. I'm just presenting."

"On?"

"Prison reform."

"Ah."

And with that, an awkward and rather inevitable silence opened like a chasm between the two men as they stood and sipped their coffees in unison.

"I know one of the main organizers of the event," Quinn said, extending an olive branch. "She asked me to do a brief segment last minute. What's your focus?"

"Water sanitation and agriculture. We work mostly in rural communities, capacity-building projects and that sort of thing. Actually, we've been scaling back our projects of late. Rumor has it that Washington is cinching up the old purse strings."

Quinn nodded, taking another sip of coffee and allowing Jimmy to talk at length about his accomplishments, of which, evidently, there were many. Every now and again Quinn prompted the man with a few thoughtful nods to avoid speaking himself, which was just fine by Jimmy, who continued his monologue, detailing the finer points of aquifer depletion in Tunisia and all of his progressive solutions.

"Hm?"

"Your talk. When are you up?" Jimmy asked.

"After the first break."

"Well, I'm looking forward to it."

"You say that now. Just wait till people find out you're USAID and start asking you to write checks."

Quinn spotted an opportunity—over the shoulder of a red-headed woman in a green sweater, a couple of groupings away. Wearing a tight gray jacket and mustard-yellow tie, Marchand, brow furrowed with concentration, was doing his best to follow a discussion, holding a saucer piled high with assorted biscuits.

"Jim, I hope you don't mind, but I have to introduce you to someone. He's our authority on all things environmental, really passionate about the topic."

"That right?"

"Absolutely." Quinn motioned with his head. "The office would be lost without him. I think you'll really hit it off."

Slowly navigating through the negative space between the crowds, Quinn sidled up to the foursome and introduced himself with a big smile. "Pardon me. I'm sorry to interrupt, but there's a gentleman here who Marchand absolutely must meet."

The redhead seemed pleased, her eyes wide as she awaited the introduction. The two Arab men alongside her, wearing identical brown suits, appeared rather indifferent. Marchand gave nothing away, but chewed a little faster now, preemptively wiping his hand on a napkin.

"Sir, this is Jim Hutchinson with USAID. He's a specialist in water sanitation projects and environmental preservation."

"Well, I don't know about *specialist*," Jimmy said, a rather awkward attempt at humility, shaking hands all around.

"Aw, don't be modest," Quinn said. "As I was saying, Marchand here, he's basically our environmental guru. I don't know where we'd be without him."

The guru forced a smile, trying to keep up.

"And with our regional manager being on the road so much—you know how it is—he's essentially our de facto head of office."

"Oh, do I *ever*," the woman said, waving a wrist. "Honestly, back at the mission, if 'Henrik Sorensen' wasn't printed on all the stationary, I'd hardly remember the man's name." Everyone smiled at this.

"Exactly," Quinn said, leaning in conspiratorially. "Let's be honest, we all know who the real leaders are, behind the scenes. Marchand, what was the latest initiative we were discussing the other day? Something about the benefits of recycling wastewater in the Sahel, reducing the costs of land irrigation, I believe."

Marchand cleared his throat, about to speak.

"Anyhow, I'm hardly an expert," Quinn said, "but I'll leave you to it. Apologies again for the interruption, I should review my notes before we get started. Nice to meet you all." Courteous nods went around the circle, with the exception of Marchand, slightly flushed in the cheeks and already being queried about his views on ground-water depletion.

Having bought himself a few moments of peace, Quinn stood off to one side and considered how best to make use of the attendees. Surely there were some officials milling about who could be trusted—a young, idealistic prosecutor; an incorruptible detective, perhaps. Earlier, he had spotted some uniformed policewomen in pressed suits and gold-trim caps, fairly certain they would be sympathetic to his cause. While he wasn't overly optimistic, he had brought along a few passports in case the proper resources presented themselves.

In the midst of the chattering crowd, a familiar face leaned out from a small cluster of women, drawing his attention. Dressed in a fashionable navy business suit and turquoise hijab, Maha tilted her head—eyes wide, brows raised—and tapped her wristwatch dramatically. He returned the look with a shrug and the most diffident of smiles, receiving a subtle shake of the head in reply, an expression filled more with relief than reprimand. A different Maha today—conservatively dressed, clipboard in hand—firmly in her element, managing proceedings.

It wasn't long before everyone was ushered into the grand lecture hall, the conference formally commencing with an inaugural photoshoot of the panel, followed rather predictably by official introductions, complete with all the requisite self-congratulation.

Six elderly men, distinguishable only by their mustaches or reading glasses, sat atop the elevated front stage. A woman in modest business attire sat off to the right, presumably to add some semblance of balance to the proceedings. A few other characters, wearing the snide, crooked-mouthed grins of seasoned politicians, stood here and there—behind the table, beside a flag, resting their hands on the shoulders of seated colleagues—while a horde of media types flocked to the back of the room, hoisting video cameras and taking photographs. The lone woman took to the podium, evidently some sort of administrator, and heaped praise on the distinguished panel.

"To his excellency, the Minister of the Interior . . . to his excellency the deputy Minister of Justice . . . representatives, distinguished guests, ladies and gentlemen . . ."

Forty-five minutes later, the audience had been thoroughly regaled with just how significant the contributions of these prestigious individuals were—so significant, in fact, that apparently there was no need for them to attend the rest of the seminar. The esteemed gentlemen were escorted back into the foyer, followed by their harem of media personnel, and when the first speaker was finally introduced, she found that her time slot had been reduced by roughly twenty minutes.

General Fatima Ibrahim Al-Hashimi was a senior member of the all-women's police force. Through a pair of crackling headphones, Quinn listened to the static-filled translation as she spoke at length of their efforts, achievements, and the challenges faced by a new female unit on the streets of Cairo. It was a passionate speech, though the mood was rather anticlimactic following the celebrity panel and camera flashes beforehand, the general appearing somewhat isolated now, alone on the empty stage.

In the agenda, Quinn scanned her biography: a master's degree from here, a doctorate from there, a member of this charitable group and that grassroots initiative, fluent in English, French, Arabic, and Farsi. However, undeniably of greatest significance was that beneath her immaculate blazer, proudly adorned with a colored service ribbon, she sported a set of large, stately breasts, promptly invalidating her every achievement, academic or otherwise.

At 10:30, the scheduled time for the first coffee break, several men stood while the general was still speaking, shuffled out of their row, and left the room. A minute later, others joined them, casually filtering out the doors. Their departure was nonchalant and seemingly without pretense, merely an honest demonstration that coffee and cigarettes took precedence over whatever this woman had to say.

As she concluded her speech, there were no questions, but she did receive rousing applause from everyone who remained seated—women, in the large majority. The general, visibly moved by the reception, stayed behind for a time to shake hands and pose for photos as the rest of the crowd retreated into the foyer for the interval.

A dense and lingering haze of smoke clung to the ceiling. Servers in smart black vests snaked through the crowd with platters of savory dishes and canapés, pausing every now and again for nimble fingers. Amidst the fog, Quinn spotted Heidi, the intern, clutching a clipboard and looking paler than usual. He felt a nostalgic pang of empathy for the young girl, a bewildered expression upon her freckled face.

"How are you holding up?" he asked.

She blinked twice, waking from her trance. "Oh, fine, just fine. How are you? Ready for your talk?"

He grunted a sort of chuckle. "You don't have to put on a show for me, Heidi. First conference? It's quite a lot, I know. You're doing great."

Smiling timidly, she looked to the floor and back. "Is it that obvious?"

"Not at all. Like I said, you're doing great. Maha speaks very highly of you."

"It's a little overwhelming. I don't remember anybody's name! We're introduced and then the next minute . . ." She looked skywards, exasperated. "I have the worst memory."

"Don't worry about it. They don't remember yours either." He glanced around the room. "I've always hated this shit, you know.

The *networking*. I don't know why they call it that. Pretending to care as some complete stranger flaps their gums. Just waiting for that opening—a position with better pay? A longer contract? *What's in it for me?*"

She laughed nervously. "Wow, how do you really feel?"

He shrugged. "Maybe it's just me. I've never introduced myself out of the blue without an agenda. Can't say I've ever had some burning desire to learn about a stranger's personal accomplishments, how little Johnny is doing in school, how they're enjoying the city. I wanted to know if they had a job for me—or if they would in the future." After a moment he shook his head apologetically. "Sorry, I shouldn't be projecting my disgruntled views onto you. You're all fresh faced and excited. Don't let me taint your perspective."

Heidi laughed. "Just how young do you think I am?" She blushed slightly. "I guess I see your point though. I admit I've had similar thoughts. It's nice to hear someone else say it. I've never been blessed with the gift of the gab."

"You'll be alright. It comes with time. You're just very polite. You can't be humble; you need to sell yourself quickly, in the briefest of conversations."

She nodded slowly, pondering this.

"Have you eaten yet? No? You should. Here, tip number two. See that plump Egyptian fellow by the door? Red tie."

She craned her neck, nodding.

"Look where he's standing, the doors. Notice anything?"

She shook her head.

"That's where the servers come out."

As if on cue, a waiter with an empty silver platter blurred along the side wall and disappeared through the swinging double doors.

"See? It's not his first rodeo; he knows. Any new plate of hors d'oeuvres that emerges through those doors, he's got first dibs. I mean, look at that gut. Clearly a veteran."

Heidi chuckled, her cheeks red, posture slightly more relaxed. "They do seem to disappear awfully fast . . ."

"Of course, we're on the wrong side of the room. We don't stand a chance over here."

"I'll have to remember that for next time. Survey the landscape beforehand."

Quinn tapped his temple. *Don't forget.*

"Well," she said, checking her watch, "another couple of minutes, and I believe you're up. Any more pearls of wisdom?"

He considered the question for a moment. "How long have you been working here now?"

"About three months."

"Have you been to the Japanese embassy?"

She shook her head.

"*Never* skip an event over there."

"Why not?"

"The food, obviously."

"Is that right?"

"It's not far from the office, if I recall. Somewhere along the corniche. Everyone always fights about going, so make sure you're on the list."

"That good?"

"Are you kidding? The sashimi." He put his fingers to his lips, kissing the air. "I swear they fly the salmon first class from Narita."

TWENTY-EIGHT

Q<small>UINN'S TALK WAS BRIEF, TO THE POINT, AND GENERALLY WELL</small> received, if a little rusty in delivery. As always, he began with something lighthearted—his grandmother once threatening to place him in a juvenile facility, thus instilling, since childhood, a keen interest in the quality of such establishments. A momentary hush fell over the room—the translator's delay—followed by a muted rumble of amusement from the crowd, setting the tone suitably enough.

He gave an overview of the project, the assessed needs of Roumieh Prison, glossing swiftly over the deliverables. He avoided any charts or graphs, a sure-fire way to lull the crowd to sleep, and spoke in layman's terms about what had been achieved, foregoing all the stuffy, bureaucratic "UN speak."

He spoke of the construction of a new wing at the prison in response to the increasing population; meetings with prison administration regarding the implementation of vocational initiatives such as sports, namely football, as well as gardening; the push for enhanced cooperation and dialogue between key actors in the criminal justice sphere and civil society; and the possibility of an oversight committee, or at least further talks surrounding the issue of human rights abuses and complaints related to such themes.

Just about the time he noticed a few backsides shifting in their seats, he ran through a slideshow of pictures taken at the prison itself: the new wing, the mess hall, the garden, the soccer field, men in suits shaking hands, staff alongside female inmates.

He concluded with an open forum, fielding a few rudimentary questions. Has anything been done about the prison's perceived notoriety? How are they coping with the influx of Syrian refugees?

Silence lingered for a few moments while he scanned the audience for any further hands, and then, from an older woman in the second row: "And just what did you do that made your grandmother threaten a juvenile facility?" Some muffled laughter rolled back through the crowd. Quinn protested his innocence, claiming he had been framed. Naturally, there was no telling how the soccer ball ended up in the flowerbed.

As the conference paused for midday, the administrator explained to the rapidly emptying hall that lunch would be held in the Sultan's Tent, the hotel restaurant on the second floor.

Quinn stood by the door, shaking the hands of passersby as he waited for Maha, who was buzzing around the room like a hummingbird, ensuring instructions were being followed and preparations were in place.

Trailing the last attendees out into the foyer, she puffed her cheeks dramatically as she approached. "I owe you one. Thank you *so* much for filling in. I know you have other things on your mind. You were great."

He brushed her praise aside. "Don't mention it."

"Here, this is for you." She held out a cotton drawstring bag, stuffed full of knick-knacks and memorabilia.

Raising a palm, he replied, "It's alright. I don't need one."

"Of course you do. Every speaker gets one."

"It's fine, really."

"Quinn, take it."

"I don't want—"

Maha reached for his hands and cupped them around the middle of the sack. "*Khalas,* don't be so stubborn. I don't care if you want it. I can't be seen giving anyone special treatment. So, smile and accept this gift, hm?" Her expression was serious despite the playful flicker of mischief in her eyes. Whatever cosmetics she was using, he noticed he could hardly see the tiny scar along her chin.

"You know, it's funny," he said, hands accepting the bag in defeat, "I recently spoke to someone who mentioned your stubbornness."

She scoffed. "What? Who would—oh, *aiya,* please, that old man doesn't know what he's talking about."

"Of course he doesn't."

"How did it go?" she asked, her mood shifting.

He rocked his head from side to side. "Making progress, I guess. I still don't know what I'm doing here." He looked around the room as a few straggling suit jackets and blouses floated toward the exit. "Here least of all."

"Doing me a huge favor. Listen, I was asking around a little bit, just a few contacts—don't give me that look; I trust them. They're like my sisters. I don't know how much it will help, but we should talk. Are you staying for lunch? Afterwards?" He hesitated with an answer, so she continued. "I'm going to be running around the rest of the day, but we're taking a felucca out tonight. Just the staff from the office, nothing fancy. It'll be nice. You should come. We can talk then."

"What time?"

"Around nine."

"Alright."

"Alright what?"

"Alright, I'll be there. Just let me know where *there* is."

"Stay for lunch. I'll get you the dock number."

The Sultan's Tent was full to capacity as Quinn passed, a warm cloud of aromas—sizzling meats and sautéed onions—emanating from the kitchen, beckoning him to return as he continued down the hall in search of the restroom.

Amidst the throng of aimless reverie, he was struck by a strange and disconcerting sensation, a familiar sense that he was being watched; that if he turned, he would surely meet the eyes of the onlooker. He continued down the hall, and as the voices of the restaurant fell away, he listened intently to the whisper of his footsteps along the carpeted floor.

As he approached the men's room, he glanced over his shoulder and saw . . . nothing. After a moment, a soft rumbling from around the corner turned out to be a waiter in the trademark black vest, pushing a rolling cart filled with rattling serving trays. The man smiled and gave an obliging nod as he wheeled past.

The feeling stayed with Quinn as he lathered his hands and stared into the mirror, unnerved and almost comically wary of any unexpected movements in the reflection. Stepping back into the hall, once more, he found no one. By the women's lavatory, a rather short, hunched woman sat on a regal chair examining the contents of her purse.

Suddenly, he stiffened, a vice gripping his shoulder from behind. He jerked to the side, whipping himself around, catching sight of the man's face—somehow, strangely familiar.

"Christ, you scare easy. It's a good thing I let you do your business beforehand. You might have shit your pants."

It was the voice more than anything—coarse and baritone—that hastened the recognition. Then the massive skull, shaved down to the wood, a fringe of gray at the sides, and set atop bulging shoulders, a thick neck virtually eclipsed by muscle. A scruffy beard, thoroughly unkempt, and sky-blue eyes contrasting against tanned, wind-burnt skin.

"Ray?"

"Took you long enough. Is that all I mean to you? A lesser man would be insulted."

Quinn exhaled in relief. "You scared the shit out of me."

Ray's booming voice guffawed loudly, his meaty palm smacking Quinn's shoulder. "Like I said, that's why I let you use the little boys' room first."

"What are you doing here?"

"I could ask you the same thing."

"Working, obviously. I just gave a talk." He sized up the hulking brute in front of him. "Did you get even bigger? A couple of inches taller and you'd be unstoppable."

"Don't worry," Ray said, hiking his belt. "I've got the inches where it counts, string bean."

"You're part of the conference?"

"Sort of," he said, glancing back down the hall. "Gimme a sec here—let me tell my guys to cover for me. We'll catch up."

It was years ago that he met Raymond Ward at an impromptu consultation in Istanbul. Quinn could still recall the tourist trap café just off Taksim Square—weak tea and dry *kofte*. Quinn and his delegation were only in the city for a few days, and Ray was easing the concerns of a particularly skittish politician, "the sleaziest kebab in Constantinople," as he referred to him.

Ray worked mostly as a private security contractor for the rich and paranoid, and he made a killing doing it, in no small part because killing was heavily implied in the job description, if such a predicament were ever to arise. Whatever assemblies, workshops, or press events required the presence of the well-to-do, Ray usually had a hand in the matter, either as part of the security detail himself or managing from behind the scenes.

Reappearing from the restaurant, he started back down the hall, looking very much like the man who Quinn had known years before. The same stiff, broad-shouldered march, an acute awareness of his surroundings, a man who moved several paces ahead of everyone else, rarely, if ever, taken by surprise.

"Are you on the job right now?"

Ray gestured back to the restaurant. "They've got it covered. Let's get a fucking drink, yeah?"

The pair descended to the ground floor, following signs to the aptly named Ottoman Bar, in keeping with the luxurious Turkish theme throughout the hotel. The bar was dark and practically empty. Dark shades of red and maroon lent a kingly ambiance, with plush ruby seats and weathered leather couches dimly lit by pendant lights and antique lamps.

A lone waitress with platinum-blond hair and broad, painted eyebrows brought two glasses of single malt to a particularly secluded part of the bar. She was pleasant and courteous, though visibly intrigued, perhaps more than just intrigued by Ray, who paid her no mind.

"You're serious?" Quinn asked.

"I am."

"You can't retire. What would you do with yourself?"

Ray's lips arced in contemplation. "Don't know. Teach, maybe."

"Teach."

"Sure."

"Teach what, exactly?"

"How to wipe a smirk like that off someone's face, for starters."

"Fair point," Quinn conceded, the smirk growing.

"Instructing is what I meant. Training. Back at the academy. Defensive tactics, firearms manipulation, something a bit more low key."

"That makes a bit more sense. It's time, is it?"

A slow, thoughtful nod. "It's time."

Quinn glanced at the man's forearms, thick and vascular, and, in terms of size, more or less rivaling Quinn's legs. "So, who are you here for? Anyone I know?"

"Maybe. It's your conference. Ahmad Salman Al-Enizi."

Lifting his glass, Quinn thought for a moment. "Saudi?"

"Yep."

"Three of 'em?"

"Four."

"Really, for this?" Quinn rubbed his chin. "Looking to get more exposure?"

"I don't pay much attention to the politics, but from what I overheard, something about improving public image. The new regime is modernizing, trying to get away from all the stereotypes, I suppose, so they're sending out envoys like this. Women's issues, climate change—pretending to give a shit, I guess. It's not the first time. There was one in Muscat a couple of months back. Another more recently in Dubai."

"Still based out there?"

"Abu Dhabi."

"That's right."

"Just working though, not based. I'm actually home now, back in Chicago."

"You're kidding."

Ray made a low, grumbling sound. "Something about this part of the world," he said, taking a sip, the glass a shiny children's toy in his palm. "I feel like I've been pushing my luck here a bit too long."

"How's that?"

"A few too many close calls. You get to thinking . . ."

Quinn nodded. "You're not going to miss it here? The Emirates?"

Another grunt. "It's a young man's game. And it's been a while since I was that. The grizzled vet now. But sure, I'll miss it. Heaps of cash. Heaps of anything you want. It's a goddamn circus out there."

"You'll have to get used to regular paychecks like the rest of us working stiffs. No more of those ludicrous contracts."

"It can be a small fortune to some. Still, unless you complete the full six months, sometimes a year, you get nothin'. You get injured, say, or shot—no one cares. You don't finish the contract, you don't get paid. Simple as that. During training, anyhow. Protection gigs are a little different. Added incentives." He shook his head, a sentimental grin behind the scruff. "They give you a menu, *additional comforts*, they say. It's just a list of races." He shook his head in bewilderment.

"I didn't care for the Emirates much," Quinn said. "We move in different circles, but it just wasn't for me."

"They're a different breed of wealthy out there," Ray replied. "Everything becomes a competition, egos of the super-rich and all that. It's nothin' but a big dick-measuring contest, except these guys, they measure their dicks by the height of their buildings. Whoever's got the tallest one wins. Manhood measured in towers and yachts." He chuckled deep in his throat. "Anyway, what about you? I haven't seen you 'round these parts for a while."

"Left the region. Left the whole job, really."

"You get the sack?"

"Actually, yeah, from one posting, but that's not it. Long story. Sick of the politics."

"If you had any gristle on those bones, I could use a man like you. Someone with half a brain, not like the meatheads I got."

"Well, despite how flattered I am . . ."

"For the best. Hell, you nearly dribbled down your pant leg when I tapped you on the shoulder." The same chuckle devolved into a phlegmy cough, Ray moving a ham-hock fist in front of his mouth.

"Listen, Ray, I'm actually glad I ran into you. I could really use some help. It's a sort of . . . delicate issue."

Ray looked up, his eyes pink and watery from the coughing fit.

"I'm not really here for work. It's personal. This," he looked to the ceiling, "is a favor. I have something else going on. And I'll be the first to admit I'm at a complete loss. I have no idea what I'm doing. Most of all, I need people I can trust. People with a few connections."

Ray nodded. *Go on.*

"You know anyone at the Ministry of Interior? Senior, junior, anyone at all? Someone reliable."

"Enough with the foreplay, Quinn. Tell me what you need." Ray had never been one for small talk, one of his many endearing qualities.

"The long and short is I'm looking for a girl. A child. She's gone missing. And this is where it gets crazy: I've actually followed her here from Bangkok." He reached into his bag, fished amongst his notes, and pulled out one of the passports, the sleeve of pictures tucked inside.

"The hell have you gotten yourself into . . ."

Quinn handed the passport across the table. "She disappeared in Cambodia initially, part of a trafficking network, if I'm right. Except now that I'm here, I'm completely out of my element."

"Who is this girl?"

"She's . . . just an innocent, Ray."

Raymond Ward was a beast of a man in every sense but one. Beneath the calloused exterior, coarse like weathered stone, his eyes betrayed a compassionate man, a man who understood.

"Didn't you work this stuff in Asia?" he asked, thumbing through the passport.

"Things work differently here. These passports—fakes. I just don't know what kind. They're the only solid lead I have. I know a bit about what goes on—child marriage, rich businessmen exploiting the poor, nothing unusual. But the country itself, the corruption, the instability, especially with what's going on outside these days, I can't risk going to the authorities. Now more than ever." He ran his fingers through his hair and tilted back the rest of his drink. "Do you know anyone?"

Ray sat pensively for a long time, tapping the passport against his stubby fingertips. "I have a daughter, you know."

"You do?"

He nodded.

"Congratulations. I had no idea."

"Thanks." He held up the passport, open to the first page, showing it to Quinn. "Same month. June."

"What's her name?"

"Ella." Ray smiled to himself. "She's two. I call her Junebug."

Quinn had never heard Ray speak like this before. If it wasn't about hollow points, bourbon, or the indiscretions of the fairer sex, it wasn't much worth discussing. It was a new window into the big man, his soft and vulnerable middle willfully exposed.

"I don't wanna get your hopes up. I might, *might*, know a guy. Junior, unfortunately, but he's a good shit. What do you need, exactly?"

"I think the passports are genuine for the most part but with substituted bio pages," Quinn said, handing him the rest of the stack from his bag. "Then again, it could just be the photos that have been subbed out. Honestly, I can't tell anymore. Anyone who deals with passports, if they can look them up, trace the document number, the issue date, something. Anything."

As Quinn spoke, Ray took out his phone and snapped a few pictures. He flipped through the rest of the documents taking shots of each entry and exit stamp.

"I'll look into it, but I gotta tell you, I have to find my guy first, that's *if* he's still there. I'm only in town for a few more days—a week, tops."

"Anything you can do."

Ray handed back the documents with a groan, reaching across the table, then sank deeply into the velvet armchair. He slipped into a daydream, lost somewhere until their server reappeared, perfume trailing, offering fresh glasses.

"*Athnan*," Quinn said, raising two fingers, "*shukran*." As her heels clicked back to the bar, Quinn noticed Ray was staring a hole through the floor. Deep canyons crisscrossed his forehead, his skin bronzed and weathered from the desert sun.

"What is it?"

"Rich businessmen . . ."

"What about them?"

"You said—what, exploiting the poor or something."

Quinn nodded. "Like anywhere else. The wealthy preying on the less fortunate. Here, many come up from the peninsula or the Emirates, purchase whatever they want. Drugs, sex. Bahrain isn't the only Vegas in the Mideast."

"Johnny Walker Bridge," Ray murmured, a glimmer of nostalgia in his eyes. He was referring to the infamous bridge that connected the conservative Saudi kingdom to the sinful nightlife of the island nation next door. Bahrain had always been an oasis for expats in the region and a paradise for rebellious Arabs alike. The pair themselves had tossed a few bottles into the sea during a return trip to Dammam.

Ray chewed on this for a while, the wheels turning slowly, methodically. "What do you know about Abdulrahman Al-Balawi?"

"Balawi. Your Saudis?"

"Yeah, but not these ones," he said, pointing upwards.

"So, who?"

"The contract isn't to protect Al-Enizi, the one with the entourage upstairs. It's Al-Balawi."

Quinn shook his head, not quite following. "Never heard of him. Where is he?"

"Depends. What time is it?"

"One," Quinn said, shrugging, "one-thirty."

"Still in bed, I'd say. With a hangover the size of the Burj Khalifa."

"So what are you doing here then?"

"He told Ahmad to go in his place. Abdulrahman's the one who's actually invited, supposed to be attending. Couldn't be bothered. He's not big on stuffy meetings, all the diplomacy. So, he insisted I bring part of my crew here to watch over Ahmad while the rest stay back at the villa. He's got his own bodyguards there too. To be honest, they couldn't care less about our presence. Dad insisted, from what I hear."

"What are you getting at?"

Behind him came the familiar scent of perfume, two fresh glasses clinking with ice, followed by an emphatic flip of blond hair, a flourish undoubtedly meant for Ray. The big man either failed to notice or just ignored her, scratching his beard thoughtfully, fingers raking across steel wool.

"First off," he said after she left, "I'm not some intel operative, alright? I know what I know. I'm a hammer. I've always been a hammer. Everything out there is just a different-size nail. So, take it or leave it."

Quinn waited patiently as Ray took a drink.

"This guy, Al-Balawi, he's," he shook his head, "he's a real piece of work."

"How so?"

"He's the definition of those modern, young Saudis, spoiled beyond all means. He's actually a prince, or related to a prince, prince's cousin . . ." He waved his mitt. "You know how it is with that family. I couldn't tell you the exact relationship, but he's connected. So, of course, *filthy* rich. I mean, all that shit you hear about—the drugs, the girls, the excess, that's him. Fleets of cars, pet lions, gold-plated AKs, the works.

"Anyhow, the new king, the reformer, he's trying to mend some political ties, spread the word about how they're *modernizing* the country. Green energy, women driving, easing up with the *mutawa,* the religious police. But, apparently, he also wants to promote a more, I don't know what you guys call it, humanitarian image? Yeah. The human rights record, all that. Hard to say you're reforming anything when folks are still gettin' the chop every Friday in the town square.

Public beheadings don't make for the best PR campaigns. He's got his people flying around the world attending these events, making it look like he's more liberal, more compassionate."

"That explains the entourage."

"It's why they're here. Waving the Saudi flag at a conference hosted by UN Women. It's great press, and all they have to do is show their faces. Well, Ahmad's face at least. Abdulrahman isn't much of a diplomat."

Quinn shrugged, "Neither am I."

"This guy, Balawi, he's different. It's not just the excess; it's more than that. He gets off on it. It's the first time my crew is working with him, but I've heard stories; we all have. Normally, I wouldn't pay much attention, but it's all true. He goes hard all the time, and he's a vicious little shit. Girls leaving parties covered in marks. Big into the dog-fighting scene in London. I even heard they shipped him off to a different boarding school back in the day when all the housekeepers kept leaving. They'd end up at the local police station or consulate trying to lay assault charges, rape charges."

"Maybe the conference was supposed to teach him something."

"Right. Well, I just had the thought, you know, what you said about rich Arabs." He raised the glass to his lips.

A moment passed, and at first, Quinn wasn't certain where this was leading. Though, what was the point of telling him if not to hint at the possibility? To say it was a leap would be giving the notion far too much credit.

"What, you think he's involved somehow?"

Ray opened his palms in defense. "I don't think anything. I haven't heard, I don't suspect, I have no clue. But you start mentioning rich Saudis with twisted fetishes . . ." He jabbed a finger on the table. "This is the guy I think of."

Quinn leaned forward, lacing his fingers together, and chewed his lip awhile. "You trust your contact with those passports, right?" Ray glared at him, ending that debate. "Right."

The pair were silent for a few minutes, Quinn considering the possibilities. It wasn't much to go on, a wealthy Saudi with a questionable reputation. Then again, it wasn't as if he were chasing down rock-solid leads either. And now this—attendees at a women's safety conference somehow involved in the sex trade. Ray's intentions were good, of that there was no doubt, but the idea was ludicrous.

"You know, we're only here for a couple more days, and he's having a party tomorrow night. Well, there's a party every night, but it's a sort of farewell event, I guess, quite a few people invited." He nodded to himself, agreeing with the idea. "If you want, I can put you on the list if you don't stay too long."

Quinn laughed somewhat messily into his glass. "And do what, exactly?" he asked, wiping his chin. "Ask a Saudi prince about people smuggling? How does that conversation go?"

"It doesn't. You wouldn't be allowed to talk to him. You likely won't even see him. But if you're curious to see what kind of circles he moves in . . ."

That *did* strike a chord. The clientele at the party would be an interesting bunch. Likely the exact type of men who Youssef had talked about: wealthy tycoons from the region in town for business meetings, mergers, maybe even the conference. Perhaps some down time as well, away from the family, far from prying eyes. Then a party hosted by a man known for his indulgences, a man who, by the sounds of it, would have few qualms about temporary marriages, if indeed such a formality were even considered.

It wasn't the worst idea. It wasn't as if he had somewhere to be or a wealth of alternatives to explore. Ray would need some time to track down his man, then see about the passports. In the meantime he'd listen to what Maha had to say that evening, and afterward, why not?

"I'd be out of place."

"No shit. If you go, you can't stay long. Believe me, if it were anyone else, I wouldn't even mention this. We'll pick a name, a backstory—you stay, maybe . . ." He rolled his head from side to side. "Half an hour, poke around for a bit, but that's it."

Now that the proposal was out in the open, it was Ray who seemed to be having reservations, wringing his palms together as if kneading dough.

"Just don't fuck this up. I'm not tryin' to scare you, but if someone figures out you're not who you say you are . . ."

"What if someone from the conference recognizes me?"

"It's not that kind of party. Trust me, nobody here is attending."

"Except for the Saudis upstairs."

Ray shook his head. "They don't take part in the extra-curricular stuff. The Al-Enizis don't really get along with the Al-Balawis. It's a tribal thing. Ahmad and his crew consider themselves more pious, and in a way, I suppose they are. They even stay at different hotels. Same delegation, but underneath there's a sort of unspoken rivalry."

"You sure about this?"

"Not at all."

"Thanks."

"I'll put you on the list and take care of the Nigerians. You get in, act like your briefs are made of threaded gold, and you get out. I doubt anyone will pay much attention. A half hour, tops."

"Nigerians?"

"His personal guard."

"Christ. What's that supposed to mean?"

"All the young Saudis have 'em. They basically buy up Nigerian kids, train them as bodyguards, and they grow up with whatever prince or whoever they're protecting. They become like brothers— keeps 'em loyal." Ray saw the look in Quinn's eyes. "Don't worry about it."

"Sure," he replied, wiping his sweaty palms on his trousers, "this sounds like a great idea."

Ray sat thoughtfully for a moment. "It is. Kids, they . . ." He cleared his throat. "You get a new perspective. What's her name?"

"Mei."

"If there's any chance this will help you find her, it's worth it." He raised his drink, "I'll let you know the address, and I'll get going on those passports." As their glasses clinked together, he said, "You owe me."

"Thanks."

"Oh, and dress like you have money."

TWENTY-NINE

That afternoon the Egyptian sun baked the capital with a fierce, unrelenting heat. While the locals took refuge indoors, stray animals hunkered beneath shadows in the cool sand. Quinn, a damp sweat on his lower back, had foolishly gone for a walk to get some "fresh" air. Without a single passing breeze to provide respite, the city's stagnant breath hung low in a thick, jaundiced fog, enveloping those who dared to challenge its dominion.

When he returned to the apartment, Mahmoud was sound asleep—was, until a power surge returned to the building, igniting his small radio with a crackling hiss and jolting the old man back amongst the living. He shuffled gingerly to the front gate, a drowsy smile on his puffy face. Upstairs, Quinn showered, changed, and called Saad for a lift down to the pier that evening.

By the time he arrived at the riverfront promenade, helping to lug a cooler onto the old wooden boat, he had the impression that it would be a marvelous night for a sail. The sun had dipped, nestling behind some cloud cover, and the city had cooled to near perfection, a warm summer's eve as inviting as any he could remember. A light wind ruffled his hair as an old man—barefoot, wearing a tattered brown *thobe*—stomped across the hull of the felucca. He had a stubbled white beard and a matching turban. Coiling a length of fraying rope, he shouted something at a young boy who, also barefoot, scrambled up the central mast like a monkey, adjusting the lateen sail. Moments later, they pushed away from the shoreline with a long oar, drifting out into the current of the storied river.

There were roughly twenty people aboard, mostly staff from the office, seated in two parallel rows among mountains of embroidered cushions. Archie made some opening remarks while one of the crewmen opened the various coolers, spreading a buffet across the long central table. There were heaps of fresh flatbreads, a variety of skewered meats, grilled vegetables and plentiful bottles of wine. After concluding his speech, Archie circled around the boat, thanking everyone individually as they sailed along the open water, a faded Egyptian flag fluttering quietly at the stern.

For a time, Quinn made small talk with a man who introduced himself as Karim, the head of the anti-terrorism unit. An amiable fellow with an easy smile, he had fat, rosy cheeks, at least in part from the wine, and was eager to discuss the prevalence of money laundering at Egyptian banks.

Later, the conversation took a darker turn, with Karim speaking in hushed tones about the ongoing political strife in the city. Tensions between the current government and newly emerging grassroots opposition: the Muslim Brotherhood, rather, what was left of it, disenfranchised and vengeful; the more radical elements of society, plotting in the shadows, biding their time; and the poor citizens themselves, still reeling from the optimism of the Arab Spring—now withered and frail, consumed by decay.

"In Cairo, we are a large pot with a great big cover," Karim said. "We are blind when the water is boiling. The cover, *yanni*—the *lid*, always it is stopping our sight. But soon the water will boil out and onto the fire, and we can do nothing to stop this."

From a hidden speaker, a mournful Arabian ballad, the vibrato of a tenor's voice singing the word *habibi* in seemingly every verse.

When Karim decided to indulge in the sweets on offer, slightly unsteady on his feet now after the merlot, Maha spotted the vacant seat. She was casually dressed, jeans and a violet golf shirt, a matching scarf draped loosely over her head, the material hovering gently with the rise and fall of the breeze. She smiled as they tapped their plastic cups of wine together.

"So, what did you think?" she asked.

"Of Karim? Seems nice enough. Convinced there's going to be another revolution."

"Not Karim, for goodness' sake —the conference."

"What did *you* think? It's your show."

"One more day. I'm holding my breath," she said, taking a sip.

"It's going to be fine. We've been to enough of these. It's obvious from the start when they're poorly planned, and we both know you're far too neurotic to let that happen."

She wobbled her head in consideration, playing along. "Well, there was that one speaker, in the middle. I didn't care much for him."

"Mm . . . just before lunch?"

"He tried making some jokes. Like some comedian. I found it very unprofessional."

"Ah, well, you get what you pay for, I suppose. There's always bound to be at least one hack at these things."

Maha looked straight ahead, smirking, hands cupping the drink in her lap. Then she looked at him, the levity waning already, a grim reality that lifted at times but never drifted too far.

"You said you were asking around?" he said. "Talking to some people?"

"Yes. A few of my colleagues, not from here." Her eyes flicked toward the front of the boat. "Some others as well."

"And?"

"Sadly, there's not much I didn't already know. I just wanted to be sure in case I led you down the wrong path. I don't know how much help it will be."

"It's alright. Youssef filled me in on quite a bit."

"Summer marriages?"

"We touched on that."

She sighed. "It's a big problem for us here. Difficult to make any progress. How much did he tell you?"

"Wealthy foreigners, impoverished families, financial transactions. Nothing about how to find these girls though."

"And that's the problem. For obvious reasons, they don't exactly advertise their services. The brokers, I mean. They're mostly lawyers but not legitimate ones, as you can imagine. Corrupt, greasy." She scoffed. "Still, they provide a service for a supply and demand that already exists."

"How open is all of this? How accessible?"

"To you? Not very. You don't exactly come across as a rich Emirati; it would make them suspicious. But as I said, the economy is there. They simply connect the parties involved and produce the documents."

"There's records?"

"Not exactly. They're fakes. Well, some are. The brokers don't just arrange the marriage certificates. They forge birth certificates as well. Any relations with a minor"—she dangled a wrist, indicating the obvious—"and they need documents, making the girl a few years older to have everything legitimate. Sometimes they bribe physicians as well, signing documents regarding their age, making it—*yanni*, the record, more authentic." She gave a dispirited shrug. "Of course, sometimes everything is fake. It depends on the situation."

"I'm assuming it's too much to ask for police to look into this sort of thing."

"They do, but even for them I have to make an excuse. It's very difficult to prosecute. They lack training, and so do the prosecutors and the judges. It's quite complicated here. You have to remember that all parties involved are benefitting from this."

"Except the girls."

"*Aywa*, except the girls. But the brokers, they make very good money. And these monsters who come from abroad to abuse, they leave happy. Often, parents will approach the brokers themselves and make arrangements, so where does an officer begin?"

"The parents," he muttered, thinking back to the orphanages in Cambodia. Thousands of miles apart, a continent removed, yet the trends of desperation remained the same.

"Some of these towns, the levels of poverty . . ." She said something in Arabic that he didn't catch, a prayer, maybe. "It's really bad. Really, very bad. If they have two or three daughters, they think, 'Maybe I can sell one to help provide for the rest.' Then they convince the daughter it's for the good of the family, so they can eat, have clothes without holes, simple things. And what does she say to her family who needs help, to her father who begs her? No? Of course not. Some of these girls, they're married fifty times before they're eighteen."

"And foreign girls—anything?"

"With them it's even more complicated." She sighed once more and looked to the bow. He noted the pained and tender look in her eyes, troubled that she couldn't deliver a more hopeful message.

An unexpected wave of guilt flooded over him. Maha's empathy was so sincere that, at times, it made his own temperament feel somehow rather disingenuous. She wasn't much unlike Noi in that sense, a compassion that knew no bounds. She was, at once, sophisticated and demure, timid in her own way, and conservative in some respects more than others. On the other hand, she had a ferocious spirit that for her entire life had confronted the endemic chauvinism in her society, not only rising to the occasion but almost yearning for confrontation, fiercely independent and ready to fight for what she believed. And somewhere between those two elements, despite the somber conversation, was a girl whose company he was rather beginning to enjoy.

"They're so much harder to find because they have no family here, no legal status. Most likely no legal documents either."

Quinn looked off into the water, soft waves splashing against the hull, a steady, therapeutic sound that could lull him to sleep. The music was slower now, a woman's voice flowing over a tranquil melody. He lit a cigarette.

"From what I know, most of this is taking place in apartments, luxury rentals. Sometimes hotels too," he said, lungs full of smoke.

"You're right. It's difficult to find a hotel room for an affair. Many places won't rent to an unmarried couple. Especially locals. The marriage certificates, even bad ones, they help get around this. I've even read about brokers going beyond facilitation. They actually deliver the girls. A verbal arrangement is made, a price negotiated, and then, she is dropped off at the suite. These are what you call high-end, fully furnished apartments. Penthouse suites." A sound of disgust escaped from deep in her throat.

He continued staring out at the horizon, the water glinting now in the light of the setting sun.

"Can I ask you something?" she said.

He nodded, turning back to her.

"Please don't take this the wrong way." Her lips parted slightly, then reconsidered. When she found the words, she spoke slowly, feeling him out. "You're not a detective, Quinn. You're, well, a consultant. A diplomat—"

"Oh, I wouldn't go that far."

"You know what I mean. I understand why you don't want to involve the police, and sometimes I think you're right, but I don't understand how you expect to . . ." She let the thought finish itself, floating it out and leaving it to hover between them. He took a long drag from his cigarette, letting the smoke char his lungs awhile, until a moment of nostalgia drifted to the fore.

"Did I ever tell you about my father?"

She shook her head.

"Mm. He was a beat cop, back in the day."

"A beat cop?"

"The *beat* was the neighborhood you were responsible for. 'Walking the beat,' they used to call it. In some cities, police used to just patrol a set area, get to know their community. 'Community policing,' they'd call it too. He passed away when I was still young—I was twelve. I remember he had bad back problems from the duty equipment. Even when he wasn't wearing the belt, he was always tapping around his waist, subconsciously checking for his sidearm, his baton. Funny the way your memory works.

"Anyway, there was a corner store we used to go to. Every Saturday I'd go with him as he ran errands, but afterwards, he'd get me a bag of candy from that store. Herschel's, it was called. It was always the last stop, and he'd make me wait in the car. After a few minutes, he'd come out with a newspaper and a brown paper bag for me filled with all sorts of stuff. Licorice, gummies, sour candies. Every Saturday.

"One day, Herschel's got robbed. Some punk kids broke into the store, used a brick to smash the window, in broad daylight, no less. I think it was a Sunday—that's why it was closed. Even as a kid I couldn't understand why they did it during the daytime. They didn't get away with much, just a few bicycle baskets full of bubble gum and baseball cards. I mean, they were kids; what more could they want? But one of them got caught. Herschel's nephew happened to be out back for some reason, heard the commotion, and came running. As the kid was peddling away, he somehow got his frayed jeans caught in the bike chain. He was going full speed, and a wad of denim got spun right up into the greasy links. Naturally, the bike came to a screeching stop, and the idiot did his best Peter Pan right over the handlebars, smacking his head on the concrete. Apparently, when Herschel's nephew caught up to him, he was dragging himself along the sidewalk in a panic, still tangled up in the sprocket."

Quinn ashed his cigarette behind him into the wind. "My dad told me about it, and I was furious. Not only because that place was my weekend treasure chest but because at least three other kids had gotten away with it. Honestly, I don't even remember what happened to the kid who got caught. I was just so mad that the others got away free and clear. My dad sat me down that night and told me, 'You're not going to like hearing this, but that's just the way life goes sometimes.' I said, 'What do you mean?' And he said, 'Ninety percent of the bad guys get away with it. That's just the way it is. We only catch about ten percent, and the ten percent we do catch are the stupid ones. And that's exactly why we catch 'em. 'Cause they're stupid.'

"I hated that answer as much as I hated those kids. I would forget about it during the week, but then Saturday came, I'd see that plywood sheet hammered across the empty window, and I'd be stewing again.

"But as I grew up, I couldn't really disagree with what he'd said. Everyone had a lot of respect for my dad—his friends, the other officers at the precinct, our little community in general. I think about it now, the memories I have of him. Everybody loved him. He was good at his job. Really good. He did what he could, always did his best, and didn't lose any sleep about what he couldn't change."

A lively tune came over the speakers with a thumping drumbeat, a few of the women clapping along with the pulsating melody. Archie, having finished his formal duties, had apparently been sampling the wine, and was now attempting his best *baladi* dance as people shouted instructions. The old sailor in the white turban seemed to enjoy it as well, seated on the bow, one leg hanging overboard, smiling a near-toothless grin and bobbing his head.

"That's your commander-in-chief," Quinn said.

Maha nodded slowly. "Yes. Yes, it is."

For a while they sat in awe of Archie's disconcerting lack of rhythm, his gyrations all the more enthusiastic as the crowd clapped in encouragement.

"I have no idea what I'm doing," Quinn said finally. "I know it's no surprise; I've told you before. And I feel I've already used up all my good luck. Christ, I remember feeling like that in Bangkok. But I'm here now. I've gotten this far. And maybe I can't do anything about the ninety percent who get away with it. Maybe that was never in the cards. But maybe, *maybe*, someone will slip up. Make a mistake."

He was certain now that he was no longer speaking to Maha but rather to himself, an internal monologue spoken aloud.

"I met up with an old friend, bumped into him out of the blue earlier today. He might know someone who can help, might be able to take a look at those passports. I think he works for the MOI."

"That's excellent, Quinn. That's great news."

"It's something, I suppose."

"And what were you just saying about your luck . . . ?"

For a few minutes they sat together in silence, the crowd carrying on without them—joyful melodies, flowing wine, platters of figs and dates. He could sense that she felt uneasy; impatient and frustrated by her own inability to do or say anything that might help, desperate for a solution that she could not provide.

"I'll get us some more wine," she said, standing up.

"Sure. Thanks." He took a last pull of his cigarette and dropped it into the cup. "Maybe a couple of fresh glasses too."

Maha smiled, more out of compassion than pity, and rested her hand on his wrist, squeezing for a moment, then let go.

The setting sun shone a bright orange, the clouds having thinned and dispersed, allowing for a picturesque view of the glowing half orb sinking slowly into the distant waters. The boulevards of abundant, green brush along the embankment faded into darkness, along with the tan, wind-swept brick dwellings behind them.

The Nile was calm, the current flowing gently, caressing the bow, every now and again a warm breeze lightly sweeping through the stillness of dusk. In the distance, a silhouette of a fisherman, dark against the shimmering tangerine waters, stood in his humble craft, carefully drawing a sodden net from the river, patiently awaiting the catch of the day.

THIRTY

QUINN FIGURED TO ARRIVE AROUND MIDNIGHT—LATE ENOUGH
to avoid a spotlight but early enough to ensure a brief window of
opportunity. An opportunity at what, he wasn't yet certain, and
while the thought of mingling with the Arabian *nouveau riche*—
eavesdropping on murky business dealings and hushed conversations—had sounded like a good idea at the time, he was increasingly unsure of what he hoped to accomplish.

He did as he was told—freshened up, dressed well, and added a
few accoutrements for good measure. Along with a cheap flask purchased at Road Nine, the rundown pharmacy on Al Nadi supplied
a Piaget watch—sparkling, magnificent, and counterfeit, right
down to the faux leather band. Then some further gravitas in the
shape of a slim designer belt—designer in name only. He paired
the items with a newly adopted, if disconcertingly self-conscious,
heir of bourgeois entitlement, and an upper lip curled staunchly
into place, smug and dripping with contempt.

As he sat in the back of the taxi, adjusting the crown on his spu-
rious timepiece, he struggled to shake the gnawing unease. Nerves,
he told himself, but it was more than that. Nagging doubts about
the entire idea—the clientele, the façade he presented—en route
to some misguided attempt at playing the private eye, an effort to

spy on a crowd with an ungodly amount of wealth and power. He removed the flask from his breast pocket and took a purposeful swig to bolster his resolve.

He needn't have concerned himself with the address. Unfamiliar with the Al Narges neighborhood in New Cairo, it was the vehicles that announced themselves. He instructed the driver to keep going, who—once past the brimming luxury automobiles parked in front of the villa—slowed around the corner on a darkened side street with a speculative glance in the rearview mirror.

For a long while, Quinn stood beneath the tree cover, shifting his weight amongst the shadows. Eventually, having drained his flask and discarded it into some construction rubble, he approached the three-story mansion—elegant balconies and a glowing rooftop terrace, a succession of showroom vehicles out front, parked in perfect alignment.

With all his might, he assumed an effortless stroll; nonchalant, as if having just tossed a set of keys to a fumbling valet. The cars glimmered in the warm light of the villa windows: the cherry-red Lamborghini Veneno Roadster, the Aston Martin DB11 in British racing green, two Ferraris, silver and canary yellow, a jet-black Bugatti Veyron, and a spotless white Hummer, somewhat appropriately parked diagonally on what passed for a front lawn in the new suburb.

A small grouping of Arabs in crisp white *thobes* and checkered red *shemagh*s were admiring the Lamborghini, a friendly debate drawing to a close as they started up the front steps to the main door. Quinn joined the procession a few paces behind, examining his phone as if responding to a pressing inquiry while the Arabs funneled through the front door, floating past the security detail.

Two African men—Nigerians, he presumed—stood like pillars on either side of the doorway in matching black tracksuits, one with a formidable gold chain around his thick neck, the other opting for a sparkling silver cross. For some reason, both wore matching aviator sunglasses. Off to one side, behind some shrubbery, he spotted a third man smoking a cigarette. Judging by his similar enthusiasm for fitness apparel, he was likely a third member of the entourage.

Cresting the top step, Quinn ignored the new cadence thumping in his chest. Eyes narrowed and focused on his phone—ever the preoccupied business magnate—he stepped confidently toward the door, the last *thobe* before him flowing past the threshold.

At what seemed an opportune moment, he twisted his lip with derision, as if having read something particularly asinine, instantly regretted his poor theater, and slipped the phone back into his pocket. With the next step, he felt a barrier descend across his chest: the bulging, ropey forearm of the doorman, capped with a fist, gold rings the size of lug nuts. Quinn stopped, not entirely of his own accord, and sneered at the impermeable aviators that gave away nothing but his own reflection. The man stood like an ebony statue of Anubis—towering, completely rigid.

"He's good," said a gruff voice from inside. They both looked toward a man in a black suit with a shorn skull and razor-sculpted beard. The man nodded, and the barrier withdrew, albeit somewhat reluctantly. Quinn required no further invitation, and after brushing some imaginary filth from his shirtsleeve, proceeded inside, ignoring the rush of blood drubbing within his temples.

"Quinn," the man said.

He nodded.

"Twenty minutes. No longer. Don't get yourself noticed."

"Like I just did?"

"Like you just did. With—" He stopped and turned his head, raising his finger to an earpiece. After an involuntary nod, he turned his attention back to Quinn. "Twenty minutes," he said firmly, then turned on his heel and proceeded outside, past the two Nigerians still watching from the doorway.

A fool's errand now, stepping into the lion's den as a result of his own desperation. Even if he had some sort of well-laid plan, which he did not, twenty minutes wasn't a great deal of time to accomplish anything, much less unearth a trafficking ring. For a fleeting moment, he almost laughed at the absurdity. Was that really what he was hoping to achieve? Heroically barge into some lavish party and expose the corrupt underbelly of the elite? He felt dreadfully out of place, and noted he was subconsciously rubbing his watch, hoping no one took a closer look.

Stepping into the grand foyer, he proceeded across the tessellated marble floor, a gleaming open space that was all white columns and towering archways. In the center of the room, he passed a flower arrangement on a round, polished stone table, which surely cost more than his imitation watch, belt, and likely his entire wardrobe.

To his right, in a secluded room, a group of men watched a boxing match, puffing their shisha and shouting at the theater-sized television. The room to the left, however, was far more lively and opened into a massive, crowded gallery with high ceilings; a room which, through its glass-walled enclosure, appeared to stretch out infinitely past exquisite gardens, sculpted fountains, and off into the moonlit desert.

The opulence was palpable, saturating the air. It was in the extravagant, ornate chandeliers that hung from above, the vibrant oil paintings in golden trim. It was in the eclectic limestone sculptures, porcelain vases, and shimmering, jewel-encrusted daggers, the exotic bouquets that bloomed in sparkling crystal. It was in the colorful mosaic area rug on which Quinn stood, self-conscious, afraid to wipe his feet. Mostly, it was the people themselves.

He cut a solitary figure, weaving through clouds of perfume, amongst silken fabrics and all their various diamond and gemstone accessories, through the effortlessly excessive wealth that filled the room. Suddenly, the room was stifling, and he struggled to draw a cool breath. He felt eyes upon him as he moved, necks craning, watching with curiosity—staring, gawking—until he came to the rather comforting realization that, in fact, they weren't.

Heaving a sigh of relief, he glanced around, confirming that the thought had been nothing more than a product of his frazzled nerves. No one, in fact, seemed to take notice as he passed like a ghost through the crowd. Everyone was otherwise engaged. Groups of Arab men stood chatting; others lounged about the soft furniture, some in traditional garb, some in bespoke vests and jackets, one character sporting a rather bizarre sort of luxury sweat suit. And each of them with an accompanying consort, stunning in her own natural beauty, or equally stunning with her purchased attributes, as exaggerated and likely as costly as the room's décor.

To his left, thankfully, the bar—a sleek marble countertop—presided over by two gorgeous women, one straining a beverage from a cobbler shaker, the other slicing thin wedges of pomelo.

Propping an elbow along the marble, Quinn cast his eye over the crowd and noted a party of six laughing gleefully, oblivious to the world around them as they lazed on gray velvet sofas, a glass coffee table between them. On the table were martini glasses, a plate of half-eaten canapés, two gold-plated iPhones, and several slivers of white powder. A puppy with blond fur, limbs splayed out and purring against the sofa, was not, as it turned out, a puppy at all. Quinn took a rather obvious second glance before registering that the lazing "dog" was, in fact, a baby cheetah, an adorable look of boredom upon its spotted face.

He ordered a whiskey from one of the models, who poured him an excellent single malt in a square tumbler. She gave him the most casual of winks, grazing his finger as she pushed the glass across the bar, and Quinn momentarily fell in love as she unwrapped a bottle of Moët & Chandon, utterly indifferent to his existence.

He surveyed the room. There was no question that traffickers came from all backgrounds, spurred on by poverty just as often as greed, but any curiosity, any *what if* scenarios that enticed him while at the Ottoman had all but disappeared. The crowd before him, this class of people, they had no need for such an enterprise. A twisted desire, maybe, some perverse yearning for power, but certainly no necessity. It was a lucrative crime, to be certain, the age-old practice of transporting persons for all manner of exploitation, but even criminal groups who excelled in the nefarious business wouldn't hold a candle to the wealth currently on display.

These were oil men, true oil men, not the pipeline moguls and CEOs from the West. These men were in a class entirely of their own. Balawi, wherever he was, connected in any fashion to Saudi royalty, required little more in life. He had *wasta*, connections, of the highest accord. The relationship alone all but guaranteed a lifetime of privilege and affluence.

The others in the room, they all had their special relationships as well. Bloodlines and tribal affiliations, all connected to Emirati investment funds, Arabian oil and gas, petrochemicals, Gulf State construction companies and development firms. The revenues generated by such regional juggernauts were so substantial that even hovering on the outermost periphery, one would be wealthy beyond words. If these characters had anything to gain through involvement in the flesh trade, the motivation certainly wasn't financial.

Outside, past the bar and through the glass wall to his left, was a hot tub in the shape of a figure eight, its perimeter a small mountain range of rough stone and rock, the water a sparkling blue from mood lights beneath. A silver tray of champagne flutes rested on a nearby wooden stool. The foursome who waded amongst the bubbles were lost in their own world. Two men with matching chest pelts and mustaches floated merrily in the shallows, gawking at their counterparts across the way. The blondes, glossy lipped and full figured, flutes in hand, splashed around gaily in front of them, swimsuits red and white like Christmas morning. It certainly seemed to be for the enraptured audience.

It wasn't the party or anything specific that Quinn could identify, but a certain unnerving mood began to settle upon him, like an ominous black sky portending a storm. The darkness closed in, bringing with it all the questions he'd feared to entertain, questions that asked if at last, after all this, he was finally losing the plot.

It was rare to have such a singular drive concentrating all the senses, the raw motivation to sever all superfluous detail and focus unflinchingly on one singular, definitive goal. Then again, such blind ambition wasn't entirely without its drawbacks. On the rare occasion that he did pause to take things into account, to look himself in the mirror, it was clear that he was well beyond his depth and had been for some time. Stubbornly, perhaps even arrogantly, he had insisted on going it alone. And now here he was. No closer to Mei. No closer to anything.

He turned his attention to one of the younger men on the near couch, light skinned with a chiseled beard and finely shaped eyebrows. Pinning a nostril with his index finger, he proceeded to vacuum his nose across the glass table.

Maybe it was time to take a step back, to withdraw and reassess the entire picture. He had been cautious not to involve anyone he didn't trust absolutely. Not here, not in Bangkok, and not in Battambang. But was his caution making matters worse? Was it bordering on some form of paranoia, an obsession that clouded his judgment and hindered his progress, a barrier to letting in those who could help make a difference?

He could rely on Maha, especially now that the conference was over. Surely, she had colleagues who could help, project officers, some locally engaged staff at the very least. It was only law enforcement that really concerned him, and, ironically, it was their assistance that would have been the greatest asset. If he was right in presuming the scale of the operation, their involvement would risk the very real possibility of a leak among the ranks, or worse. A simple tip would undo everything he was rather hopelessly trying to cobble together. In his mind, this perceived element of surprise, whether real or imagined, was the only advantage he possessed. The last thing he needed was word getting out to the wrong people that someone was sniffing around.

Maybe it *was* time for a change. Corruption plagued the authorities; there was no question about it, but he couldn't paint everyone with that brush. Maybe it was time to stop playing the detective, stop pretending he was some sort of private investigator with any inkling of how to track down missing persons. Across an ocean, no less. Bangkok had given him a false sense of confidence, and he was paying the price for his naiveté.

A vision of ruby materialized in his periphery, and he turned to meet the smile of a voluptuous blonde in a painted red dress, looking like some sort of femme fatale from a film noir. She was tall, even without the heels, with an ample bosom on full display and dark lashes that extended outwards like geisha fans. She mewed something at him, a question judging by her tone, though he wasn't paying any attention. He had already turned to what had caught his eye before: a crowd gathering at the far end of the room. Over by the immense stone fireplace, heads were swiveling around, the conversation gathering pace.

It took him a moment to notice that the lights had dimmed, a restless hush sweeping through the room. While the crowd shuffled about, he spotted a grouping of four men wearing all white *shemaghs*, standing prominently like snow-covered mountain peaks in the wild. Taking his seat on a plush leather armchair was a young man whom he assumed was Al-Balawi. He wore a plum colored blazer over a white dress shirt, a sparkling wristwatch the size of an apple, a self-satisfied smirk painted across his tanned face. Slouching on his throne, a chore to be attending yet *another* party, he indulged the commentary made for his amusement and, on occasion, contributed a few quips himself, much to the delight of his pandering entourage; a sultan holding court.

Then, a drumbeat. A piercing timbre building from somewhere behind the bar, echoing throughout the room and maturing seamlessly into a melody, the bass joined incrementally by vibrant, wavering strings and the sensual voice of a soprano. All eyes focused on the foyer entrance, the anticipation growing.

A petite brunette appeared in the doorway to a chorus of rousing applause. A bewitching smile spread across her crimson lips as she stood shimmering, spectacular in the bejeweled, silken dress that draped around her figure. She tapped her bare foot to the beat, then began to clap, nodding and encouraging the crowd to join. Slowly, to the mesmerizing beat of the drum, she floated to the front of the room and began to dance. Her sparkling gold robe left her arms and midsection bare as she swayed her wide hips this way and that, a sensuous rhythm punctuated by rapid gyrations. Her belly, toned yet soft, churned in and out, mirrored by the slim, delicate folds on either side. She had a curvaceous figure in keeping with the mood of the dance, and long, wild hair, which she tossed about every now and again, much to the pleasure of her adoring crowd. The thrusting of her hips and the heaving of her chest sent the men into an uproar, cheering raucously for her wobbling assets while the women, at least the large majority, looked away detachedly, masking their disdain at the new competition. The femme fatale said something else to which Quinn simply nodded. Evidently, she wasn't particularly keen on the new center of attention either.

The music built to a frenzied crescendo, then back down again to its final few bars as the woman's movements slowed. It was a soulful and exotic dance but a tiring one, her cheeks glistening with sweat during the final graceful moments as she set about seducing the room with her gaze. Her eyes, painted dark and mysterious, hidden in shadow, enchanted those upon whom they lingered as she swayed to the rhythm like a majestic cobra, summoned by the delicate notes of a snake charmer's flute.

As the crowd watched, entranced, the performance drawing to its conclusion, Quinn noticed something else about the room, another theme that was evident throughout the soirée yet had somehow eluded him until now. He looked around, confirming his suspicions that all the women, with the exception of the dancer, were blonde.

The marriage consultants, sleazy, second-rate lawyers who facilitated the summer unions only existed, at least in part, because of a unique cultural requirement, relations with minors notwithstanding. Clients sought to legitimize these relationships, at least in some regard. How one rationalized such abuse was another matter entirely, but at least the veneer of lawful matrimony existed once all the requisite paperwork was signed—religious morals accounted for, everyone's virtue still intact.

Here, there was no place for such a façade. No self-deception, no theological window dressing, no need for any marital pretense to avoid committing transgressions. If the cocaine and high-end liquor didn't speak loudly enough, the women sashaying about in skin-tight slips certainly did. No one had any illusions about the company they were keeping or the prices associated with such a provocative guest list.

Blondes. All of them. Not natural, of course, but bleached along the entire spectrum, from botched, off-color dye jobs to brimming shades of platinum. Most importantly, they were all of them, very clearly, willing participants.

These were hardly impoverished young women looking to make ends meet, idling on street corners in Cairo's rundown slums. These were high-end escorts, mature women, paid well, and for good reason. With luxury handbags to match their diamonds and pearls, augmented busts and collagenous lips, they were more business-women than prostitutes—they knew their worth, and who had the money to pay them.

It couldn't have been more obvious. There was nothing to be found. No predators amongst the men, no victims amongst the women, at least not in the vein of what he was searching for. These were business transactions. By one definition or another, these women *wanted* to be in attendance and more than likely made their living by finding their way to such parties with regularity.

The dance having finished, the lights were brought up, and the star of the show, after many bows and kisses blown, took a seat. Quinn had all his questions answered about the man in the plum jacket as the dancer seated herself on his left thigh, head tilted back in coquettish laughter. Perhaps the possibility of a private showing later.

He was tired. Deeply so, in his very bones. Tired of chasing shadows and fumbling in the darkness, grasping at air. Maybe it was time to consider a more realistic perspective, one without such well-intentioned delusions. Maybe it was time to listen to what everyone had been saying so very clearly all along. Not in the words they spoke—Noi, Maha, Youssef—but in the pity he could see so clearly in their eyes, that intolerable look of sympathy. He'd been pushing away the thought for weeks now, refusing to open the door to that darkest of cellars.

He threw back his drink, relishing the sting at the back of his throat and the glow in his belly. The lady in red, pouting her lips to steer his attention, had murmured something else, though it hardly mattered. Given the storm brewing within, he didn't bother feigning any interest and simply stared at her, then turned and started back toward the foyer. Behind him, she scoffed rather loudly to make sure that he heard.

On the way out, the Nigerians were less concerned with his appearance than earlier; however, they too were being entertained by some new company. It wore a silver dress with an open back, open-toed Louboutins, and apparently did not enjoy sharing the spotlight inside the villa. He walked past the guards, past the vehicles out front, past the neighboring villas that lined the unpaved road, and then walked some more. In time he would surely find a taxi, but for now was content to wander the streets alone, a quiet rage smoldering deep within.

The roads were lined with contrasts, from stunning estates and palatial manors to abandoned construction sites—concrete piles and crumbling scaffolding—slums with cluttered balconies and homes without rooftops. Skylines of rusty rebar where "unfinished" dwellings enjoyed exemptions from property taxes.

Eventually, he found a lone taxi who took him most of the way back to Maadi, though they stopped as soon as Quinn recognized some landmarks along El-Nasr Road. He walked the dusty streets of the unusually quiet Egyptian metropolis, an otherworldly ambiance to the silent city at night. By a roadside ravine along Sekat Hadid Al Mahager, he saw a pack of wild dogs, spindly and malnourished, muzzles buried in bags of trash torn asunder. The female stared at him as he passed, his footsteps drawing her attention. With cloudy, wounded eyes, she watched him, her left ear a swollen mass of scar tissue, sagging teats covered in dirt and sand.

Mahmoud was asleep when he arrived, though Quinn couldn't blame him considering the hour. He let the old man rest, snoring like a locomotive on a sullied mattress beneath the staircase. Braced against the sycamore, Quinn hoisted himself over the brick wall, coming down on the other side streaked in dirt and debris but otherwise unscathed. He was thankful that Mr. Shafiq hadn't employed the region's traditional security features along the top of the ledge: shards of broken glass embedded in smears of concrete.

His eyes took some time adjusting to the darkness. Somewhere between navigating the staircase and unlocking the front door, he realized the power was out again. Not that he minded. By the sliver of moonlight that shone through the kitchen window, he grabbed a bottle and a glass and made his way carefully back to the living room. He poured several inches, slumped back on the couch, stared at the glass awhile, then buried his face in his hands.

Suddenly, a flicker of life, violent and incendiary. He swatted the glass aside, heard it splash and shatter somewhere amidst the darkness. For good measure he stood, took a step, and kicked the tufted ottoman with all his might, sending it tumbling across the floor and careening into the far wall with a hollow thud. His chest heaved for a minute or so before he sat down, lowering his head. He ignored the burning welt on his shin, the scent of whiskey in the air, and let the darkness envelop him.

THIRTY-ONE

IT WAS A COOL, OVERCAST DAY, MEEK RAYS OF SUN SWALLOWED UP by gray cloud, gusty winds kicking up sand and swirling litter along the streets. Quinn walked along Qasr El Eyni, rubbing something granular from his eye, traffic inching alongside him as the road congestion grew, ever closer to Tahrir Square.

Along the buildings he passed, scars of the revolution remained: spray-painted murals, portraits, and graffiti. Rebellious slogans had been hurriedly streaked across the concrete, the artist's hand tremulous for fear of being discovered. Other images stayed with him a while longer: stencils of young martyrs caught up in the chaotic times, eyes closed, prayers scrolled nearby, justice demanded in capital letters. Men with saintly angel wings floating above the ground where withered flowers lay beneath their feet.

As he entered the square, traffic slowed to a near standstill. Cars crept through the central roundabout, a grassy oasis amongst the concrete, an Egyptian flag fluttering proudly on high. Conspicuously absent was perhaps the most famous symbol of the great uprising—the charred concrete remains of the former headquarters of the National Democratic Party. Originally founded by Anwar Sadat, it was most famously associated with the iron-fisted rule of Hosni Mubarak, a reign democratic in name only and lasting nearly thirty years. Quinn remembered watching the news on an icy January morning, images of a torched and smoldering building in central Cairo, thousands chanting, singing, waving flags in the night sky.

Though the eyesore had been demolished, so long a reminder of the hope that blossomed with the Arab Spring, it didn't seem as if much had changed. Soldiers remained stationed at roundabouts, regular protests followed the weekly *Jumu'ah* prayer, and now, according to Mahmoud's grainy television set that morning, there was even news of government troops firing upon demonstrators.

Across the square stood the famous Museum of Antiquities, standing out not so much for its *beaux-arts* architecture but more for the odd salmon color of the structure itself. It was a beautiful, old building, built in the neoclassical style though standing rather incongruously amidst the dull, mud-brick beige of the ancient capital.

He crossed the square and, once inside, bought a ticket at the entrance booth. There was a surprising lack of security upon entry, but after some consideration, he realized there wasn't anything surprising about it at all.

Gazing around the entrance hall, he was struck by the amount of natural light that poured in through the windows, illuminating countless statues and artifacts. Yet, the afternoon rays were hardly enough. The museum's own lighting was poor and outdated, leaving many pieces obscured in shadow. There was a distinct, musty odor throughout and a coating of dust that had settled on certain sarcophagi more than others, the entire building in a sad state of disrepair. Still, the ground floor was remarkable in terms of the priceless antiquities on display, the sheer size of the monuments, and the intricate craftsmanship from Egypt's ancient civilization. A colossal monolith of Amenhotep III and Queen Tiye sat high above, the royals watching over the room, missing a few bits and pieces here and there, slowly eroding like the building around them. It was at once the most magnificent and underwhelming museum he had ever seen.

Having arrived early, Quinn took his time, strolling through the ground floor and up the stairs, studying awe-inspiring examples of a great lost dynasty. He perused artifacts through smeared glass display cases and was often guided along by paper signs, directions scrawled by hand. It was quiet throughout, perhaps due to the season, perhaps due to the political atmosphere. The country had never quite recovered from the events surrounding Mubarak's fall, tourism barely returning and certainly without the same enthusiasm, the industry upon which so many Egyptians depended.

At long last he found himself by the mummy exhibit, a separate room cordoned off by stanchions and fraying yellow rope, another handwritten placard in both English and Arabic that read, "Closed for Renovations." A grouping of Chinese tourists followed their guide back down the hall, their disappointment evident even in the foreign Mandarin.

Quinn watched the last of the group turn the corner before he tilted one of the stanchions aside and slipped past, stepping silently into the dimly lit exhibit hall. The room was quiet, eerily so, or at least it would have been but for the metronomic whisk of a sweeping broom. He startled a young woman who looked as if she'd seen a ghost, or perhaps a mummy, come to life, and called out softly to the far end of the room. Maha popped her head up from behind a sarcophagus, wearing the same blue hijab as her colleague. She rounded the display case with a spray bottle and rag in hand, warmth radiating from her familiar dark eyes and broadening smile.

"You found us," she said.

"I did. I feel like a spy, sneaking in here for a secret meeting."

"Oh yes? And where's your briefcase full of money?"

"Nearby. You show me the stuff, I show you the cash."

Maha said something to her friend, now standing with a mischievous grin on her face, scrutinizing Quinn before nodding at the pair of them and shuffling away, broom in hand.

"So," Maha said, motioning around the room. "What do you think?"

"It's nice. A little morbid, but nice. I can't imagine they make for good company."

"It's not so bad. They don't interrupt, and they don't talk back. They're very good listeners."

"I can see that."

"This gentleman here," she said, leading him to an empty display case, "he's actually out for a day at the spa. What we call the laboratory. He needed a few touch-ups." She patted her cheeks with her fingertips.

"Of course, of course. So many people taking pictures, one can get self-conscious. In fact, it looks like there's a few others lying around who could use a bit of work. They look . . . dehydrated."

She raised a finger, assuming the tone of a schoolteacher. "That's the most important part of your skin-care routine, you know. Hydration."

"Naturally."

She examined his face like an esthetician, then said, "Whiskey doesn't count."

"Sure it does. It's liquid, isn't it? What about this girl here?"

They turned to face one of the rare female royals on display, her skeletal frame covered with a thin shroud, a charcoal complexion completely at peace.

"This one could use a different shade of lipstick."

"Mm . . . some blush perhaps."

The two of them stood together, smiling, gazing down on the embalmed queen, a skull with open sockets staring back at them.

"How long have you been working here?"

"Oh, it's not work, really," she said, spritzing the glass and wiping it down. "There's not too much we can do. Most of the restorations are done in laboratories with scientists. It's quite complicated, fixing something that's two thousand years old. But we help out where we can."

He caught the subtle smile on her face. "But you enjoy it."

"Yes. Yes, I do. It's almost like going back in time. I love to think about the lives they led, you know? Who they were. I think about the jewels they wore and which were their favorite. Who poured wine from this vase, who wrote what on this piece of papyrus. It was our golden age. A long one too. Sometimes when I get frustrated with the Egypt of today, I like to come here and remember what we once were. The envy of the world. Well, maybe envy is not the right word . . ."

"One of the greatest civilizations the world has ever known. There's no denying that."

"It's strange, almost like therapy to be here, but then I remember what's happening outside, and it can be so depressing. Even the beauty inside here is at risk. This old building itself is one of the artifacts now, falling apart everywhere. Over a century old, this museum, did you know that? The government gives no money to help because it has no money to give. At every historic site in Egypt you see signs: funded by Germany, funded by Poland, funded by Japan. Our history is maintained by the world, not by us. We even had those . . . those brutes who came smashing and breaking," her eyes turned fiery as she spoke, "stealing things and even destroying mummies. Can you believe this?"

"The looters. I remember seeing it on the news."

She shook her head. "Monsters. I was there, you know, joining arms together outside to stop them from entering. Selling off their own culture, their own history, for what?"

"Mob mentality, I suppose. Desperation."

"Idiocy, more like."

"Fair enough, that too."

She took a deep breath, composing herself. "Look, now you've got me started."

He chuckled. "Do you have a favorite in here?"

"Mummy?"

"Anything. Mummy, artifact, time period."

She smiled once more, a glint in her eye. "Hatshepsut."

"Hm . . . I figured Cleopatra."

"Too cliché. Hatshepsut was the original strongwoman. She was pharaoh fourteen centuries before Cleopatra."

"Fourteen?"

She nodded, then glanced at her watch. "I need a few minutes to finish up here, then I'll give you a history lesson over lunch."

THIRTY-TWO

Outside, the clouds had begun to disperse, beams of sunlight, glowing and insistent, revealing thin slivers of blue sky. The air remained cool, an occasional blustery wind hinting that a storm lay somewhere in wait, unforeseen beyond the horizon.

Maha waved farewell to some of her co-volunteers as they walked past the museum's outer gate, an imposing column of tanks in desert camouflage parked along the perimeter.

"I thought we could walk," she said. "It's not far."

"Sure," he replied, sheltering his cigarette from a gust of wind. He poked his chin toward a crowd of demonstrators who had gathered in front of the Mogamma building to the south of the square. "What's going on over there?"

From a distance they could only make out the colors of a few placards bobbing above the group, the metallic shrill of a bullhorn echoing nothing more than static and white noise.

"The same as always. Every week now. The problem is that ever since we filled the square, even big demonstrations seem so small. No one pays attention."

"It's been a bit tense lately, no? They woke me up the other night, marching down my street."

"It's more common in recent months. I don't know why

exactly; the complaints are still the same. The problems from before remain unresolved. And, of course, they're legitimate problems. But every once in a while the protests become more serious. They, *yanni* . . . flare up? Yes. On Fridays they gather in front of their local mosques and plan their routes. Like they did before, leading to Tahrir. But the more aggressive they become, the harder the pushback. Our government does not wait to take action; they act, and when they act, people lose their families. In the prison or the grave. You remember Rabaa al-Adawiya, the clearing of the square?"

He nodded. "Awful. What was it, five hundred casualties?"

"Eight hundred. They like to ignore the numbers from Human Rights Watch. Anyway, enough of that talk," she said as they crossed the street. "How are things with you? With Mei? Any progress?"

He took a long drag of his cigarette and scratched his stubbled chin. "You know what? I don't really feel like talking about it. Not right now, anyway. It's been a rough few days. I'm starting to feel like maybe . . ." He searched for the words, found them, and decided on another lungful of smoke.

Maha waited a few steps before saying anything. "I'm sorry, Quinn."

In the air hung an all-too-familiar silence. Out of respect, words of comfort went unspoken. Thoughts of all the most likely outcomes were too raw, too painful to discuss.

"It's alright," he said after a while. "After this I may need your help though. I have some passports that I'd like some of your colleagues to look at, if possible. I was thinking maybe you could put me in touch with the general who spoke at the conference. Al-Hashimi, I think it was."

"Fatima, yes. She's terrific. Of course." She paused for a moment. "I know you don't want to talk about it, but if there's anything else I can do, just say it. I feel I've not been much help to you."

He forced a grateful smile, then shook his head. "What more could you have done?" He flicked the nub of his cigarette into the air and watched as it dropped behind a mound of debris by the roadside. "Now, I believe you said something about a history lesson?"

"Ah, yes, that's right. It seems I have to educate you about our great queen, Hatshepsut."

"Will this be a lesson based on fact or opinion?"

"Shh—you see? This is the problem. People don't know how important a ruler she was. This great woman's legacy was almost lost because of others taking credit for her achievements."

"I know of her temple. The big one with the columns, near the Valley of the Kings?"

Maha closed her eyes, smacking her palm against her forehead in jest.

"I'm pretty sure I saw it on a postcard the other day."

"Deir el-Bahri, yes, her famous mortuary temple. One of the most famous sites we have. And she deserved a grand temple, of course. You know she ruled longer than any other Egyptian woman. Over twenty years. Centuries before Cleopatra, like I said."

"That Cleopatra. Always stealing the headlines."

"She wasn't so bad, but not truly Egyptian like Hatshepsut. Cleopatra was from the Ptolemaic dynasty, the Greeks. Or Macedonians, depending who you ask." She turned to him, her finger raised. "But not Egyptian. Hatshepsut was one of the most successful pharaohs ever to rule ancient Egypt. Famous for building monuments and temples. Statues. Obelisks. For establishing trade in the region, bringing gold and ivory and perfumes. And, most importantly, peace throughout her reign. Twenty years of stability in such an age. Can you believe it? Here we've had two revolutions in less than a decade."

"Well, when you put it that way . . ."

"And you know what they did? You know why you haven't heard of her? Because they tried to erase her from history. They took credit for the temples she built and carved away her portraits from the stone. They even destroyed statues of her and tried to remove her name from historical records."

"Who, her successors?"

"Yes. Well, there's some debate about this now. That her stepson, Thutmose . . ." She paused and put a finger to her lips, then waved her hand dismissively. "I can't remember which one, the second or third Thutmose; there were many. He was jealous of sharing the throne with her. So, this was his revenge. And *his* son, Amenhotep number . . . something, he defaced her hieroglyphics as well, they say maybe to prevent women from holding so much power again. She claimed to be the daughter of the great god Amun."

He scoffed. "Men."

She nodded fiercely. "Exactly. Always trying to hold us back."

He chuckled. "Well, you can't blame me for what jealous pharaohs were doing a thousand years ago. My people had nothing to do with that. We were far too busy raping and pillaging up and down the Baltic coast."

"Oh, yes," she said, rolling her eyes, "you Vikings were so sophisticated."

"We certainly were. Plundering was very much à la mode back then. I'll admit it's fallen slightly out of fashion in recent years, but there was a time when women would swoon at the sight of a hulking brute swinging an axe."

Maha shook her head, hiding her smile. "You're unbelievable."

A gust of wind carried the low sound of agitated voices from somewhere up ahead. As they approached a small intersection, the voices grew louder, the rhythm of the chorus more familiar. To their right, down a narrow, cobbled street, an old mosque stood in the distance. In front of it, a mass of men and women chanted in unison, the odd fist raised defiantly in the air. The march was just beginning, slowly spilling out into choked lanes of traffic.

Soon, wave after wave of bodies clogged the intersection, drivers responding by honking their horns or shouting from open windows. The drivers could barely be heard over the growing cacophony. Quinn watched as an old man with hunched shoulders pushed a wooden cart of assorted herbs away from the demonstration.

"We should go back," Maha said, apprehensive. "We can find a different restaurant."

He nodded. "Where are they going?"

"Probably south, to Tahrir. To join the others."

Passersby increased their pace, moving swiftly away from the boisterous mass of protesters. A rusty Skoda attempted a three-point turn and was enveloped by the crowd. As it inched forward, several men reacted angrily to the intrusion, shouting and slamming their palms on the hood of the vehicle.

"Quinn . . ."

At first, it was difficult to tell where the screams were coming from. A couple of men turned their attention toward Quinn and Maha, faces contorted with anger, then, eyes wide with surprise, pointing, shouting. Maha instinctively grabbed his shoulder.

He felt it before he looked, the hair on his neck, the dry choke of his throat. Again, voices, different voices, coming from elsewhere now. The men weren't pointing at them—they were pointing *past* them, behind. The first man ducked as a brick soared through the air, a frightening thud as it crashed behind him. Another gray blur arced overtop, catching the second man in the shoulder with a puff of dust, spinning him violently to one side like a ragdoll.

Quinn turned and spotted streaks of color sprinting down a sloping alley toward them, a rabid mob following closely on the heels of those leading the charge. He hardly noticed their faces, his eyes drawn to the pieces of rebar in their hands and the glass bottles leaving them, pitched forward, hurling through the air.

Maha cried out and dug her fingers into his arm. He twisted to the side, snatching her out of the way, just narrowly avoiding the berserker run of a hooded man clutching a tire iron. As he pulled her aside, something struck him from behind, a force charging through him like a rampaging bull. For what seemed like a long moment, he was weightless. Then his palms scraped across the pavement, the rest of him following, thudding heavily against the ground.

He tried to draw breath but couldn't, his lungs empty and crumpled in the pit of his stomach. Glancing up, he saw the chanting voices from the mosque collide with the roar of the opposing mob, bodies slamming together like bowling pins, toppling in all directions, limbs swinging wildly. A boot came down on his leg, and he hollered in pain, his breath returning through clenched teeth. All around—the shuffle of feet, the scrape of gravel, the chime of smashed glass, the grunts and shouts of men.

He couldn't get to his feet, so he crawled, fought his way to one side, the occasional kneecap clipping him as it charged by. At one point a man fell on top of him and was met with a fury of wild fists and elbows—Quinn swinging upwards in a blind panic until the man slumped over to one side.

Out of the main thoroughfare, he scrambled unsteadily to his knees, then stood and looked around. He searched for the beige sweater and the navy hijab, but all he saw was a blur of beards and scarves, boots and fists. He forced his way along the side of a building, scanning the brawl that was unfolding across the intersection, the chaos spilling out in every direction, individual scrums taking on a life of their own amongst the greater melee. He spotted a flicker of blue amongst the crowd, his heart stopping as a splash of crimson colored the face before it disappeared from view. Tearing at shoulders in front of him, he looked on, breathless, until a clearing revealed the grimace of a young man in a brown jacket, his nose bleeding profusely. Relieved but for a moment, he flinched when another projectile fell from the sky and crashed into the windshield of a parked car.

Then he saw her. To his left, maybe ten feet away, swatting at an older man with a distended belly. Fighting his way in her direction, Quinn's progress was slow as he tore at throats and collars, clamoring from behind in vain. Bits of cloth would slip from his fingers, the mass of bodies heaving forward and back, rising and falling like an ocean swell, pushing him closer, then carrying him away.

He looked on helplessly as the heavy man pinned her against the wall, his thick hand smacking her across the face. She responded in earnest, reaching up with her free hand and pulling a pin from her hijab. She raked it across his face, leaving a dark, burgundy streak. As he pulled away, clutching his cheek, she swung again and again, settling into a fierce, lashing rhythm.

Moving ever closer, a wooden club caught Quinn beneath his chin—clusters of stars, iridescent, danced before him—until he shook his head, then ripped the splintering two-by-four from a set of hands. The hands attempted to seize it back, the owner catching the butt end firmly in the chest before staggering backward and disappearing into a knot of bodies. Quinn swung his new instrument before him like a sledgehammer, cracking walnuts as he went, clearing his path.

He forced his way through until Maha was within touching distance, flailing against her attacker, who had rallied himself. His face was twisted into a snarl, eyes wild and enraged, crimson rivulets dribbling along the length of his cheek. He lunged forward but was met with a crack of lumber that whipped his skull to one side. A puff of sawdust floated above his head like a magician's spell as he went limp, crumpling to the ground in a heap. Tossing the weapon aside, Quinn grabbed Maha who cried out and recoiled in fear before meeting his eyes.

"This way!" he shouted, pulling her along the edge of a storefront, back toward the intersection. The mob was a singular heaving mass, everyone engaged with one another, outliers scrambling away from the scene. They slipped along the edge of the chaos, Maha screaming as yet another man tumbled into them, nearly sweeping her legs out from underneath.

An unmistakable sound stopped them dead in their tracks. The staccato burst of an automatic weapon froze the entire crowd, everyone ducking instinctively. A second spray of bullets sent bodies scattering in all directions. Quinn couldn't tell where the shots came from. He looked forward and back again, trying to find a clear path in any direction.

"Hold on," he said, kicking over a display table of tomatoes and stepping onto an overturned crate. In the middle of the intersection he spotted a grouping of uniformed men, a wall of black with helmets and plastic visors. Riot shields moved together in unison, forming a great barrier that, on occasion, separated here and there to release the vicious swing of a black baton. A cloud of smoke had formed at their feet and drifted upwards, obstructing the view of everyone in the vicinity, lending a distinct advantage to the newest arrivals.

His first thought was tear gas, and yet, no one was reacting. Those caught in the thick of the haze fumbled around for their bearings, frightened and confused but not incapacitated. A flare, perhaps. The smoke grew, enveloping the front of the crowd, who were now blind to the batons that rained down from the fog. Peering down the lane, Maha caught sight of the shields as well and pulled at his shirt. She looked up at him, eyes welling with tears, and shook her head. *Not that way.*

They went back. Tripping over eggplants and other fresh produce, caroming off bodies that grappled with one another, weaving their way through the storm. Maha's hijab had unraveled, and she tore it away, casting it aside as she went. She was quick and agile, her small frame able to elude the obstacles that appeared endlessly in their path. Quinn's height made him more of a target as he struggled to keep pace. They crept by a wall, a brief opening between bodies, and were eventually funneled along the sidewalk by a row of parked cars. The sound of distant gunfire ripped through the street once again, eliciting shrieks from the crowd. Quinn grabbed Maha and forced her head down as they pressed forward.

A few feet in front, he spotted a gap, the smoke clearing and the crowd thinning out into tentative onlookers and the wounded, tending to their injuries. Maha tripped, falling to the ground, but recovered quickly, and he pushed her along towards the opening.

When he looked up again, the shouting, the scrambling, and the erratic gunfire suddenly ceased, the din replaced by the hollow tolling of a bell, the chaos before him now a serene scape of blue sky and billowing clouds.

He blinked slowly, noting that all the sounds were actually still there, muffled and echoing around him, but the ring of the bell was far more soothing, and he embraced it. Maha's face appeared before him, looking down, concerned, more than concerned, saying something, perhaps even shouting.

He preferred the sky. The clouds. The way they floated lazily in the atmosphere above, drifting amidst the faded blue until it turned to dusk. It was tiring, watching the clouds, exhausting, and it wasn't long before the dusk, rather swiftly, darkened along the periphery, and turned to night.

Ghonlaat,

How are you? I am well. I think that my English is improving! We have a teacher now from England who is helping us at the weekend. She is very nice. Her name is Katie. I think Katie is very charming and also very beautiful. She is not married, and I think she needs a good husband. I told to Noi that maybe when you come and visit us again you can meet Katie and think she is beautiful! Will you visit again on Christmas this year? Noi says you are very busy with working so I understand if you can't. I love the snow picture you send of your home and the snowman. One day I will build a snowman. This is my dream. Today it is too hot. I think the snowman should give me a hug! Today I drew a picture for you of me and the snowman. I hope you like it. Okay, bye for now,

Mei

THIRTY-THREE

Somewhere in a distant dreamland, a man sang to Quinn from a remote mountaintop. The melody floated down a sandy peak, along the sun-bleached cliff face, and drifted into his consciousness, gently rousing him from slumber with every new stanza. For a while he simply lay, savoring the delicate notes of the Arabian harmony, letting it wash over him.

He opened his eyes, thick, tired lids squinting at his strange surroundings. For a moment he remained motionless, observing the peculiarities of the room until his senses began to return, realizing that he was, in fact, in his own bedroom, back in Maadi. He was awake, of that he was certain, yet the man who was serenading him from the mountaintop continued his song, the voice drifting in through an open window. It was dark out, and he realized it was likely *isha'a*, the melodious call to prayer lingering in the wind from a nearby minaret.

And then, he remembered. He tried to prop himself up, though his elbow caught a small dish on the nightstand, knocking it to the ground. The sharp clatter hurt his head as much as the wincing. He felt the soft tissue of a bandage above his brow and, a moment later, heard the pitter-patter of footsteps down the corridor.

Maha appeared in the doorway, a familiar look of concern on her face, followed by relief as she exhaled. She was wearing his white dress shirt and khakis, the top billowing like a parachute and the pants cinched to the tightest belt notch above her slender waist. Her hair was wrapped in a white towel and sat like a turban on her head, the body of a giant cobra draped down her back.

"Nice outfit," he said, flinching slightly as he explored his bandage.

"Still you make jokes?" she said, incredulous.

He shrugged. "We might need to find you a tailor, but generally, I think it works. Desert chic."

She made a disapproving sound with her tongue, then picked up the dish and wet cloth from the floor, seating herself at the edge of the bed. She was self-conscious now, draping her arms around herself, clothed and yet not, sitting in his bedroom.

"Are you alright?" he asked.

She nodded.

"Sure?"

"Yes, I'm fine. How are *you* feeling?"

"Like my head is two sizes too big."

"That's just your ego."

He smiled. "Now who's making jokes?"

It came as a relief to both of them, slipping back so easily into their little routine, despite the fact that Maha remained visibly shaken from the experience, whether she admitted it or not.

"What happened?"

"What do you remember?"

He thought about it. "Running. The noise. Then . . . nothing. Waking up here."

"You took a nasty blow to the head. I didn't even realize until you weren't behind me anymore. I looked back and saw someone dragging you to the side."

"Who?"

"Some men nearby. Everyone was going in all directions, and those who stayed were helping the injured. You were, well, honestly I didn't know what to think just then." For a moment her emotions got the better of her, and she rubbed her palms together in distraction. "One of the men offered to drive us home. He said there was a curfew. You woke up for a few minutes, do you remember? No, I didn't think so. You didn't say anything. You were looking around but not really seeing. The man and his friend helped carry you up the stairs."

"Curfew?"

She nodded. "Military curfew. From seven at night until six in the morning. What we saw, that was only a small part. They say there were riots like this all across the city. Some worse than others. The police were ready and waiting. At least fifty dead, who knows how many injured. The numbers will be higher by the morning. Events like this, you can always tell when our government is becoming worried . . ."

"Who started it? I mean, there were two groups we saw, right?"

She shook her head, neatly folding the damp cloth in her lap. "I'm not sure. It feels very much like 2013 with the Muslim Brotherhood. But after Morsi fell, all of them were arrested—well, the most influential ones. Maybe they've regained their numbers, I don't know. Or it could be another group like them, tired of the way the country is being run. They wouldn't be the first to think this way, and they have good reason to be upset, angry. Sometimes they take action. Then there are those who defend the government no matter what they do." A beleaguered sigh escaped her lips. "*Wallahi*, sometimes I don't know what is happening to this country."

"Is that why you're here? The curfew?"

"Also you were unconscious and bleeding on my shirt."

"I didn't mean it like that."

"I know. I found some first-aid supplies in the bathroom. You have a horrible gash on your head. It looks like a fig. We agreed you didn't need stitches, so I cleaned it as best as I could. I wanted to put more ice, but it was soaking the dressing."

"Thank you."

"By the time I finished, I realized the curfew had passed. I called my family to let them know I'm safe, but, if you don't mind . . ."

He gave her a look, and even the slight curl of his brow stung the wound. "Of course. Don't even mention it."

When she reached up to adjust her towel, he caught sight of a nasty scrape the length of her forearm. He held her wrist and angled it toward the light.

"It's nothing," she said.

"Where's your bandage?"

"I was about to put it on."

"I can do it."

"It's alright."

She folded her hands in her lap, straightening her posture. "I was just doing some laundry; that's why I'm wearing this. There was a lot of blood. It was all over my shirt. Yours too."

"Sure."

"I'll go check on it. Are you hungry?"

"Not really."

"Me neither. I'll make some tea."

And with that, she stood and left the room. Quinn did his best to sit, at first propping himself up on his elbows, successfully this time, and eventually, with some effort, swung his legs out from under the sheets. The floor was cool, and he sat for a moment weathering the storm that had gathered in his head, the rush and pulsation of blood just above his right eye. He heard a faint click in the air, the sound all too familiar as the power went out yet again, followed by a whispered curse from Maha in the kitchen.

Eyes adjusting to the darkness, he stood, propping himself against the wall, and carefully slipped on a shirt. He had finished with a single button when he heard a booming explosion, the building itself shuddering, windowpanes rattling. Then, the same blood-chilling eruption of gunfire, much closer than whatever had detonated in the distance. He heard a yip from the living room and fumbled down the hallway where he heard voices shouting from the street.

Maha was at the window, the same one where he had stood a few nights before, gazing at the raucous mob below. From her silhouette he saw that her hair was down, long and unruly, still damp from the shower, and she wore glasses with thick rectangular frames. He joined her, and they stood side by side observing a similar procession, although this time the mob was far more aggressive, determined. No one walked casually now; they marched. No one came along simply for the fresh air; they raised fists, arms fervidly thrusting into the black sky. Whatever they chanted was different now—they spat the words with vitriol, shouted so their voices carried from the Red Sea to the Mediterranean.

"This is not going to end well."

"What are they doing," she said, a statement, rather than a question. "They'll be lucky if they find themselves in a jail cell. The police won't hesitate to fire on them if they feel threatened."

"Maybe if they stay along these backstreets—"

Someone toward the rear let off a flurry of automatic rounds, rippling the air, a sequence of violent muzzle flashes in the darkness. The sound startled both of them. Maha clutched his arm, pressing herself against him as Quinn held his breath. The crowd cheered as the man held the trigger once more, throwing his head back defiantly as he punctured the night sky.

They stood, mesmerized by the march that flooded past, the shouting and riotous chants muffled through the glass. Maha clung to him as their breathing, offset, was the only sound in the still apartment. More gunfire, erratic and unnerving, a second gunman, already out of view, making his presence felt.

They didn't speak, and as Quinn held her, their inhales and exhales settled into a harmonized rhythm, bodies tense and watchful. After a long while—as if half the city had joined the demonstration—the crowd finally thinned, echoes of the insurgent mantra fading as the mob retreated back into the darkness from where it had emerged.

Maha didn't move, so neither did he, his arm still cradling the small of her back, all too aware of the scent of her hair and the swell of her breast, rising and falling between them. Having waited long enough, he turned his head and gently lifted her chin with a finger, her eyes meeting his. He slipped off her glasses, revealing the dark, precisely shaped arches of her eyebrows, her eyes, golden, like liquid toffee in the ambient light. He traced the crescent moon scar on her chin.

"What's this?"

"I was young."

"Mm . . ."

"Coffee table."

"Clumsy."

"*Nam.*" She swallowed. "Yes."

He kissed her, and he meant it. Holding back, he awaited her reaction, for a moment unsure, until she slowly pressed her pursed lips against his. A soft kiss, he felt her trembling through shallow breaths. Mouths closed, another, then another. Mouths open, he cradled the back of her neck as she sank into the moment, wrapping her arms around him, folding into the embrace. They moved against the wall, shallow breaths now deep and long, the world falling away behind them. She cupped his face in her hands, studied him, hungrily explored the contours of his shoulders, and he, drinking her in, caressed the length of her figure, grazing her petite breasts, nipples taut beneath the thin fabric.

Down the hallway, eager hands, fiddling with buttons, grasping at sleeves, the brush and chafe of cotton. She smelled of a floral bouquet, fresh from the shower, though he caught a subtle whiff of himself, old sweat now a bitter musk. Even so, she didn't seem to mind. In the darkness, an echoing thud sounded as he bumped his already tenderized skull against a door frame.

"Christ," he exclaimed.

"*Ayy*, are you alright?" She cradled his head, stifling her laughter. "How many times . . ."

She caressed the bandage and brought his attention back to her, then, with the slightest hesitation, placed her mouth on his. Standing in the cool, dark hallway, they held one another. When he released her belt buckle with his thumb, the pants, several sizes too big, crumpled to the ground in a heap. And as they fell together on the bed, the old springs strained beneath the sudden weight.

The bedspread was an obstacle; the comforter pushed aside, pillows swept onto the floor, in their own world now, tugging at what little clothing remained. Maha gasped as he slid his hand in between, nestling her face into the nape of his neck as they slowly embraced. Rocking in unison, she whimpered the most personal of sounds in his ear, stirring his head, senses overtaking him. He felt her warm, shallow sighs as she neared, clutching at his back, grasping his hair and then, a moment suspended, before quivering beneath him, and he, breathless, following thereafter.

The silence of the evening was occasionally broken by the rioting that enveloped the city around them—the stillness of midnight interrupted by political fervor that would not sleep, would not know peace until the early hours of dawn. And so, the pair spent the night listening to the crackle of distant gunfire, sweat on their skin, blissfully tangled in fine Egyptian linens.

THIRTY-FOUR

A HEAVY KNOCK ON THE DOOR. QUINN STIRRED, OPENING HIS EYES, pleased to see that it was morning, pleased that she still lay by his side. They faced one another, heads pressed into their pillows, retrieved from the floor at some point in the night, neither saying a word. The morning rays that shone from the window illuminated every speckle of dust that hung in the air, motes like tiny constellations drifting above their heads. He could tell she had been awake for some time, watching him, a shy, little smile, half hidden behind the sheets.

Another knock.

"I'll get it," he said finally, then winced as flecks of dried blood clung to the pillowcase.

"Stay. I ordered breakfast." She swung her legs out of bed and, making sure he got no view at all, pulled the comforter clean off, wrapping it around herself like a giant robe. On the way to the door, she threw a towel over her head, tucking her hair beneath it with one hand as if she had done so a thousand times.

As she paid the deliveryman, Quinn peeled away his bandage, feeling around the hot, tender walnut on his forehead. She returned and sat on the bedside with a brown paper bag and a tray with two coffee cups. The aroma was heavenly, freshly roasted beans and fragrant cardamom.

"Breakfast in bed?"

"Why not?" he replied, propping himself against the bed-frame, only then realizing his left shoulder was slightly out of sorts as well.

"Here, this will help."

He took a sip of the strong black coffee as she laid out paper plates with crisp falafel, oily hummus, fragrant *ful*, and slices of bread and cheese. The food was delicious, and they ate in nearly complete silence, realizing only then how famished they were. When they finished, they folded everything back into the paper bag and put it aside. Maha remained seated, wrapped to her chin in the duvet, though her long hair flowed down around her in thick, natural waves. The meal was no longer a distraction, and she struggled to find her words.

"Last night," she began, "I don't, I don't want you to think, I've never—"

"I've never been in a riot either. We're more about peaceful protests where I'm from."

She rolled her eyes, unamused, so he took her hand. "I know," he said, then made sure he had her attention. "I know."

After a moment, making certain of his sincerity, the same bashful smile curled the left side of her mouth. She looked away. "Well," she said, changing the subject, "it wasn't *my* first riot."

"No?"

"Tahrir, 2011. We were all there."

"That's right."

He rubbed his thumb back and forth across her hand, interlaced his fingers with hers. When he kissed her, she tasted of salt and cumin, and she breathed in deeply when he tugged at the duvet, and let it fall from her bare shoulders.

In the languid afterglow, the conversation flowed as smoothly as it did before, as it always had. Maha's comments about the protests had piqued his interest, and they spoke of her first experience during the Arab Spring, the revolution that had gone so wrong for Egypt. He found that, much like himself, she was somewhat disillusioned and rather cynical about all that went on in Cairo. In 2011, there was an optimism that had permeated society, a powerful sentiment that this was their moment. It was an exciting time when Egyptians came together from all creeds and walks of life, unified, a chance to forge something new, to create real, lasting change. Tragically, the opportunity had been squandered, devolving into the usual bickering amongst political egos. And it was the people, as always, who suffered the most, destitute and unfulfilled, their dreams, having shone so brightly, turned to ash.

She expressed particular disdain when he mentioned the hope that had surrounded General Sisi's ascension. Her voice hit a fever pitch when she spoke of the infamous "red carpet fiasco." While statistics showed the country's dire poverty levels, and the general, now president, spoke of economic reform, even his motorcade received special treatment. A giant carpet was woven for the procession, four kilometers long, because heaven forbid the tires of the presidential convoy touch the cracked, filthy streets.

They talked of Mei and of Quinn's favorite memories, which, to his surprise, he found comforting, despite his initial reticence. Trips to Battambang and local excursions thereafter; Noi's frequent updates regarding Mei's progress in school, particularly in English; the money he sent, without hesitation—whatever she needed or wanted; the sketches and paintings that arrived in the mail, envelopes crinkled and sooty from the long journey. He would read the letters of an innocent, having escaped a terrible fate by the skin of her teeth, only to have her bright future clawed back once again. It wasn't long before he deflected the conversation, the topic grating on him, disconsolately spoken in the past tense, words flowing as if in eulogy.

"What will you do now? Will you go back to work?"

"I'm not really sure where *work* would be," he said, shrugging indifferently. "It's been a little while since I've been gainfully employed."

"What do you mean?"

"I was taking some time off—a few months—before I got the news about Mei. Not really sure where I'd fit in at the moment."

"Is that what Marchand was saying, about the Philippines?"

"Sort of. I wouldn't put much stock into what comes out of his mouth."

"No one does. That's why I'm asking you."

"Well, I didn't get fired. I quit."

"Isn't that what people usually say when they're fired?" she asked, playfully arching a brow.

"Don't get me wrong—I definitely would have been fired for what I said. But that's not the point."

"What *is* the point?"

He shook his head, gently. "I'm not sure I'm ready to go back just yet."

She rested her head on his chest, and they lay together for a few minutes. Through the open window drifted a calming breeze; the city silent and tranquil, a respite from the previous evening's furor. Somewhere in a neighboring garden, a family of sparrows chirped gaily.

"It wasn't just about Mei, really. It started long before that."

"Being so cynical."

He nodded, slowly, deep in thought. She reached up and held his cheek in her palm, turning his attention toward her. "What happened to make you such a grouch?"

"What happened in Tahrir to make you so—"

"Nothing happened in Tahrir. I should say, nothing happened *after* Tahrir. That was the problem. And *realistic*, I think, is the word you're looking for."

He smirked, quite enjoying the little flashes of attitude that she continually shot his way.

"Tell me about Manila."

"Like you said, it's what didn't happen. Pass me my cigarettes?"

"You don't need those."

"Says who?"

"Says me."

"Christ . . ."

"Leave him out of it."

A brief and rather stubborn staring contest ensued, broken only by the weight of Maha's curiosity as she reluctantly handed over the pack of Camels with a cluck of her tongue.

"Well, as these stories usually begin, there was a girl—not like that, not at all." He tapped the pack against his palm. "Just a visa applicant, like any another. Sophie. Sophie Reyes. I was on assignment to enhance security screening checks for work visas. It was just an assessment, really. Get the lay of the land, find the gaps, make some recommendations, and then, inevitably, listen to them moan about the lack of resources. The usual.

"So, it didn't take long before it was obvious that the screening process was complete garbage. I mean, anybody could get a travel document. The post was overwhelmed with applications, so the reviews became even more brief. Submissions were scanned, glossed over; there wasn't any time to do in-depth screening or much desire either. At one point they were toying with the idea of skipping the interview process altogether, simply accepting submissions at face value. The level of fraudulent applications coming in was already sky high, and there they were, considering mailing visas without even speaking to anyone."

He tore a match from a booklet, lit his cigarette, then took an empty coffee cup for an ashtray.

"Anyway, instead of slowing down, they ramped things up. More approvals meant more income, new immigrants, a boost for the economy, etcetera. But the worst part of it was, when it came to domestic workers, the live-in caregivers, they weren't screening the employers either. They were pumping out permits so fast the ink hadn't dried, and they had even less information about the reception.

"So, I reported all this back, but obviously, they weren't concerned. Some days they replied saying I was doing a great job, buttering me up, other times . . ." He let out a sigh. "They heard what they wanted to hear, and they were too scared to tell their superiors any different. Heaven forbid someone ends up with a blemish on their immaculate record. After all, no one gets a promotion by speaking the truth. Then, one day, I was overseeing some of the interviews in person, routine applications for the live-in caregiver program."

"This is nursing—at home."

"Exactly. There's millions of them. From basic domestic work to at-home patient care, there are Filipino women all over the world doing this. It's one of the country's biggest exports. Unfortunately, they often end up in places like Saudi or Kuwait, or with families in Hong Kong, Singapore. It's a roll of the dice for them, really. There's a lot of horror stories that come with this type of work."

"We have it here too. Filipinos but also Indians. Bengalis."

He took a long drag and blew a plume up at the ceiling. "There was a break in the interviews, a couple of no-shows, but there's this girl, waiting in the lobby. She was over an hour early. She was maybe twenty but looked all of fifteen—just over five feet tall, braces, little ponytail, bubbly personality. How she was so positive, I still have no idea, with everything she'd been through.

"She told us how her family had been victims of Typhoon Haiyan, which devasted the region. The Visayas were hit particularly hard, and, even though she escaped from Cebu to Manila, the family lost everything. House, belongings"—his palm cut through the air like a scythe—"everything. She finished school and wanted to work abroad as a nanny but figured she could earn more money for the family as a caregiver.

"She was so excited about the opportunity but nervous as all hell. She answered the questions, her voice quivering the entire time, 'Yes sir,' 'No sir,' hands folded in her lap, nodding politely, eyes as wide as dinner plates.

"And, that was that. We did most of the interview for procedure only; of course, there were no concerns. Later that week I sent my routine email back to headquarters—employer screening, we need to do more, the same bullet point suggestions, no response." He took another drag. "And you know, I'm pretty sure I never would have thought of her again."

Maha sensed the shifting mood, the distant gaze that glossed over his pale blue eyes. She propped herself up on an elbow.

"It was maybe, a year later, more or less, when I got this email. 'Do you remember this case? Such and such girl. Sophie Reyes.' No idea, to be honest. Filipinos have such unique names, some of them, and hers was fairly standard. I opened the passport photo in the attachment, and there she was. Braces. Ponytail. I scanned the email, didn't really understand what I was reading, or maybe just didn't want to. I clicked the link to the newspaper article and read that instead.

"Sophie had her application approved, of course, and according to the article, ended up working for the Sayyid family. As the live-in caregiver, it was her responsibility to take care of the elder Mrs. Sayyid, the bedridden mother of Farooq, a middle-aged man who ran an electronics store. Farooq's wife, Zainab, was apparently too preoccupied to tend to her mother-in-law's needs—with what, I don't know. She was a housewife, after all, yet Sophie did all the housework. All of it. If the list of chores was not completed, she was beaten and had her wages confiscated. She was made to sleep in the laundry closet for her disobedience, or at least that was the rationale that was given to the police.

"A few months into her stay, she committed the grave sin of becoming pregnant. In the end, it was determined to be Farooq's child, although DNA from his brother, Ahmad, was found as well. Zainab disagreed with the rape charges, claiming it was the girl's own fault for seducing them, acting like a shameless whore. Again, this was how they justified it to the police.

"Solving the problem didn't seem to involve any real head scratching. In the end, it was Farooq who caved in her head with an antique tea kettle. Her little fingers had been polishing that silver kettle nearly every day since she arrived. Forensics determined that, despite the head trauma, her body showed signs of repeated abuse—cuts, burns—likely since the very beginning. It hadn't taken them long to find the body in a nearby park, at the bottom of a small ravine, hidden under a pile of brush and leaves. It was the neighborhood dog walker who found her—one of the dogs, anyway. The coroner said she still had silver polish beneath her fingernails."

He took one last draw and swished the butt around in the cup, a final gasp of smoke spiraling into the air. "After that, it was a little difficult to come to work. I wondered if there wasn't more I could have done. I knew who I held responsible. I knew the system was inherently flawed, but it wasn't enough. I'm not surprised Marchand got wind of it. I had a bit of a meltdown about a week later. They called it insubordination, which is putting it lightly. I should probably be thankful for that. I just didn't care anymore. What was the point? All the signs were there—I knew it, they knew it, and they didn't care. No one did. And in the end, it was that poor kid who paid for it. Last I heard, they went ahead and stopped doing face-to-face interviews. Overwhelmed with applications, they just take submissions as they are now."

It was clear that Maha didn't know what to say. There were no words of comfort for such situations. She laid a hand over his, the best she could manage.

"I quit. Ended up, well, eventually, in Costa Rica. Drinking myself into a stupor. A week turned into a month, a month into . . ." He sighed, running his fingers through his hair. "I don't know how long, to be honest. I wasn't at my best. And, that's when I heard about Mei."

Her eyes searched his, a look of contemplation as she pieced the missing elements together, making sense of the man lying next to her—the raw, scar tissue that marred his psyche, the obsessive, all-consuming need for redemption, no matter how misguided.

For his part, he realized he wasn't altogether uncomfortable telling her any of it. He hadn't spoken about Sophie to anyone, not since the shouting match in a boardroom in Manila. He never much wanted to, either. He liked that Maha wasn't saying anything. He preferred the quiet moments with her, hidden away from all the cold, unforgiving realities of the outside world. And the way she looked at him now—perceptive, empathetic—he knew she understood, at least as best as she was able.

Outside, the sparrows had been silenced by some local children kicking a soccer ball, the scuffle of shoes across the dirt, an occasional yelp, the pang of a deflated ball against brick. Yet the breeze remained, soft and welcome, bringing with it the muted sounds of life beyond the bedroom—only a hint, so as not to disturb the silence.

A sharp knock on the door split the air.

THIRTY-FIVE

Mahmoud stood in the doorway, beads of sweat on his forehead, a look of distress on his weathered face, more crevassed than usual.

"Mahmoud. Can I help you?"

He held an envelope in his hand but was more concerned with Quinn's visible contusion, extending his arm outwards, then motioning to his own forehead, wincing theatrically.

"It's alright, Mahmoud."

"He was very concerned last night when they carried you in," Maha said from down the hall. "I ordered him some breakfast too. Did he get it?"

Quinn noted the remnants of hummus smeared in the corner of the old caretaker's frosted mustache. "He got it."

"Good? Good?" Mahmoud inquired, even the singular syllables heavily accented.

Quinn knocked on his forehead and gave a thumbs up, *"Mafeesh mushkileh.* Is that for me?"

Mahmoud handed over the envelope excitedly. "Good! Good!" Visibly relieved, a hand across his chest, he turned and started back down the stairs.

"Shukran, Mahmoud."

"*Afwan*!"

In the living room, Maha joined him on the couch as he sliced the blank, white envelope with a key.

"What is it?"

"No idea," he said, sliding out a postcard. The famous pyramid of Djoser stood nobly before the setting sun, a pair of camels seated in respite in the bottom-left corner. He flipped the card over.

No go on docs. All authentic, reported stolen, lost. Barcodes often faked, but document numbers check out. Sorry, brother. See you on the other side.

"Who is it from?"

He sighed heavily, pinching his nose with his thumb and forefinger, then tossed the card on the coffee table. "A friend. Someone looking into the passports for me."

Maha heard him curse under his breath as he went looking for his cigarettes and read the card for herself.

"He says barcodes are often faked?"

"I guess so," he called back from the bedroom, retrieving the stack of passports. "Something might be off with the MRZ."

"MRZ?"

"Machine-readable zone, the barcodes at the bottom." He fanned the documents across the table, handing one to her. "At the airport it's what the machine scans and reads, brings up all your personal information on the officer's screen." He squinted, taking a closer look at the passport in his hand. "I was hoping there would be something more to go on than this."

"What are we looking for?"

He held a page up toward the window, tilting it to one side, searching for any ambient light. "And why change them?" he wondered aloud. "Would the machine even . . ."

"Quinn?"

"Can I borrow your glasses?"

She carefully pulled them off her head and away from a stubborn lock of hair, handing them to Quinn who, angling the frames against the page, used the lens as a sort of magnifying glass.

She placed a hand on his wrist. "Tell me what I can do."

"Sorry, I'm just looking to see." He picked up a different passport. "Could you compare the English to the Arabic lettering and see if anything jumps out at you? Any discrepancies at all? They should be mirror images."

They sat for a time, examining the pages for any hint of inconsistency, meticulously combing through faded visas, scribbled pen marks, smudged ink blots. They sat as two stamp collectors, peering at their wares, twisting the documents left and right, upside down, turning the pages with scrupulous delicacy.

"These birthdates," he said, "this is the third one now, January zero-one. Does that mean anything to you? Look, this one too, January first—zero-one, zero-one. Only the year is different."

She took the passport, already shaking her head. "I don't think so. In many of the rural communities, they don't record their birthdays, they're just assigned the first day of the year for documents. Sometimes, depending on their interpretation of Islam as well, although I can't say for certain." She shook her head, tight lipped. "It's not uncommon."

Several hours later, the pair occupied the floor, Quinn lying on his back, still flipping through tableaus of numbers, letters, and Arabic script; Maha, cross-legged, diligently scribbling her lists, cross-referencing anything that piqued her interest. The passports now formed a cluttered semi-circle, at one time organized by citizenship, then by birth year, and later, patterns of travel history.

"Hold on."

"Mm?"

He dropped the passport he had been holding and swept his arm along the floor, grasping at whichever document came to his fingertips. "Does your"—he flipped to the front page—"does your code match the biodata?"

"English, Quinn. Or Arabic."

"Sorry. The barcode. Look. Between all the arrows."

She shuffled over to take a closer look.

"Here's the country, EGY. These numbers here are the birthdate. Then, the document number, matching this one up top. All the letters and numbers among the symbols mean something. They correspond to the information above, written here. But these last digits . . . I don't know. Do they match anything in Arabic?"

After a while a slow, if uncertain, shake of the head. "I don't see anything."

"They all start with this LXDX, but mine follows with ZAM, and yours, look, HEL. Then, more numbers. Maybe it's something with the computer program, not the individual. And these two are the exact same. Here"—he held up two pages side by side—"both of them, LXDXHEL0211. Identical."

With a new vein of inquiry, the process commenced once more; documents strewn about the floor gathered, sequenced, and divided into stacks, a fresh set of criteria to be dissected and examined.

"These two have nothing at all," she said. "You see? It ends. The LXDX part is missing."

He nodded. "I was looking at those two before. I didn't notice because, well, there's nothing there." He rubbed his palms into his eyes, a piercing headache setting in, perhaps from hours of squinting at microprinting, though more likely from the throbbing welt on the side of his head. "None of this makes any sense," he said, sighing in exasperation.

"Could it be some sort of code?"

"The strip itself is the code, it's meant to—"

He stopped. Froze. Sat still as a statue.

"Meant to what?"

He raised a hand, then turned back to stone. A gargoyle with a look of consternation upon its face. A creature that spoke only in half sentences. "Code, but not . . . if it's meant, if it's not supposed to . . ."

He turned to face her. "Youssef. Youssef said something about code words, using them to move girls from place to place." His eyes flickered in recollection. "Not for the computer. A code for the border. For the handler."

She looked down at the document in her hands. "A handler." Removing her glasses, she weighed the thought. "But telling them what? If they change this, won't it affect the machine? What if it doesn't scan properly?"

He was still once more, then spoke. "Maybe that's the point. Maybe they don't need to scan the document if the border guard is part of it, part of the operation." He nodded slowly to himself, considering the idea. "I read an article about it just a few days ago. Border officials at the airport, here in Cairo. Working with Saudis to smuggle in domestic workers from, Indonesia, I think it was." He looked back to Maha, "It's a stretch, but if the officials are part of it . . ."

"What do you think the letters mean?"

"Could be anything," he said.

"LXDX. The flight number?"

He shook his head, collecting every passport in the near vicinity. "That would be on the ticket, the boarding pass. And it wouldn't matter. They would have already landed."

"It can't be so easy to alter these documents. What if the flight changes, or is canceled?"

"That too."

"What about a connecting flight?"

"Mm . . . maybe," he said, wishing he could ignore the possibility. If they were transiting onwards, he would have wasted all his time in Egypt. The city was a regional hub, after all. Hadn't Youssef said something to that effect? Transit routes to Israel and up into Europe. Then again, more documents would likely be required. He leafed through the Syrian passport in his hand, searching for a Schengen visa.

"Or, where they're going? Here in Cairo."

He nodded. "Could be. Where to take them after they've cleared customs. If they've transited . . ." He sighed. "There was nothing in the travel history, was there? Nothing consistent."

Maha flipped back a few pages in her notepad. "Not really, no."

"Someone would have to meet them, put them on the next flight. If there was a next flight. Youssef said they often use the Sinai."

Maha nodded.

"So, trucks, in that case. Or boats, north."

"Now we're speculating too much, I think."

Reluctantly, he agreed. "We don't know what we don't know."

"Exactly."

"Alright, let's say it's something to do with Cairo then. The letters."

"A lounge," she mused.

"Taxi stand. Plate number."

"LX. For some reason it makes me think of Lux, the soap company. I use their shampoo."

"Those apartments . . . the short-term rentals." He stood and went to retrieve his laptop from the nightstand.

"And what about the passports that don't have anything at all? No letters. Maybe those haven't been changed."

"What did you say about shampoo?" he called from the bedroom.

"It's called Lux. They make soap, shampoo. Bath products. You have some in your shower. It's meant to sound like luxury, I suppose."

"Luxury . . . luxury." He rolled the syllables on his tongue. "If you had strip clubs here it could be something."

"Why—they're meant to be luxurious?" she said flatly.

They resettled on the couch, the computer open in front of them. "They always have names like that. But why does that sound so familiar? Lux—"

"Wait."

"What?"

"The other letters."

"Which?"

"Look. SHU. HEL. And this one, NAS."

He looked from the passports back to Maha, a blank expression on his face. "What am I missing?"

"Shh . . ." she scolded, silent and still, her mouth slightly agape. Then, she reached for two more, comparing one against the other, in her own world. "*La . . . la.*" She shook her head. "These are the same." Glancing at the document in his hands, she pulled it closer. "GAR." She looked up, her expression shifting, a lock of hair falling across her brow.

"Garden City. Quinn. They're all neighborhoods in Cairo."

He began to speak, then realized he didn't yet have the words. Instead, he stared blankly at the picture of a dark-skinned girl with green eyes.

"SHU. Shubra. HEL. Heliopolis. And here. Nasr City. The first three letters. Quinn, they're directions."

He snapped out of his trance. "The apartments. The goddamn apartments." Frantically, he began to type on the laptop, swatting at the keys, scanning up and down the screen like a hawk. The Internet was torturously slow, loading pages like the sands of time.

"They may have blocked communications," Maha said.

"What?"

"After last night, they may be cutting the Internet. Censoring text messages, social media, like they did in 2011, to stop the protests."

"It's doing something. Come on, come on."

After a moment, the screen came to life, loading its images at an agonizing pace, and he scrolled down the listings as fast as the page would allow.

"What are you looking for?"

He sat back, instinctively drawing his palm across his mouth. "That's it," he said, pointing. "Luxury Deluxe Serviced Apartments. How the hell did I miss this?"

"Luxury Deluxe . . . LXDX."

He leaned forward, tapping the screen. "Nasr City. Like you said."

Quinn shot up from the couch like a coiled spring, wincing slightly as the blood rushed to his head wound, then swatted the passports into his bag. "I have to go."

"To the apartment?" she asked, not hiding her concern.

He didn't respond, spinning around the room, snatching his keys and belongings as if she weren't even there.

"Are you sure about this? We don't even know if—"

"We do know, Maha. You were right." He stood by the door, turning to face her. "This is what they do. They rent out suites like this, a couple of months at a time. They keep moving around, so no one catches on. And it's right there, just like you said. Look at the screen. There are several apartments—it's a chain. That first one is Nasr City, but I'm willing to bet the others correspond to the passports."

"How do you know which?" she asked. Then, "You're planning on going to all of them, aren't you?"

"Let's hope I don't have to."

"And these numbers at the end . . ."

His expression darkened, an ominous shadow moving across his face. "Room numbers. Floor and room. Or," he shook his head, "I don't know. I'll find out."

She rose and met him by the door, then hesitated. She brushed her hair aside, revealing a look of genuine anxiety, a look that he'd never seen before. "I don't know what to say."

"You're not coming with me. I can't let you."

"You shouldn't be going."

"I'll be fine."

"Listen to me. I'm not stupid enough to try and stop you . . ." She whispered something to herself in Arabic. "Maybe I am. You need to be careful."

"I will."

"I'm serious, Quinn. Your heart is in the right place, but maybe it's best for the police to look into this now. I know that's the last thing you want to hear. It's strange to say it, I know."

"Not a chance. You think something like this would be high on their list of priorities with everything else going on now?"

"That's exactly what worries me. The curfew. If it's after seven o'clock, and they find you, *yanni*, poking around, if they catch you . . ." She trailed off, looking away, a foreboding silence left hanging in the air.

"I'll be fine, Maha. Why are you so worried?"

"Because I know the way you are," she snapped. "I see the look in your eyes. And I know my country, what's happening outside." She flushed for a moment, cupping her hands around her nose before taking a breath. "They won't ask questions now," she said, her voice wavering. "Not if you're caught outside at night. The entire government, they're paranoid like this. They'll arrest you—even worse, they'll say you're an American spy and then throw you in prison. It's not like back home, Quinn. There are no rules here. Not now."

The raw emotion caught him off guard, giving him pause, but in truth, there was little she could say to deter him now. There was little anyone could do, he thought, to stop him from walking out the door. He pulled her close and held her tightly, tucking her head beneath his chin, but she remained rigid in his arms, unyielding.

When he finally let go, meeting her eyes once more, she dabbed at a stray tear with her index finger and inhaled deeply, composing herself. Then, she held his wrists and squeezed them, her dark eyes glistening.

"Just don't be a fool."

THIRTY-SIX

An hour later, standing behind the front desk of an otherwise deserted hotel lobby, a polite yet wary Filipina named Mary-Joanne keyed some numbers into her computer. She was sweet as honey and exceptionally courteous, finishing each sentence with a sing-song "yes, sir," but despite her efforts, she struggled to conceal her reservations.

The man standing in front of her was unshaven, a gleam of perspiration across his forehead where, just above his right brow, an inflamed purple gash made her wince every time she gave it a curious and involuntary glance.

"The room is not currently occupied. Would you like to see it, sir?"

"Yes," he replied, matting his hair into place with his palm. "Please."

"I can have my colleague take you up, sir." She looked to another Filipino—a man of similar height and build as her own—with a brimming smile and an eager nod.

"That's great, thank you."

It was the last thing that Quinn wanted to hear. The best pretext he had fabricated on the hour-long ride from Maadi was that a friend had stayed in the suite once before and recommended it highly. Before making a deposit, he figured he would take a quick tour and see if the space was to his liking.

Now the room was confirmed empty, but for how long? A good sign, perhaps, that no one was there. No harm, no foul. Then again, maybe not. Just the opposite. Had he arrived too late? One step behind, a step too slow.

The bellboy made some overly chipper small talk on the elevator ride and then escorted him down the hall to room 204. For some reason, Quinn held his breath as the key card unlocked the door—a deft click, a flashing green light.

Inside was a spacious family suite; a sparse but practical kitchen to the left, the living room also simply furnished, cozy if a bit tired, a clichéd painting of the Nile and a Bedouin campfire on the far wall. The bellboy showed him around and gave him a compressed tour of sorts, along with a sales pitch highlighting the rooftop gym, hot tub, and some other amenities that Quinn brusquely ignored, poorly masking his lack of patience.

It soon appeared as though Quinn were leading the tour, the diminutive Filipino man trotting along behind as he paced around the room, searching for anything that might pass as a clue. However, the more he looked, the more foolish he felt, all too aware that there would be nothing to find and, even worse, that he had no idea what he was looking for.

As he opened and shut dressers, poking his head into every closet, making his escort increasingly uncomfortable, he found himself consumed with melancholic reverie. The hapless, half-wit detective, without a clue both literally and figuratively. Even if there were something, anything out of place or carelessly left behind, the cleaning staff would have taken care of that long ago. Who knows how many times they would have been over the space, dusting and tidying, removing every trace of any previous occupant.

Back downstairs at the front desk, he paced while a family of four checked out—a courteous Dutch family whose redundant questions had him alternately puffing his cheeks and, after several more minutes, grinding his molars.

"How did you like the suite, sir?" Mary-Joanne asked, the same bright smile and apprehensive demeanor.

"Perfect. Thanks. I was wondering, could you do me a favor? When was the last time the suite was booked, do you know?"

"Oh, I'm—I'm very sorry, sir, but I don't think I have that information."

"Would you mind looking it up for me?"

"I'm sorry, sir, but I'm not allowed to release that information to you." Even this came with a delightful smile.

"Mary-Joanne, I really need . . ." He shook his head. "There's nothing you can do?"

Cheerful as she may have been, there were clearly limits to her influence. "Unfortunately, sir, I cannot, and our manager has left for the evening. If you come back tomorrow, he usually arrives at nine, maybe you can ask—"

"No, no, it's alright, thank you."

Pushing the issue wasn't a good idea. He wasn't keen on drawing any unnecessary attention to himself. He still had three other hotels to search. If he got really desperate—desperation only a relative concept now—he could return and badger the manager the following day.

He glanced at his watch. Rush hour was fast approaching. A different kind of rush altogether now with the government curfew, likely several hours of mayhem on the roads, everyone hurrying home to beat the clock.

"I'll come back tomorrow. Thanks for your help. Would you mind calling me a taxi? In fact, never mind."

Heliopolis was a comparatively short ride north from Nasr City, though in the end, he spent about as much time in the taxi as he did in the hotel itself.

At the counter sat a young clerk with pockmarked skin and a sweaty upper lip. He wore a gray dress shirt whose buttons strained to hold their contents at bay, creeping sweat stains encircled by salt rings beneath his arms. He apologized profusely while relaying to Quinn that the room he wished to see—indeed, the entire floor— was undergoing construction and had been for some time. Both the third and fourth floors would be ready for use once again the following season, as they were "upgrading the deluxe experience," according to his script.

Quinn had no reason to doubt him, a jolly fellow with an easy smile who seemed genuinely eager to please. Still, after turning to leave and proceeding back through the lobby, he glanced over his shoulder and swiftly exited through a stairwell door.

Climbing a couple of flights, he didn't hear any construction but then recalled it was the weekend and getting rather late in the day.

Pulling open the door to the third floor was like uncovering a hidden chamber to a warzone. A cloud of dust and debris coated his head and shoulders as he stepped forward. The walls were gutted and bare, the floor a puzzle of concrete chips and jagged slabs, garbage bins overflowing with assorted rubbish. There were pinwheels of carpeting, thick coils of black and silver wire, and, farther down the hall, a rickety piece of scaffolding made of splintered wood and rusted metal. Another dead end.

By the time he reached the third hotel in Shubra, he didn't bother with anyone at the front desk. The taxi had barely rolled to a stop when he threw the door open, sprinted up the front steps, and promptly located the elevator bank. When the doors slid open, he was greeted by a whirlwind of a family, a mother and father hastily shepherding two young children into the lobby while lugging a variety of bags and suitcases. The daughter, skinny as a beanpole with golden hair like Rapunzel, was teary-eyed and a couple of octaves shy of a full tantrum. As Quinn stepped past, pushing the button for the seventh floor, the father doubled back into the elevator, muttering under his breath.

"If we miss this flight over a stuffed rabbit, I swear . . ."

Quinn hovered his finger over the buttons.

"Yeah, five, thanks. My god, what a week. You leavin' too?"

"Hm?"

"The city. You have a ticket out?"

"Sure. Tomorrow."

"Well, make sure you leave plenty early. The traffic here, *whoof.* And they say they might be shuttin' down the airport now too. Egypt. Unbelievable. I told her, we should have gone to Greece."

"What's that?"

"Yeah, my family, they're Greek, well, half, my brother's—"

"No, no—the airport?"

"Oh, this morning on CNN. They're saying some flights have been delayed for hours. They're even talkin' 'bout chartered evacuations now. Well, for some," he said, suddenly coy, uncertain if Quinn held the right passport.

The elevator jerked slightly as it came to a halt, the doors sliding open.

"Well, good luck, buddy. Safe travels."

"Yeah. You too."

Room 714 was at the far end of the hall, tucked in a corner by the fire escape, its door wide open along with that of its neighboring suite. A housekeeping cart blocked the entrance, overflowing with bedsheets, spray bottles hanging on a steel railing beneath a pillar of folded towels. From inside, the chatter of feminine voices, a faucet running in the bathroom, the restocking of miniature toiletries, and the dramatic theme song of an Arabic soap opera playing on the television.

The third hotel now and the same seemingly inevitable result. For a moment he was rooted to the spot, too disheartened to move. It was the endless waves of dread that washed over him with increasing regularity, the crushing doubt that had plagued him for weeks now—and he felt further adrift than ever before. With every empty hotel room, the all-too-familiar anxiety, a constant companion, simmered within him, never far from a rolling boil, churning like a storm and sapping his strength. There was a price to pay for the faint hope that resurfaced every now and again—a half-clue, a novel theory. It slowly carved away pieces of the soul, and there was precious left upon which to draw.

He considered the garbage bag on the cart, recalling stories, anecdotes from different vice units, detectives specializing in prostitution and sex crimes. Hotel rooms with trash bags full of tampons, pads, pregnancy tests, used condoms and ointments for yeast infections. The routine deliveries of fast food and take-out, another indicator that could have been something—could have, if it weren't for the fact that this bag contained nothing more than balled tissues and plastic bottles. The cleaning ladies themselves would be of little assistance—the state-funded projects used to train housekeeping staff on potential clues, tell-tale signs of sexual abuse, now a world away.

He contemplated returning to Nasr City, to Heliopolis, retracing his steps in case he had missed something. As if somehow it would have been possible to ignore the grim reality that mocked him at every turn. He stood, a sort of paralysis setting in, stemming from an altogether new type of fear. Not the compulsively negative thoughts, the dreadful predictions, flashes of where she was, what she'd been forced to endure. This was a novel fear, a dread of the final act and what would happen to both of them once the curtain fell. A fear of what awaited him in Garden City.

THIRTY-SEVEN

THE TAXI DIDN'T HAVE A CLOCK ON THE DASHBOARD. ALTHOUGH, to be fair, it was hardly a dashboard by most definitions—missing vent slats, melted plastic, a few stray wires collecting dust, hopefully of no immediate importance. The box of tissues and dangling prayer beads completed the tableau, drifting in and out of focus before him.

Khalid, his driver, had reminded Quinn of the looming curfew, not that anyone in the city needed reminding, Quinn least of all. It was late, in more than just the hour; late in every sense. He figured it must have been around 6:30 when they arrived, rolling to a stop beneath the familiar hotel emblem on an unfamiliar street.

Stepping inside, he made it just past the sliding glass doors before a roving bellboy greeted him with an overly enthusiastic smile. Unable to shake his pleasantries, they proceeded together to the front desk where, turning his back to the greeting party, Quinn trotted out his well-rehearsed theater once again. As the clerk queried his database, Quinn took note that the Garden City residence was quite refined, polished with a chic ambiance—abstract paintings, potted birds of paradise, a lingering scent of bergamot in the air—and he wondered if it was the chain's flagship location.

"I'm very sorry, Mr. Lindstrom, but the room is currently occupied. I can show you room 302 if you like. It is one floor below. Same style. Very nice. Very beautiful."

Occupied.

The moment lingered, as did Quinn's vacant expression, prompting the concierge once more.

"Sir?"

"No, it's . . . it's alright, thank you."

Turning away, he almost resented the slightest flicker of hope; impassive now, refusing to let any false positive lead him astray.

As he came upon the elevators on his left, he locked eyes with the overzealous bellboy who still followed his every move with the same obsessively cordial gaze, the attention as inconvenient as it was uncomfortable now that he required a different avenue upstairs. A diminutive, elderly couple—Malaysian, if he had to guess—stood by the elevator doors, the man bitterly scolding his partner about some trivial affair and drawing the attention of more than a few sidewise glances.

Quinn decided to keep walking past the elevator bank, hardly breaking stride, then continued reluctantly past the stairwell, all the while consumed by a curious and absurd sense of paranoia; breathless, mind racing, his cheeks flushed.

Ask to see the fitness center, or the pool, he thought, though such a tour would surely come with an escort; in all likelihood, an escort in the exact shape and size of the all-too-attentive bellboy. He could book a room—any floor; it wouldn't matter—just a key for general access. Though they would surely require a credit card on file, a passport. Room 402 was occupied, and while he wasn't certain what he might find, if anything at all, there was one guarantee: he knew even less about how he would react. The thought frightened him, and while he preferred to remain anonymous, in truth, it was more than just a preference—it was a necessity. He recalled what Maha had said about foreigners poking around and found himself scanning the ceiling for security cameras.

He was nearly out the door when, ahead of him, a young man in a bright shirt and cap caught his attention, a vision of canary yellow with a black delivery bag slung over his shoulder. The logo on the bag was familiar, ubiquitous throughout the city, one of the more popular food-delivery outfits. He followed the man beyond the glass doors and down the steps to a rust-colored Honda that, at some point in time, had likely been red.

"Hamed!" Quinn called out. Then, a little louder, "Hamed!" The young man paused, turning slightly. Quinn looked up and down the street, which was practically deserted as the curfew neared. He sputtered a few words of awkward Arabic, which seemed to cause more confusion than anything, the perplexed teen promptly responding with his own heavily accented English. Stealing a quick sideways glance in the passenger window, Quinn proceeded with a clumsy pantomime routine, communicating that someone at the front desk was calling after him. The order—something was wrong—an item missing, perhaps? Incorrect change? The boy looked unsure, eyes flicking back toward the hotel, but finally gave a rather insouciant nod, removed his phone from his pocket, and proceeded back up the steps.

Quinn watched him go and, as the glass doors slid shut, reached for the passenger door handle. It clicked open, the gentle *pop* in his hands providing a cathartic release. On the seat, amongst a pile of soda cans and empty cigarette packs, lay a crumpled yellow shirt and matching hat. Acting more on impulse than with a definite plan, he snatched what he needed, shut the door, took a quick glance back at the hotel, then opened the back door and retrieved a deflated black duffel bag.

The fact that the yellow uniform was several sizes too small didn't help matters as he yanked, pulled, and stretched the fabric over his torso. Slinging the bag over his shoulder and pulling the cap low over his brow, he forced a deep breath, then exhaled.

Up the steps, eyes down, his range of sight now limited to a foot or two in front of him. He tugged at his shirt, which rode up past his waist, wondering if he looked as ridiculous as he felt. The doors slid open, the cool waft of air conditioning greeting him. More voices than before. Or, maybe he was simply more attuned. He tensed with every step.

What a stupid idea. They wouldn't have looked twice at him before, but now—what, impersonating a deliveryman? How could anyone answer that? He could have found his way upstairs one way or another and simply pretended he was lost. He could have come up with any number of more plausible explanations before slipping on this absurd costume.

He forced the thought from his mind, lifting his head slightly from the tile floor. Some feet at the front desk, some chatter to his left. The bellboy? A few more steps, and he stopped next to a grouping of shoes and sandals waiting by the elevator bank.

He waited, and waited, then waited some more. Seconds passed like hours as he stood motionless, burning a hole through the floor. Would the delivery boy notice him on the way out?

A gentle *ding* was followed by the muffled sound of sliding metal as the elevator opened, his counterparts shuffling forward. They seemed to move in slow motion, and he felt a bead of sweat dribble the length of his cheek. Patiently, he followed, resisting the urge to bowl them over, then turned at the front of the group, never looking up as the doors slid shut.

The fourth floor was quiet, unnaturally so. Not a sound from anywhere; not a shuffle along the carpeted hall, not a television program behind closed doors. Eerily silent. Only his own footsteps, the brush of his shoulder bag until he came upon the room: 402.

Utter silence as he looked left, then right, leaned in, and placed his ear to the door. He could faintly hear something inside but only just. There was motion, some sort of activity, but he could discern nothing further. He noticed that he was rubbing his fingers together the way a cricket might stridulate its appendages, and wiped his palms across his shirt, hands cool and clammy.

He took a deep breath, swallowed heavily, and braced himself. His fist was already clenched as he raised it to knock.

Once. Twice. Three times.

He listened. The motion inside stopped, then, started again, moving toward the door.

They were taking too long.

He stepped to one side, out of sight from the peephole, then reconsidered, standing directly in front, adjusting his cap. A delivery boy, nothing more.

Inside, the chain rattled and dropped, scraping against the door like a pendulum. The handle made a heavy *ka-chunk*, rotating down and back up again. He lifted his head as the door swung open, his ears ringing, chest pounding.

THIRTY-EIGHT

"*Ja*? Can I help you?"

"I have a delivery."

"I don't believe it's for me, my dear, but hold on just a moment, will you? Hermann? Oh, Hermann?"

Quinn wasn't entirely certain what his mind was telling him. His heart was still racing, his face almost certainly flushed, though the narrative was shifting now. Something wasn't right. The lady standing before him looked to be in her sixties and, by her accent, German, or at least some cultural variation thereof. She wore tan pants—a light hiker's fabric, and a breezy white blouse.

"He's just getting out of the bath, but I don't believe he ordered anything. Hermann, dear, did you call for room service?"

Quinn studied her like a piece of artwork: the frizzled grayish hair, a touch of sun on her thin nose, the warm, welcoming crow's feet when she smiled. She had bright blue eyes that had once surely sparkled like sapphires, slightly duller now with age, and thin red lips with perfectly symmetrical teeth—lightly tinctured from years of afternoon tea and the occasional bottle of pinot noir, the well-deserved indulgences of retirement.

"No, I'm sorry, are you sure you have the right room, dear?"

"Ah, maybe not. I'll have to double check. Your accent," he said, tilting his head, "German?"

"Austrian, actually. But don't worry, I won't take offence to that." She winked and patted his arm, such a warm and unexpected gesture that it derailed his train of thought. "And while we're on the topic of nationalities, you seem a bit fair haired to be Egyptian."

He wasn't expecting a question. "American, actually. I'm . . . interning here. Groundwater depletion, aquifers, that sort of thing."

"An internship? Here, in Cairo? Oh, how delightful. What an adventure!"

It was.

"My husband and I have always wanted to visit but never got the chance. Life passes you by, you see—work, then children." Her wrist floated about as if she were conducting an orchestra. "Of course, we've been everywhere in Europe. Peru as well. That was truly something. The Incas—magnificent. But the pharaohs have always called to me," she whispered this last part, as if it were a secret between the two of them.

Just then, a pot-bellied man with a cloud of white chest hair and a pink pin-cushion head strolled casually past in a loosely tied bathrobe. He bent down with a groan and began rummaging through a suitcase on the floor.

"And how are you finding the city?" she asked. "Have you been here long?"

"A few months. It's busy. A lot of work. And now, a little tense."

"Oh, yes. Tense. Mm-hmm, most definitely. Still, you know . . ." She shook her head and raised a set of bony fingers to her collar. "I must admit, I can't help but feel that it's all just a little bit exciting, wouldn't you say?" Her eyes widened, accompanying a wicked little smile. "Of course, I don't wish to see anyone in harm's way, not anything of the sort, but, you must admit, it certainly adds to the adventure, don't you find?"

Not really. "Yes. I think so."

"Anyhow, look at me going on and on. I'm sorry about your wasted trip. I'm sure it's delicious, whatever it is you're bringing." She sniffed the air. "But it's not for us, I'm afraid."

"Not a problem. Wrong location, most likely. Easy to fix."

"We flew in . . . when was it now, Hermann, last Thursday?" Hermann was already back in the bathroom, unconcerned with whatever was taking place in the doorway. "So, just over a week, and the food has been our favorite part! We've got another few days before our cruise down to Aswan. Although I hope they're still in operation, to be honest. Who knows what will happen in the coming days."

"Sounds nice. I should probably get this to the right address, before it gets cold."

"Yes, of course, of course. Do be careful out there, dear."

In the lobby, a thin plume of smoke drifted upward from Quinn's hand, a length of ash, flaccid and crumbling, hung nearly as long as the cigarette itself. When the amber finally singed his finger, he winced, the slight sting bringing him back to the quiet, empty parlor. On the coffee table in front of him lay the yellow hat, absentmindedly tossed aside, a seemingly appropriate ashtray. He smeared the bright fabric with a smudge of black.

For a long while, he simply sat, numb, ruminating on the faintest sliver of comfort that he still possessed. He wasn't nearly as upset, not as devastated, as he'd expected. There was no blinding rage, burning hot and electric, nor was there any deep sense of tragedy, dragging him down to untold depths with guilt and sorrow. The steady undercurrent of melancholy remained, though somewhere amongst the endless streams of nicotine, he realized that most of those emotions—the sorrow, the frustration, the hatred—had all left him long ago. Slowly parceled out since that first phone call from Noi, little by little, almost unnoticeable. In the solitude of Mei's room, in front of the abandoned storefront off Sukhumvit, during the grueling, ten-hour flight to Egypt, with every knock on a hotel room door.

He knew the truth, had felt it for some time now, and kept it hidden from himself, buried deep and distant. Had he known from the very beginning? A lost cause the moment she was taken. And now, almost in spite of himself, he felt his own mind seeking solace, a consciousness exhausted by the weight of it all. Sophia. Mei. A patchwork of a career comprised primarily of self-deception and childish illusion, a laughable attempt at making a difference. A grown man, old beyond his years, and yet still a naïve, idealistic fool.

On the table, next to the sullied hat, several pamphlets were fanned out across the glass, promoting the hotels. Collages of only the happiest families at Luxury Deluxe serviced apartments—children splashing in the pool, well-rested travelers nestled in plush duvets, fine dining at La Papillon.

It wasn't a stretch to suppose his entire theory was wrong. How implausible it all seemed now; the letters, which could have meant anything, the numbers too, easily coincidental. Did they really correspond to this floor, that room number? Or had they been molded, distorted to better fit his own expectations, filling a void out of desperation? Square pegs in round holes.

He wanted it to be true, *yearned* for it, and as proof, he now sat alone in a tranquil lobby in Garden City. He lit another cigarette and picked up one of the brochures, leafing through the glossy pages. Daily excursions available: sunset felucca tours, explorations of ancient ruins, couples on camelback in the Valley of the Kings. Locations to suit everyone's needs. Heliopolis. Shubra. Helwan. Garden City. Nasr—

Wait.

His eyes focused. He brought the brochure closer, no longer halfheartedly scanning the words, suddenly aware, senses heightened. Helwan. For a moment the world stopped turning. Ambient lights darkened while a spotlight shone on the letters. Tunnel vision. Not Heliopolis. Helwan. HEL. The same letters.

Helwan.

He was up and out of his seat, lifted into the air by a sudden rush of adrenaline. A moment later he was outside, scanning the street up and down, dark and still, the curfew now in full effect. With the city indoors, the soft light of apartment buildings cast their faint amber glow upon the deserted sidewalks. To his right, three young boys kicked a soccer ball along the asphalt, defying the curfew more out of boredom and curiosity than any rebellious intent.

He walked for a time, the neighborhood silent but for the occasional rumble of a car engine somewhere in the distance, not everyone abiding by the army's new regulations.

After a few blocks, beneath the canopy of an age-old weeping fig, he spotted two men, as ancient and weathered as the tree itself, sipping tea, plainly unconcerned with the politics of the day. It was hardly the first display of military might in their time, citizens of a land where conflict swept through the streets like the ebb and flow of the tide. It would take more than some military posturing to wrest them from their evening routine.

Eventually, under the dim glow of a streetlamp, he spotted a small grouping of young men, smoking shisha in an otherwise deserted café patio. They slouched in their seats, jocular and defiant, yet close enough to a nearby tenement, a likely destination if forced to flee.

They observed him as if he were a wild animal, bewilderment etched across their faces as the blond-haired man emerged from the shadows, a frightful gash on his forehead, wearing the uniform of a delivery boy. It took a few minutes to convince them that a drive to Helwan was worth the risk, a decision made easier at the sight of some crumpled American bills. For a moment Quinn waited anxiously as one of the boys muttered something about helping *his* kind. The other, arms crossed, added his own insight regarding the increasing prevalence of American spies in the city.

In the end, the money won out. Tariq, slim and likely still in his teens, wore a navy blue tracksuit with sandals. He agreed to be Quinn's chauffeur, though he warned that the trip could take some time. The risk of being spotted by the army didn't appear to be a concern, Tariq shrugging at this while he lit a cigarette. Rather, it was avoiding the main roads and traversing mud-rutted alleys that would account for the long journey.

His black Nissan was parked just behind the café and, after a brief debate amongst the group regarding which route was best, the two of them set off onto the first of many side streets, headlights off, a slow, tentative roll around every corner.

It was a long drive, as Tariq had warned, dark streets behind apartment complexes, dirt roads alongside construction sites. Dusty streetlights illuminated shadowed cobblestone and sand-swept pathways, few signs of life amongst closed, shuttered shops and graffitied walls. Tariq never appeared nervous but left the stereo off and clucked his tongue from time to time when traversing a wider intersection.

When they finally slowed to a stop, obscured beneath a first-floor balcony, Tariq pointed across the street. He didn't ask a single question throughout the trip, but once at their destination, scanned his passenger up and down, trying to make sense of it all. *Was it really espionage, as his friends had said?*

In that moment, Quinn realized he was still wearing the yellow polo shirt and started looking around the car—the back seat, the glovebox, everywhere—for another prop. In his haste, he had left the duffel bag in Garden City. A crumpled plastic bag was tucked deep into the side door pocket, which he unraveled and whipped open.

"Can I have this?"

Tariq nodded, more confused than ever, his thin eyebrows converging.

"Thanks."

"Well come."

As the black Nissan rolled around the corner and out of sight, Quinn briefly surveyed the area. It was as quiet as anywhere else. Light from the hotel lobby streamed through the glass doorway onto the steps, fading out into the street. As far as he could tell, there was no movement inside. He stooped to gather some dead leaves and a flattened soda can from the curb, stuffed them into the bag, and tied the ends together.

Once inside, he made for the elevator bank as nonchalantly as possible, releasing an exaggerated sigh when he pressed the button—a routine workday like any other. The lobby, despite being somewhat run-down, resembled the others: tile floor, potted plants, framed prints of dramatic Saharan landscapes, and, on this occasion, a heavier-set Filipina behind the front desk. She eyed him inquisitively, casting a subtle glance at her watch.

"Evening."

"Evening, sir."

"Last delivery of the day," he said, embracing the role. "On the way home, at least." His attempt to look somewhat ragged from a long shift required little effort.

She wore black glasses, a short ponytail, and had a kind face with full, dimpled cheeks. Confused, maybe, but not overly concerned, yet even from a distance he could tell she was curious about the dark contusion slashing across his forehead.

"Ah, this," he said, pointing, "football." He jerked his neck to the side. "Tried to head the ball, ended up heading my teammate."

She winced, making a hissing sound with her teeth.

"Looks worse than it is," he said trivially.

"What room number?"

He hesitated for half a second, but she didn't catch it. Her plump face had an enchanting smile, just making conversation.

"505."

The chime of the elevator echoed through the empty lobby.

"Ah, yes. A little late today, no?"

He shrugged. "Traffic. With the curfew it's pretty bad out there."

"Oh," she replied, somewhat bemused, then went back to scribbling something on the desk. "It's just . . . usually you're much earlier."

He planted a foot firmly in the elevator, the closing doors jarringly halted, then sliding back open in defeat.

"I'm sorry, earlier? I'm fairly new," he said sheepishly.

"Room 505?" Her glasses lifted with her eyebrows. "Your deliveries are usually earlier in the day. Breakfast and lunch."

A wave of trepidation washed over him. "That's right." His dry mouth fumbled with the words. "I forgot. Someone mentioned that earlier."

"Fahad isn't working tonight?"

He made a face. *Fahad! Of course.* "He's off. Visiting family. Just dropping this on the way home, like I said."

She nodded happily. "Ah, yes, that's right. Well, I hope you live close. Not safe to be driving around so late. Not tonight."

Another quiet hallway, silent as a tomb. No tourists anymore, at least none that made any noise. The adrenaline coursed through him—shallow breaths, tight chest—as he counted down the room numbers; cautious, purposeful steps across the carpet.

There were no guarantees. He had certainly learned as much. Some unfortunate soul with a bad case of Cairo belly, perhaps, hardly uncommon for first-time adventurers. A honeymoon gone terribly awry. Still, it didn't feel right. It felt as though he were reaching. For once, it wasn't hope that felt unrealistic, but all the other potential scenarios. Surely most of the relatively sane travelers had steered for calmer waters by this point—ill or otherwise—the turmoil unfolding like wildfire across the city. If they were bedridden, they would have had ample opportunity to watch the news, make alternate arrangements. What had that man said in the elevator? Something about chartered evacuations.

Here was someone who valued their privacy. Someone who clearly didn't want to be bothered, a flimsy plastic sign hanging from the door handle. A stick figure in bed with a trail of "Z's" floating above, gold-and-black lettering in English and Arabic:

"Do Not Disturb." He likely would have done the same if he were unwell, but now, the hour late, he was tired of waiting.

No need to rehearse anything; he would make it up on the spot as he'd been doing all along. He ruffled the plastic bag and pushed his hair back over his forehead. Taking a deep breath, he raised his fist to knock and nearly jumped out of his skin as the evening call to prayer swelled from a nearby minaret. The tinny echo of a *mu'azzin*'s voice split the silence and reverberated throughout the hallway as he took a moment to recover with heavy breaths. He cursed, silently to himself. *Isha*.

THIRTY-NINE

He rapped his knuckles on the door.

No answer.

Stepping closer, he pressed his ear against the cool frame for a moment, then thought better of it. Too suspicious.

He knocked again—once, twice, three times—then stood back, cradling the plastic bag in both hands. Did he hear something? Shuffling. There was someone inside. Of course there was.

An agonizing few seconds passed again. A stalemate. Would he leave? Would they answer the door?

Once more, three forceful cracks, his knuckles stinging and red.

Apparently, the disturbance could no longer be ignored, the muted baritone of a male voice coming from somewhere inside the room. The voice spoke in Arabic, gruff and evidently irritated, the muffled tones through the door impossible to understand.

He held up the plastic bag to the peephole as an offering. "Delivery. Room 505?"

He heard the door unlock, opening only a couple of inches, just as far as the lock chain would allow.

"Wrong room. We didn't make order," the voice said. Quinn caught a thin glimpse of the man inside: stubbled face, thick eyebrows.

"Room 505? Mr. Mansour? Are you sure?"

"*Nam!* Sure. You don't see sign?" The voice more than just irritated now, the tone angry, on edge.

Quinn began to recite an imaginary bill off the bag, testing the man's patience even further. "Half chicken, rice, bakla—"

"I said no!" the man thundered, the door slamming shut. Then, from inside, "*Ayreh feek . . .*"

Quinn didn't so much knock as hammer his fist against the door. The man could have been an angry guest, could have been anyone with a hot temper to say what he had, but that hardly mattered now. At the very least, Quinn no longer cared. He banged on the door again, relentlessly, and this time, heard something else. Something different. Voices? Several voices. Or just the television? It didn't matter. Whatever had been simmering inside was now at his throat, the pressure nearly choking him. He pounded on the door, his fist hot and inflamed until he heard the same voices, more clearly now, followed by heavy footsteps stomping toward the door, a tirade of insults.

He took a step back.

The handle turned, the chain cinched taut, and Quinn's boot slammed into the center of the door, snapping the brass links. The door flew open, met abruptly by a heavy thud on the other side. A chorus of sounds erupted all at once: a low-pitched groan, shrill voices in the distance, and the brush and scuffle of clothing as Quinn forced himself through the guarded entryway.

Everything moved in slow motion now, picture frames flashing before him, grainy and unclear. He looked past the shadow in his path. Lights. Countertop. A family on a couch in the corner.

The specter grew, blurry, moving closer. Still he looked past. Pillows. Blankets. Not a family. Children. Holding one another.

The blur came into focus before him, his tunnel vision revealing a heavyset man, face twisted into a snarl, arms outstretched, reaching for his throat. Quinn was late to react, powerful hands grasping his shirt collar and throwing him into the side wall. The man was shorter by about a foot but powerfully built—sturdy, thick, with heavy bones.

They grappled. Palms swatting at the air, grasping at fabric, the strain and tear of collars and thread. Flecks of spittle through clenched teeth, hoarse grunts between gasps. A thumping, hollow dent in the wall was followed swiftly by a tumbling crash into the opposing side.

Quinn managed to free his right arm, maneuver himself just so, and bury a heavy fist into a soft, exposed belly, stopping the man in his tracks as he let out a heaving wheeze. He recovered quickly, slapping at the air and grabbing hold once again, the pair twisting around like a whirlwind in the front hall. The man was clearly still struggling to catch his breath, fighting a secondary battle with his own diaphragm.

For a moment their off balance *pas de deux* halted in a corner, the angle opening just enough to give Quinn a clear view of the thick bridge of his opponent's nose. Pinned against the wall, he was enveloped by the man's hot breath—rotting sardines—while fleshy fingers deftly maneuvered around his throat. Quinn rotated his arm around and, fist cocked to one side, waited for the opportune moment. Just as the man's grip began to tighten, Quinn landed a blow, buckling the cartilage and causing the man's head to snap back, a torrent of bright red streaming down his face. A peculiar sound followed the snap of the nose: a whimpering dog, his paw having been stomped by an unexpected boot.

The man crumpled into the wall, slipping to the floor as shrill voices behind him cried out in terror. As Quinn began to turn, he was suddenly blinded—sweaty hands cupping around his eyes, then clawing at his face. A rabid animal pawed at him from behind, latching on like some sort of frantic creature, feverishly scratching and growling. He hollered in pain as nails tore at his skin. He reared up like a bucking bronco, pivoting left and right until the beast slid off into the air and cracked something delicate against the countertop. He turned to see the slumped body of a middle-aged woman, a purple hijab torn to one side, black-and-gray hair matted and exposed, a trickle of blood along her cheek.

Heart pumping furiously, he tried to gather his wits and turned his attention to the frightened cast of young girls on the couch. "Is there anybody else?" he shouted.

They were huddled together, five of them, arranged by size like *matryoshka* dolls. He didn't recognize any of them. The younger ones clung tightly to the eldest in the middle, who cradled the others like a mother hen, herself no older than fifteen. They had Asian features, darkly tanned skin, and were dressed in mismatched tank tops and pajama bottoms. Some were caked in unnatural masks of lip gloss, mascara, and rouge. An assortment of stuffed rabbits and teddy bears lay strewn at their feet, limp and inanimate. Others were held tightly, their plush bodies contorted beneath an arm or clutched between tiny fingers. On the end table was a glass bowl of individually wrapped candies.

He realized what a sight he must have been. The girls who weren't already sobbing stared at him, wide-eyed, looks of terror on their virgin faces. He kneeled, slowly extending a hand—palm toward the ground—as an offering, a sign of peace. Lowering his voice, he spoke softly, barely audible over the whimpering. "Someone else? Inside?" He pointed to the two closed doors to his right, but the girls sat unresponsive, eyeing him warily, at least those who weren't bleary eyed, too frightened to look at all.

He moved carefully toward the first door, hesitant in his approach, then figured anyone who would have heard the earlier commotion would have already come running. Slowly, he turned the knob, stepping into the bathroom. Inside, the tile floor was a pigsty of sullied towels and discarded clothing, the garbage bin overflowing with tissues, wrappers, and used feminine products. The counter was grimy and cluttered with makeup: bristles and brushes, powders and creams, cracked paint palettes and half squeezed tubes. The mirror was stained with greasy smears and water driblets, and the toilet bowl had a sickly, jaundiced tinge. By his feet, a cardboard box, once filled with orange soda, contained an assortment of sex toys.

Suddenly, he heard something scratching along the outer wall, accompanied by an unnerving crescendo, a rising chorus of cries and whimpers from the couch. Turning his head, he spotted the beaten man struggling to his feet. He was unsteady—a knee on the ground, a hand on the wall—spewing wet and unintelligible profanity from an oozing red mouth.

Quinn spotted a laptop and mounted camera that sat invitingly on the kitchen countertop. A few steps later, he held the computer in his hands, relishing the weight of the device. He swung it with venom, a swift arc that caught the man's chin with a sharp crack, the laptop fragmenting in his hands as limbs tumbled together beneath him. It was only when the man began to raise his voice once more, defiant and snatching at his pant leg, that Quinn resolved to finalize the matter. With a lift of his heel, he brought his boot down hard, cringing at the sensation: the rubber sole pressing flesh, the muffled snap of bone against tile.

The room fell quiet. An unexpected sensation swelled in his chest, then tightened rapidly around his throat, saliva gathering, bile rising. He hunched over for a moment, stifling the retch with his forearm, gathering himself. Rather unsteadily, he made his way toward the second door.

Stepping into a poorly lit bedroom, he immediately locked eyes with yet another child seated in the center of a faded floral-print bedspread, hugging her knees. She was maybe ten, he supposed. They held each other's gaze, the girl somewhat indifferent to his presence, a veneer of detachment coating her visage. Her hickory brown hair was tussled and unkempt, a smattering of tiny freckles matching her spotted orange dress. Next to her lay another girl with her back to the room, facing a mural of hand-scrawled images, colored and etched into the wallpaper.

Pillows without pillowcases littered the floor, as did several blankets, crumpled in heaps. The wrinkled sheets upon the bed appeared blotchy and soiled, their edges untucked, the near corner of the mattress exposed. The room was stuffy and smelled of old sweat and cheap aerosol spray. When he spotted the electronics—recording equipment positioned on the carpet like an amateurish film studio—his stomach turned. A small television, laptops, wires and cables, mounted spherical webcams, recording devices on tripods.

He rounded the far side of the bed, kicking and stomping the paraphernalia as he went, rampaging like some aggrieved fairy-tale giant. He approached the girl who lay still on her side, head flat against the bare mattress, a vacant stare at the near wall. She wore neither socks nor pants, only underwear and a pink shirt with thin shoulder straps, palms cupped together and nestled between her knobby knees as if trying to keep warm. He knelt beside her, peering through the black hair matted across her face. Her heavy-lidded eyes stared straight ahead, impassive, deep into the scribbled tableau of trees and stick figures on the wall.

He didn't recognize her. Not her features, not the strange, vacant expression, not anything. A different girl before him now. Her image had haunted him for so long—memories, nightmares—the tangible and intangible blurring together, obscured in the dim lighting and his own delusion.

"Mei . . ." he whispered. He placed a hand on her shoulder, shaking her ever so gently. The freckled girl looked down on him, passively observing with the faintest curiosity, a Siamese cat perched on a windowsill.

And it was something about that girl that made him remember. The freckles, the orange dress, something about the way she looked at him. He imagined her as she was before, a lifetime ago. He pictured the sun upon her face as she ran barefoot through the long grass, the reeds gently whipping at her knees, birds scattering in the tree line, flocking away into a cloudless sky. A bright and dimpled smile, streaks of yellow *thanaka* spread across her cheeks to keep her cool and lessen the sting of the sun's rays. Her hands still wet; sticky and sweet from the ripe lychee that had dribbled the length of her wrist when she peeled back its stubborn shell. She ran toward the outer edge of a grove, mature trees with plump clusters of fruit, prickly green lanterns of durian suspended amongst the canopy.

He turned his attention back to the girl who lay before him, running his hand down the length of her left leg, scrutinizing every inch. From hip to heel, only a faint bruise on her shin, green and fading. Nothing more. Then, he gently pushed the limb aside, sliding it back just enough to expose her calf, part of her inner thigh, just enough to reveal the coffee-stain blemish that marked the skin above her right knee.

The durian fruit.

He collapsed against the wall, cupping a hand around his mouth, a shallow breath escaping his lips, sharp and involuntary. Anchored now, immovable, a state of disbelief. As the tears welled, blurring his vision, a chuckle of relief from somewhere within, confusing and unexpected, followed by a few more, a strange fit of maniacal sniggering as he sat on the carpeted floor.

The birthmark, not much larger than his thumb, was the most innocuous of markings—a rounded discoloration, the object of childhood ridicule and youthful insecurity. Now a blessing. A lifeline.

She took shape before him, the familiar features and contours. When he brushed her hair aside, he finally recognized the tightly hooded eyes, albeit with new, dark crescents underneath. The same curt button nose, nostrils chafed and red, cheeks no longer fully plump with baby fat but slightly sunken now, tired and wan.

But it was her. It was Mei. Finally, somehow.

He blinked with purpose, regaining focus, dragged the back of his hand under his nose with a snort, composing himself. He moved swiftly, snatching one of the larger blankets from the floor, draping it overtop of her, tucking in the edges along the outline of her tiny frame. He rolled her onto her back, pulling the fabric through beneath, folding and wrapping until she was bundled into a snug, polyester cocoon. When he hoisted her into his arms she hung like dead weight, her head lolling backwards until he steadied her, the freckled girl silently watching as he carried her out of the room.

She was lighter than he would have guessed, but he wasn't certain how far he would have to carry her, hardly inconspicuous now. His head was pounding, pulsating since the scrum with the unconscious man, recalling how it caromed against the wall as they tussled.

Stepping over the bodies still motionless on the floor, he turned to face the *matryoshka* dolls—silent, unmoving—staring at him as they had from the outset, still mesmerized by the evening's incomprehensible turn of events. A man who entered their lives like a sandstorm—a blur of violence—now appeared to be leaving with one of their own. He looked down at Mei, still staring off into a void, and then back to the girls.

"Do you know how to call the police?" he asked the eldest.

There was no response, no reaction of any kind.

"Police?" he tried once more. "Policia? Pol—" What was that, Spanish? What use would that be? Arabic, doubtful. Tagalog, maybe. Perhaps Thai.

The eldest girl's features seemed to soften for a moment, a dry swallow followed by a tentative nod.

"Thai?" he gambled.

Another nod, more certain this time.

"Police. Telephone." He hoped he'd pronounced it right. He balanced Mei against his chest and mimed a phone call with his free hand. "One two two. *Neung. Song. Song.* Alright?" He jutted his chin toward the telephone on the corner desk.

He waited, holding her gaze. Was he really about to leave them, huddled together in fear? What else could he do? He wasn't going to wait around for the authorities to show up, if someone hadn't called them already, having heard the disturbance from down the hall. And he certainly couldn't take them with him.

He spoke again, slowly, nodding with every syllable, "*Neung. Song. Song.*"

Without a sound, her lips parted, mouthing the numbers back to him.

Cradling Mei with one arm, he opened the door. It was wobbly now, hinges bent. He stuck his head out into the hallway, looking both ways down the empty corridor. He gave a final glance at the painted dolls behind him, a last nod to the mother hen, her wings still shielding her young.

She nodded back.

Down the hallway now, footsteps muffled on the carpet, racing toward the exit sign that glowed at the far end.

Once out in the open, the exposure was, if nothing else, stimulating, and it propelled him forward. In his mind's eye, the image of a crudely drawn police sketch flashed before him. Then another, a still frame, black and white and granular, the kidnapper and his victim fleeing a local hotel, caught by a surveillance camera.

Thankfully, nothing but silence as he sped, legs pumping down the hall. Nudging the metal crash bar with his hip, the door swung open into the yellow glow of the stairwell, the warm air thick with the reek of stale smoke.

He cursed himself as he hurried down the concrete steps. Cursed himself for being so reckless, doing exactly what Maha had warned him against. She would know exactly where to take Mei and find her treatment, but he couldn't involve her now, not after this. Breaking and entering, assault—two counts at the very least, possibly on Egyptian citizens. And who knew how they would tie him to the girls back in the room? It was their word against his, and the state wasn't exactly known for its impartial judicial process. Another image flashed in his mind: Tariq and his mustachioed friends pointing and yelling, mouths twisted with hate. *"Jasus Amriki!"* American spy.

His lungs burned as he sucked the thin air, sweat pouring as he descended the final staircase. On the one hand, he was exhausted, acid pumping in his legs and thighs, but the little girl was still as light as a feather in his arms, clasped tightly to his chest.

Carefully opening the door, he stepped out into the darkness—a side street, quiet and still, shadows scarce in the dim moonlight. His eyes adjusted to his surroundings: storefronts with padlocked metal shutters, rusty air conditioners hanging from darkened apartment windows. Graffiti scrawled across the brick building in front of him, the contours of its old, arched entryways barely visible. A few steps away, a back alley beckoned.

A warm midnight breeze floated through the alley without so much as a whisper, and he listened to the gentle flutter of bedsheets, hung on a clothesline several stories above, forgotten during the rush of the day or perhaps simply left out to be collected at dawn. For the time being, the alley would have to do, and in truth, it was as good a spot as any given the circumstances, given his rash behavior. As good a place as any, while he waited.

FORTY

Huddled in an obscure corner, Quinn crouched by a low wall of crumbling brick that jutted out into the lane. Surrounded by loose stone and trash bags, the shadows cascaded overtop at just the right angle, melding the pair of them seamlessly into the side of the building.

The sounds of the city still echoed now and again, carried on the wind from a distance, but for the better part of an hour, Quinn listened to the soothing flap of linens from the clothesline on high, a welcome sound for his frayed nerves. He brushed Mei's sweaty bangs aside, her eyes closed now, perfectly still, asleep. At one point, an anxious moment, he tucked his head down next to hers, relieved to feel her warm breath on his ear. Every few minutes he adjusted the blanket around her, tucking this and folding that, simple acts that made him feel that at least he was doing something, trivial as it might have been.

For a long while, time stood still in that darkened space. Then, emerging from a shallow slumber, his ears pricked up, senses homing in on a foreign sound on the street at the far end of the alley. The grind and churn of sand and loose stone beneath the wheels of a car. There were no headlights. He tucked his chin into his chest, folding deeper against the wall, holding his breath.

Peering into the distance, he saw the silhouette of a dark truck roll into view, pause for a moment, then turn its nose down into the side street. The vehicle slowed, stopped, and the engine cut. He watched the door open and a dark figure emerge, hunched over in the darkness, searching left and right, quiet footsteps on the pavement. Then, the familiar gravelly voice. "Mr. Quinn? Are you here?"

He let out a deep sigh of relief and tried to stand, his legs tingling and numb from the hard ground. He lifted Mei, carrying her out of the shadows and into the crepuscular light.

"Saad. I can't thank you enough."

The Sudanese had a swift and determined stride, his arms outstretched. "Give her to me. Okay. *Y'allah*. We go."

Quinn opened the back door of the SUV, and Saad laid her carefully on the leather seats. The pair climbed in the front, Saad having made sure the dome light was off and hushing his passenger as they gently shut their doors. The engine started up again, turning over smoothly into a low hum. Saad placed his arm behind the passenger headrest, craning his neck to look behind as he reversed, glancing down at Mei.

"What is her condition?"

Quinn looked back as well, his face solemn. "I don't know."

As they pulled out onto the street, he turned and faced forward as Saad shifted the truck into drive.

"But I know someone who will."

It was the deepest hour of night, nearly three in the morning when Quinn crested the final landing, carrying Mei to the fifth floor of the apartment stairwell. A pendant bowl light hung from the ceiling, the glass speckled with a collection of dead flies, casting an apricot glow throughout the hall.

He paused in front of the familiar door and motioned toward it with his head. Saad, following just behind, nodded and joined him. He held up a large black fist and paused for a moment, just long enough for the two men to exchange a look, then rapped on the heavy door. They stood perfectly still, listening, until Saad's knuckles clapped along the heavy wood door once again, the rattling sound echoing through the empty hallway.

Quinn put his ear to the door and thought he heard some stirring inside, though the sounds were swiftly drowned out by voices across the hall, activity in a different room. Saad moved toward the far suite just as the door handle creaked and turned, hands already raised, whispering that there was no cause for alarm.

Quinn heard the deadbolt snap open behind him and turned to meet Youssef's droopy, sleep-filled eyes as he squinted through the slight opening into the hallway.

"I didn't know where else to go."

The old man opened the door wider, taking a moment to appraise the situation, looking down at the sleeping girl, mouth open, bundled in cloth, then back to the haggard man cradling her in his arms. He stepped aside. "You came to the right place."

Quinn looked back at Saad who, glancing over his shoulder, gave a hasty nod, then brusquely waved him onward, still working to deflect the prying eyes that peered from the doorway: a husband and wife, heads bobbing, curious to see what all the fuss was about.

Once inside, Quinn lay Mei down on the couch, the men speaking in low whispers, though it did little to assuage Noor—lights on in the bedroom, impatient words for her husband. Youssef soaked a cloth in cold water and handed it to him before capitulating to the angry voice that beckoned. "A moment," he said, hobbling back down the hallway, his wife's Arabic—staccato and harsh—demanding an explanation.

Quinn knelt next to the sofa, wiping Mei's forehead with the cool, damp rag, dabbing her cheeks, swathing her neck. When Youssef returned, he carried a brown leather physician's bag, a stethoscope dangling from his neck. He winced, moving at a quicker pace than he was accustomed, a pivot in his gait without the cane, limbs stiff from being woken unexpectedly in the night.

"Bring me my stool, if you please."

The doctor seated himself and exhaled heavily through his nostrils, squeezing Mei's thin wrist and looking her up and down, clinical and meticulous.

"This is the girl," he said, more a statement than a question.

Quinn nodded.

"Where did you find her?"

"Hotel room."

"Forgive me, I cannot recall her name."

"Mei."

"Yes, of course. Mei."

With his thumb and forefinger, he gently opened her eyelids, inquisitively assessing, then, inserting his earpieces, placed the silver diaphragm on her concave chest, sliding it left, then right, then left again.

"I will need to examine her," he said, matter-of-factly. He looked up at Quinn. "It may be better if . . ." He trailed off, the situation calling for a certain delicacy. Then, he paused for another reason entirely, taking in the full picture of the man standing beside him: eyes red-rimmed, suspended above dark semi-circles, sallow cheeks and an unshaven face—pale as moonlight, but for the inflamed purplish contusion above the right brow, some raw nail marks across his jaw. Quinn swayed gently on his heels, a withered oak teetering in the breeze.

"Mr. Mills?"

Quinn sniffed sharply and shook his head reflexively, back amongst the living once again.

"I'm thinking perhaps you could use an examination yourself."

"I'm fine," he said, clearing his throat. "I'm fine."

"Down the hall on the left, you will find a balcony. Maybe you would prefer to take a moment. You can see my cigarettes on the table before you go outside. You can help yourself."

Pushing open the slatted wooden shutters, Quinn stepped out onto a small, tiled platform with a waist-high railing. A rustic kitchen chair occupied most of the balcony; a wooden stool held an ashtray and a potted jade plant. Youssef smoked Cleopatras, apparently, a portrait of the famous queen herself on the pack. He took half a drag before realizing he had put fire to the filtered end, spitting a curse and tossing it aside.

He leaned forward onto the railing, taking a few deep breaths, trying to focus on the rhythm of his diaphragm, something Maha had suggested the night before. She used the technique whenever she was frustrated with men, she'd said, employed rather frequently in Archie's office. A curious yet endearing Buddhist quirk of hers. He focused on the rise and fall of his chest, savoring the cool air he drew in and the hot breath he let out until the pain in his head distracted him. He lit another cigarette instead, properly this time, and put his mind back to work—back to getting out of Cairo, and Mei safely out of Egypt.

FORTY-ONE

"I NEED A STRAIGHT ANSWER, YOUSSEF. TELL ME."

The old man rose unsteadily, Quinn helping him to his feet. He nodded thoughtfully, the faintest arc on his thick lips as he reached out, gripping Quinn's shoulders. "It is much better than I thought, my friend. I feared the worst, but I think there is no need."

Quinn shrank where he stood, the relief palpable, washing over him, pulling him to the earth. He took a step back and sat down into the sofa cushions, gathering himself for a moment. "So, what now?" he asked. "I mean, how is she? What do I need to know?"

"Mostly, it's good news. The most common injuries are not there, the ones we might have expected, the ones we may have feared. She seems to be largely unaffected, certainly no tears or abrasions of any kind, and, to my eyes—my *old* eyes—there are no genital or extra-genital injuries that I can see. Swelling or erythema of the labia, the hymen, the posterior fourchette, I don't see anything of what you might call the more frequent traumas.

"Now, of course, I am limited with the tools I have at my disposal"—he motioned to the open leather bag—"a timely examination is crucial. We're not sure how much time has passed or if there was any kind of prior abuse. However, I am optimistic from what

I've seen. Physically, she has several bumps and bruises but, nothing to worry me, although you can see here . . ." He raised Mei's limp arm, holding up her hand, fingertips raw and specked with blood. "They have cut back her fingernails, deep into the nailbed, most likely to keep her from scratching. They are raw, but they will heal with time."

Quinn nodded along, a strange sensation of relief and fury warring within him.

"Unfortunately, it is not all good news. As you know, the psychological ramifications can be . . . wide ranging. I cannot speak to this, so I will not make assumptions. Tell me, Mr. Mills, you mentioned a hotel room?"

He nodded. "With other girls close to her age. I told them to call the police as I left but, I'm not sure."

"There are others?"

"I have the address, the room, but you shouldn't call yourself, at least not from your home. I didn't . . ." He shook his head from side to side. "I didn't exactly leave quietly."

Youssef's eyes drifted to the gleaming welt. "I can see that."

"This isn't"—he thought better of it—"it doesn't matter now. I'm on camera at the hotel, and it doesn't look good. I can't take my chances having to explain any of it."

A look of concern had begun to creep across Youssef's face, knotting his brow, the old man perhaps wondering what he had gotten himself into and if he shouldn't have heeded the warnings that came from the bedroom.

"I'm sorry to get you mixed up into this," Quinn said. "I know I'm asking a lot here, but if you could give me a couple of hours, just until morning. I couldn't take her to the hospital—the questions, and with everything going on outside, there was nowhere else."

Youssef pinched his eyes shut, waving his hand. "No, no, of course not."

"And I wasn't about to leave her there. It's bad enough the others—"

"It's alright now. What's done is done. As for me, I may be old, but I'm not without my connections, you know. Don't worry about that. Now, tell me again, the room, did you happen to see any medication? Tablets?"

Quinn shook his head. "I wasn't exactly shopping."

"There are no indications that she's been abused. However, I'm concerned about her heart rate, her breathing. She's been unresponsive like this since you found her?"

"She goes in and out. Dazed. I don't think she knows."

"They may have given her something, some sort of CNS depressant, perhaps . . ."

"CNS?"

"Central nervous system —barbiturates, benzodiazepines— sedatives, essentially, something as common as sleep medication, perhaps, for cold and flu, like this . . ."

"To calm her down, keep her docile."

"Most likely."

"So now?"

"Do you remember what time you found her?"

He thought for a moment, "What time is *isha* prayer? Nine?"

"*Nam, tis'a*—yes, that's good. It has been several hours then. She is most likely out of, what is this expression, the forest?"

"Woods."

"The woods, yes. Out of the woods. She is dehydrated and will need fluids and rest but, *yanni*, overall, Mr. Mills," he exhaled, "this is something of a miracle."

Quinn nodded in agreement, though only out of courtesy. "Well, we're not entirely out of the woods just yet. I need to get her out of Cairo as soon as I can." Then, he added, "In fact, I need to get myself out of Cairo."

"You believe you're somehow implicated in this?"

"I don't know what I believe. It wouldn't be difficult. There were cameras everywhere in the hotel room. Laptops. They were filming, broadcasting. At first I wasn't sure—everything happened so fast—but it fits. It's why she's . . . not worse off than she is."

Youssef pondered this for a time, "So then, a different type of exploitation, two sides of the same coin."

"It's like the Philippines. All you need is a camera and an Internet connection. Few people coming in and out, little overhead, and the profits are," he shrugged, "exponential. And because it's all online, legally, they're in the Stone Age trying to enforce anything."

"And the girls, they are like your Mei, from abroad?"

He nodded, chewing his lip. "None were local from what I could tell. Maybe they move them on later, as you said, across the Med. To Israel, maybe. But for now, that was the operation."

"Something for their pockets before they are moved again."

"They have me in the room, Youssef, leaving with one of the girls. It would be my word against the couple who was in there running everything."

"Egyptians?"

"Couldn't say. Arab. Arabic speaking."

"Mm."

"It was the passports. They have a code, not overly sophisticated but clever enough. I stared at those goddamn things for how long and didn't see it." Restless, he began to pace. "I don't know if they altered the documents on their own or if the entire operation is more institutionalized."

"You believe the state is involved?"

"Not necessarily the state—members of it, maybe." He combed his fingers through his hair. "I don't know what to think anymore."

"I love my country, Mr. Mills. I am a proud Egyptian. But I cannot say that all who represent us have the same character. The country is poor, and those at the top find every means to line their pockets." He laid a hand on Quinn's shoulder, steadying him. "You need rest, Mr. Mills. You look, if you don't mind my saying so, quite terrible."

Quinn gave a weak grin, would have laughed had he been able.

Youssef placed his palm over his own heart and blinked slowly. "I am only thankful you are both alright, *hamdullah*."

"*Shukran*, Youssef, *shukran jazeelah*. I promise we'll be gone at first light. I know I haven't done you any favors," he added, casting a guilty look down the hall.

"She will understand. She worries, you know, in times like these. We Egyptians are no strangers to this," he said, motioning to the far window. "But still, it can be unnerving. The ordinary becomes unpredictable. I will help as much as I am able, Mr. Mills. Do you know where you will go next? What you will do?"

"I have an idea," he said, his eyes on Mei. "Something of an idea."

FORTY-TWO

At dawn, the clouds nestled low to the ground, heavy and still, hardly any movement in the yellowish-gray sky. The air was thicker than usual, dense with smog and dust, and above all, petrol fumes, the taxi's open windows allowing the noxious exhaust of the gridlocked city to flood into the cab.

It had been forty-five minutes and they hadn't even made it to Ring Road. They had yet to encounter any government roadblocks; rather, it was the primitive neighborhood defenses that clogged the narrow lanes of Maadi. Local collectives of men, grabbing whatever rudimentary weapons they could—bricks and broom handles, pipes, small mounds of rocks—constructed barricades with household wares to ward off looters and bandits should they try and test their luck.

They crept along, hemmed into the endless queue of cars, buses, and motorbikes as pedestrians rivaled their pace: a shuffling old woman, hijabed in black and hunched with plastic sacks weighing her to the ground; a street vendor, one hand carefully balancing a tray of *aish baladi*—Egyptian flatbread. When the salesman's obstinate stride pulled him ahead of the taxi, Quinn muttered under his breath, cathartic words aimed at the universe. From the rearview mirror, apologetic eyes glanced at him nervously, and he dismissed the driver's concerns with a shake of the head, his quarrel elsewhere. The man behind the wheel, slim and rather timid, slouched back in his seat with a sigh and, after a moment, threw a hand up toward the windshield in solidarity.

Traffic was worse than he had anticipated, and he had anticipated it to be awful—stifling and congested, but nothing like this. Anxious tourists flocking toward the airport, passionate voices marching defiantly toward mosques and local squares, the army tense, on high alert at every intersection, the city in a frenzy while many locals simply carried on about their day. The honking was incessant, a relentless dissonance even by Cairo's standards, everyone pounding their steering wheels, waving their arms, shouting commands, and admonishing transgressors.

They had left early and made relatively good time at first— Quinn wouldn't have bothered returning to Maadi if it weren't for his passport—and yet there was a very real possibility that he wouldn't make the flight. He could only hope that Saad was making better headway. Maybe the flights were delayed, like the man in the elevator had said the night before. Delayed, but not canceled, a slim margin for hope.

The congestion was nightmarish in that it also forced him to sit and contemplate every decision leading to that very moment, a prison of his own making, obliged to face his anxieties in painstaking detail. There was no longer time to do anything other than consider all his mistakes, every detail overlooked. He could only shift his weight and fidget, churning over hastily laid plans that had seemed far more sensible the night before, plans that appeared rather exposed now, increasingly desperate in the sober light of day.

As the lanes began to open up, nearing the outer reaches of the city, he stared into the distance where a cloud of drifting black smoke unfurled above the sunbaked roofs of dusky condominiums.

A skyline of beige brick, swaying clotheslines, and rusty satellite dishes. The smoke moved slowly, billows light and airy, not some blazing inferno in need of dousing but rather a smoldering pile of debris, somewhere off in the desert horizon.

He thought about the cameras. The hotel would have had many, surely, overlooking the entrance, the lobby, possibly the hallways as well. What would they have seen? He shuddered at the thought, not for the first time. A lone man, blond, six feet tall, well past the evening curfew, wearing a bright yellow delivery shirt, waltzing up the front steps. He might as well have worn a beanie with a propeller on his head.

"Idiot," he muttered.

And the nosy couple across from Youssef's apartment. He hadn't asked when he called Saad that morning. How much would they have seen in the dim light across the hall? He could hear the conversation, irresistible gossip over tea and *basbousa*. "A Western man carrying a young girl? The middle of the night, you say? To think, at times like these. And to Dr. Nasser's front door. Impossible. I can't believe it. What could the good doctor have to do with someone like that? Well, yes, I suppose so, he is a physician after all. Still, with all the trouble out there. And accompanied by a bodyguard, no less . . . an American?"

They weren't far now, having kept a steady pace since they left the inner city, flying down the open lanes, but as they turned onto Airport Road, the highway was slowly choked off once again. Would they close the airport? It had certainly happened before. More than likely it would be the flights that were canceled, grounded for security precautions. Then what?

Then, it was only a matter of time. His mind kept returning to the same question, weighing the selfish choices that he had made and how he had managed to implicate all of them—Maha, Youssef, even Saad. But what else could he have done? It was undeniable; they needed to get out now for everyone's sake, before the inevitable questions were asked, before the authorities started looking, if they weren't already.

How long before police attended the hotel, investigating the scene? There was a distinct possibility that they were already there, piecing the evening's events together, interviewing the clerk, pulling the footage. And then? His face, printed on flyers, distributed at shift briefings at every precinct, photographs plastered in customs inspection booths. He could no longer differentiate a rational concern from his own creeping paranoia.

It was difficult to gauge the temperature of the city and how close the rising simmer was to boiling over into full-scale upheaval. The Spring was still vivid in the nation's memory, as was Morsi's demise and the ensuing fallout. The violent protests the other day could have been the peak, the apex of long-standing tensions, a necessary release of the pressure valve. Then again, it could have been just the beginning.

The army had been brought in, as it often was, to demonstrate its might and to keep the citizenry from erupting as it had before, although he couldn't tell if the protests were just pockets of inflamed emotions or part of something larger. Was the curfew a precaution, or reactive panic by the old guard? Surely, he wasn't a priority for anyone now. The jails would be full of demonstrators, possibly looters, and vandals. More than likely, innocents too, in the wrong place at the wrong time, just as Maha had warned. Would the police be wasting time with someone like him, even if they did obtain a proper description? Would they not have other orders now that the city might be on the brink of revolution?

Quinn was pulled from his reverie as they slowed, spotting the seemingly endless line of taxis queueing along the ramp. He counted out some crumpled notes, pinned the small bundle against the driver's shoulder, and threw open the door as the cab was still rolling.

He forced his way through a crowd blocking the entranceway and, once inside, found himself in the midst of a frenzy. A mob of humanity clogged every artery of the terminal, the air reeking with the stench of mothballs, old garlic, and pungent body odor. Contorted faces shouted in every direction as he navigated carts with stacks of luggage, backpacks that swung around unexpectedly, carry-on baggage rolling along, clipping ankles and heels, an obstacle course amongst a sea of bodies.

An especially large grouping had gathered by the Egypt Air desk, exasperated faces checking phones, poking heads up to see if the line had moved, strangers inquiring with other strangers, the rolling of eyes and shrugging of shoulders. The airline staff appeared just as unapprised, uniforms and hairstyles still starched into place, but expressions weary and numb. He stumbled, tripping over a grouping of backpackers who had unfurled their sleeping bags in a not-so-secluded corner. A teenage girl shot him a look for daring to pass through her makeshift dormitory.

He continued to push through the crowds, using his height to his advantage, maneuvering left and right, navigating through the moving hurdles in his path. Finally nearing the coffee shop, he tried to pick out faces, scanning for the dark features behind circular frames, the snowy-white hair. He surveyed the crowd until a blurry motion caught his attention by a palm tree, an arm frantically waving.

Saad's eyes were wide, beckoning him forward. In the next moment, he was motioning toward the security gates instead. Quinn wasn't as polite now, using his shoulders to part the bodies when they stood their ground, everyone absorbed with their own concerns.

Saad puffed out his cheeks, a dramatic exhalation, a single ticket in his outstretched hand.

"Where are they? Everything good?" Quinn asked, panicked eyes darting around.

Saad nodded. "We could not wait any more. I thought maybe you don't make it. The plane, she is on time, but you must go."

"Thank you again for everything, I can't even tell you—"

Saad would hear none of this, shaking his head and waving his hands in front of him. When Quinn tried to pull out the last of his bills, his wrist was held in place by an iron-like grip.

"I'm serious," Quinn said. "What you did for me, for us . . ."

"What kind of man does nothing in this situation?" Saad relaxed his grip and planted a firm hand on Quinn's shoulder, looking toward the security gates. "This girl, I give thanks to Allah this is not my child. But . . ." He raised a finger. "This is a child of Allah. You understand my meaning?"

Quinn felt himself smiling from the corner of his mouth, "I understand your meaning, Saad."

The man let his grip linger for a moment as Quinn caught his breath.

"*Matara shayala*?" Quinn asked.

Saad laughed heartily from his belly, blinking slowly with a great, beaming smile. "*Matara shayala*," he replied, nodding.

The men embraced, Saad's powerful arms smacking Quinn's back. "Maybe five minutes before they went. Go now, *y'allah*."

As Quinn made his way through security, the tedium of the screening process clawed at him, every excruciating and needless delay. An elderly Chinese woman, stubborn despite the language barrier, refused to relinquish her bottle of tea. An oblivious Canadian woman, still wearing her watch and money belt, was apparently without a passport, until Quinn pulled it from beneath her purse. When she thanked him profusely, he simply pointed to the body scanner, the same scanner whose one-at-a-time queueing policy mystified an Indian family of four, harried and scolded by two stern officials.

His pace quickened for only a moment before he was halted by the tail end of another queue, this one even longer, an immigration officer at the far end stamping exit visas. He found himself in the middle row, flanked by the same impatient travelers he had waded through on the public side, a few signs of relief amongst the crowd—the first hurdle overcome, another checkpoint closer.

Scanning the masses, it was far more difficult this time around: columns of ponytails and sunhats, backwards caps and headscarves. Had they already passed through? His eyes lingered over any black garb in sight: a sport jacket, a sweater. *There, a burka*! No, not them. A single woman with another man. More *niqabs* to the right but too many, likely a mother and her daughters.

As time wore on, a sense of dread began to creep, a slithering feeling of unease that refused to dissipate no matter how hard he willed it away. *Had they been caught?* No. Impossible. Not that fast. Still, they wouldn't be able to confirm anything at the booth. *An interrogation room?* Taken elsewhere, out of sight, avoiding any public melodrama, the proper resources at their disposal.

Another black hijab! A moment suspended in time until the woman rose from the suitcase on which she sat, helped by a man in a white *shemagh*.

How could he have ever put them in such a position? The absolute epitome of stupidity. He had found her, somehow, against all odds, mainlining good fortune as though he might have even deserved it. And now, he had risked it all, for what? Because he didn't trust the police to find those accountable? Because of a thousand unfounded ruminations, tugging his mind in a thousand different directions? Because he didn't want to end up in an Egyptian prison? He would make the trade a thousand times over without a moment's hesitation.

For a fleeting moment, he had a tender, comforting thought. Maybe they had gone through, swiftly, with minimal screening, no concerns whatsoever. Already en route, past the queue, past the booth, past the flight board with gates and departure times, past the duty-free shops with sparkling bottles and seductive fragrances, past the washrooms, the lounges, the cafés, and currency exchanges. Past the departure gate and into the cabin, along the tarmac and into the clouds, soaring high and away into the endless blue sky. Far and away, headed back home. Headed anywhere at all.

There. Right there. The left-hand column, by the booth. A pair of tourists gathered their documents, and a slim figure in a black abaya materialized at the front of the queue, stepping out from behind a group of broad-shouldered backpackers. She moved toward the passport control, a furtive glance back at the crowd. Judging by the height of her *niqab*, she had pinned her hair up in a bun, dark eyeliner accentuating her only visible features. Maha looked back once more, shoulders sagging with relief as they finally locked eyes, the weight of her emotions tangible even from beneath her garb. Beside her, Mei, identically clothed, shrouded from head to toe in black, following hand in hand as Maha led her to the officer's desk.

It was a strange confluence of emotions. Relief washed over him. They had made it, at least this far. And yet, now was only the beginning. The *niqab*, the passport, the improvised deceit, if there was a time to feel genuine relief about anything, this was certainly not it.

Squinting from a distance, he watched Maha remove the passports and boarding passes from her purse, sliding them across to the official. Hers would be fine, of course; everything hinged on the other. Of the dozen or so passports he had found, only two remained unaltered, or at least appeared as such. On the bio page of the first was a photograph of a girl several years older than Mei. She had South Asian features and a much darker complexion—perhaps Indian or Bengali—hardly a match for even the most bleary-eyed customs official.

Not that the second document was much better. The girl was younger, closer in age, but it would still require quite the imagination to align any of Mei's features. However, the biggest gamble remained with the authenticity of the passport itself. There were no signs of the additional alphanumeric coding designating hotels, room numbers, and who knew what else. It could very well be that the barcode, unadulterated, was still valid. It certainly matched the document's validity date, good for a couple more years, well past the six-month mark that raised questions at certain borders. And it certainly wouldn't bother anyone on Royal Jordanian—no visas required for a friendly neighbor state, just a mother and daughter visiting relatives in Amman.

Some nodding back and forth, a shake of the head from Maha, likely answering some basic questions. *Where is your husband? And what business does he have in Jordan?* Mei stood, motionless, staring at the floor. The official leaned forward in his chair, peering down at her, then turned his attention back to the passports. He flipped a few pages in one, then the other. Typed something into the computer. Some more questions.

Quinn realized the fragility of his hopeful daydream when the man barked something at a female officer passing by, waving one of the passports, beckoning her near. Quinn watched in horror as the document changed hands, the female officer ushering Maha behind the booth and out of sight.

He felt the blood drain from his face. Then, weakness in his knees. He steadied himself. The man in the booth leaned back in his chair, contemplating whatever he saw on the monitor, glancing to and fro from the passport to the screen. A moment that stretched on in perpetuity as Quinn held his breath, or didn't. It was difficult to tell anymore.

He gasped in relief when Maha reappeared, adjusting the veil around her cheeks, seemingly nothing more than a routine identity check. The female officer handed the passport back to the official as Maha gestured to Mei, a hand on her shoulder. *And my daughter?*

It was in that moment that Quinn realized he should have never doubted her. The officer gave a gentle shake of the head, followed by a wave of the hand. Clearly, there was no need to examine the young one. Maha responded in kind with a measured nod—*wa alaykumu as-salaam*—and the officer continued on her way down the line.

She wrapped an arm around Mei, pinning her close against her waist, standing for what seemed like an eternity yet with faultless composure. The immigration official kept looking back at his monitor, with either scrutiny or boredom—impossible to tell, given the distance—then flipped through the pages in the documents once more. Finally, a small, dark object appeared in his grasp, and he slammed it with vigor several times. He slid the passports back across the counter and slouched back into his seat. Maha slipped her belongings into her purse, crouched and whispered something to Mei, then led her forward by the hand.

Through the shifting crowd, Quinn caught glimpses of black *abbayas* side by side, snapshots and still frames, appearing and reappearing between the rows of customs booths, eventually drifting out of sight, fading into the bustling milieu of the terminal.

The passage of time was strange, Quinn mused, creeping along at a glacial pace while his heart pattered wildly in his chest. Then, a rush of euphoria—the queue flooding forward like a turbulent stream, the current pulling him along until he found himself, a dazed look upon his face, handing his passport to a hulking, square-jawed official.

The officer leafed through the document rather casually, reached the back cover, and began once more, turning the pages more carefully a second time.

"Where visa?"

"Sorry?"

"Visa. Where."

"It's in there," Quinn assured him, the guard peeling apart two pages clinging together from blotches of dried ink.

Quinn looked out into the terminal, into the crowds that, having overcome their screening ordeal, now meandered lazily, passing the time. He tried to be subtle about it—a sideways glance here, a casual peak there—to see if they were waiting for him. They should have been well on their way to the gate by now, if not already boarding. He checked his watch. Maha knew not to wait. He had insisted on that.

The click-clacking of the keyboard had stopped, and the man was reading something on his screen, eyes scanning right and left for longer than made Quinn comfortable. Then, he splayed open the passport with his thumb and raised it in front of him, lining up the picture with Quinn's head. His eyebrows creased as he looked from the page to his traveler, and back again.

"You change your hair."

He keyed something else into his computer and shifted in his seat, straightening his posture. A phlegmy cough erupted from his chest, then another. All the while he gazed at the screen.

This was taking too long.

Unexpectedly, he rose from his seat, taller than Quinn had imagined, then turned and stepped out of the booth. As he came around the side, he kept his head down, eyes ever on the passport, turning the pages methodically.

"Come with me."

Quinn thought he misheard. "What?"

The officer stopped and raised his eyes, a cold stare, inconvenienced by the halt in his stride. "I don't ask again."

FORTY-THREE

Far and away from the bustling hum of the terminal, removed from inquisitive eyes, perusing shoppers, and the travel-weary public, Quinn followed his chaperone down a white-walled corridor—silent, but for the hollow echo of their footsteps. They stopped before an unmarked door.

"Wait here," the man said, turning the handle and stepping inside.

Quinn swallowed drily, almost coughed from the sensation. He forced himself to think of Mei, of Maha. They were through, free and clear, and at the very least he could stall until the plane pushed back. The delay wouldn't be long; no checked baggage to offload. That was all that mattered now. They couldn't be tied to him, not unless . . .

The plane tickets. The booking would have been made as one, the three of them linked. And if—

The door swung open, the guard standing off center, jerking his head, motioning him inside.

The heat was the first thing he noticed, the room suffocating with foul air: burnt tobacco, stale onions, acrid body oil. The walls were white but for where they met the ceiling, a blotchy yellow stain encircling the room. Behind a metal desk—faded army-green—sat a heavyset man, clearly of some importance despite his state of attire. He wore a white button-down—no epaulets or medals—spread open to reveal an undershirt sprouting tufts of black overgrowth. A thick face with sagging jowls, a few strands of hair remained on his skull, smeared across a greasy scalp like neglected railroad slats. It was unclear if he was losing his hair or if the follicles had simply migrated south to his bristling eyebrows. An impotent white plastic fan whirred on the desk, stirring the warm air.

The guard motioned once more to the seat as his superior examined Quinn's passport. The supervisor had stubby fingers and chewed fingernails, a half cigarette smoldering beside him in a silver ashtray. He didn't say anything, so neither did Quinn. It wasn't an interrogation room, he thought, though not exactly standard procedure either.

To his left, a black-and-white portrait of President Nasser, waving to the adoring masses. To the right, an aerial photograph of Mecca, an ocean of humanity encircling the *ka'bah*—less a pilgrimage of devotees than a solar system, a galaxy with infinite stars drifting in orbit.

"Mistair . . . Mills, yes?"

Quinn nodded.

"Ferst time in Egypt?"

"Second."

"And for what purpose, may I ask? Business or . . ."

"Tourism."

"Of course, of course. Was the trip to your, hm . . ." As he searched for the words, he picked up his cigarette and took a heavy drag. "Satisfaction?"

"Sure."

The man gave nothing away. Neither did the guard, whose presence Quinn could still feel, standing somewhere close behind him.

The silence that lingered worked as intended, prompting Quinn to volunteer a concession. "You have a very beautiful country," he said.

A gracious tilt of the head. "Beautiful, yes, but poor." He opened his palm. "But, this is part of our charm, no? Mm . . . so, tell me, what did you see?"

"What did I see?"

"Tourism, yes? Tell me," he said with a shrug. "What have you seen in Egypt?"

Quinn shifted in his chair, twisted around to get a good look at the guard behind him, then faced the front. The bushy caterpillar eyebrows were raised, expectant. *Well?*

"Camels and sand traps. Does anyone want to tell me what's going on here? I have a plane to catch."

The tone of the room shifted. Behind him, heavy boots shuffled forward, closer than he would have liked. A palm lifted, somewhat reluctantly, no more than a couple of inches off the desk, halting the boots in their place. Quinn stared straight ahead, his interrogator's mouth tightening almost imperceptibly, though his cheeks had reddened. Clearly, not a man accustomed to suffering an insolent tone.

"Pardon me," Quinn said, shaking his head, a retreat, of sorts. "It's been a long day. I'm just a little confused as to why I'm here. I'm sure you can understand my concern. This doesn't seem like your typical airport lounge."

"You are correct, Mistair Mills," the man said.

"Quinton, please. And, I didn't catch your name?"

"You can call me Amir."

"Amir. I think there might have been a misunderstanding, maybe some confusion . . ."

Amir's attention had drifted, staring now at Quinn's forehead. Slowly, he raised his hand, bringing his index finger to his own brow. "Maybe this," he said, "is reason for your confusion?"

"An accident."

Amir grunted.

"I got lost, ended up somewhere I shouldn't have been, and—"

"And, what?" Amir blew two columns of smoke from his nostrils, "Misunderstanding?" he drawled.

His client subdued for the moment, Amir reached for the passport once again, leafing methodically through the pages. After a moment, he said, "Your visa is no good. It is, *khalas*, *yanni* . . . is expire."

"That's impossible."

Amir gave the most indifferent of shrugs, casually turning the pages, a look of exaggerated boredom on his face.

"Can I see it?" Quinn asked.

Amir waved his request away with a couple of fingers, the cigarette nub tucked in between. It hissed when he crumpled it into the silver tin.

"How long are you in Egypt?"

"A few weeks."

"Where did you get this?"

"The visa? Here. On entry."

Amir made a clicking sound with his tongue. "This, you would not get here. No. This, you bought somewhere else."

"Bought? Where would I buy this? And why? What are you talking about?"

"These days, we are having some problems with visas, my friend. We find many of them now. Fake. *Not genuine,* as you say in America."

"I don't know what you're talking about."

Amir leaned back in his chair. "As you can see," he began, speaking matter-of-factly now, "we are having many problems in my country at this time. There are those people who do not like the men in power, trying to take power for themselves." He shook his head solemnly. "This is a mistake. You see, I grow up with many of these men. I know them. We are, Egyptians, like brothers. The men, they have . . ." He clenched a fist. "Energy, *passion*. But, they are not organize." He pulled a face, then shrugged. "They are too separate. With power, they do not know what they do not know. You understand? As you can see, they cause many problems like this. You have seen, the world has seen, what happened with President Mubarak."

He coaxed a cigarette from its package with fleshy fingers, the guard circling from behind Quinn to offer a light.

"There are those in our government who think my friends, my people, with this passion, they cannot do like this themselves. They cannot organize by themselves. There are people who think"—he lowered his gaze, narrowing his eyes at Quinn—"that there are others who help them."

"Is that an accusation?"

Amir opened his palm, followed by a shrug of implication. Quinn leaned forward to stand and immediately felt a vice clamp down in the crook of his neck, forcing him back into the chair. He grabbed the man's hand, twisting it until the guard broke free.

"*Khalas*!" Amir bellowed, motioning the guard back as the two men glared at each other, chests rising and falling. "Mistair Mills . . ."

Quinn kept his eye on the guard, who stood defiantly, his neatly trimmed mustache twisted into a menacing sneer.

"Mistair Mills, perhaps now I have your attention. Why are you in Cairo?"

"I already told you."

"The American tourist."

"Hardly the first."

"Tell me what happened to your face."

Quinn jabbed a thumb behind him, "One of your *brothers*."

"In the wrong place, you said."

"I'm here now, aren't I?"

"Traveling alone?"

"Does it look like there's anyone else here?"

Amir's patience was wearing thin. His cheeks flushed once again and he folded his hands on the desk. "These are strange times for Egypt. The country's security is our highest priority. It is difficult to know who to trust."

"Then I'll save you the trouble. You don't need to trust me. I'm leaving."

Amir paused just long enough. "Leaving . . . and you are certain of this?"

Quinn maintained his composure, but the tone of the comment struck a nerve. The threat hung in the air, looming over him as he contemplated his next move. The plastic fan swiveled and blew a small puff of ash from the silver tray onto some paperwork, the soft whir of plastic blades keeping the room from absolute silence.

Amir had gambled, though Quinn had just enough information that he could afford to call the bluff. It wasn't just the visa, but it was clear they didn't know about the girls. At least, that would be *his* gamble. Amir's face had turned the shade of a harvest tomato, and he still hadn't hinted at anything substantial, though that didn't mean the threats were idle. Maha had warned him about that, too. Still, he was willing to play along, and he had the feeling this was something different altogether.

"If you're looking for spies, I suggest you look elsewhere. You said yourself that my visa was expired. Then, you said it was a fake. Well, which is it? And either way, does that sound like the mistake a professional would make? Let his visa run out, or have one so bad that it gets noticed? Of course not.

"If you're looking for some *baksheesh*, I've got maybe . . ." He reached into his pocket, examined some crumpled notes, then dropped them on the desk. "Two hundred pounds. That's what, ten bucks? It's not much, but it's what I've got. Ask your lapdog here to buy you some more cigarettes. If you're looking to shake down some ignorant tourists, there's plenty more out there. You've seen the crowds, the confusion. Easy money to be made if that's what you're after."

Amir tilted his head back as he sank into his chair, exhaling a thick plume of smoke that drifted upwards, swirling around as it met a gust from the fan. The crinkled bills drifted a few inches along the length of the desk.

"It's your decision. You can let me catch my flight or call my embassy and prepare a statement for Al Jazeera about why you detained me without my rights."

This prompted a loud guffaw from deep in Amir's belly, the chortle filling the small room. "Your rights? *Your* rights?" He leaned forward, propping his elbows on the desk. "This is Egypt, my friend. And right now, Egypt is a very . . . complicated place. You have seen outside what happens. People get nervous. And we, the government, the police, *we* get nervous. Some people, they are causing trouble, problems for the country. So, we react. Sometimes, there can be violence. People become hurt. People go to jail. Sometimes, people . . . they disappear, in this confusion." He waited a moment to let the words sink in. "And you talk about your rights? You believe your *ideals* matter here?"

"Maybe not as much as they should, but I'm still willing to bet it's easier to keep skimming a few pounds off naïve tourists than arresting me."

"Mm . . . maybe. Maybe not. Maybe I tell Hisham to take you and throw you in a cell until we do, how you say . . ." His lips pursed together into a sarcastically pensive expression. "Background check."

Quinn said nothing.

"Our computers, you know, they are slow. Sometimes, these checks, they take some time."

Quinn ignored the sweat beneath his hands, resisted the urge to swallow, which would give him away. "That's your decision."

Amir slouched in his chair, the springs creaking as he rocked back and forth. A sliver of a grin crept along the side of his mouth. "I'm beginning to like you, Mistair Mills. It's a rare thing for me to meet a man with . . ." He trailed off, making a face and weighing some imaginary stones in his hand, then wagged a finger. "No one speaks to me like this in my country. Do you know why? It is not wise."

Quinn remained silent, waiting him out.

"Al Jazeera . . ." He snorted. "You would not make my daughter's school newspaper."

The office went silent for a few moments, but for the fan that continued to whir, tumbling bank notes further down the desk. "*Y'allah*, Hisham," Amir said finally, closing his eyes and giving a subtle jerk of the head. *Get him out of here.*

Hisham hesitated until Amir gave a second, rather heavy, authoritative nod. Quinn listened to the bootsteps make their way back to the door, the slow twist of the doorknob.

He rose from his seat, sliding his passport from the desk and watched as Amir leaned forward, gathered the crumpled notes in his fingers, and tucked them into his breast pocket, meeting Quinn's eyes with a self-assured stare.

At the door, Hisham's chest was puffed out, broad shoulders drawn back, a scowl painted across his face. For a moment, Quinn was reminded of Marchand.

He glanced back toward the desk. "I thought I was a spy."

Amir took a final puff of his cigarette, fading momentarily into a drift of cloud. "Spies mean paperwork, Mistair Mills," he said, butting out the filter in the ashtray. "I hate paperwork."

FORTY-FOUR

HE RAN. THE SOFT PURR OF WIND IN HIS EARS MUFFLED THE hollow announcements almost certainly calling his name. He couldn't make out the sounds, his boots rhythmically drumming a beat on the terrazzo floor, passengers turning their heads and moving aside in anticipation, instinctively hustling left and right, alerted by the sound of galloping footsteps.

There were only a couple of close calls along the way: a rogue child, having shunned the grip of his mother's hand, darted out amongst the crowds, a gasp from the mother as Quinn vaulted to one side. Later, an oblivious couple in their teens, cellphones and lattes in hand, inches from lattes on the floor and on their person.

He whipped his head left and right, the yellow signs above nothing more than a blur of letters. Just as he slowed, reaching for his boarding pass, he spotted a pair of gate agents in the middle of the hall, wide-eyed and searching, bobbing their heads back and forth, then waving frantically when they caught a glimpse of him dipping in and out amongst the crowds. They were, in fact, calling his name, and when he arrived at the gate, one of the agents stopped his announcement mid-sentence, and proceeded to launch into the final boarding call. "All passengers should now be on board for Royal Jordanian Airlines flight 502 to Amman."

They glanced at his passport for only a moment, knowing all too well who they'd been waiting for, tore his boarding pass, then gestured through the glass doors and down the bridge. Still he ran, frayed nerves and anticipation spurring him onwards, even though there was little need, even as he tasted copper from somewhere in the deepest cavities of his chest. Soaked in sweat and short of breath, he slowed by the plane door, a flight attendant in a crimson dress, mauve hat, and perpetual smile, the warmest of welcomes ushering him aboard.

In the cabin he was greeted by a few sets of rolling eyes, some clucking of tongues, and a disapproving shake of the head from business class—a snooty, old thing with too much jewelry and a frightful perm—irritated and relieved that *this* man, surely the culprit responsible for the delay was, at long last, aboard. Most of the passengers simply busied themselves as they usually did: sleep masks on, mouths slightly agape, already drifting into slumber; parents entertaining children with jangly toys and sweets, or left entranced by mesmeric screens and moving pictures; a couple of men, sweaty and determined, still struggling with the physics of large, oversized bags in small, overhead compartments, pulling and shoving and slamming panels closed.

Quinn jostled past them down the aisle, negotiating his way row by row, section by section, to the tail end of the plane. For a moment he paused, a flight attendant in his path assisting an elderly couple with a temperamental seatbelt.

Not more than ten feet away, he could see the second-to-last row: three seats on the left-hand side, two occupied with the aisle seat remaining vacant. By the window, his view partially obscured by the preceding row, he spotted a swirl of dark hair bobbing above the headrest. He waited, patiently, for once in his life, watching the dark locks shift and sway, attending to someone in the middle seat—a much smaller someone.

He didn't mind waiting. When Maha finally looked up, he realized he had been smiling for quite some time. Peering just over the seat, her eyes, smoky and dark as always, were full of relief as she beamed at him, laugh lines creasing. By the time he reached his seat, her eyes glinted with tears. Beside her sat Mei—*niqab* also removed, swimming in black cloth, her right hand resting in Maha's lap, fingers intertwined. She stared straight ahead, as she had when he found her. As she had with Youssef.

He took his seat carefully, delicately, laying his bag on the floor, hesitant to even graze her sleeve. The weight of the world should have been lifted now, but it was another peculiar emotion. Exhausted in more ways than one—in most ways—and now here she was before him, almost an illusion. An apparition, as if he reached out for her hand, she might evaporate, a puff and whorl of smoke, drifting into oblivion. Or would she turn to face him, a stranger staring back, a face he no longer recognized. No longer Mei, a different person altogether.

Maha pressed her head back against her seat, gazing at him, eyes glistening with tears that had yet to fall. She pursed her lips as she smiled tightly, holding her emotions at bay.

"Sir? Your seatbelt, sir. You need to fasten it, please."

"What? Oh, sorry, yes."

"And your bag, sir, it must be under the seat. There is no more room overhead."

"Of course."

He looked back to Maha, who nodded gently toward Mei, urging him on. "Go ahead," she said, softly. "Mei, our friend is here. Do you remember?"

Mei didn't move. After a moment, an announcement from the pilot broke the silence. The weather was slightly overcast in the Jordanian capital. Despite the delay, they planned to arrive as scheduled.

"Mei?" he said, leaning forward. "It's Quinn." Still she sat, facing forward, immobile.

As the plane rumbled along the tarmac, Maha watched over Mei like an overprotective mother. She adjusted her seatbelt, fastening it snugly, loosened her collar, then redirected the overhead air vent so the cool air ruffled her bangs. Mei closed her eyes at the sensation, lifting her head ever so slightly, allowing the gentle breeze to take her away. Maha caressed her head, combing her hair with her fingers, tucking the loose strands behind her ears.

When they made the final turn onto the runway, Quinn reached into his pocket, removing his wallet. He unfolded a picture, the edges worn smooth, a cross-sectional crease through the center of the image, ink faded white. He held it out in front of him: a younger, fresher version of himself, Noi, stout and proud as always, and Mei, pigeon-toed in her school uniform, a smile teetering on the edge of laughter.

"Mei . . . do you remember?" He held the picture in front of her, moving his index finger across the image. "This is you. Do you remember?" He slid his finger to the middle. "And *Khun* Noi."

He was about to put the picture away when she slowly turned her head, acknowledging his existence for the first time, or at least the existence of the photograph. She stared at the image for a long while. He pointed to the left side of the photo. "Do you remember?"

She raised her head, looking up at him with weary eyes.

"*Ghonlaat*," he said, pointing to himself and forcing a grin. "*Ghonlaat*."

Her gaze appeared to focus for a moment, no longer looking through him but shifting now, from one eye to the other, up, and then down, before finally returning to the photograph. He leaned in, watching as she mouthed the word to herself, softly, without a sound. *Ghonlaat*, cockroach, the most absurd term of endearment imaginable. Even in Khmer it seemed foreign upon Mei's chapped lips.

She reached out, her arm too short for the long black sleeve of the *abbaya*, and laid a small, clothed hand on his wrist. He felt the sting of tears welling in his eyes, filling them, blurring his vision. And when she leaned in toward him, resting her head against his shoulder, the warmth flowed silently over his cheeks, streaking down his chin.

The twin engines roared to life, propelling the aircraft forward, pinning everyone against their seats. The plane juddered as the turbines spun, the wheels speeding along, gathering pace down the runway, until the nose lifted into the air. They felt themselves lift along with it, suspended in space and time, the tarmac, the earth, and the entire world falling away beneath their feet.

MATEJS KALNS was raised in the Latvian community of Toronto, Canada. He holds degrees in History from the University of Ottawa, and Human Security & Peacebuilding from Royal Roads University. He has worked in the fields of education and human rights for over ten years. Beasts of the Night is his first novel.

www.matejskalns.com